ECLIPTIC

KRISTIN TRAVIS

THE ROGUE QUILL

Cover by Kristin Travis and Red Thread Co.

ISBN 979-8-9883211-2-5 (Paperback)

ISBN 979-8-9883211-3-2 (Ebook)

Published by The Rogue Quill

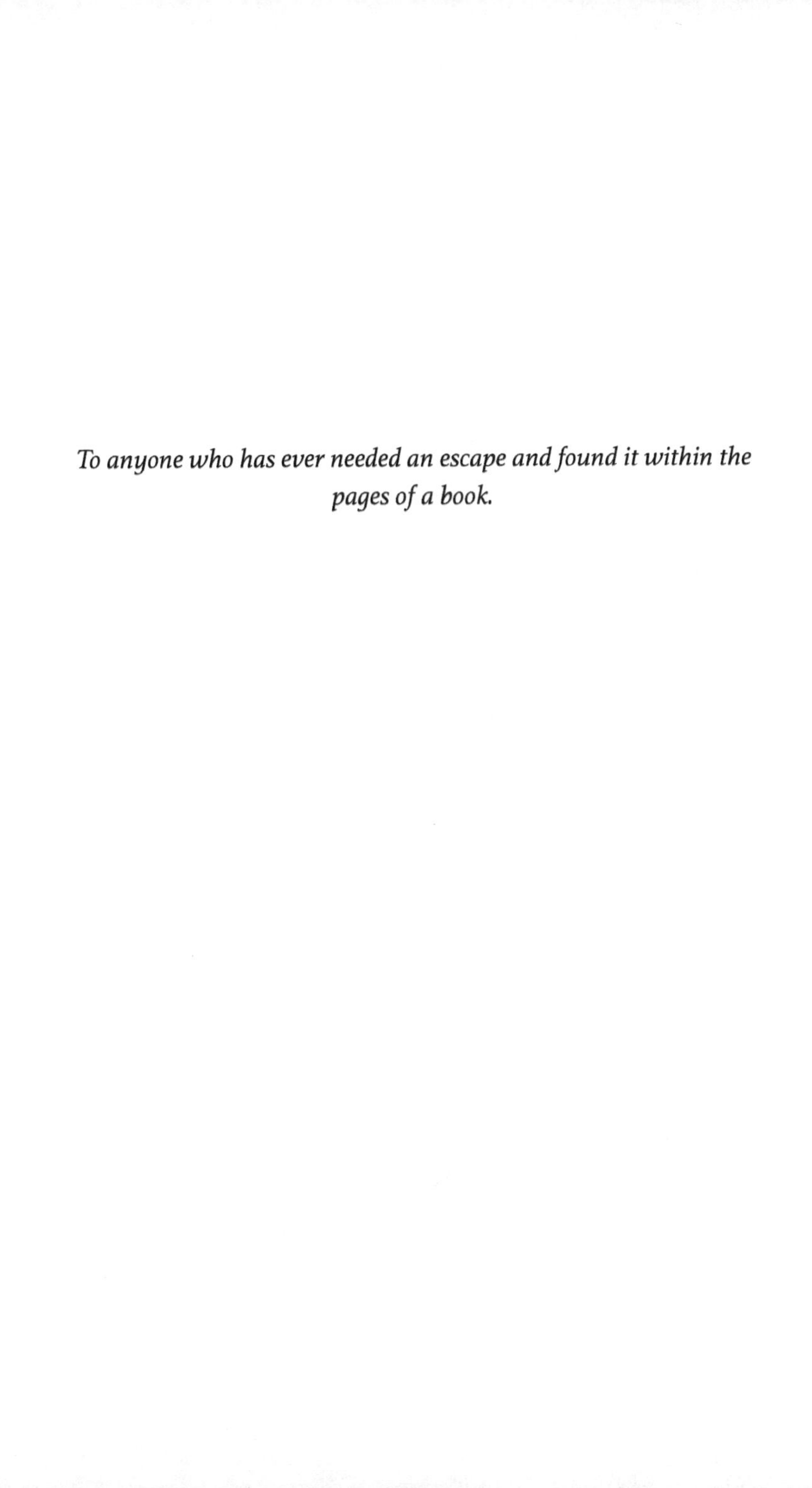

To anyone who has ever needed an escape and found it within the pages of a book.

Keira Copeland hasn't dreamed for as long as she can remember. Now, her nights are filled with darkness, shadows, and monsters that haunt her every step. One night, Keira meets the mysterious stranger Rowen in a misty forest.

Attempting to forget Rowen's forbidden touches and the land that calls to her blood, Keira goes to a nightclub with Natalie and Harlan, where she has a strange reaction and flickers between the nightclub and the forest from her dreams. Rowen attempts to save her through her waking nightmare but can only do so much from one side of her reality, and Keira must rely on the electrical shocks emanating from her body to save herself.

Keira fears she is losing her mind until she wakes with an unexplainable bruise on her wrist and realizes every dream, look, and touch is real. Keira learns she has been unknowingly astral projecting to the ethereal world of Luneth, a land suffering from a failed prophecy. As the land slowly dies, villages go missing without a trace. Keira finds refuge in the Wyn village as the Dark Spirit Erovos and false queen Aliphoura hunt for the one the Synodic Prophecy spoke of—The Marked destined to bring Light and life back to the dying lands.

Keira's feelings for Rowen grow, but he pulls her close one moment only to push her away the next. Keira meets Dyani, the fierce Wyn Warrior, and her twin brother, Demil. Keira grows weaker as her astral form is torn between worlds. Takoda, the village healer, prepares a Hymma ceremony where Keira can heal her body, but instead, she finds herself lying comatose in a hospital bed.

Hearing her parents discuss her condition, Keira discovers they have been drugging her with a powerful cognitive suppressant that has kept her from astral projecting. Keira returns to Luneth whole, shedding the darkness of her past while revealing a Light bestowed upon her by the Elder Spirits.

Back in Luneth, Nepta, the Elven-head of the village, sends her on a quest to revive an extinct noxlily. On the journey, Keira heals Rowen from a poisonous wound, and in a secluded cave, he nearly kills her, thinking her to be the mysterious woman, Fou.

Snapping out of the hallucination, Rowen kisses Keira in a devouring kiss, which he later admits was a mistake. Heartbroken, and on their way back to the village, Keira feels a chill from a mysterious crevice where she comes face-to-face with a trapped spirit. He attacks Keira, but before he can overtake her, she blasts him with the Alcreon Light.

Keira and Rowen return to the village in time for Celenova. Rowen admits to saving her from the monsters she'd roused in the forest, and Keira realizes she is in love with him, even though he is holding back.

Keira is kidnapped during a fire by Caeryn, a man claiming to be the false queen's favored. Brought to the Crystal Crypts, she is beaten and tortured by Rowen's ex-love Aliphoura (Fou). She meets the friendly face of Rayal, a woman who brings her food and feels the power of her blood. Rowen finds Keira and heals her with the petals of the noxlily. Fou threatens to kill Kiera unless Rowen sacrifices his body to her, and the false queen admits to cursing and spying on Rowen through his mother's necklace.

Keira summons the Light within her to blast the false queen but misses, causing the Crystal Crypts to cave in. Just when all seems lost, the Wyn blast through the Crypts, having followed Keira's trail of blood turned to evergreens. In a bloody battle with lives lost, Keira, Rowen, and the Wyn Warriors defeat Aliphoura, saving the missing souls trapped within the Crypts. Keira returns to the village where Rowen confesses his love to her, and they intertwine in heart, body, and soul.

Demil betrays Keira and leads her outside the village, using Ven and Sabra as pawns. Determined to save the man, new family, and land that ignited her dormant heart, she takes Erovos' hand and vanishes with him into the mist.

CONTENT WARNING

Dear Reader, please be advised this book contains scenes involving depression, anxiety, violence, abuse, explicit language, and sexual situations (both consensual and nonconsensual). Your mental health matters.

Eclipse: the obscuring of one celestial body by another

1

"No wandering out tonight," my mother said as she tucked me into bed. "We'd hate to lock you in your room again."

"We mean it, Keira," my father scolded beside her. "You upset your mother when you get out and come back a filthy mess, dirtying up the house."

Last night, I'd accidentally left a trail of muddy footprints across the carpet. The stained impressions of my soles were a faint reminder of my disobedience.

"I'll try, Daddy," I said, not wanting to upset him. But no matter how hard I tried, I found myself walking the paths of an enchanting forest almost every night. Then, I would suddenly appear in my room, covered in mud, twigs, and scratches, not remembering how I managed any of it.

My mother shot my father a quick stare, but he remained stiff with his arms across his chest. "If you could just tell us how you're doing it, honey. I promise we won't be mad."

"I told you," I groaned, my little fists balling in frustration. "I close my eyes, and I fall through stars."

"Keira!" my father shouted, making me flinch. "You are eight years old now. Enough with the lies, or we will take away your telescope."

"No! Please, Daddy," I cried, leaping up from the bed. "I won't go anywhere, I promise."

It was a promise I couldn't keep, but I would say anything to keep my telescope. Most children had a stuffed toy or blanket, something soft to chase away the shadows. Some even had parents they could run to. Not me. I was scolded for leaving my room and giving in to my fears. Any disruptions led to more rules, stricter punishments, and longer sessions of questioning in my mother's office.

All I had was my telescope.

Every night, I planted my gaze through the eyepiece, losing myself within the glittering map of space. The long black tube became my faithful companion while the velvet night enveloped me like a quilt.

"I think we'll take it tonight, just in case," my mother said, gathering the one thing I counted on. "If you're good, we'll return it to you in a week."

My heart plummeted. There was no way I would last that long.

I rushed after my parents as they closed the door, ready to beg and plead, but when I turned the knob, it wouldn't budge. Terror choked me as I realized they'd locked me in.

I pounded on the door, unable to hold back the tears as they spilled down my face.

It wasn't until my palms were sore that I slumped down and curled up at the bottom of the door. My body turned heavy, then weightless, and I began to drift. I tried not to chase the lights that always found me—carried me. But the pull was too strong, and I soon found myself under the biggest disk of a moon I'd ever seen.

A comforting breeze swirled around me, drying my tears

into salted crystals upon my cheeks. The gentle wind ushered me to my feet, and my toes sank into the plush ground beneath me.

I marveled at the massive lunar pendant above, its glow casting a silver enchantment over the forest. I found I preferred this sky over the one I saw out my window every night.

It wasn't home. It was my sanctuary.

I surrendered to the forest that knew nothing of walls or locked doors and pushed my impending punishment far, far away. I hummed with the melody of the woods, skipped on pools of moonlight, and danced with the trees.

When my parents learned of this, who knew how long they'd keep me locked away. I might as well enjoy every second of this freedom while I had the chance.

Suddenly, a squawk echoed through the forest and stopped me in my tracks. My eyes darted through the branches, searching for the animal that seemed to call for help.

Labored chirps led me over and under moss-covered roots and through long-hanging vines until I came upon a bird shimmering like a comet.

I was unfamiliar with the creature, though it looked to be about the size of a peacock. Upright feathers flowed from its head like a twisting fern, and its tail cascaded in a long, glittering plume. The bird's watery eyes pierced my soul as it chirped helplessly.

I rushed to the feathered ball of light, and my heart sank as I realized it was trapped in a net.

The poor thing had struggled to escape, further tangling its delicate wings and feet in a jumbled mess. It was afraid, shaking, and exhausted.

"It's okay. Don't be scared. I'm going to help you," I said, carefully unbinding its legs. But I must have pulled a little too hard because the bird reared back and slashed its talons through my white nightgown, causing blood to well on my shoulder.

I bit back the pain radiating down my arm. "I'm so sorry. Just a little more, and you'll be free," I coaxed, working to untangle the last bit of rope.

Shedding its confines, the animal unfurled its wings like a curtain of jewels, and my mouth hung open in awe.

The bird didn't fly away. Instead, its body relaxed, and its intelligent eyes held my gaze as if thanking me. Its iridescent feathers shimmered in the moonlight, and as I reached out, its neck stretched to meet my fingertips.

Beneath the foreign sky, I stroked the magnificent creature who had trusted me enough to save its life.

It cooed and trilled at my scratches, then hopped back, padding its feet.

"What is it?" I asked—a perfectly sensible question to ask an animal.

It squawked again and ruffled its wings.

I checked for more injuries, but the bird swung its head, motioning for me to follow. The forest was full of life, light, and energy, but my eyes snagged on the dark tunnel twisting with thorns and heavy shadows.

"You want me to go in there?" I asked, unable to hide the quiver in my voice.

The creature let out one last chirp before swooping through the tunnel in a flash of light.

I waited with bated breath, hoping it would return, but it had been several minutes since the glint of its tail vanished in the darkness.

I tugged at the hemline of my nightgown and gnawed on my lower lip. I was already in so much trouble; what would a little more exploring hurt? It was clear my new feathered friend wanted me to follow. And even though I was barefoot, bleeding, and terrified, I knew I couldn't leave the creature to be hurt or trapped again.

I dipped a toe into the tunnel, testing the whorls of darkness. Goosebumps rose along my skin and drained my warmth. I wished I could withdraw from this place, just as the sun had long ago, but I wouldn't leave without knowing if the bird was safe.

I pressed on as thorns scratched me and ripped my nightgown and hair. A lump of dread formed in my throat, and my teeth clattered inside my head. I wrapped my arms around myself, attempting to protect my heart from the destroyed forest.

Just when I thought the dark had swallowed me whole, a flash of light arced before me like a shooting star. "There you are!" I cried as I ran to the bird perched on a fallen log, its gaze honed onto something in the distance. I peered over the trunk, following its star-lit eyes.

Ahead soared the most majestic tree I had ever seen. A canopy of gold, green, and pink leaves flourished from the towering titan. The bark looked healthy and strong, and the tree seemed to stand on its roots, creating hollow chambers within its trunk.

Inside the cavity, a man hung by his wrists, his head limp and shoulder blades protruding.

A scream charged up my throat, but the bird turned its head in warning, and I clamped my hands over my mouth.

Suddenly, a figure darker than the night materialized before the captive, and my whole body froze in terror.

The cloak of shadows leaned forward and placed his hands on either side of the man's temples, forcing his gaze up. "Now that I've given you time to think, I hope your memory's jogged. And know this, I shall not ask again," said a booming voice that raised the hairs on the back of my neck. "Are you the Synodic Son?"

"I t...told you. I have no idea who that is. Please," the chained man begged.

"Very well," the figure droned, and his shroud of darkness shifted to reveal a man with pale skin and volcanic eyes that churned with unending destruction.

His mouth opened wide as the skin around his face and hands veined an inky black before dissipating into his pallid complexion. The prisoner's back was to me, but I could tell by his shrieks and writhing body that something vital was being stolen from him.

Blood pooled on my tongue as I bit back my screams.

After what felt like forever, the screaming ended, and the dark being removed the shriveled corpse from the chains and threw him onto what appeared to be a pile of clothes. But as I peered closer, I realized it was a mound of bodies littering the desolate landscape.

Terror jolted my legs into action and propelled my feet as I ran back through the dark tunnel. Branches lashed at my face, and my bare feet split open beneath me, but the fear surging through my veins dulled the pain. I followed the ball of light to safety, running until I collapsed from exhaustion.

The bird gracefully landed beside me and gently pecked at my hair.

"Why did you show me that?" I cried into my arm. I couldn't comprehend what I had just seen. It was so unnatural. So wrong. It was as if the captive had been siphoned of everything that made him...*alive*.

The flutter of wings brushed against my skin, and when I lifted my head, a flock of glittering birds encompassed me. Some shivered from within their nests, while others protectively draped their wings over sparkling eggs.

The creature had led me to a small patch of greenery surrounded by darkness and devastation.

Deep within my roots, I knew this was the shadowy man's doing. He was the cause of the dying forest and was destroying their home.

"You need help," I whispered as the birds curiously shuffled toward me. "You all need help."

I wished I could give more than comforting words and scratches beneath their beaks, but it was all I had to offer.

Suddenly, the creatures unfurled their feathers and squawked in unison as if something had startled them. Their eyes glistened with fear as their wings snapped in a flurry, blowing my hair and nightgown around my body.

Had the dark figure followed me?

Whatever it was, I felt it now, too, rushing at me like an avalanche. I spun to see what came at me with a vengeance, but my eyes were blinded by a light that engulfed me like the birth of the sun. The luminosity pierced my skin and seeped into my every pore with a frigid intensity that was so cold, it burned.

And I screamed as the Light consumed me whole.

····(· C · ● ·) ·)· ————

My screams echoed through a tunnel of time as I staggered back to the present and swayed on my feet.

"Ah, there she is," came the voice of a man whose crimson eyes were twin harbingers of death. "Thought I lost you there for a moment. I was holding your body but nothing more. Where did you go?"

"I remember you," I said, reeling as my childhood nightmare faded.

Had I astral traveled to my past? It was the only explanation for why I remembered. And I remembered *everything*. They weren't delusions at all, not even nightmares. They were memories of my earliest astral projecting.

I walked between worlds before I ever possessed the power of the Alcreon Light. It was during one of my projections when the Light found me. Had it known I was *other*? Known I wasn't from Luneth and that it would be safe in a world far from Erovos' reach?

My mind tumbled as I tried to remember how I ended up by the Dark Spirit's side.

I'd been stolen away.

No.

I'd come here willingly.

"My little light," he said as his thumb stroked the back of my hand. "I told you it wouldn't be long until you were mine."

2

———

Erovos' hand was frigid and smooth, like glass fired from the first strokes of lightning upon the sands of time. My fingers slid further into his grasp as he yanked me closer.

"Where did you go?" he asked again, each drag of his gaze leaching the warmth from my skin.

"The past," I whispered, withdrawing my hand as if I'd been burned.

"Ah," he smiled, revealing his sharp teeth. "So your talents aren't to be exaggerated."

I tore my eyes away from his threatening stare, and when my surroundings came into view, horror punched up my throat. I hadn't gone anywhere. Only a second had passed, yet it had been over fifteen years.

I was standing in the same barren landscape as my childhood memory, only now, the once strong and magnificent tree stood twisted in tragedy. Its deformed branches were coal black, bare, and sharp, sagging with an indiscernible weight. It would have been unrecognizable if it weren't for the distinct hollow through its trunk.

"What did you do?" I seethed, mourning the forest that was

now steeped in death and despair. The bird had tried to warn me all those years ago, but was it too late? Was *I* too late? "The creatures that lived here. What happened to them?"

He ignored my question, curiosity engulfing his face. "Where in the past did you go?"

"I answered one of your questions. Now answer one of mine," I demanded.

"Oh, the starwings?" he asked with a sinister smile. "I haven't seen one in quite some time. Extinct, I suspect."

A choked sob caught in my throat as thorns pierced my heart.

"Where in the past did you go?" he asked again, this time with less patience.

"Here," I ground out, despite the devastation wracking me from the inside out.

"Of course," Erovos said, his ever-shifting cloak of darkness obscuring his pale face and body. "This tree has called to you many times."

"Why?" I asked, my gaze snagging on the familiar chains dangling from the internal cavity. Not only was this the tree from my memories, but it was also the tree I'd traveled to during my Hymma ceremony, where I'd gathered my astrally torn body from across the cosmos and returned to Luneth whole, healthy, and teeming with celestial light. Even now, it glinted off my skin like a moonlit lake.

"She is Indrasyl, the Sylvan Mother Tree. It is her roots that bind this world. Her arms stretch far and wide beneath us, connecting every living thing on Luneth."

Everything is connected, Takoda's words whispered in my mind. At the time, I'd thought it a comforting sentiment, but now I saw it for the beautiful curse that it was.

I ran my hands along Indrasyl's ruined bark, searching for

any signs of life. Every living soul on Luneth depended on the health of this tree.

"All the dying forests and suffering people lead here. But why?" I asked, sending a pulse of Light through the sheath of her trunk with my illuminated palm.

Erovos snatched my wrist in a bone-crushing grip. "Indrasyl has served her purpose well. Luneth is nearly drained. For it is through her by which I feed."

My eyes widened in disgust. "What are you?"

"I am a being that cannot be sated. My hunger grows and knows no end. And you, my little light, are making my mouth water."

Terror gripped my spine as sure as the hand around my wrist. I breathed in through my nostrils and wrangled in my fear. My gift from the Elder Spirits was foreign, the full scope of my abilities was still a mystery. I could try blasting Erovos with my Light, but the way he eyed my shimmering skin told me he might enjoy such a thing.

I had no idea how to escape the Dark Spirit's clutches. My best bet was to keep him talking.

"Why string up the men and . . . and drain them within her?" I asked, a captive in his dark aura.

"You know the first half of the prophecy, I'm sure. *The lost light of Luneth shall return to its synodic beginning when the first six stars align with the stones of shattered ruin. Through blood, bone, and crystal, the marked son will breathe life anew unto the deadened lands of darkness.* But were you ever told the second half? It is much more interesting in my opinion."

When I didn't respond, the Dark Spirit continued. "*Shall the lost light fall unto those who feast, darkness will reign an unending beast. Worlds have fallen, and so they shall remain as a Sylvan door opens to a universe unrestrained.*

"It is whispered amongst the stars that many Sylvan Mother

Trees exist throughout the galaxies. See the passageway through her trunk?" The Dark Spirit motioned to the hollow with a sweep of his hand. "It is rumored to be a portal, connecting all worlds through a canopy of cosmic branches. For all her greatness here on Luneth, Indrasyl is but a small sapling within the infinite web of space. I hoped the Alcreon Stone would invoke the portal's opening, allowing me to pass through. Rich and viable planets are not easy to locate. They are rare gems scattered throughout the void, but with Indrasyl's interconnecting system, feasting on plentiful worlds will be effortless."

He released my wrist and surged toward me like a toxic cloud. I thought he swirled with darkness, but I was wrong. He was absorbing whatever light was around him, distorting the air and making it impossible to discern his true shape.

"You're a monster," I choked, falling back against Indrasyl, and even in her destroyed state, she caught me as I fell. Terror seized my muscles as I clung to her. Erovos didn't just feed off life or light; it was existence itself.

"No. You misunderstand," he replied. "I am a cosmic conquerer. Worlds have succumbed to my hunger. But don't fret. The energy I accumulate does not go to waste."

I couldn't stop the bile as it roared up my throat—he had replicated this destruction with other planets? My eyes bore into him as I wiped my mouth with the back of my hand. "You're a world eater, a black hole."

The power I'd seen him wield against the helpless man, along with the abilities Aliphoura had displayed in the Crystal Crypts, functioned like a controlled black hole. They both drew energy from any living being, siphoning their life to be repurposed into raw power.

Rowen told me that Fou had learned such teachings from Erovos himself. Even Caeryn had used a dark tunnel when he'd abducted me. How many students did this world eater have?

"What will you do when there is nothing left to conquer?"

"Darkness was first, my little light. And it will be last," he replied, his gaze simmering with arrogance. "It took me centuries to find where the Elder Spirits hid the Alcreon Stone. But your fearless leader shattered the crystal at the Battle of the Breaking, and the Alcreon Light was lost. I was outraged until I remembered an ancient prophecy about a lost light. The prophecy spoke of a Synodic Son, and I've spent every day for the past sixteen years searching for potential males who I believed could be the one. They all ended up being a waste of time. It wasn't even worth the effort to drain them. Some would scream and howl while others held their cries for as long as they could. They all begged for death in the end, and I always obliged."

Erovos pulled the ever-shifting hood from his face, revealing the smooth ridges of his head. The prominent angles of his jaw and cheekbones accentuated the depths of his eyes that held twin torches of destruction. Even though his features were alluring and hypnotizing, his countenance repulsed me.

"Very few understand what is on the other side of destruction. But I do. It's creation. It takes breaking something to make another thing possible. And I have every intention of breaking you."

Terror surged through me, but I held my voice firm. "Light can bend to darkness, but it never breaks. *I* will never break."

"I really think you will."

"You've killed so many," I hissed. "All for what?"

"I am creating something quite grand with the energy I have stored. Although you won't be around to see it," he said with a sinister smile. "The Elder Spirits think they were the first, but they weren't. It was I who reigned before, and the more they create, the more my energy grows. They are fueling my armies of primordial darkness."

"Creating more of your tracker demons?" I asked, remembering it was his creations that hunted me when I began astral projecting again. Shortly after my encounter with the star-wings, my parents had drugged me into oblivion. The poison they created suppressed my abilities and kept me trapped on Earth, but now my bloodstream ran with untainted celestial light.

As if sensing my thoughts, Erovos caged me in against Indrasyl. "The Light in you is potent. I think I'll try a little taste."

Erovos' eyes churned, and his jaw hinged open, revealing rows of jagged teeth. He was a cosmic beast ready to feast. On me.

I squeezed my eyes shut and turned my head away. Images of Rowen, the man I loved to the core of my being, filled my mind.

"Erovos!" a voice shouted from the shadows, and the Dark Spirit's maw snapped shut an inch from my neck. I squinted my eyes open.

The body of a bronze warrior emerged from the darkness, his silver-sleek hair matched the warrior circlets on his arms. It was Demil, the traitor who had put me in this position in the first place. "You know one little taste won't be enough. You'll feed from her until she is dead, and you need her abilities to leave this world."

"You," I seethed, wanting to rip his black heart from his chest. "I trusted you."

Tears of rage clouded my vision as I recalled Sabra's lifeless body and Ven's tear-stained face. Two innocents used as leverage to get me to take Erovos' hand and disappear with him into the darkness. I wondered if Rowen had realized I was gone. Had Dyani noticed her twin brother was missing, too?

Ven most likely told the village what had happened, seeking help for his lifeless wolf. I just hoped no one would come after me; it would defeat the purpose of everything I had just done—

everything I had just sacrificed. I couldn't bear it if anyone else was hurt or killed because of me.

After being held prisoner in the Crystal Crypts, I'd returned to the Wyn village. I'd only had a few days of healing before Demil traitorously led me beyond Nepta's borders. My life had gone from empty shadows to overflowing darkness, and no matter how hard I tried, a peaceful existence remained a delicate ornament hanging just out of reach.

"The traitor might be right, and I may not be able to stop myself. Though I do wonder how long it would take to drain you dry," the Dark Spirit said, bringing my thoughts back to the dead forest.

My mind clashed with horrors old and new. "You're both sick."

Without taking his eyes off me, he said, "Demil. Come." And the man I had once seen as a beautiful warrior, who would do anything to protect his people, walked towards the world eater. A much larger silhouette followed him, and I immediately recognized the giant, Graem. "Your traitor tells me you are an astral traveler. A walker between worlds. No wonder you were so difficult to find." He stared at me, his eyes never blinking. "And thanks to you, I have my next destination. I'm sure there is a tether leading right to where you're from. For as I've said before, Luneth is nearly all used up, and I grow so very hungry."

Horror twisted my gut.

Erovos said it himself, he'd already left a trail of stellar corpses in his path. The Elder Spirits tried to slow him, but if he gained the ability to travel through a gateway of connecting trees, the swiftness with which he could turn the galaxy into a graveyard was unimaginable. And now his sights were set on Earth.

"You may have the power to destroy worlds and extinguish light, but you can never take away hope. Luneth will fight you until its dying breath," I gritted through bared teeth. "And you will have to go through me."

"That is precisely what I intend to do."

I had no idea what he meant by that, but I was no longer near the village. The fear of hurting innocents was as far away as the man I'd abandoned in bed.

Who cared if I self-combusted and took everyone along with me?

The Alcreon Light thrummed in my fingertips as if begging to be unleashed. I refused to hold it back any longer. I raised my palm and hit the world eater with a formidable blast of silver light. Unlike in the Crystal Crypts, when I missed the False Queen, my aim rang true, and I hit the Dark Spirit square in the chest.

He didn't stagger or even shirk from my blast. Instead my Light stretched and distorted as he absorbed my power whole. Never to escape.

He rolled his shoulders and stretched his neck. "Your Light alone cannot defeat me. And should you try that again, I will be forced to destroy that little village you are so keen to protect. Shall we begin?"

"Begin what? Doing to me what you did to all those men?" I asked, my voice broken from the realization that my Light didn't affect him at all.

When I'd left with Erovos, I thought there would be a way to defeat him. A way to use my Light when I was far away from the village. But I was wrong. I had over-dealt my hand, and I now stood before a world eater with no weapon and no plan. Despair snuffed out any flicker of hope as realization sank in—Erovos had no weaknesses.

"Not quite," the Dark Spirit said, his churning vermillion eyes trailing up my body. "Now, remove your clothing."

3

"Wha...what?" I stuttered. Of all the things I expected from my willing abduction, stripping wasn't one of them.

He studied me, unfazed. "I said, remove your clothing."

Graem stepped up beside me, and my spine stiffened in dread.

"No."

"I have something for you. Never in my years of searching would I have imagined a woman to be the bearer of the Alcreon Light. I've been envisioning this moment since I first laid eyes on you."

"I don't want anything from you," I spat, hatred dripping from my every word.

"You agreed."

"I said I would come with you, not do everything you demand."

I had agreed to go with Erovos, and because I'd given him my word, he hadn't restrained me. We both knew I wasn't going anywhere. Not when he could destroy everyone I cared about.

"Now, now. We mustn't seem ungrateful, must we? I've been preparing for this a very long time, my little light. Try not to spoil the mood. Seeing your skin covered in my darkness has been quite a fantasy of mine. Now, take off your clothes. I'm starting to lose my patience."

"After years of failing and waiting, I'd think you'd be used to it by now."

"That tongue of yours is going to get you in trouble. If you don't obey me, I'll have Graem assist you."

My lip peeled back into a snarl. He knew full well that he could make me do whatever he wanted, but he would make me agree to every sick step along the way.

"Fine," I seethed. The thought of Graem undressing me curdled my stomach. "Turn away."

"No," he stated, mirroring my tone. "Now, you'll do as I command, or I'll slowly torture the man I can smell all over you. What was his name again, Demil?"

Demil cleared his throat and shifted, his hands clasped behind his back. "Rowen Damascus," he said, his warrior stance faltering.

"Ah, yes. The little lord."

"Don't you dare touch him. Don't even speak his name!" I shrieked, launching myself at the Dark Spirit with unrestrained fury.

Graem's massive arm shot out and grabbed my wrist in a vice-like grip, halting my momentum. He yanked me back. Hard. And I cried out as my shoulder twisted.

"You have my word that he is not to be harmed. But you must cease this feral behavior and do as I say," Erovos said, his jaw twitching as he noted the look of pain on my face.

I ground my back teeth, the pressure nearly shattering my molars. "I'll do it for you, but the giant and traitor have to go," I rebutted, bargaining however I could to get fewer eyes on me, less enemies seeing me vulnerable.

"Graem, leave us," Erovos ordered. "The traitor will stay."

The giant released me and obediently walked away.

"Oh, and, Graem?" The servant stopped and turned back to look at his master. Erovos released a whip of darkness and lashed him across the face. "That is for hurting her."

My insides lurched as the giant cried out and touched his wounded cheek. "Go!" Erovos shrieked, and Graem hobbled off into the dark forest whimpering.

Once his massive frame disappeared, Erovos stepped toward me. "See, I am not above compromising and look how well we work together. Now, hand me your clothing."

My chest heaved with each fuming breath as I slowly peeled off the terracotta robe. After our bath underneath the stars, Rowen had wrapped me in this dress. Before he'd removed it again to taste, lick, and kiss every inch of my skin. And how—after he fully claimed me, body and soul—I had put it back on to surprise him with breakfast in bed.

I fisted Erovos the robe with my head held high, and he took my clothing from my outstretched hand.

He inspected my naked body without a hint of lust. He looked at me as if I were a piece of clay waiting to be molded. Reshaped.

I refused to shy away and cower even as my insides screamed and revolted. There was only one artist across all the galaxies I'd want to see me this way. And he was back in bed, tousled in the sheets, waiting for me to return.

Demil cast his eyes downward. Despite the small act of decency, I despised him down to his rotten core. Though I wasn't sure why he acted ashamed. This was all his doing.

Suddenly, Erovos' veins ignited into black ichor as he redirected the flow of his power into my robe. Billowing smoke poured from him, turning the cloth into a black cloud that engulfed me.

I cried out as it surrounded me, reminding me of the drug-induced dreams I used to have when my mother and my room-mate poisoned me.

It was as if I were back there, fighting an invisible darkness. I couldn't breathe, couldn't see. And I choked as black ribbons swirled around me, dipping between my breasts and over my shoulders, brushing against my skin in frigid strokes. They coiled and fused, shaping themselves into a gown of black smoke.

Panting, I inspected how Erovos' darkness settled over me. The fabric was sheer, with slightly thicker panels around my hips and breasts. Though the dress was floor length, the see-through gossamer did little to conceal my form.

A daring cut-out at the chest left my breasts on the verge of spilling out. The lace fastened at my neck with a hook-and-eye clasp, exposing almost my entire chest.

I pried at the choking collar, but no matter how hard I tried, the misted fabric remained in perfect form. The gown hugged my every curve but did little to guard against the chill that wafted around me and sent tremors through my body.

I pressed my hands to my mouth, but there was nothing left in my stomach to purge, and I heaved. I would rather stand naked than be dressed in a gown fashioned from stolen lives. I wondered who, or what, had died for the energy to fashion it.

"You wear my darkness now, little light," he said, beaming with pride, but Demil's gaze remained on the ground.

"Look at her!" Erovos screamed, and Demil obeyed, his light-yellow eyes snapping to mine. Pleading.

"I'm so sorry, Keira," he said, dressed in the earthy fabric of the Wyn people. His unique silver circlets glinted in the darkness.

He used to be a welcoming sight, but now, he made me sick.

"Fuck you."

"Filthy mouth but beguiling form. I can see why she interests you," Erovos said, wrapping an arm around the warrior's shoulders. "Look upon what I promised you, Demil. She is what you asked for? Your reward for delivering the Alcreon Light into my hands. We made a deal: I possess her Light, and you possess her body," he stated as he motioned to me. "Well, take it."

Demil's eyes darted in confusion. "Right now?"

Erovos nodded.

"N-no. You promised I could have her after you removed the Light," Demil stuttered, his square jaw tensing.

"I never specified when, just that you would. And do you honestly believe anything will be left of her when I'm done? I am bound by my word, but I have a much greater use for her than your petty desires. Your moment is now, and it is fleeting."

Disgust swarmed my veins. Erovos had given Demil permission to rape me in front of him, but it wasn't his authority to give.

I stood tall before both men. "Touch me, Demil, and it will be the last thing you ever do. The Light may not hurt him, but it will fry the shit out of you."

"Keira, I . . . I wouldn't. I won't," Demil said, shaking his head in disgust as if his original plan had been any better. "I thought he would travel to the next world and leave Luneth be. I thought I was saving us."

"You forfeit your prize then, traitor?" Erovos bellowed.

"I do," Demil replied.

"Very well, then. Give us our privacy, won't you?"

The whites around Demil's eyes widened as Erovos' gaze swirled like twin black holes—a celestial anomaly. Suddenly, the Dark Spirit conjured a portal in the same manner Aliphoura had in the Crystal Crypts, and Caeryn the night of the fire. It was also identical to the one that had brought me here. The energy taken from the earth and its people was used to create these dark portals, and the fact that Erovos had made two in less than twenty-four hours was horrifying.

How many had to die for him to wield such power? An inconceivable amount, yet somehow not enough to find other worlds without the help of me and Indrasyl.

My thoughts vanished as Erovos hurled Demil into the dark portal with no more than a flick of his wrist.

Dread gripped my lungs as the once vibrant warrior vanished. I couldn't grasp how it was the same man who helped lift me up after his sister kicked my feet out from underneath me and knocked me to the ground. He was a brilliant warrior who offered to train me and fought to free the missing villages from Aliphoura's wrath. He ultimately wanted to save Luneth but had chosen the worst way possible and failed.

"Where did you send him?" I demanded, not sure why I was so terrified of the answer.

"Graem will keep him in line for now. Who knows, I may have further use for him." Erovos gripped my shoulders as he eyed me up and down. "You do make quite the sacrificial vessel, my little light. Now, let us begin."

4

I tensed as Erovos seized control of my body with whips of darkness. Smokey tendrils ensnared my wrists one at a time, forcing my hands into the shackles that swayed from Indrasyl's cavity. My tendons strained as I resisted the dark power that controlled me like a marionette doll.

With the final clink of the irons, my arms were wrenched apart, drawn taut within the hollow trunk.

I had always known my wrists were destined for these chains. And now here I was, strung up and decorated like the sacrificial lamb I'd been reduced to.

But I wasn't alone; Indrasyl and I were both prisoners to Erovos' devices. I had seen the dying Mother Tree after my Hymma ceremony, where I thought I'd met the Dark Spirit for the first time. Though, according to my repressed memories, this was where my childhood night terrors had played out one by one.

I lifted my gaze to find Erovos, his eyes gleaming with the anticipation of receiving everything he'd ever wanted. The cost being me, my body, and soul. "How many men did you string up like this before me? Killing them for something they didn't possess?"

"It took mountains of corpses to find you," he said casually, inspecting the dark smoke against my skin, and I flinched in disgust. "I'm glad you've finally decided to see things my way and cooperate. It wasn't easy getting you here."

Erovos stepped into my space, eyes on fire with a gravitational hunger that pulled at the edges of my skin. He placed his finger on my cupid's bow, his touch cold, hard, and unflinching. My gaze burned with revulsion as he traced a finger down my mouth and paused at my lower lip. I snapped at his hand with my teeth, but he grabbed my chin in a bone-crushing grip. "Don't bite the hand that is about to free you."

"Interesting words to say to someone you just shackled," I said, staring back into his eyes defiantly.

"Oh, Keira, it is not these chains that bind you. Can't you see? It is this body that imprisons you," Erovos said, loosening his grip to trace his fingers over my chin. My breathing was rampant, my chest heaving as his finger continued to slide down the column of my throat.

"Where does the Alcreon Light reside? Is it in your spirit? Your mind? Or is it here?" he asked, tapping his finger at the swell of my left breast. His touch lingered over my pounding heart, which simultaneously surged with life yet shattered with grief. "I guess I will just have to use all of you to find out."

At least my heart had known Rowen's, however fleeting our time together had been. He finally confessed his love for me and explained why he'd kept it hidden for so long—why so much time had been wasted. He had done it to protect me from the woman who had cursed and abused him.

I needed to get back to him. That couldn't have been all the time we were allowed after baring our souls and claiming each other's bodies. I would forever resent the Spirits if that were all the time we were given.

I thrashed beneath Erovos' icy touch, desperate to find a way —any way—to stop him. But I had willingly brought this upon myself, and he relished every second of my fight.

His amused expression turned hungry as his orange eyes glinted in the night. "Such a pity that one so beautiful must be destroyed," he said, his hand latching onto my shoulder. "I can put you back to your true form. You were never meant to be trapped in this fragile body. Can't you feel it failing all around you?"

I squeezed my eyes shut and thought of Rowen. No matter what happened, I would keep thinking of him, of our few perfect nights together. I would let the memory of his fingers and breath on my skin give me strength.

"Beings of my kind made you. Therefore, it shouldn't be without too much difficulty to unmake you. You should be thanking me."

"You underestimate the Elder Spirits," I said, ignoring the dress that clung to my skin like a shroud of crawling spiders. "They chose me for a reason. Maybe this was their plan all along, and you're falling right into their trap." I was grasping at straws, but how could I defeat a being with no weaknesses?

The Dark Spirit smiled, a horrifying sight on his smooth, pale face. "The Elder Spirits have made many mistakes. As well as your fearless leader Nepta. When she broke the Stone, the Light sought a vessel from another world, though why it chose one so fragile is beyond me. You might just be another mistake, but I must admit, you were the last place I would ever look."

Erovos lifted both hands and placed them on either side of my face. His touch was gentle, almost like he was pulling me in for a kiss. Disgusted, I wrenched my head in his grasp, but his fingers dug in deeper. I may have agreed to be here to save everyone I loved, but I refused to be toyed with any longer.

"Do what you mean to do, and let's be done with it," I spat.

"Very well. Goodbye, Keira, bearer of the Alcreon Light."

A splitting pain unlike anything I'd ever felt erupted in my skull. It traveled down my neck and back in chasms of agony when, suddenly, a blast of light shot out of my arm like a bullet hole.

I blinked in shock before another silver beam shot out of my chest, then my shoulder, stomach, and hands. Bright streaks erupted all over my body, covering me in pinholes of searing Light.

I yanked against the bonds, uselessly thrashing as Erovos' fingers pressed into my scalp. I only knew I was screaming from the tearing sensation in my throat.

I'd emitted power out of my body before. But this? This was different. It was as if the Light was being pulled from the very essence of my being. My legs gave out, forcing my wrists to take the brunt of my weight.

Tears streamed down my face as I retreated somewhere deep inside, where I wouldn't feel this . . . this destroying.

"Watch as I free you," Erovos said, forcing my gaze back to his. His focus was steady as he dug his nails in so deep, I swore blood dripped down my temples. "Watch as I bend your body to my will, reshaping you into a gateway—a tunnel of light through which I can travel."

My eyes widened in terror as agony pierced me to my marrow. He was deconstructing me down to the purest form of Light.

My flesh burned out of existence as more streams of celestial brilliance shot out of my body. I barely registered the breathtaking sight before I whipped back in a violent arch; the Light engulfing me like an exploding star.

I was losing feeling, going numb, which was bad. Very bad. I tried focusing on my wrists where I still felt the cold metal shackles, but even that was fading.

Suddenly, the pain vanished. All of it, and the chains that once bound my wrists now hung limp and empty.

The body I knew was gone.

My pearlescent glow bloomed like a noxlily, my silver petals unfurling to connect with the sides of the tree, looking for something to grasp on to.

"Fascinating," Erovos marveled as his eyes grew wider, a shimmering pool of Light reflecting in his irises.

Me.

Somehow, I could still see and hear even though my senses were distorted without a body to anchor them. I should have been terrified, but it was oddly freeing. And for a moment, I considered giving in. I had already lost.

Or could I harness this new form? Use it to my advantage?

If Erovos intended to turn me into a gateway of Light, then I would be just that. I would decide who and how they passed. No one else.

Step through, I coaxed the Dark Spirit's mind, shocking even myself with the sound of my voice.

Erovos hesitated, astonished that I could speak to him. My caressing of his mind had defied his expectations.

What are you waiting for? Isn't this what you wanted?

Erovos remained where he stood, his billowing cloak of darkness brushing against his bare ankles.

Why wasn't he moving?

I couldn't lose this chance and let him slip away, not when I was slipping myself. I could barely remember why I was here, only that I desperately needed to contain this Dark Spirit before his blight spread through the cosmos.

More power awaits you, I lied, not letting my voice reveal how frightened I was, terrified that he might change his mind.

"You are under my command. And you will take me where I wish to go," he said, dipping his hand into my pool of Light.

My new form wanted to recoil, but I quickly latched onto his hand. *I will take you where a hungry being such as yourself deserves to go.*

Erovos tried to pull away, but my Light held firm. He yanked again, his expression twisting in fury as he realized I wasn't letting go. "Release me," he demanded, and when I ignored him, he thrashed like a wild animal, desperately fighting to break free.

You thought I was weak and easily manipulated. But you have unleashed me, I said, surging with unshackled power.

However strong I felt, Erovos was an Elder Spirit with formidable power, and I was losing my grip in our battle of wills.

You shall travel where I see fit for you to go, I said, struggling to hold on to Erovos' thrashing body, gnawing for release. I couldn't keep him like this forever. I would have to send him somewhere.

I shifted my attention, searching for a familiar prison, even though it already harbored a guilty man. Or what was left of him.

I frantically searched for the lightning-shaped crevice that had once opened just for me, revealing the astrally torn spirit of Maddock Mosa. His fractured mind had called to me after the connection we'd forged in the hospital where I'd tried and failed to save him. The echo of pain guided me to the place where all our destinies would intertwine.

I needed to hurry before I lost my hold on Erovos, which was weakening by the second.

At last, I found the crevice—dark and jagged, just as I

remembered it. And now, it would be the eternal resting place for both Erovos and Maddock.

But before I could transport Erovos, he wrenched free, and my heart plummeted like a cliff falling into the sea. The failures of my life stacked before me like a crumbling wall, waiting to bury me under the weight of my guilt. Maybe Erovos was right, and I was a mistake.

I failed not only Luneth but Earth as well, and any other planet Erovos deemed worthy enough to drain. Because the Dark Spirit would not give up; he would find another way to travel to distant worlds, returning here to use me once I'd forgotten who I was.

Suddenly, a bronze warrior burst from the shadows, barreling into Erovos with the force of a charging beast. Demil lunged out of nowhere, his momentum unstoppable as he locked the world eater in a tight embrace.

I could only watch as they both fell through my tunnel of light.

How had Demil returned so quickly? Had he slain Graem? The giant was colossal, but Demil was a fierce warrior. Had it come to deathly blows, or had Demil escaped, returning for one last shot at redemption?

"Unhand me!" Erovos shrieked as they plunged together into the crevice. The once handsome man who'd lain next to me in the ICU would be there to greet them. Though his physical body was comatose in a hospital bed, his astral body was stranded in the cave I now banished the Dark Spirit to.

But I didn't have the time or luxury to feel regret over Maddock and Demil. They had chosen their fates.

I extended my Light in a swirling vortex, pushing the traitor and world eater deeper into the crevice.

Erovos fought and gnashed, but Demil's arms squeezed tighter, never letting go of the Dark Spirit. The warrior's yellow eyes quickly traced over my glimmering essence, so out of place in this nightmarish cave. "Get out!" he screamed, his silver circlets stark against Erovos' black robes.

I pulled away, reeling in my current of Light as Demil held the Dark Spirit back, buying me precious time to escape. But I couldn't just leave. I needed to seal the rock shut.

With unspeakable strain, I tried to close the chasm, and to my disbelief, the sound of grinding stone filled the air. It was as if the earth was aiding me, helping me imprison the being that had fed off it for years. The lightning-shaped crevice closed, trapping all three men deep within the mountain.

Relief surged through me as I fell back and settled into my crushed diamond energy, letting it become all that I was.

Cradled within Indrasyl's hollow, I silently slipped away, and I knew no more.

5

I was peaceful. Nestled between the endless worlds that stretched out beyond me.

I spiraled in a dance of diamonds, dust, and moonlight. Infinity surrounded me as I floated on a sea of stars.

Had I always been like this? I tried to remember, but I let the thought drift away like petals on a pond. This existence was peaceful. There was no more pain, anxiety, or betrayal.

An echo fluttered at the edge of my awareness, stirring something within me. I hummed at the presence, sending a gentle wave in return before turning away. This peaceful bliss was all I wanted. All I was.

Nothing could hurt me within this chrysalis of time and space. I was safe here.

But then, it happened again—that echo that pulled me away from my serene void. Whatever it was, it threatened to create waves on the smooth surface of my existence. I had no intention of being disrupted, so I turned away and fled.

But the hum found me again and slowly morphed into a pleading whisper. *Keira,* it seemed to say, but the word held no meaning. It was an elusive glint, vanishing each time I tried to grasp it.

A caress rippled through my being, igniting the innermost flame within me.

Wait. I'd ached for this touch. Reveled in it, even.

It was someone I once cared deeply for, but who?

Suddenly, this solitude felt unbearably calm. I desperately yearned for ripples and waves and hands that knew how to handle me, touch me.

Rowen!

He was calling to me.

I spun to where I felt his touch, confusion overwhelming me as painful memories broke through my protective shell.

I remembered now—flashes of how I came to be here hit me like a tidal wave.

Erovos thought he tore my power from my body, but he hadn't. He'd just altered my state of being. I was still me. *Changed and altered, yes*, Rayal had said deep in the belly of the Crystal Crypts. *But never taken.*

I'd sealed the Dark Spirit deep within the crevice, but it wouldn't hold him forever. It was only a matter of time before he escaped. I had to get back and warn the others. This battle was far from over.

I needed to pull away from these tranquil waters and return to the life I knew. Yes, there would be pain and heartbreak but also unspeakable love and joy.

And Rowen.

I would claw my way back to him if I had to. I could still feel him there, feel his pain. I wanted to go to him, comfort him, but my new form held me back.

Suddenly, another sound echoed through me, soft yet layered with the harmony of several voices intertwined. *Light*

Bearer, you wish to return to Luneth? Even though you shall lose this peace?

My Light instantly recognized its maker. *I need to get back. No matter the cost,* I pleaded to the Elder Spirits.

When our Light found you in the forest, you were just a youngling, yet you contained more compassion and courage than many who have lived beyond your years. They hummed in accord. *That is still true of you.*

The Spirits confirmed I hadn't been born with the Light. It had found me. *I just wanted to help.*

One nebulous entity flickered beside me, but many voices spoke. *Yes, and we will need your help yet, but your body has been broken beyond repair. You will not be able to return as you were.*

Something in me shifted in agreement. I couldn't stay here a moment longer.

Very well. With what little power the Elder Spirits possess, we will grant you a gift. Thanks to the noxlily petals beneath your skin, we have anchor points to restore your body. You will not merely carry the Light. You will be reforged in it.

An astral gateway appeared before me.

I gathered my incorporeal self, summoned my courage, and pushed through the silver veil of light.

6

—————

I stepped out of Indrasyl's hollow and opened my eyes to a dark forest, my body bare like a wolf in the moonlight. As much as I wanted to run and howl with the energy swirling through my limbs, I knew I needed to return to the village.

The black dress Erovos had fashioned for me lay in a destroyed heap on the ground. I refused to put the horrid thing back on my body, but I couldn't return to the village wearing nothing.

A notion struck me. If Erovos could create a dress of darkness, I could create one out of light.

I summoned pinpricks of Light upon my skin, allowing the specks to create luminous paths along my body. Heavenly jewels draped down my chest and torso like liquid moonlight turned to fabric. The Light clung to my waist and hips, sparkling against me until it flared out and trailed behind me in a radiant train.

I was dressed in a glimmering gown that looked as if millions of diamonds had been painstakingly placed upon my skin one stone at a time.

My senses were keen, hyperaware, and my ear twitched.

There were eyes on me.

My sharp gaze darted to a massive figure hiding behind a tree. His dull, mossy stare looked frightened and unsure.

"You can come out," I said to Graem, and he slowly emerged from behind the tree.

"Master?" he asked, somehow looking filthier than when I saw him a few minutes ago. He always wore tattered clothes, but now they were threadbare and barely hanging on. Demil must have done a number on him when he escaped.

"He's gone," I said plainly.

"Master?" he asked, gesturing to me.

"No. You no longer have a master, Graem. Is there somewhere else you can go?" I asked. I didn't want to hurt him. I knew he had been under Erovos' control all this time.

He nodded his misshapen head, and for the first time, a spark of light shone in his flat eyes.

"Go there and never come back. Do you understand?"

He nodded again, his body twitching with eagerness.

"Good. Now, go!" I commanded, and without hesitation, he ran into the woods. The ground shook and trembled as he fled from what I could only assume was a life full of suffering.

I turned away from the giant and closed my eyes.

Home, I thought with the merest of whispers, and thousands of beautiful threads unraveled before me in a celestial chandelier. I gently searched through the strands until I found what I was looking for.

The shimmering thread to the Wyn village came easily. I gave it a gentle tug and rushed through a channel of stars until my feet landed on solid ground. I marveled at the grace with which I arrived just outside the village. I'd never traveled with such speed and elegance before.

My hair and dress tousled around me as I settled from my crossing in a beam of light. It came so naturally, unlike before when traveling had been such a struggle.

I welcomed in the sight of the village—a place I had come to call home since learning the Alcreon Light flowed within my veins. Teardrop domes bloomed on the horizon like wooden flower buds, and the forest brushed against the purple-and-sapphire sky.

I took a deep breath and curled my toes into the plush grass, but my brows knit together in confusion. The ground was pokey and dry—an odd sensation for a village that was perpetually verdant.

My gaze darted up as a bounding white wolf charged toward me, and I dropped to my knees. "Sabra!" I choked out. My heart soared at the sight of her.

After she attempted to save Ven, Graem had hurled her into a tree, where she'd lain lifeless and unmoving. The sound of her snapping in half still haunted me, but now she ran without the slightest limp.

How had Takoda mended her so quickly? The healer told me his medicines worked best on flesh and that bones were another matter. The only plant capable of mending Sabra was a noxlily, but Rowen had used the last one on me in the Crystal Crypts. Not enough time had passed for Takoda to grow more of the healing flower.

I batted the thought away. Who cared how she healed? The wolf was here, strong and magnificent. That was all that mattered. The desire to run my fingers through her billowing fur overwhelmed me, but as the wolf neared, she slowed, avoiding my outstretched hand. Her nose sniffed the air as she circled a wide berth around me, not letting me touch her. Amber eyes blinked at me from a distance, and she lowered her head and whimpered.

Fear immediately gripped me. The beautiful beast never faltered at my touch.

"Sabra, come here, girl. What's wrong?" I asked, patting the dry grass. I reached for her again, but she turned away from me with a flick of her snout.

I watched in confusion as she darted back to the village. Disappointment quickly morphed into elation as I saw Rowen sprinting towards me in a desperate fury.

"Keira!" he shouted my name from across the field. Emotion swelled in my chest like an overflowing chalice, choking up my throat and welling in my eyes. Members of the village rushed behind him to greet me.

"Rowen," I cried as I ran to his outstretched arms.

Rowen closed the distance between us and gathered me into a fierce embrace. But as soon as his hands landed upon my skin, he flew from my fingertips.

He catapulted across the sky, slamming into a tree with a devastating grunt. Fear cinched around my ribcage as I hunted for whoever attacked Rowen, ready to turn my hands on them and incinerate them into dust.

When I saw no one near, I sprinted towards Rowen, my dress trailing behind me in a stream of light. He let out a groan as he struggled to pull himself up.

I placed my hand on his arm, my murderous eyes scanning for whoever did this, but as soon as my skin touched Rowen's, his eyes rolled into the back of his head, and he convulsed violently in my arms.

Repulsed, I yanked my hands away, realizing I was the one inflicting pain on the only person I had ever loved.

Ever since Rowen had emerged through the mist of my dreams, I felt an inexplicable pull toward him. What began as a delusional attraction evolved into an earth-shattering love that spanned across galaxies. But the man who owned my heart and soul wasn't breathing, and something deep in my chest whipped in fear.

"Keira," he finally gasped, and the breath I'd been holding

loosened at the sound of his voice. "When I told you to learn to knock me on my ass, this wasn't what I had in mind."

A ragged laugh puffed up my throat.

I turned to see the entire Wyn village gaping in terror, their star-kissed hair gently blowing in the midnight breeze. I whipped my head back to Rowen.

His gaze trailed up my body, but the more he took me in, the more his brow furrowed in confusion and awe. "You're so beautiful," he rasped. "Are you all right?"

"You're worried about me?" I asked incredulously. "You're the one who was just hurled into a tree."

"I'm okay," he grunted as he sat upright, clutching his shoulder.

The light from my dress cast a glow upon the dark hollows of his face, revealing a trail of blood dripping from his nose.

The red stain upon his skin curdled my insides, and slowly, I took in my surroundings. The villagers looked horrified; the plants that used to shimmer in my presence were dead, and the dried grass poked at me like needles.

The once lush village was dying.

Suddenly, darkness bubbled up inside me—thick, heavy, and rotting—taking root within me like a seed of decay.

Death enveloped me. It was everywhere, all around me. *Within* me.

Erovos was right; my body was failing. I could feel it dying a little more with each passing second.

Tears flooded my eyes as anguish crept up my throat and choked me. When suddenly, lightning struck a nearby tree and shook the earth.

The Wyn elves gasped as they dodged the violent bolt.

I could feel more than see Rowen reach for me, just as he always had. "Don't touch me!" I screamed, tears streaming down my face and clouding my vision. "I don't want to hurt you."

Another bolt of lightning pierced through the nearest dome like a skewer. The Wyn scattered, trying to escape the sky. Escape *me*.

Takoda suddenly appeared beside me; his healing hands remained by his sides. "Star-touched, breath. Control yourself," he soothed in my ear, but the death was too strong, and growing, and lightning struck again. I was harnessing the Alcreon Light in bolts of lightning, but I wasn't controlling it.

I had no control.

Rowen's impossibly strong arms clasped around me, his fingers interlocking behind my back. We were chest to chest, fully flushed, and he shuddered against me as I shocked him unwillingly.

"Keira," he grunted in my ear, his body stiff as every one of his muscles strained from the current running through him.

My hair cracked and whipped around us as the sky roiled. The veins in Rowen's neck bulged dangerously. I tried pushing him off me, but he didn't budge. The stubborn bastard wasn't letting go.

Rowen was going to stop me, or he was going to die trying.

The light in his green eyes faded as the ground erupted and splashed around us. His eyes couldn't close; I wouldn't let them. Whatever I was feeling right now would multiply if Rowen died—there would be no stopping my rage. But the more I tried to gain control, the more I lost it. There was nothing I could do.

Suddenly, foreign arms wrapped around me from behind, trapping me between two walls of muscle. Both bodies pressed against me in an attempt to smother my celestial storm. Fear bolted through me as I waited for whoever was behind me to start convulsing.

But they never did.

"Stop," a familiar yet unfamiliar voice begged against the

curve of my ear. The stranger squeezed me tighter, his fingers digging into my skin. "You're killing him."

"I don't know how to stop," I cried as the two bodies pressed against every inch of me, but the men's strength was no match for my raging tempest. I was inconsolable as more light exploded in chaos and destruction.

"I'm sorry," the voice said before I was blasted with a Light that was mine yet wasn't. It pulsed through me calmly, peacefully, and my body went limp.

The last thing I saw before I blacked out was Rowen crumpling to the ground in front of me.

I collapsed into the stranger's arms, and the darkness I feared yet welcomed blanketed over me and carried me away.

I woke with a gasp, my body aching from the unforgiving surface beneath me. A breeze tousled my hair, and I winced as the sun beamed into my eyes.

"Careful, star-touched," Takoda said, his hazy silhouette coming into view. The healer regarded me with soft, worried eyes. "We were unable to move you. You remain where you fell."

Bits of last night flashed before my eyes in violent strikes of lightning and earth. Panic erupted in my chest. Not from barely escaping Erovos or the presence of death that picked at me like crows on a carcass, but by the pain I had inflicted on Rowen.

Was he still alive?

"Rowen?" I pleaded, my fingertips searching for him. Those nearest to me jumped back and avoided my arm.

"I'm here," came the deep voice that called to me from across the galaxies, but it was strained. Hurting.

My vision expanded. White-haired members of the Summit hovered over me, their faces creased with concern, and I noticed several warriors nearby, resting their hands on their weapons.

"Do not touch her," Takoda warned as Rowen pushed

through the crowd. Despite his emerald presence filling my view, a painful distance lingered between us. It mirrored the moments when he'd held back, the times he feared his true emotions would put me in danger.

When the false queen Aliphoura cursed Rowen, she vowed that if she couldn't have him, no one could. And the forced separation felt like a painful reminder of our past.

The air pulsed with energy as I examined his exquisitely sculpted face. He appeared exhausted, with a thicker beard, new worry lines, and deep purple smudges under his eyes. It looked as if he'd lived a thousand tortured lifetimes since I'd been gone. "Keira, you . . ."

"I shocked you," I whispered, guilt hanging from my heart like an anvil. I'd launched Rowen into a tree as if he weighed nothing, which was a feat, considering his body burgeoned with strength and power. His size had always been intimidating, but now it was fearsome. It was as if he'd doubled in muscle mass overnight. "That explains why Sabra wouldn't let me touch her. Though I'm not sure why this is happening."

"Whatever transpired with you and Erovos, it has caused the Alcreon Light to surge to the surface of your skin," Takoda said, his tone clinical yet concerned. "Without a proper channel to guide it, the Light is spiraling out of control, threatening to overwhelm you."

Wonderful. Where my Light had barely come to me in the past, it was now a weapon I couldn't control. Even the beautiful dress I'd fashioned was gone, flashed out of existence like a broken bulb, and I realized I was completely naked beneath a linen blanket.

"We were unable to dress you," Takoda said solemnly. "Or even move you to my dome. We quickly made you as comfortable as possible, hoping you would wake soon."

I sat up, clutching the blanket to my chest. The destruction I had wreaked upon the Wyn village surrounded me. The shame sat heavy in my gut.

My gaze darted back and forth, taking in the once vibrant landscape, now dull and dying, to Rowen's changed appearance. "How has all this happened in one day?"

"Keira," Rowen breathed my name. His gaze traced over my face, drinking me in like I was a long-awaited oasis. "You've been gone for nearly three moons."

"That's not possible," I choked out, clutching the sheet tighter. "I went with Erovos yesterday."

Rowen released a ragged breath.

"It has been a season's turn, star-touched. Rowen speaks the truth," Takoda said, resting his hands on his knees.

I was going to be sick. My existence as the Alcreon Light had only felt like moments, not a robbery of time. "Is Ven alright?"

"Ven is well. He is the one who told us you left with Erovos to save him and Sabra," Rowen said, his features twisting. "I searched for you every night in the Hymma. I thought I found you many times, but then you would slip through my fingers like liquid starlight."

During my time as the Light, I'd felt Rowen's touch ripple through me, and I'd turned away. "Erovos changed me, deconstructed me down to the purest form of the Alcreon Light. It took me a while to remember what—who I was. I'm sorry I couldn't remember sooner."

Rowen's face paled. "Don't apologize, my flame. You're here now. That's all that matters."

I gathered my legs beneath me, keeping the blanket wrapped around my body. My hair was somehow longer, thicker, and billowed around me like an underwater forest. Even my nails, normally bitten down to the quick, had grown long, healthy, and strong. The Light's influence had changed me from the inside out.

When I came to my feet, I remembered I hadn't fallen at all. I'd been caught. Someone had come up behind me and wrapped me in their arms. But they hadn't been affected the way Rowen had. "Who stopped me?" I asked, remembering that the stranger had a power like mine, and he'd used it against me.

"It is difficult to understand . . ." Takoda began as Rowen wrapped an overcoat around my shoulders without touching me. His welcoming scent enveloped me in a cloud of charcoal, musk, and sandalwood.

"One of our prisoners," Nepta, the Elven-head of the Wyn answered, her commanding voice strong yet tinged with grief.

What happened since I'd been gone?

"We don't know how the prisoner escaped to get to you. To lay his hands on you," Rowen seethed as his temples pulsed with fury. "There was no damage done to his cell. He may have used a dark portal to get to you."

"Who?" I asked, utterly perplexed.

"A man who claims to know you personally. He won't tell us any more than that. He says he will only speak with you," Takoda replied.

I wracked my brain. "I don't know anyone here. Unless it's someone who escaped the Crystal Crypts."

"Possibly," Rowen said as his fingers itched toward me. "It's quite a coincidence he showed up the exact morning you left."

My mind reeled. "The day I left? I don't understand."

"It could be a trap from Erovos, or the false queen. Her body was never recovered," Alvar, the captain of the Wyn warriors chimed in, his prominent brow furrowing over dark brown eyes. "The interloper refuses to tell us anything. His lack of coopera-tion does not bode well. We have no idea what his intentions are. He is not to be trusted."

Curiosity clawed at me. The Wyn village had been imprisoning a man for months. One they feared enough to detain yet somehow knew me. "Take me to him," I said, brushing the long, unruly strands of hair from my face.

"The prisoner can wait. No one is to see him until the best course of action is decided," Nepta said, her quartz headdress displaying the authority of her decision. "He is well guarded. It is more urgent that we know what happened with the Dark Spirit?"

"Oh. Of course," I said as I relayed how Erovos rid me down until I was nothing but Light, intending to use me as a gateway to other worlds. I recounted how I'd trapped him in the crevice, buying whatever time I could. How I'd been the everything and nothing of the Light for the last three months. And how the Dark Spirit had been using the Sylvan Mother Tree to drain Luneth dry.

"I should have suspected Erovos would use the sacred Mother Tree. It is a great and unforgivable sadness," Nepta said, the creases around her marble eyes deepening.

"The crevice won't hold him forever," Alvar remarked, managing to sound somewhat impressed.

"No," I agreed. "It won't."

The war captain traced the scar on his chin with a weathered finger. "Much has changed since your disappearance: the earth trembles and quakes. And now we know why. The Dark Spirit is fighting for release."

I stiffened in dread. Even though I already knew it wouldn't hold him forever, guilt swarmed me. I should have thought of a better prison.

"You did well, child. Had Erovos escaped to other realms, there would be no stopping him. At least now we have a chance," Nepta said, somehow sensing the remorse that engulfed me. The crystals from her headdress swayed around her neck. "Did you learn of any weaknesses?"

I pulled Rowen's coat closer. "No."

"And Demil? Where is that coward?" Rowen snarled.

"He helped me in the end, and I . . . I locked him away with Erovos," I said, my voice containing no emotion. I wasn't sure how I felt about Demil sacrificing himself. Was I grateful or remorseful? Both felt wrong, considering he put me in that position in the first place.

"He will most likely be tortured," Alvar commented solemnly.

"How I would like to torture him myself," Rowen said, a fire darker than anything Erovos could conjure flaring in his eyes. "Though I hope Erovos does a skilled job of it."

Nepta's stare passed through mine and latched onto something much deeper within my soul. "You are quite a force, child, battling two warring dragons within. One breathes great life and healing unto this world while the other wields destruction. You must choose which beast to nourish, the one who heals or the one who destroys."

Nepta's words chaffed. The line between ruin and renewal was thin, and I feared I had lost the boundary altogether. But both the beasts inside me agreed on one thing. We needed Rowen's touch. Desperately.

As if reading my mind, Rowen stepped directly in front of me and said, "I would like to try touching you again."

"Rowen, you only woke moments before Keira. She did quite a number on you. I've only just managed to slow your heart rate and stop the bleeding from your nose and ears. Not to mention how I had to put your shoulder back into place," Takoda said, motioning to his propagated medicines and supplies.

I felt the color drain from my face.

"We will test it again," Rowen offered me with a weak smile.

Takoda sighed. "You must be able to pull back, Keira. If you hold on for too long, his heart could give out."

I blanched, but Rowen cut in before I could refuse. "Keira, I trust you."

"That makes one of us!"

"Please," he begged. "Try."

"As lightly as you can," Takoda instructed.

I was terrified of injuring Rowen again, but I was willing to try. For him. And I nodded reluctantly.

The healer glanced at the warriors surrounding us. "Others, brace him. We don't want him flying into the trees again."

The warriors latched onto Rowen's shoulders, their arms holding him in place. His deep-cut, linen shirt was low enough that it exposed his skin. His massive chest, dappled with dark curls, rapidly rose and fell with each desperate breath.

Surely, the spirits weren't cruel enough to keep me from Rowen once again, especially after having left him alone and frightened for three long months.

I reached out and touched him as lightly as I could, barely pressing the pad of my finger to his chest.

Rowen's eyes immediately rolled into the back of his head. He convulsed violently, triggering a chain reaction that struck the line of warriors with my current. I jerked back in horror, helplessly watching as they all struggled to regain their balance.

Takoda darted to one of the warriors who had fallen to the ground. "Keira, I am sorry, but you are to touch no one until you have mastered your powers. And no one is to touch you. Not even your soul flame," he said with a pointed look at Rowen.

So the spirits *were* that cruel.

"No," Rowen growled fiercely as he swayed on his feet. "We have a few sprouted noxlilies. Give her one. Heal her," he demanded as the veins in his temples bulged.

"Rowen, she is not ailed," Takoda said with pained honesty. "She is uncontrolled."

I grimaced. I'd been called similar names by my parents. The treatments they put me through, *forced* me through, still pained me like a break that would never heal. I couldn't believe I was reliving the same situation, only this time with people who truly felt like family. And as if on instinct, a protective shield raised around my heart.

"Perhaps I could brew a few petals into a tea, but the flowers are slow to bloom and should only be used for grave injuries. Like Sabra. It is only because of the noxlilies that she is healed."

"He's right, Rowen," I whispered, my body aching to hold the man I was forbidden to touch. "Save the noxlilies for those who need it."

Rowen's jaw tensed, but he nodded in agreement. We'd only been given a few precious nights to touch and hold each other the way we'd always wanted to but had been denied. And though our separation only felt like days for me, it had been months for him.

My heart plummeted with a gut-wrenching force, but I agreed with Takoda. If my touch was hazardous, it was out of the question for me to get too close to anyone, even if it was the man I loved with every shattered and broken fragment of my being.

Nepta turned her regal stare to Alvar. "Now that we know the cause of the quakes, and where they originate, we must gather warriors to guard the crevice. Have them report any movement from our enemy."

Alvar's scarred chin dipped in compliance. "We will be the first to know if anything slips through the cracks. The mare must dress and show us the way," the war captain said, keeping with the nickname he'd granted me.

Rowen tensed beside me. "She's not going anywhere tonight. She just got back."

"I know the way," Takoda interjected before Alvar or Nepta could refuse. "I shall show you. Let them rest."

"Yes, get some rest, Keira. But your powers mustn't go untamed for long," Nepta said in an unspoken warning, and the air rang with the words she didn't say, *for if you don't, who knows what's to become of you.*

8

Rowen and I made our way through the low-lit village to his dome. Our dome? Hell, I didn't even know anymore. We hadn't had a chance to discuss living arrangements since he'd claimed me, body and soul.

"What happened to your clothes?" Rowen asked with a strangled moan. "Did he touch you?"

"No," I replied, and the tension in his shoulders released like a bowstring. "But he dressed me in his shadows."

Rowen's eyes darkened, rivaling the black cloth that had once adorned my skin, and a low, murderous growl rumbled through his chest. "He sought to mark you, that sick bastard. If you hadn't imprisoned him, I would torture him slowly and with frightening efficacy, leaving him alive, but only just, in agonizing pain until he begged for death."

"He's done so much damage," I murmured, recalling the lifeless forest, dead bodies, and extinct starwings. "Erovos destroys everything in his path. He deserves to pay for his crimes, but I have no idea how. My Light didn't hurt him, Rowen. He doesn't have any weaknesses."

Rowen's face paled, but he remained resolute, offering me

strength where I felt I had none. "We will find a way. Your brilliant mind found a way to trap him once. If he escapes, you will be able to do it again."

"I don't know how I managed it," I said, grasping for handholds as I fell down the well of my mind. "And now that I'm back, I can't make sense of anything. Everything feels so . . . dark."

Rowen's eyes flashed with empathy. "Keira, no matter how dark it gets, remember there is a way to find your Light again. Even if I have to make you find it myself."

"I'll hold you to that." I smiled, keeping a far enough distance to prevent any accidental touches. It defied everything in my nature to pull away from Rowen physically. "How did you know I was back?"

"A bright light, similar to what I've seen you do before, filled the sky. It was the most intense I'd ever seen it. The flash of light was there and gone, like how you used to appear to me in the night." His jaw clenched. "I *knew* it was you, Keira. After not being able to breathe for months, seeing your flash of light in the sky lifted a weight from my chest. Sabra sensed you as well. She hasn't left Ven's side for anything. When she charged towards the light, I knew it had to be you."

"I've never felt so powerful yet entirely useless," I said, my bare feet padding along the dry pathways. "I knew something was wrong when Sabra wouldn't let me touch her. I'm just glad she's all right. I didn't think she'd make it."

"Thanks to the healing noxlilies you brought back to life. You are so much stronger than you are giving yourself credit for. Your power—I saw it. You were magnificent, Keira. You looked like a goddess raining down from the heavens in your dress of stars, but then I saw you descend into doubt, and you disappeared in a haze. You were a being of pure light, as if the moon rested just beneath your skin. I charged into your glow, and it was the last thing I saw before I passed out."

"Passed out" was a nice way of saying knocked out. *By me.*

My abilities were out of control. I once had to beg for the Light in me to surface, but now it raged like an exposed wire above my skin. I was a live, walking, and talking electrical shock waiting to happen. I wasn't strong enough to contain it.

"Your hair. It's longer," he said, his fingers reaching to touch my lengthened tendrils, but he stopped midair. "I'm told it nearly covered all of you until Takoda placed the blanket over you. But your other changes, Keira. I think you're a—"

"Don't," I said, barely a whisper. "Not yet."

The changes in my appearance troubled me, but as Rowen's dome came into view, a lump of emotion formed in my throat. I wanted nothing more than to disappear within its wooden walls.

Rowen opened the circular door, grimacing as he led me through. The beautiful dome was in shambles. The canopy that once hung from the ceiling lay in a heap on the ground. Books, paper, and weapons were thrown and scattered on the floor. My gaze slid to his, knowing exactly what had happened.

Rowen appeared embarrassed and cleared his throat. "I was not doing well with your absence. Excuse the mess. I will take care of it while you rest."

"You don't need to apologize. I'm sure I would have done way worse."

"I shouldn't have done it, but your scent lingered on the sheets for weeks, slowly fading every day. I nearly brought the whole dome down the day it disappeared completely."

"You don't need to explain." I gulped. It seemed so unfair that what only seemed like a few days for me had been months and months of agonizing torture for him. "What I would like to know is how you managed to get bigger. It seems like you've done nothing but work out. You're huge! So is your beard."

"Trimming my hair was not high on the list of things to do while you were missing. Pushing my body to the brink of death seemed like the preferable option."

"I'm so sorry. I wish I could give you beard scratchies to make up for it," I said, my nails begging to run through his thick hair.

"Beard scratchies, huh? So, you like it then?" he hummed.

I crinkled my nose with a smirk. "Did I say that?"

"That's a polite way of saying you prefer it as it was." He grinned, a crooked smile pulling at his full lips. "I'm beginning to see you have very specific desires for my facial hair. The last time I shaved it off, you nearly punched me in the face."

I laughed, remembering how furious I'd been when he'd gotten rid of it. "Don't mess with perfection."

"Spirits, how I've missed that laugh," Rowen groaned, his voice a husky whisper filled with longing. Every part of his body, essence, and awareness reached for me, but he remained where he stood, fighting the urge to claim me as if it were the greatest battle he'd ever fought. "I've missed every part of you. Your smile, your taste, your laugh, your strong-willed spirit."

"I've missed you," I whispered, scanning every perfect line of his face and body, fighting my own silent battle.

Rowen approached me with the tenderness of a man handling a delicate yet wild creature. He removed his overcoat from my shoulders and eyed the blanket covering my body. His jaw ticked through his dark beard. "How I wish I could strip you of this and touch every inch of your skin that I uncover." His voice was rough yet fluid, like a tumbling of unpolished stones.

"I wish that too," I exhaled with a breathy moan when suddenly, memories of Erovos making me strip in front of him flashed through my mind, and I clenched the sheet tighter.

Rowen's emerald eyes didn't miss a thing as he assessed my body language. "What is it?"

"Erovos made me take off my clothes in front of him."

With a darkening, murderous gaze, he asked, "Do you need me to override that memory?"

I nodded, grateful he knew the exact treatment that would heal me. I wanted his precise and wild love to guide me away from this darkness. I needed his hands, mouth, and tongue to bend my body and pleasure to his will. "Yes."

"Then undress for me and only me," he commanded, his eyes blazing with a fire that promised to both scorch and heal me. "Anytime you remove your clothing, you will think of me and no one else. Do you understand? That memory will hold no power."

Knowing we were playing with fire, I eyed him with a hunger that wouldn't, *couldn't*, be sated tonight. I lowered the sheet over my bare shoulder, revealing my collarbone and the swell of my breast.

His eyes darkened thunderously. "Don't toy with me, Keira. Take it off. At least let me admire what I can't touch."

I let the blanket tumble down my body and pool at my feet. A low groan rumbled deep within him as I stood in his full view, allowing him to drink me in. "You are so fucking breathtaking," he said without taking his eyes off my alabaster skin.

He stepped toward me, the air pulsing between us. His breath washed over my face and chest, and he watched with satisfaction as my nipples hardened and my breasts turned heavy.

An unrestrained moan passed through my lips as he lowered his mouth to the soft flesh just under my ear. I was so sensitive that even without his touch, my body still responded to him. "Lie on the bed," he whispered, his lips hovering painfully over my skin as he trailed a breath down to my pebbled nipple.

Coming out of my trance, I asked, "While you clean?"

He chuckled. "I said I would do that while you rest. Right

now, I have other plans for you. I need your scent back in my sheets."

"How?" I asked, gesturing to the distance between us.

"I don't have to touch you to make you come, Keira."

My brows furrowed in confusion.

He chuckled again. This time, darker, deeper. Depraved. "Your hands will do my bidding," he said as he stalked toward me, forcing me back until my legs hit the bed.

Realization dawned on me as warmth pooled between my thighs. "Oh," I said as I lowered onto the sheets without breaking eye contact. I'd never done anything like this before, but my aching body begged me to try. "I might be bad at this."

"That's impossible," he said, his gaze pinning me to the sheets. "Just do as I say. I want to watch as my words make you unravel. Now, lie back and run your hands along your body."

His voice radiated through me as I laid down and traced my body with my fingertips. I watched his eyes taking in every inch of me, leaving no part of my skin uncharted.

All his intense focus was centered on me. It was intoxicating.

I arched my back as I drowned in the power of commanding such a formidable warrior. My undoing was the only thing that could claim his complete and utter attention.

"My hands are at your perfect breasts," he said, and my fingers found and pinched my nipples. "Good girl," he praised, his voice a tortured gravel.

"More," I moaned.

"My hands are tracing along your waist, lowering to your hips, where I squeeze you," he said, and my hands mirrored his orders. "I'm grazing past your hipbones, slowly teasing open your pretty thighs. I'm in between your knees now, pushing them apart. Further."

I shamelessly spread my legs wider, my mouth watering for

more of his commands. Rowen's nostrils flared at the scent of my desire. "Don't stop," I begged.

"By the spirits, you take my breath away," he said in a throaty rasp.

I writhed under my own touch as his words caressed me with powerful energy. But would it be enough?

"I can see how wet you are from here," he hummed approvingly. "I'm going to touch you now. Slowly, as I trace you up and down. That's it."

My touch lowered to my aching core, mirroring his every word.

Spirits. I *was* wet.

After a few strokes, I touched myself where my budding need demanded it most.

"Uh-uh, Keira. Aren't you impatient? I want to take my time with you." The absence of his touch tortured me, but the fear of him telling me to stop ached just as badly. I needed his words, needed them as badly as I needed oxygen. My fingers would be his instrument as he played me like a fiddle. "Don't you dare speed up."

"Please," I groaned, stroking myself. His mouth hovered over my pussy, his breath washing over my wet thighs as my whimpers filled the dome. I was begging for the missing fullness that should be buried deep inside me.

"Open yourself for me," he ordered, and I obeyed, easing out my throbbing clit. "How I wish I could feast on you, Keira. Kiss those lips until I lose myself in your taste, but until I'm able, I think I should like you to take a finger."

I whimpered as he made me deny myself, but it was as if I was possessed and he was inside my brain, controlling me.

I knew what I needed for release, but his words held me captive as I slipped a finger inside myself. My hips bucked the air in front of him, and his eyes watched with a dark fire that blazoned my blood. It was his own private show, one that he was orchestrating from the front row.

"So tight," he hummed. "How I wish it were me sinking inside of you."

"Rowen, please," I begged for mercy as I slid in and out, my finger coated in my arousal. I was floating, throbbing, begging him to let me speed up.

"Take another finger," he commanded.

I groaned uncontrollably as I filled myself with my own fingers, small and delicate, not nearly as rough and calloused as I needed.

"Can you feel me, Keira?"

"Yes," I panted. "Yes, I can."

"Don't stop. You're so close. Show me how you like it."

His eyes, words, and commands touched me in the way his body couldn't, and my hips jerked against my palm. "Come with me," I begged. I was so under his spell I couldn't see straight, but the thought of him coming undone from watching me sent me over the edge.

I heard the metallic clink of his belt.

"Yes. Look at me," I breathed, hypnotizing him with my body.

A primitive growl erupted from his chest. "You're so beautiful. Don't stop."

The depravity of how I lost myself in front of Rowen was exhilarating. My legs spread farther apart as I pleasured myself. There was no shame, no embarrassment. Only the tether of his voice orchestrating me, building me up for a crescendo that I prayed would come soon; otherwise, it felt like I would die.

"You're going to make me come, Keira. I won't last much longer," he rasped, stroking himself.

"Yes. Oh God, yes," I panted as I took my other hand and pressed where my blood demanded it most.

We cried out in unison as our bodies convulsed side by side in waves of ecstasy. Our pleasure collided across the distance that separated us. In the fabric of space, where our pleasure met, we were together. At least there.

My peaked breasts heaved as Rowen crashed down beside me—an eternally long twelve inches apart.

"When I get my hands on you, I'm going to take you in every way. No part of your skin my tongue won't taste, no part of your soul I won't mark, no hole in your body I won't fill," Rowen ground out, his chest heaving.

"Yes," I whimpered, my inner walls still contracting. Every part of me screamed for Rowen's touch, a soul-deep desire that raged for his words to become reality, but the aftershocks of my orgasm pulsed torturously around nothing, and I was left empty.

As my shaking subsided, the aching distance between us grew. The inability to hold each other was an echo of our past, when Rowen had been cursed from touching me, loving me, fucking me.

Now, it was I who was cursed, uncertain if I would ever feel the warmth of Rowen's touch again. The thought hung between our soaring bodies like a weight, making our fall back down to earth that much more painful.

9

———

After a long, restless night, I woke to a clean room. The canopy was re-hung, and the fabric swooped around me in a sheer embrace. The bookshelves were restored and decorated with his books, knives, sketch pads, and journals. He'd even hung up a few of his favorite sketches. The wooden frames contained drawings of mountains, forests, and the streets of his hometown, Viltarran, before Aliphoura destroyed it. But most of them were of me.

"How did I sleep through all of this?" I asked in amazement, hearing Rowen move about the dome.

It had taken me forever to fall asleep. I worried all night that I would accidentally brush up against him and stop his heart. When I did manage to sleep, it was haunted with dreams of black holes, bloody noses, and dying trees.

"Once I got out of bed, your tossing and turning stopped, and you slept like a hibernating mawcat," he said, bringing in a tray from outside. His thick beard was gone, trimmed down to a perfect stubble. "Drooled like one too." He grinned as he placed a colorful platter on the bed; the aroma of fresh bread, berries, and amber syrups made my mouth water.

"At least I don't snore," I rebutted.

"You do that too." He grinned.

I wrinkled my nose. "Do not."

Rowen grabbed a note from the tray. "It's addressed," he said, his eyes scanning the letter. "It's from Takoda. He says to enjoy and to get your rest. No visiting the training grounds or the prisoner."

"They may as well throw me in the cell with him," I replied, tearing into one of the brown loaves. "It's no less than what I deserve for last night."

Rowen's brows furrowed as he folded the note and lay beside me, resting his weight on his elbow. "He most likely wants us to avoid high-stress situations," he said, digging into the delicious spread, our fingers careful not to touch. "And seeing you locked behind bars? Well, let's just say that wouldn't be a good thing for either of us."

"Do you know what the prisoner looks like?"

"I have not seen him."

My chest deflated. "Whoever he is, he used my Light against me."

Rowen's jaw tightened, and his eyes darkened.

"And I've done nothing but rest for months. It's the last thing I want to do right now," I continued as I plopped a ripe berry in my mouth. The flavors exploded on my tongue in a burst of earthy sweetness, and a moan slipped past my lips. The food landed in my empty stomach, and I realized I hadn't eaten in months. I hadn't needed to, but the jarring thought made me realize how hungry I was.

I devoured another berry and moaned again.

"If that isn't one of the most beautiful sounds," Rowen said, his eyes softening as they locked with mine. "Your absence took the joy from my world. Made everything *less*. Less beautiful, less colorful. Less flavorful. Everything tasted of stale wood chips."

I chuckled. "Glad I could help your appetite."

"In more ways than one," he said, giving me that lopsided grin that melted my insides.

"Ugh," I groaned in frustration. "We can't touch. We can't train. We can't visit the prisoner. What can we do?"

"We could try resting. Just for today," he suggested noncommittally.

I knew Rowen was worried about me, and I couldn't blame him. The way I'd lost control terrified me too. Despite our smiles and laughter, the memory of last night lingered like a storm cloud, casting a pall over our morning.

I could lose control at any moment. It was a miracle no one was hurt from my dangerous panic attack last night.

I would try the healer's suggestion, and if nothing worked, I would have to leave the village. I couldn't risk hurting anyone. Takoda said even one more touch could kill Rowen.

I threw myself back on the bed. "Okay, now what?"

"Now, we lie here," he said, his voice deep and caressing, and I flushed as I recalled how he'd guided me through my self-given orgasm. Remembering how his words had been penetrating, powerful, and commanding.

I watched Rowen through half-lidded eyes, my bare breasts heaving as his tongue darted out to lap at the berry juices dripping down his fingers.

I was entirely mesmerized, wishing it were my finger he sucked between his lips, and a desperate moan escaped me as my hands tightened in the sheets.

We lay side by side, our chests heaving from the palpable tension.

"This is torture," I said, scooting off the bed through the curtains. The memories of all the ways Rowen had touched and claimed me in these sheets were too potent to push aside. "How is anyone supposed to rest like this?"

He ran his hand down his newly trimmed beard, letting out a pained groan. "Resting is shit, isn't it? How about we go for a run?"

I perked up, immediately loving the idea of his company in an activity I'd always done alone. "Tell me more."

He sat up and watched me through dark lashes. "You mentioned you liked the competition of it."

"You want to race?" I asked, a shocked smile spreading across my face.

"By the spirits, I've missed that smile. I . . . I've been wracked with grief, Keira. When I woke up, you were nowhere in sight. I searched the village in a panic, turning murderous when Ven told me what you'd done. What Demil had done."

"I wonder how Dyani is," I said, curious how she'd been dealing with her twin's betrayal.

"I'd say she trained as hard as I did. Who do you think I sparred with? She wanted me out of the village and challenged me to a duel. She blamed me for what happened between you and her brother. I wanted to hate her, but I recognized her suffering. Our pain wasn't so different, hers and mine. We battled for hours with no clear winner, fighting until our injuries were too great to continue. Neither of us said a word as we limped off to tend to our wounds. We just met the next day and repeated it all over again, channeling our shared grief into every strike of our blades."

My heart ached as I listened to Rowen describe how he'd endured my absence. "I'm glad you weren't alone. Though I'm sure you two put on quite a show."

"We did end up attracting a crowd," Rowen said as a glint of violence flashed through his eyes, recalling the desperate measures he'd taken to cope. And at that moment, I realized I would go to any lengths to ensure his happiness.

"So, about that race?" I asked, moving to give him a playful bump with my shoulder. But my whole body recoiled with an unnatural, against-all-laws-of-physics jerk as I stopped myself.

Rowen noted the unnatural flinch of my body and said, "Let's get the fuck out of here."

I dressed in a woodland-blue vest, fitted leggings, and boots. I tugged at the material rubbing against my skin, realizing I hadn't worn proper clothes in months. Though the garments were soft, I found the fabric restricting and uncomfortable. Would I ever get used to being human again? Or whatever the hell I was?

I knew there were changes to my new body. I could feel them. But Rowen, being patient and understanding, knew not to rush me to face them. His willingness to distract me with one of my favorite hobbies filled me with gratitude.

Rowen, dressed in his usual form-fitting pants and loose linen shirt rolled up to his elbows, led me to a secluded section of the village. As he fidgeted with the flint stone he'd pulled from his pocket, I studied his adept hands, missing the trail of his fingertips along my skin. Though he'd made me pleasure myself last night, my slim, smooth fingers hadn't been enough. I needed his rough, calloused palms scratching my skin and his broad fingers entering me, curling up, and stroking my—

"Keira! I can practically taste your arousal in the air," Rowen said roughly. "Let's begin the race before I do something foolish, like commanding you to ride your own hand right here, where anyone could see you."

"Sounds tempting," I said as my mouth watered and my thighs rubbed together. My body didn't seem to understand why it was deprived of Rowen's touch, and I bit my lip as I warred against every fiber of my being.

"By the spirits, Keira. Don't do that. It makes me want to take your lips in my mouth and taste you before tracing my tongue along every inch of your body. Pleasuring you until I drop from exhaustion."

I released my lip with a moan, ignoring the bone-deep desire to be reunited with him in every way. To claim and be claimed. "I guess I will just have to find other ways to exhaust you," I said, desperate to turn the conversation away from my aching core. "Should we make bets on who is faster?"

"What would you like to bet?" he asked with an inquisitive arch of his brow.

"Loser has to serve breakfast in bed for a week."

"The last time you went to get breakfast in bed, it took you three months to return. With no food in hand, I might add."

"Okay, so that's out," I said, picking up a small branch and drawing a line in the sand. I tossed the stick and wiped my hand on my pants. "Where should we race too?"

"There," he replied quicker than expected, pointing to a tree in the distance.

"Sounds good," I said, lowering into a crouch.

"Copeland, what are you doing?"

"I'm getting into a runner's start. You might want to pay attention," I said as I settled into position. "Place your hands along the line and get into a nice, balanced base. When I say 'set,' you raise your hips. Like this."

I felt Rowen's eyes tracing over all the wrong areas of my demonstration, not observing the angles of my knees or the placement of my feet. "I do enjoy watching your ass in the air like that," he said, confirming my suspicions.

"Focus. I don't want any excuses when I beat you."

"Apologies. Please, continue."

"Then you wait for the signal to, 'go'," I said, relaxing out of my stance. "Starting like that enhances the speed of your take-off. The first step is the most important. It's how you shoot out that really sets the tone of the race."

Rowen mirrored my positions. "How do I look?" he asked with a crooked smirk.

His massive thighs and firm ass flexed as he lifted his hips, and the tendons in his forearms bulged as he distributed his weight. I couldn't help but admire his form. "You make a perfect student."

"Don't let me distract you now," he said, jolting me from my admiring.

"You wish," I said, situating myself back into position. "On my mark . . . set . . . Go!"

I exploded from my stance as muscle memory kicked into place. As much as I loved running, it also filled me with terror. I had conditioned myself to believe that I was safe when I ran, that fleeing from everyone and everything was the only way to escape the threats closing in around me. But now, as the rhythm of my footfalls harmonized with the man beside me, running changed. It was no longer a solitary journey but a shared path with the man I loved.

Rowen was a formidable opponent, but I beat him to the tree with a few moments to spare.

"Best two out of three?" he asked with a wild grin.

"I know what the loser gets to do," I panted.

"What's that?"

"Sleep on the floor."

"Absolutely not," Rowen said as if the suggestion were criminal.

"What if I accidentally touch you? Takoda said one more touch from me could stop your heart."

"I've had to live believing I lost you. Twice now. Living through that type of anguish shredded my soul. I don't think I could live through that again. And I'll be spirits-damned if I won't be as close to you as I possibly can."

My eyes trailed up the tree that Rowen had selected so quickly. But it wasn't one tree at all; it was two, spiraling around each other in a tender duet. "This is the entwined souls tree," I said, recalling the story Ven had shared with me on one of our adventures. He spoke of how, when Rowen first came to live in the village, many elves invited him to the tree that looked like two lovers embracing, growing together, and supporting one another. Forever intertwined.

He had declined every invitation, and I could see why. The entwined souls tree was a symbol of love, unity, and everlasting commitment.

"It is," he replied, a deep fire burning in his eyes.

"Oh. We can go. I know you like to avoid this tree."

"I want to be here," he said, his expression sincere and anchoring. "With my soul flame."

My breath caught in my throat. "You and Takoda have said those words before. *Soul flame.*"

My eyes locked with Rowen's, and our breaths quickened. We were nearing the precipice we'd been edging toward since that first day in the forest. The anticipation thickened in the air like honey, sweet and heavy, knowing that once we fell, there would be no turning back. "Yes," he said in a low rumble. "How does that make you feel?"

"It sounds pretty intense," I whispered.

"You had to travel from another world for me to find you. That's as intense as it gets."

"What . . . what is it?" I asked, gulping as I read the look in his eyes that, in one glance, shot across the universe as it landed on me.

"You know," he said, his voice like a finger trailing down my spine.

"I know we are *something*," I replied, my knees trembling.

"We are most assuredly more than *something*," he said as his gaze held mine infinitely, and I shivered. "You are not just my perfect match but the beacon to my soul. And I to you. We each carry a piece of each other's innermost flame, forging a celestial bond that transcends worldly limitations. It's the deepest connection two souls can make. I always suspected, but it wasn't until I joined you in the Hymma that I knew for sure."

"The Hymma joining," I barely breathed. "Takoda said it's dangerous to join another's Hymma, that..."

"That only soul flames are capable of such a thing."

The golden fire that lived deep within me flared. "That was a pretty big risk you took on a hunch. We could have both been lost. Trapped within the darkness of my mind."

A wounded grunt escaped his lips. "I'd do it all again, Keira. I never thought I would be able to claim you as my soul flame, but I'd be spirits-damned if I was going to watch you shatter," he said, so raw, open, and honest with no traces of the mask he'd once hidden behind. "I was a soulless corpse before I found you. I would rather walk lost within the darkness of your mind than take one step upon this earth without you."

"If anything happened to me, you could find another."

"Never say that. Never think it. There would be no one else. Ever. Soul flames are so rare, they were thought to no longer exist. That's why I took you to the entwined souls tree. I want you to know, you are, and will forever be, my soul's flame."

That golden light erupted through my body, and I smiled, bursting with happiness. Rowen leaned in closer, his breath sweeping across my neck, causing a drip of desire to shiver down my spine.

"I felt the flare of our bond the second I stepped out of the Hymma," I said, reveling in the one thing that felt safe—my connection with Rowen.

"As did I," he said, looking like the last piece of his soul had found its way home. "It was one of the best and worst days of my life. Knowing you were mine but unable to take you in my arms and hold you forever." His incandescent expression slowly shifted, and his brows furrowed. "Keira, you need to know. Though our bond fully snapped into place that day, something has happened to it."

My heart plummeted. "How do you know?"

"When Aliphoura held you prisoner, I should have been able to locate you immediately," he said, the words mangled as they left his lips. "Our connection should have surpassed her curse on me, but it didn't. And again, when you were with Erovos. I should have found you much faster."

"Is it my fault?" I asked, my hand flying to my chest to protect our bond.

His gaze softened. "I don't believe so. But we will figure it out."

The golden light within me shattered and rained down on my insides. Even though our bond was strong and enforced with celestial light, there was the possibility that we might never touch again. "What if I can't get myself under control? What if I'm always on the brink of an attack that could stop your heart and snuff out your flame forever?"

"I'm not going to let that happen," Rowen vowed.

"How?" I whispered, my eyes trailing up his towering frame, locking onto the green pools of his eyes.

"We will find our way back to each other. We always do," he said, his voice low and unwavering, like a promise forged in the depths of his soul. "I will hold you again. Have you call out my name in ecstasy as my fingers and tongue are deep inside of you." He looked me up and down, clearly recalling the way he could make my body writhe and beg beneath him.

I nodded, trusting that our bond was strong enough to bring

us back together. That our shared beacon of light would guide me back to myself, to him.

Eventually, the best two out of three races turned into the best three out of five, and so on, until we both lost count of how many times I'd beaten him.

Sweat poured off Rowen's body as he held the stitch at his side, laughing through the pain. Whereas I had barely broken a sweat. Which was odd. I'd always been a sprinter and hated running for miles on end.

"Do you have the waterskin?" I asked, my throat mildly parched after hours of running.

"Yes, but drink sparingly," he replied, handing me the water.

My eyebrows creased as I took a small gulp. "Why?"

"Since your absence, the condition of the village has worsened. Our water supply is dwindling as the rivers run dry. We have been suffering from drought."

My face paled. No wonder Nepta looked so worried. The blight she'd managed to keep at bay had finally breached her home.

I stood in disbelief, weighing the canteen that wasn't even half full.

"We all knew this could happen, yet now that it's here, it feels unreal," I said, somehow believing the Wyn village was immune. "But when it comes to a world eater, nowhere is safe."

Rowen's eyes glistened with understanding. "Let's get you cleaned up. There is still water to wash up with, though not much."

"I barely broke a sweat," I said, wanting to preserve as much water as possible. "I can meet you after."

"Keira, I think it would be best if you came to the bathing suite," he said, straightening from his crouch. His eyes traced my body with the same look he'd given me the night I'd returned. "There are things you need to see."

I nodded, knowing he was right. But it was comforting to pretend everything was fine, if only for one afternoon. Once I looked in the mirror and faced myself, it would all be real.

We made our way to the bathing suite when suddenly, the ground trembled beneath our feet. I grasped onto the nearest tree to keep from falling into Rowen's arms.

The violent tremors seemed endless as they shook the earth in a deafening grumble. When the ground finally settled, my eyes narrowed. "Erovos."

"Yes, he has been doing that for months, and they grow stronger still."

Anger flooded my veins. "It's as Alvar said: Erovos is fighting for release from the crevice."

"And from the feeling of that quake, I'd say it won't be too much longer until he escapes."

"I need to be ready for when he does," I said, still holding onto the tree.

Rowen's gaze lowered to the spots where my fingers dug into the bark; my grip formed two scorched handholds within the wood. Strength appeared to be yet another gift bestowed upon me by the Light.

His eyes met mine, brimming with concern and wonder.

I withdrew my hands from the trunk and continued on in silence, wanting to pretend just a little longer that I was still human.

10

The outdoor bathing suite was a sorrowful sight. The lush foliage had faded, leaving significant gaps in the forest walls, and the water ebbed at dangerously low levels. The white stone bath and cascading waterfalls were mere shadows of their former glory.

The last time I was here, the space overflowed with light and life, and Rowen had been able to touch me. He bathed me, washed my hair, and ran his hands along every inch of my skin —made me come with the touch of his hand. Strange how that felt like a lifetime ago.

Now, we took turns bathing, cautious and separate. I wasn't a scientist, but it didn't take one to know that bathing with an electrical conductor was a risk not worth taking.

The sound of trickling water filled the silence between us. Rowen must have sensed I wasn't ready to talk. Not yet.

Our separation was already proving to be torturous. And with each swipe of the eucalyptus bar, my body felt . . . different.

Finished with our baths, we descended the floating steps and wrapped ourselves in the plush robes that awaited us. We entered the anteroom, a vanity and chair seamlessly carved into the tree trunk. As much as I wanted to avoid the mirror, I knew it was time to face what the Elder Spirits had done to me. I lifted my eyes and drew in a sharp breath.

I knew I had changed, but the Light had reforged me with more than I could have ever imagined. I brushed the thick forest of my hair back, revealing slender ears that came to a sleek point. Starlit freckles adorned my new ears in what looked like studded diamonds.

I traced the outer shell of my ear in disbelief. *What the fuck!*

The Wyn had tapered ears and were referred to as elves many times, but mine looked completely different. The Wyn's ears arched up with a subtle flare like the tip of a leaf, while mine were longer and more tapered.

I moved my face back and forth under the moonlight, my freckles gleaming with a faint, ethereal glow. My silver-grey eyes stared back at me in disbelief. "This is insane. I recognize myself, but I don't. Why don't I look like the Wyn?"

"I've read stories about the elves from the old world. They were said to have similar features. It could explain your enhanced strength and endurance. But I'm not sure."

I let out a strangled gasp.

Rowen was right behind me, offering his support through his eyes in the mirror. "There is more, Keira. Lower your robe."

I let the robe slide to the ground.

I inspected my body, taking in the changes the Alcreon Light had given me. I would have to cut this hair soon. It was way too long. And this morning, I'd bit my nails down to the quick only for them to grow back long and healthy.

The other changes to my body were more subtle. I'd always had a muscular build from running, but now my muscles felt stronger, bigger, yet somehow lighter, more agile. It was an odd sensation, feeling extremely powerful yet on the verge of a complete breakdown.

As my search continued, I noticed a scar on my ribcage. It looked like a swirling galaxy of molten silver upon my skin. My finger traced over it lightly before noticing more marks on my stomach, arms, and legs.

"Those are all the places I healed you with the noxlily," Rowen said, inspecting my marks. All other blemishes and scars were gone, except where the noxlily petals absorbed into my skin like shimmering tattoos. They were everywhere.

I'd given myself tunnel vision to ignore these obvious changes, but now, the memories flooded back. "The Elder Spirits mentioned Erovos broke my body beyond repair," I replied, and a tortured sound left Rowen's lips. "They used the petals as anchor points to bring me back. And now it looks like . . . like I'm . . ."

Rowen clenched his jaw. "The Marked."

I nodded before counting ten more glimmering marks, and that was just what I could see. I knew there was one at the base of my skull. During my brutal time in the Crystal Crypts with Caeryn and Fou, I'd sustained a severe head injury along with a myriad of broken bones. Rowen had treated my concussion first, forcing me to feel and fight for my life as he brought me back from the brink of death, healing petal by healing petal.

The Spirits tried to warn me that I would return with more power, but they gave me too much! They'd had to alter my body to handle it, but even with these changes, it was still a burden I struggled to bear.

It was, as Takoda said, *overwhelming me*. But I was determined to prove myself, Takoda, and Nepta wrong. I needed to show that I could handle the new power within me.

The bathing chamber once overflowed with glowing blossoms, but now, it housed only a single flower, its petals wilting at the edges. "Keira?" Rowen questioned as I rushed over to it, my heart aching for its fragile state.

My light had been known to grow vegetation, spark moon-blooms, and even bring extinct plants back to life. The least I could do was help one withering flower.

I gently cradled the indigo plant, the precious life flickering within my palms. My heart soared as it recognized me, but then, like a creeping tide, the wilting edges washed upon my consciousness in brutal waves.

Suddenly, I was drowning in death. It was everywhere, not just in the flower but in everything. In *me*. It overcame my body, and before I could let go, the decay spread, drying the petals to a burnt crisp.

The flower was already dying, yet I had sped up the process and killed it faster.

Tears burned in my eyes, blurring the dead petals in my hand. I thought I had the gift of life, but I was wrong. I had the penalty of death.

I couldn't see anything as storm clouds gathered overhead, but the air was parched. Not even my tears could summon the rain we so desperately needed.

"Keira," Rowen yelled over the thunder. "Breathe. You're okay. It's okay."

The panic had taken over, blinding me. I couldn't stop. Everyone was right to handle me with care. I was unstable.

"Breathe with me," Rowen called from right beside me, but I couldn't wrangle myself in; my thoughts spiraled in death. "Be here with me. Please."

"I don't want to feel like this," I cried, the sense of doom looming within me. I was thankful that Rowen wasn't trying to touch me; if I hurt him, I would never recover. "I'm scared of what is happening to me. I'm losing all control. Losing myself."

"My flame, it's all right, you're all right," Rowen soothed as I choked on feelings of dread and terror. "Be here with me in this moment. Now this moment. And this moment."

Second by agonizing second, Rowen helped me back to myself, and I tried the age-old trick of breathing in through my nose and out through my mouth.

"Good girl. You are here with me in this moment," Rowen assured as the wind calmed and my hair fell around me in thick tendrils. My eyes snapped to my soul flame, looking terrified yet relieved as I came back to myself.

I collapsed to my knees, my hair floating around me like billowing seaweed. "I'm so sorry."

"You have nothing to be sorry for. We will get through this. You are the strongest person I know."

"I have no clue what to do."

"Just keep being yourself. That is all you can do."

"I'm trying," I said, hoping I could stay myself while everything slowly slipped away and darkness crept in.

"Will you be okay to dress while I gather the Summit? They will know more about your changes and markings than I," Rowen said, his strong and unwavering presence offering me comfort.

"Yes, I'll be okay. It will be nice to have a moment to gather my thoughts."

"You are safe here."

"I know," I said with a weak smile, holding my arms around myself.

Rowen quickly changed into his dark breeches and shirt and fastened his holster around his waist with a few deft clinks of his belt. "I'll be back for you."

"I'll be here."

A part of me was scared to learn the truth. The possibilities terrified me, but there was no more denying it, no more running from it. The truth had to be faced. The body I once had was gone, the woman I knew vanishing before my very eyes, something terrifying taking her place.

I hoped the Summit could help me find answers. If not, I feared I would aid Erovos in bringing about the destruction of us all.

⸱⸱ ᴄ ⸱ ● ⸱ ᴐ ⸱⸱

Dried and dressed, I sat at the wood-woven vanity and picked at my nails.

"They await us at the Sacred Vale," Rowen said, his comforting aura filling the powder room. His dark hair framed his face in perfect waves, and the hollows at his temples flexed as he took in my nervousness. "Are you ready?"

"No," I moaned, burying my face in my hands.

Rowen exhaled and then approached me with deliberate steps that commanded my attention. He towered over me before he dropped to his knees, his eyes locking with mine.

He placed his hands on either side of the chair, his fingers so close to brushing against me that my thighs squirmed. It reminded me of the night at Prism when my drinks had mixed with the opiates in my blood, and I'd been drunkenly relegated to sitting on a stump in the middle of the forest.

He was careful not to touch me then, and he was careful not to touch me now. "I know it's hard and frightening, but once we know what is happening, we can move forward. It's as you said, the first step of the race is the most important. It's what sets everything else in motion. This is that first step, Keira. Let's take it together."

I smirked up at him. "Look at you using running analogies. And here I thought you weren't paying attention."

"Only at first." He grinned, his full, white smile on display.

"Well, when you put it like that," I said, standing in a cobalt dress that flowed to the ground. The back was open, plunging all the way to my tailbone while braided straps draped across my shoulders. Even though the fabric was soft, it chafed against my overly sensitive skin.

Rowen's eyes trailed down my body, caressing my skin with his gaze.

A low growl emanated from his chest. "The sooner we figure out how I can touch you, the better."

11

We ventured toward the tucked-away path of the Sacred Vale, guided by the light of the stars and luminorbs. "I should warn you. It looks much different," Rowen said as I followed him across the shimmering stones that once hovered on water. "Though the waterfalls are gone, we still walk upon sacred ground."

I nodded, missing the sapphire pathway that was now a dried riverbed.

We entered the Sacred Vale, the stones transforming into a natural bridge that connected to the floating island. My heart sank. Rowen was right; where dozens of waterfalls had cascaded into misty chasms, there were now only silent, barren cliffs.

Though so much had changed, myself included, the ruins of the Alcreon Stone still hovered above us.

My first time here, I had a vision, or perhaps a memory, of the Alcreon Stone in all its former glory. It radiated in an ethereal light that seared my eyelids before returning to its shattered state.

At the Battle of the Breaking, when Nepta had freed the

Light, she'd broken the stone into pieces. I couldn't help but wonder if that was what happened to my body when Erovos altered me. Thankfully, the pain had spared me from truly witnessing the transformation.

"Hi," I said to the Summit members gathered around the marble table. I was sure it sounded as strange as it felt, but what else was I supposed to say after disappearing for three months and finally returning with deadly panic attacks?

"You are ready to face your changes," Nepta said, snapping me back to the Vale. The Elven-head sat in her chair of woven moonlight, surrounded by the members of the Summit.

"I am," I said, brushing my hair aside, revealing one pointed and light-studded ear, and a unified gasp rose from the table.

"The Ancient Elves," Driskell whispered in awe. The second-in-command's long hair, adorned with twisted braids and crystals, swayed as he shook his head in disbelief. "She has the ears of our ancestors. I've only ever seen them rendered in scrolls."

"It can't be. The Ancient Elves disappeared long ago. There has been no sign of them for over a millennia," Takoda said, glancing at Nepta.

"Who?" I asked, missing the reassuring hand that once held mine under the table. Even when Rowen was cursed from loving me, he'd found little ways to comfort me. Those brief, hidden touches had kept me going, but now we were deprived of even those small gestures, and I dug my fingertips into my knees.

"The Ancients were the first to nurture the newly budded world after the Elder Spirits sang life into existence," Nepta began, her voice and eyes distant as she recounted the primordial melodies that brought Luneth to life. "In the new, wild world, the Ancient Elves gathered the teeming life and gave it purpose and direction. It was they who discovered that the earth could be sung and manipulated into other masteries."

"What happened to them?" I asked, eager to learn more about the elves who first governed Luneth.

"They lived for an age in harmony with the natural world. Their hearts pure as they cultivated a deep connection with the land. However, as the time of man and tainted hearts grew, they retreated into the land and disappeared without a trace. But now that trace has returned," Nepta said, her eyes latching onto something deep within me.

My heart pounded. "The spirits warned me that I would be reforged. I just never imagined how profoundly they would change me. Though I guess it makes sense. I wasn't born with the Alcreon Light. It found me when I was eight years old during one of my projections to Luneth." The Summit leaned in intently, and it felt nice to finally have some answers to share. "I helped save a starwing, and it led me to Erovos and Indrasyl. The Light knew I wasn't from Luneth. I think it was desperate. But there is one thing I still don't understand. You said the Battle of the Breaking happened two hundred moons ago. That's sixteen years. That means I was seven when you shattered the stone. It doesn't add up."

"The Alcreon Light chose a benevolent host," Nepta said, unsurprised. "The Light must have wandered the land for a year until it found you, keeping itself well-hidden until it felt safe. It was no hasty decision, my child. The Light saw something in you."

My breath caught in my throat as I imagined the Light unprotected and alone. So vulnerable and afraid. The same as me. "I was only a small human child."

"Be that as it may, you have always had celestial influence, a connection to nature and cosmic forces," Nepta replied, her tone laced with respect. "The Elder Spirits saw fit to intertwine your abilities with our ancestors, enhancing your body to better hold the power to meet the severity of our plight."

I gulped, trying to suppress my guilt from rising to the surface. I once had the power to guide dormant plants back to life, but now my touch only granted death.

Takoda shifted in his seat and added, "I agree. Luneth wasn't in this dire of a state when the Light was bestowed upon you. Back then, the changes were significant but not insurmountable. That time has passed, and we are on the brink of destruction. Erovos' darkness has fully taken root, and it is only a matter of time before he is unleashed into the cosmos. Now that the earth falls evermore dire, the Light and power in you have grown to match our need."

Rowen gave Takoda a worried glance. "Will she be all right?"

The healer heaved a sigh. "She looks to be in perfect health. Though without a full examination, I have no way of knowing."

"Could this body protect her, or is it slowly overtaking her?" Rowen asked, voicing my concerns.

"I do not know," the healer replied solemnly.

"My body is stronger," I said, remembering my finger divots in the tree.

"A dangerous combination indeed—an untamed wyvern with too much spirit," Alvar, the war captain said, toying with the scar on his chin.

My eyes narrowed. This guy couldn't make up his mind! "You once saw me as a weakened mare and now an untamed wyvern. Well, which is it?"

"Ah, yes, Rowen. Your soul flame is still in there. Her sharp tongue has not changed. Perhaps a mare in wyvern clothing," he said, his eyes trailing up my new body.

"There is something you still keep from us," Nepta said, and my heart lurched. There was no way she could know about the flower I killed. Could she? "I can feel the shift in both of you."

My gaze collided with Rowen's. "Our soul flame bond?" Rowen offered carefully, and my face heated.

"Indeed," Nepta said with a regal dip of her chin.

"Like Althea and Donis," Driskell whispered in a state of shock.

"Who?" I asked, wondering if I could possibly digest any more information tonight.

"Althea was an elven princess born of sea foam," Nepta explained, her weathered fingers steepled on the table. "It was said that a small piece of the Light lived within her, shining upon her ears like celestial jewels, much like your own. And Donis was the son of an Elder Spirit. Such beings are known as the Vassi and are born of the sky.

"The waters of Luneth used to run wild, drowning lands and valleys. Althea spoke to the chaotic waves and shaped them into oceans, lakes, and rivers. She created waterways and channels that brought balance to the land. The elven princess spent hours by the ocean, swimming and playing in the waters she had tamed. One day, as Donis soared over the sea, he chanced upon her bathing. Enthralled by her beauty, he assumed a human form and waited for her on the shore. Althea was captivated by the being in the distance and swam to him. Despite their differences, much like that of a fish and a bird, their love was fierce and powerful.

"But Althea's father, Arkan, did not agree with the match. He had promised her to Tor, the king of the Stonefist Giants. He forbade her from seeing Donis again, declaring it was her duty to bring peace amongst the races.

"Donis was horrified for Althea. Such a union was not only unwanted, it was dangerous. The Stonefist Giants were enormous creatures, their bodies incompatible with that of the elves. It was cruel of Arkan to betroth his daughter to someone she didn't love, much less to someone who could kill her during mating.

"Althea refused to marry the giant and claimed Donis as her mate. But when Tor learned of the betrayal, he declared war on the Vassi. Donis and Althea begged for peace, but there were no agreements to be had. Tor refused to relinquish his claim on the princess, and Donis refused to let Tor, or anyone else, touch Althea ever again.

"The battle of the Stonefist Giants against a Vassi was immense. It tore imprints into the ground and splashed up rock and debris as their colossal footprints gouged into the land. As a descendant of the Elder Spirits, Donis was strong and mighty, but after a fortnight of fighting, the giants overcame him. Althea watched in terror as Tor went to land the killing blow. Refusing to watch her love perish, Althea channeled a flood to scatter their enemies. When the water cleared, Althea held an injured Donis in her arms."

My heart stopped. I knew all too well the terror she must have felt, watching as her love was nearly killed. I leaned in closer as Nepta continued the tale.

"Tor regained his bearings and charged toward his betrothed and her lover. Althea and Donis knew they only had moments left together, but they were unwilling to be separated in this life. With the moon, elves, and giants as their witnesses, the lovers withdrew a piece of their soul fire and gently exchanged their flames, offering a part of themselves to the other. A cosmic connection formed as their fires intertwined, and they became the first soul flames. Their bond forever immortalized in lovers whose devotion burns just as fiercely."

My bond with Rowen flared as we made eye contact. The tale of the first soul flames sent comforting heat waves throughout my body.

"When the dust finally settled, the earth was reshaped, and the Sillarial mountain range was formed. Tor could not dispute the love of the soul flames and realized he wanted a love as fierce as the one he had just witnessed. Appalled by his actions, he ordered the giants to disappear into the mountains their war had created. They have never been seen since, but I suspect Graem is a descendant of the Stonefist Giants. Though in ancient days, they used to be much larger."

I wondered if Graem had returned to the mountains. I hoped so.

"What became of Althea and Donis?" I asked, comforted that even though I couldn't touch Rowen, I held a piece of him within me. Even when I'd been gone for months, Rowen still felt me. It was how he managed to search for me every night in the Hymma. I was forever grateful for the connection the two lovers had forged.

"Donis eventually healed from battle, and the soul flames lived the rest of their days in peace and happiness. As a Vassi, Donis could not die, and though the Ancient Elves lived longer than most, Althea's flesh would eventually succumb to time. After two centuries of wedded bliss, they refused to be separated on the princess's deathbed. Donis forfeited his mortal body and returned to the heavens as Althea surrendered to the ocean. Their soul flame bond endured as they returned to their true forms, their connection and pull so profound, it created the horizon. Their love forever found where the sea meets the sky."

A tear slid down my cheek as my soul flame's eyes met mine.

"It seems you have still not mastered control of your new form, causing your attacks. It is imperative you remain calm," Alvar said, ruining the moment, and I swore if one more person told me to stay calm, I was going to explode.

The otherworldly Light swam in my veins, remaking my body and blood, but now in an elven body that could sustain and wield such power. I kept the information that I killed a flower to myself, and Rowen didn't mention it either. Let them keep their hope a little longer.

"We are allowing you to stay within the village, but with great trust that you will learn to control your emotions," Nepta said, standing from her chair and retreating to the edge of the vast chasm.

I understood her completely. I couldn't risk another panic attack.

I silently pleaded to the Elder Spirits that I would find my footing before I succumbed to the death growing in us all.

·(· ☾ · ● · ☽ ·)·

After the gathering, I watched the Summit members leave one by one, waiting until Nepta was the last to remain.

"Rowen, I will meet you back at home," I said, his gaze darting to Nepta in her quartz headdress and simple frock, her back turned to us. He nodded, understanding that I would like to speak with her alone.

Silently, I walked to Nepta and stood by her side, gazing at the extinct waterfalls that no longer filled the Vale with music. We stood shoulder to shoulder. "I'm going to do everything in my power to help. But I need your blessing to visit the prisoner. He might be the key to solving all of this."

"Keira, my child," Nepta replied, our gazes facing forward. "He is in detainment. I am sorry, but you are not to see him. We do not know his intentions nor why he is here. What if he wants to use you as a weapon, or you have an attack? Either way, I see no positive outcome from your speaking with him at this time. It is out of the question until we know more and your powers are under control."

"But I think it will help—"

"I felt your storm cloud brewing overhead just moments ago.

You are unstable. It is as clear as day. I have spoken on the matter, and my word is final. You are to do nothing until you have mastered yourself."

My mouth was left agape as Nepta turned from me and left me to my thoughts. But my inner well was as empty and desolate as the lost falls.

12

———

The following morning, I woke in a sea of white sheets. After Nepta's firm ruling, I was in shock. I didn't even remember my walk back to the dome. Not to mention, I learned the Elder Spirits reforged me in the likeness of the Ancients.

I struggled to master the powers I had, and now, they were enhanced tenfold. Everyone wanted me to remain calm, but how could I under this immense pressure?

"How are you feeling?" Rowen asked, rolling over onto his side to face me.

I popped my head over the barricade of pillows I constructed, my hair no doubt looking a wild mess. "Trying not to think too hard about anything, honestly. Thinking is a slippery slope these days."

"How about we enjoy breakfast on the beach today?" he asked, resting on his elbow with his head in his hand. He smiled at me, though it didn't quite reach the corners of his eyes. "To help get your mind off . . . not thinking."

"Am I even allowed?"

"I guess we'll find out."

87

We ate breakfast at the beach pavilion, soaking in the serene ocean views. It was hard to fathom how there could be so much water yet not a drop to drink.

Thanks to the drought, food was scarce and mainly consisted of salted beans, seaweed, and dried berries. Our welcome-home feast must have been a delicacy saved for a special occasion. And though this spread wasn't nearly as appetizing, I needed to eat. My metabolism in this new elven body was through the roof.

Rowen finished the food on his tree ring plate and immediately began sharpening his ax.

I was a much slower eater than Rowen. I had to plan and construct every bite to perfection, eating in a clockwise manner and ensuring every rotation ended with a dried berry as a palate cleanser. Whereas Rowen mixed it all together, not even glancing at what he shoveled into his mouth. What a barbarian!

"I think your ax is sharp enough now," I said, realizing he still ran his blade over the whetstone.

He lowered his hands to his lap, squinting at me through the sunlight. "I need to find ways to keep my hands busy. If they are idle too long, I start getting funny ideas."

"Funny ideas?" I asked, finishing up with my plate.

"Ideas like running my hands along your body, hiking up that dress, and tracing my touch up to your pretty pussy."

A barbarian indeed!

"Under any other circumstances, my mouth would be wrapped around your cock with talk like that," I said as my inner walls clenched around nothing.

"Your mouth will be the death of me," he groaned, adjusting himself in his pants. "How will we keep our hands and minds occupied today?"

I was forbidden from seeing the prisoner, but the mystery of his identity kept me up all night, and here I was, counting berries at breakfast. It was ridiculous! I had much bigger things to focus on.

"I have an idea," I said, tucking my legs beneath me and facing Rowen.

"Uh-oh. You have that look in your eye," he said, mirroring my excitement.

"Takoda and Nepta said I couldn't visit the prisoner. Not that I couldn't just happen to walk by and see who it is. They never said I couldn't *look* at him."

"Remind me to be on my guard with my wording around you," he said, pocketing the whetstone. "I love your cunning mind."

I grinned. "I love your willingness to join me in my schemes."

"Always," Rowen replied as he holstered his ax. "I have been forbidden from speaking with the prisoner as well. I haven't even tried. When Nepta took me in, I swore to abide by the laws of the land. But it seems you have found a loophole."

"I'm going to enjoy corrupting you," I replied, hiking up my skirt to stand.

Rowen eyed the slip of my leg and groaned, his eyes dancing with heat. "Spirits, I can't wait to get my hands on you. I'd like to explore the full scope of your corruption."

⸻ ·(·☾·●·☽·)· ⸻

My soul flame led me to the prison, guiding me to the far back corner of the village. My pulse was in my ears, and my tongue was thick in my mouth. The suspense was agonizing.

I held my breath as we rounded the corner, but instead of coming face-to-face with the intruder, we were met by two armed warriors.

We halted in our tracks.

"What brings you?" asked the warrior with the long, tight braids.

Damn. I should have known there would be security. They stood beside a white stone wall, which I assumed was part of the cell.

"It's a nice day for a walk," Rowen said casually as if our presence was a mere coincidence.

"Well, keep walking," said the warrior with a pixie cut. I immediately recognized her from when I'd seen her spare with Dyani. If she was close to Demil's twin, then she most likely hated me.

"She is forbidden from seeing the prisoner," the first guard said, his fist tightening on his spear. "As Minroe said, keep walking."

"Best be going on your way now," Minroe agreed as she motioned to the path with the tip of her blade. "And don't get any ideas about night walks. The guards switch out at sunset."

"Sorry to have bothered you," I said, knowing I wouldn't be able to return later tonight. Nepta had ordered twenty-four-hour surveillance on this guy.

Who was this prisoner? And why was Nepta so afraid of him?

I chewed on my thumbnail. Whoever this dangerous interloper was, he had stopped me from killing Rowen. But why? Why would he care about me and my soul flame?

He also wielded a power similar to mine and used it against me. The prisoner was able to catch me when I fell and held me until he was detained.

"What if he's an ally?" I asked as we continued our walk. "Someone wanting to help us defeat Erovos."

Rowen stroked his stubble in contemplation. "Why not just say that and share his intentions? By not doing so, he's earned the ire of the whole village. Wouldn't it be better to be honest?"

I bit the inside of my cheek. Because he refused to communicate, I was forbidden from seeing him at all.

There was no way I could let this mystery persist. "We'll just have to find another way."

⸺ ·(·☾·●·☽·)· ⸺

I was sprawled in the dirt of the Crystal Crypts, the mica twinkling above me like the night sky. I must have blacked out from another of Caeryn's beatings. Blood streamed down my face and clouded my vision. I raised my pounding head, knowing who sat upon the throne, watching with glee. I shot the false queen a seething stare, but she wasn't alone. Erovos stood beside her, his darkness thick and billowing around a pair of flaming orange eyes.

Indrasyl, the Sylvan Mother Tree, grew proud and strong behind me, magnificent in her healthy form. Her leaves shimmered in hues of gold, pink, and green, and reflected on my skin like an iridescent canopy.

The Crypts were filled with the missing villagers from around Luneth. Innocents led here under the false pretense that Fou was their savior. Their terrified eyes glistened and pleaded for help.

I scanned the crowd for Rowen. Though I could barely see through the blood, sweat, and grime dripping down my face, I spotted him in an instant. He was lying on a luxurious four-poster bed, so out of place on the dais. He was shirtless and drenched in sweat, his arms and ankles bound to the posts. His mouth was gagged as he writhed and struggled to break free.

The false queen approached Rowen and trailed her fingertips along his inner thigh. "You have to choose," Aliphoura said, wearing a blood-red gown that matched her plump lips. "You can only save one. Is it going to be Rowen, the innocents, or Indrasyl?"

My heart plummeted to the floor. I couldn't save them all, especially not in my current state. I was wounded, barely able to walk, and my vision blurred in and out from my concussion.

Fou slithered her nails up Rowen's torso and chest, his muscles tensing as he fought her touch. "Would you be selfish enough to save Rowen, condemning all these innocents to die? Or is his life worth sacrificing for the greater good?" she asked, removing his gag.

"Keira!" Rowen bellowed.

"Don't worry, I'll take good care of him," Fou said before tracing her tongue along his mouth.

"No," I pleaded, running to rip her off him, but my broken leg couldn't withstand the weight, and I collapsed to the throne room floor. No matter what choice I made, someone was going to get hurt. My limitations were sealing all our fates.

"Or you can choose the Sylvan Mother Tree, saving the world but murdering everyone in this room," Erovos said, suddenly beside Indrasyl. He placed a palm on her split trunk, and with a swirl of his orange eyes, he began to drain her dry. As he pulled the life from her, from the earth, from us all, she withered and turned to blackened stone.

Desperation clawed at me. "Stop. Please," I begged as Indrasyl's leaves rained down on me like ash. In my periphery, Fou joined Rowen on the bed.

"You don't have much time to choose," Erovos hummed, his pale skin stark against his black cloak. "The Alcreon Light chose a worthless vessel. I told you your mortal body was dying all around you."

I gazed down at myself, gasping in horror. My skin was rotting and decaying off my limbs. Death. I was death and dying. And there was no escaping it.

Caeryn, the red man who'd kidnapped and beat me, appeared in a gust of flames. "Choose quickly," he said; the gash I'd given him across his face was bloody and raw. He stalked toward the crowd and grabbed the nearest innocent. He held the man flush against his front, and I realized he was dressed in Wyn clothing. My gut twisted in a sickening knot. Though his hair fell in his face, I swore he was familiar, as if I knew him from a different life. But before I could recall who he was, Caeryn drove his ruby-red blade into his back.

"Stop!" I cried, my voice trembling with desperation. I willed the Light, the Elder Spirits, anyone, to help me. But there was nothing and no one. I was utterly alone, the impossible decision mine to make.

"Choose," they all seemed to say in unison. "Choose."

"Stop. Stop. Stop!" I screamed, the Light in me building to a furious crescendo. I had no control as it shot out of me like a supernova. The explosion erupted with blinding force, splintering the stone above us.

The cave collapsed, its crushing weight plummeting down and destroying us all.

I woke with a jolt, my heart pounding.

I immediately checked Rowen by my side. Once I was sure he slept soundly with no gags or bindings holding him down, I frantically scanned myself. My skin was perfect, not a single blemish or spot of rot to be found.

I let out a relieved exhale, but the tightness in my chest remained. It wasn't real, yet I couldn't ignore the impending panic attack. My heart refused to slow down, as if in preparation for the oncoming storm.

Careful not to wake Rowen, I pushed off the covers, tiptoed across the floor, and slipped out of the dome. Once I quietly closed the door, I noticed a storm brewing overhead. I sprinted towards the field where I had once faced the giant Graem. The clearing offered a sense of safety. If I did strike the land with my Light, no one would get hurt.

I staggered through the village, my nightmare flashing through my mind like a carousel of death. The smell of blood, rot, and sweat clung to my skin as if the horrors of my dream had followed me into the waking world. Nausea coiled in my stomach and surged up my throat, gagging me.

Before I reached the center of the field, I doubled over and expelled everything in my stomach. Violent heaves wracked my body as bile burned my nose and throat, and tears stung my eyes.

I gasped for air and wiped my mouth.

It wasn't real. It wasn't real.

I wanted to focus on something tangible, but I had to ignore the grass beneath me—I couldn't risk feeling it dying through the soles of my feet.

I finally stumbled to the heart of the clearing and fell to the ground. I curled into the fetal position and begged my spiraling thoughts to stop.

Suddenly, a shadow flashed in the distance—stealth, strong, and aware. I didn't need to raise my head; I knew the gaze tracing over every inch of my skin like a night hawk. I buzzed with electrical awareness as the green eyes from the forest caressed my body.

Rowen's presence reached out to me from the trees, as he had done long before I ever knew he was there. During my nightmares, he had been my silent guardian, protecting me from the sidelines. But now, I was intimately aware of his watchful eyes offering me strength from a distance, and a warmth pulsed in my chest. He must have sensed that I didn't want him to get too close—in case I lost control.

And I did. I lost it all as lightning struck down around me.

13

Over the next few nights, my nightmares persisted. I'd wake up terrified with my heart pounding out of my chest and my body drenched in sweat. I tried not to wake Rowen, but no matter how gently I left the bed or how quietly I closed the door, he always appeared at the tree line, ensuring I never faced my panic attacks alone.

His presence was a steady, reassuring force that anchored me, but I felt guilty that I was causing the deep purple smudges under his eyes. "You don't have to watch," I said after the third night in a row. Once the attack came, there was no going back to bed, so I began dressing for the day. "I feel bad for waking you. I know it's not pretty watching me like that."

Rowen's eyes, usually sharp as a falcon's, softened, and his throat bobbed in a tortured swallow. "Not being able to touch you is surely the Spirits' way of punishing me," he said, his voice slightly breaking. "That I have to stand by helplessly and watch you suffer when all I want to do is take you in my arms and comfort you. Take away your pain. But I can't. I can't even get close because I know it will only cause you more distress. If my eyes are the only way I can give you strength, please don't ask me to look away."

His voice caressed over my body, causing my skin to pebble. He sensed even my smallest disturbance, his intuition finely attuned to my every need. My heart soared through the golden clouds and fiery sunset of our bond. No one had truly ever cared for me this deeply, this intrinsically. "I won't ask you to look away," I whispered, my heart, soul, and body yearning for the touch of my soul flame.

"Would you like to try talking to Takoda? I've recently begun mind-mending sessions with him," Rowen said, the muscles in his jaw hammering through his beard. "To help me through all I endured in the Crypts. Before and with you."

My night terrors shot to the forefront of my mind. In every one of them, Rowen was tied to a bed as his ex stroked him, touched him, and violated him in front of me. It was no less than what she'd done when she held us captive. She'd used me to lure him back into her web and bartered my life for his body. Aliphoura had licked, groped, and kissed him—made him say that I was nothing to him.

I knew it haunted him, as it haunted me too, and I was glad he sought help in whatever way was best for him. But my experience with therapy had been deeply traumatizing. Every word I spoke was twisted and used as ammunition against me.

Even though my sessions were with my parents, I could never shake the loneliness and fear that filled the room. I'd been forced to endure questioning and hours of testing. Just thinking about it made my palms sweat and my chest tighten.

"I've tried a type of mind-mending therapy before. It didn't work for me. It did more harm than good," I said, my eyes trailing up Rowen's body. I took in his hands, fisted by his sides. The restraint it took not to wrap me in his arms and do to my body whatever he needed to assure himself that I was alive and well was commendable. Each day, the struggle grew more and more unbearable.

He tightened his belt around his waist and slipped his ax into the holster. "I understand, my flame. We'll find another way."

"Maybe being allowed back on the training grounds will help—be my new form of therapy," I said, finishing up the lacings of my boots.

During the day, my pleas to visit the prisoner were brushed aside. Nepta was well aware of my nightly attacks. They weren't easy to hide, but maybe she felt bad for me because she finally granted me access to the training grounds for light exercises only. Nothing that could get my heart rate up or cause an attack.

It was beyond embarrassing that I had to be monitored, but I didn't want to seem ungrateful. Not being able to do anything drove me crazy, and I was thankful for this one small freedom.

As we arrived at the training grounds, my gaze fell upon the rows of targets, blades, and weapons. The determination I'd once felt on this field surged through me. My initial goal for self-defense had evolved into a broader aspiration. I was determined to be prepared, so that when the time came, I wouldn't have to choose who to save like in my dreams. I could rescue them all.

The area buzzed with movement as partners and groups engaged in sparring exercises. The clashing of weapons and the thuds of arrows hitting targets filled my ears. I was no stranger to the sweat, perseverance, and time it took to master such techniques. It reminded me of my track days. The dedication to honing one's craft was the same, whether with warriors or athletes.

My hands itched to grab a blade. Nepta had forbidden me from holding weapons of any kind, but there were other ways to train in the meantime.

I sat on the ground and stretched. Rowen joined me,

working on his own mobility exercises. When suddenly, a dark shadow fell over me. I glanced up, my eyes meeting an unlikely pair.

A fierce, feline warrior stood in her practice leathers. The sun was at her back, casting her silver hair and blades in a white-gold light. "I would like to speak with you," Dyani said, her hands poised upon her dual blades.

"Of course," I replied, but Dyani's shoulders remained tight, her eyes flashing to Rowen.

My soul flame didn't move, his eyes landing on her hands gripping her knives.

She scoffed. "I'm not going to hurt her, Damascus. Don't be so dramatic."

"It's okay, Rowen," I assured. "I don't have a weapon. She won't hurt me."

"Your whole body is a weapon," she shot back.

I flashed her a look. "Not helping."

Rowen didn't move, holding Dyani's stare.

Finally, the warrior released her weapons.

"That's better. I'll meet up with you later," Rowen said, leaving to give us privacy.

"I . . ." Dyani faltered. I knew she wasn't one to communicate with soft words and gentle expressions, but she didn't even know how to broach the subject of her twin's betrayal.

"I'm sorry about your brother," I said, knowing the look of pain etched around her sharp eyes. I could only imagine the rage and hurt boiling beneath her cold warrior exterior, but her twin's disloyalty would not affect the strength of her stance.

"What happened to him?" she asked, fighting the lump in her throat.

"Demil betrayed Erovos in the end. He helped me imprison the Dark Spirit within the crevice. Then, he gave me the time I needed to escape without becoming trapped myself."

Still, she didn't falter. "Do you think he is still alive?"

"I don't know."

Dyani's razor stare flickered down then returned to me with no less cut. "I've never liked you, but I am sorry for what he did. What he did to us all. He made comments about wanting you. He believed you should be his. I discouraged him at every turn. I thought I got through to him. Spirits know I tried beating it out of him."

"Thank you, but it wasn't your fault. I know he truly wanted to protect you all from Erovos."

"Be that as it may, I would like to know if Demil is alive. Do you think the prisoner is working with Erovos? He might know what happened to my brother. I've tried talking to him, threatened him even, but he refuses to speak to me," Dyani said, eyeing me in my runner's stretch.

"I'm forbidden from seeing him. I've practically begged Nepta to let me talk to him."

"The prisoner contains answers. He might know of Erovos' plans."

I let out a sigh. "I've tried to see him, but he is heavily guarded."

Dyani transferred her weight onto her other foot, glancing around. "I can help you and Rowen get to him. I know the guards."

"You would help me?" I asked, my eyebrows pulling together.

"I know how important answers are. Nepta has enough on her plate. She is a wise leader who sees so much, but in this, her judgement is clouded."

"She believes it could be a trap," I said, easing further into my stretch.

"If it is, then let us be ready for it," she replied, her muscular arms flexing by her sides.

I smiled. "I couldn't agree more."

"Don't think this makes us friends." She glared at me, her pinched face narrowing. "Go to the prisoner tomorrow just after high sun. I'll make sure you get in."

"I don't know what to say."

"Don't say anything. Literally," she replied, her umber eyes glancing around the grounds warily. "No one can know I helped you. Find the answers you need and get out. We need to be prepared for what's coming. I refuse to repeat what happened here at the Battle of the Breaking. I was just a youngling, but I remember the destruction it wreaked upon the village. Upon my mother. What it did to her when my father died. I swore to her that I would protect our family. I failed Demil, but I will not fail our mother."

With that, she turned and walked away, her white ponytail cascading down her back.

I wanted to trust Dyani, but a fearful thought whispered through me. Could I trust her, or would she betray me just like her brother?

14

———

"Are you sure you want to do this?" Rowen asked the next day as we made our way to the prison.

"I'm sure," I said, my strides echoing with determination. The intruder's identity swirled in my mind like an annoying gnat, one I couldn't bat away no matter how much Nepta or the Summit wanted me to. "I need to know who it is. Trap or not."

"I'm right here if you need me," he assured, and a wave of gratitude washed over me. Rowen had always been by my side, protecting and shielding me. Even when he'd been cursed from loving me, his priority had always been to keep me safe. Never knowing the greatest threat lay at the hollow of his sternum.

But he no longer wore the necklace Fou used to spy on him. He was finally free, and the thought of me facing the prisoner with him by my side sent a surge of courage up my spine.

"What did you do with your mother's necklace?" I asked, realizing I hadn't been there to support him as he gave up his last treasured possession.

"Caeryn may have snapped Fou's neck, but her body was never recovered," Rowen said, and it broke my heart that his eyes darted to the trees as if he feared she was still listening. "I didn't want to take any chances, so I buried it outside the village."

"I'm sorry I wasn't there for you. That must have been hard," I said, my gaze tilting to his exposed chest where his charcoal-grey shirt billowed open. He now only wore the beaded necklace made in Wyn fashion.

"It was like burying her all over again. And I prayed to the spirits that it wasn't a funeral for two. Pleading I hadn't lost you as well. It would take me days in the Hymma to find you, only for you to slip away."

"I hope you can wear it again one day," I said, knowing what it was like not to own anything from your old life but wishing you had one thing of value to hold on to.

Rowen offered me a small smile. "Me too. Though I would much rather have you than any possession," he said softly. "Maybe one day I can take you to the ruins of Viltarran. Show you where my mother raised me."

"I would love that," I replied with a sincere smile.

Suddenly, our eyes snapped forward as the prison guards came into view, their imposing stances doing little to help my nerves.

Dyani had wanted Rowen banished from the village, and I worried this was her plan to get us both kicked out. Was her friendly demeanor at the training grounds a distraction? Was she earning my trust now, only to stab me in the back later?

We approached Minroe and another guard, their stern faces offering nothing. It felt like my heart was beating out of my chest as we stepped within their line of sight. Even if I had to use the excuse we'd planned for being here, I doubted they would believe it.

But without a word, the guards parted, letting us pass with a nod.

Rowen and I let out a shared breath of relief.

Dyani had told the truth.

I'd never seen the Wyn prison, much less knew they had one. Over the last few days, I'd convinced myself I'd find a suffering man in a cold, dark dungeon, but when we rounded the wall, and the cell came into view, I halted, my eyes widening.

Despite the entwined branches forming a prison around him and the two armed guards, it looked like the prisoner was basking in paradise. The sun and ever-glowing stars cast their radiant beams upon his face, illuminating his features with a serene glow. He looked peaceful, idly rolling a flower stem between his fingertips.

As if sensing my presence, his eyes snapped to mine.

"You," I seethed as I charged the wooden bars, Rowen following in my footsteps.

The prisoner *smiled.* Actually grinned at me as if we were friends.

"How?" I demanded.

"Well, hello to you, too, Keira," said a voice I'd only ever heard in agony and torment, but now, it sounded light, happy. Free. "It's nice to meet you. Officially."

"Unfortunately, we've met before," I replied to the man with onyx-black hair, angular eyes, and a square jaw. "When you violated my mind, remember? How did you even get out of the crevice, much less back into your body?" I asked the stranger who'd once lain beside me in the hospital. Who I'd met again in the crevice when he'd tried to possess my body with his astrally torn soul. "How the hell did you get here, Maddock?"

"Keira, is this . . ." Rowen's voice cut through the tense silence, and the prisoner's gaze shot to my soul flame. A fleeting expression flashed in the depths of his eyes before returning to me.

"Madds."

"What?"

"I prefer to go by Madds," he stated matter-of-factly, lounging in the comfort of his well-lit cell. "'Maddock' always felt a bit too stuffy. Father loved it, though."

"I don't give a flying fuck!" I screamed at the man who I'd caught sunbathing in one of the most pleasant cells I'd ever seen.

Rowen bristled beside me in a shockwave of fury. "This is the man from the crevice?"

"It is," I seethed through a clenched jaw. I'd pictured this man paying for his violent crimes in the crevice with Erovos and Demil. Seeing him here, twirling flowers and smiling, sent my mind thrashing like a wild bull. There were no chains or irons, only twisted branches fashioned into a small yet comfortable prison; the space was furnished with a simple wooden chair, bed, and desk. The view was open and refreshing, giving him a clear panorama of the Sillarial Peaks.

I didn't need to see this.

"Keira," he said as I turned to leave. "Please don't go. Let me explain." He charged the wooden bars and grabbed me. I shot a glare at his fingers wrapped around my arm, and a surge of disgust boiled up inside me. Yet, after months of no physical contact, his touch felt . . . warm.

Rowen charged the prisoner and yanked his hand off me. "Touch her again and you will no longer have hands," he snarled, exposing the peaks of his canines. "If you weren't Nepta's prisoner, you would already be dead."

"Ow! Jeez. Yeah, you must be the boyfriend," Maddock said as he shook out his wrist. "Got it. No touchy."

"How can you touch me when no one else can?" I asked with a putrid taste in my mouth. I hated asking him anything, but my curiosity outweighed my pride.

Maddock's eyes flashed to Rowen. "You can't touch her?"

I flinched, scolding myself for accidentally giving away too much information.

"Answer the question," Rowen growled, unfazed by my slip-up.

Maddock tore his eyes away from Rowen, a hint of sympathy in his expression. "Whatever power or ability you used against me that day in the cave, I believe I have it now, too."

My mind short-circuited. "Wha—how is that possible?"

The memory of Maddock invading my mind stole the breath from my lungs. There was no helping him. When I'd found him in the crevice, he was astrally torn. A phantom seeking to overtake my flesh and possess my body. He would have succeeded if it weren't for the Alcreon Light blasting him out of me.

"When you hit me with that light, my hooks were in you pretty deep," Maddock confessed, and Rowen tensed beside me, fisting his palms so tight I feared he'd pop a vein. "I saw . . . many of your memories, Keira. Some were very confusing, jumping in space and time. But even as you hurled me from your mind, my grip on you tightened, and I didn't let go. I-I accidentally took some of you with me. Some of your light."

"You stole it, then used it against me," I seethed, not sure if I wanted to cry or scream.

"In case you forgot, you were killing your boyfriend over there," he said, jerking his chin in Rowen's direction. "Remember?"

"Remember when you violated my mind and nearly stole my body?"

"What I did to you plagues me every day," he said, toying with the simple linen shirt and trousers he'd been given to wear. "I am truly so sorry."

"Yeah, you look real sorry. I walked upon you, basking in bliss. *Smiling.* Why wouldn't you tell anyone who you were?"

"You would have never come if you knew it was me."

"You're right. I'm leaving and not coming back. Enjoy your life sentence."

"Wait. I know I don't deserve it, but please, hear me out," he implored, his eyes darting from me to Rowen, pleading. And I noticed for the first time that his eyes were a rich shade of brown, a detail that somehow added warmth to the face that haunted me.

"As you know, I was deprived of much in that cave: the sun upon my face or the feeling of something as small as a twig between my fingers. Little things I thought I would never feel again."

"Are you trying to play the victim? It doesn't excuse what you did to me."

"I know. I was a desperate man, but look, you defeated me." He grinned as if this were all a game. "While in the process, you also healed me."

"I see," I said as my eyes darted to his head, which no longer dangled with bits of flesh from his motorcycle accident. His once skeletal body now rippled with muscle and strength, and I hated that I recalled how his body felt pressed against mine. "How did you get here?" I asked, gesturing to the hidden village surrounding us.

"You healed me almost instantly. I woke up in a hospital and simply walked out. It was a miracle. *You* are a miracle."

I scoffed and rolled my eyes.

"I should have needed rehabilitation for my deteriorated limbs. Months and months of it. But I awoke in perfect condition with a string of light connecting me to you. I followed it, wanting to apologize to you. Or thank you. Hell, I didn't know! Didn't even know if the memories were real. But I couldn't stop thinking about the beautiful woman with long, brown hair and a shimmering aura of light."

Rowen gripped his hatchet, raising it an inch out of the holster in warning.

Maddock eyed the weapon and winced. "Got it. No compliments either," he said before continuing. "It plagues me that you tried to help me and that I returned the favor with nothing but horror. It took me a minute to get the hang of drifting, but once I did, it led me right to this village. And from what I assessed, you've been missing. Even when I tried to find you again, it was like you were everywhere and nowhere all at once. I've been imprisoned all this time, waiting for you."

"It's called traveling, not drifting," I corrected sharply. "And a three-month sentence seems like you got off easy, especially for the crimes you committed against me. And the ones I'm sure you committed on Earth."

I gloated as he grimaced, but I didn't relish the sight as much as I thought I would.

I'd felt a moment of regret locking him in the crevice with the Dark Spirit. But now, as I remembered his ghostly fingers clawing into my mind and stealing my body memory by memory, I tensed in fury.

"Why haven't you traveled back home? These bars aren't really keeping you, are they?" I asked, remembering Rowen and the Summit had no idea how he'd escaped the night I returned.

"No," he said. "They aren't."

"You're an astral traveler too. A walker between worlds," I barely whispered. "That's how you ended up in the crevice. How you escaped this cell."

"All my life, I had the weirdest dreams, often finding myself sleepwalking or ending up in strange places. I just attributed my *traveling,*" he emphasized the last word with a smile, "to my frequent bouts of intoxication."

I huffed. "Of course you did. Don't forget, I saw your memories too. I know what a piece of shit you were back home. All your cheating, lies, and manipulation. It's all up here," I said, tapping my temple. I wanted to tell him his presence here was wasting precious food and water, but I refrained. I had already divulged too much information. But still, I needed him gone. "Me healing your body doesn't absolve you of your past. You're a thief who stole a piece of my Light and violated my mind. A coward I never want to see again. If you were expecting to find forgiveness here, you are sorely mistaken. *Drift* wherever you want, just make sure it's the hell away from me."

Before I could hear one more word of his pathetic excuses, I turned and left the prisoner to continue basking in his cell.

·(C · ● ·) ·)·

Dyani appeared on the organic pathway. "Did you talk to him?"

"Yes. He doesn't know anything," I said, not wanting to stop and talk. I was still fuming.

"Are you sure?"

"I am."

"Who is he then?" she pressed. "He has to know something."

"Look, he doesn't know a thing. But you and the other guards should know those bars aren't really holding him. He can escape at any time. It's all just for show. He's a traveler like me—a walker between worlds."

"Why would he want to stay in a cell if he can escape?" she asked, crossing her arms over her chest, making it known she had no intention of letting me pass.

I realized I hadn't stuck around long enough to find out. "I have no idea."

"Do you know how hard it was to organize that meeting, and you didn't think to ask?"

"I don't care what he wants. I just want him gone."

"You know he's not going anywhere. Especially if he's been able to leave all this time. That doesn't make you curious?"

"Not really," I lied, trying to step around her.

"You're going back," she said, blocking my path again.

"No, I'm not."

"Yes, you are," she said, finally letting me pass. "You are going to see him again tomorrow at high sun."

Without looking at her, I stormed away and mumbled under my breath, "No. I'm not."

15

————————

The next day, I sat at the training grounds as the sun climbed towards its zenith. Despite Dyani's behests, I had no intention of visiting Maddock. The thought of him sitting in that cell, waiting for me, made me gloat.

I hoped that if I never visited him, he would eventually give up and leave. Though something told me, he wouldn't. He'd already happily sat in prison for over three months.

It aggravated me beyond belief that a man behind bars could appear as happy and free as he did. Meanwhile, I wandered the open air, feeling more imprisoned than he looked. The mental chains around my mind seemed worse than his actual cell.

I half-heartedly stretched on the dry grass by myself. Rowen felt comfortable leaving me on my own because of how adamant I'd been about never seeing the prisoner again. So he'd taken this time to meet with Takoda for a mind-mending session.

Rowen asked if I would like to come, but I declined. I didn't need someone poking around in my head. It was a frightening place I wouldn't want to subject anyone to. I'd rather be doing the poking.

The thought hit me like a ton of bricks. The sun had just

reached its peak; there might still be time for me to slip in and talk with the prisoner. I hated that Dyani was right. I was curious.

I made my way back to Maddock after swearing I would never step anywhere near him again. For a moment, I was worried I had waited too long, but true to Dyani's word, the guards parted like water, letting me pass yet again.

I don't know what I expected the prisoner to be doing, but what I saw was beyond my worst expectations. Ven, my inquisitive little friend, was engaged in conversation with the Wyn's number one prisoner.

Fury surged through me as I charged toward Ven and his white wolf, Sabra. "Don't you dare talk to them," I said, stepping between Ven and Maddock. Would this kid ever stop getting into trouble?

"They were talking to me!" Maddock proclaimed, gesturing to the majestic beast seated innocently at his feet. It pissed me off that Sabra was letting him pet her through the wooden bars.

"No, they weren't," I said for no other reason than to disagree.

"Yes, we were," Ven replied innocently, and I shot him a glare, realizing he'd had a growth spurt since I'd been gone. The soft roundness of his cheeks had faded, giving way to the sharper planes of his maturing face. And where he and Sabra used to be about the same height, he now towered inches over her.

After our encounter with Graem, when I feared the giant would snap his neck, I was filled with joy that Ven was aging. Yet I desperately hoped he would never outgrow the wonder he held for the world, that spark of mischief and curiosity that made him so uniquely him.

I refocused my anger back on Madds. "You hanging out behind these bars is ridiculous. Why haven't you left?"

"Looking for free rent," he said with a grin, scratching Sabra behind the ears.

My eyes nearly bugged out of my head. "I hate to break it to you, but nobody wants you here."

"Remember when nobody wanted you here either?" Ven asked, popping his head around my arm. "No one would talk to you or look at you. Then I showed you around and—"

I stepped in front of him, cutting him off.

"Ven, do the guards know you're here?" I asked, already knowing the answer.

"Um, no. I know a secret way in. And the guards check on him at the same times every day," he answered, feeding Sabra a treat from his pocket. "They really should be more unpredictable."

I attempted to look furious, but deep down, I was genuinely impressed. Why didn't I think to ask Ven to do a little spying for me? Of course he had a secret passageway to the forbidden prisoner. "Then I suggest you go out the way you came in. It's good to see you, but don't let me catch you here again."

"It's good to see you too," Ven said before skillfully sneaking back into the wall of trees, quietly opening the branches for Sabra to pass through.

Maddock chuckled as the boy and wolf vanished into the foliage, leaving no trace that they were ever here at all. I huffed and shook my head, my eyes snapping back to the prisoner.

"So you've been in my situation before, huh?" Maddock said, rising to his feet from where he pet the wolf that wouldn't even let me touch her. "Ven was also telling me you happened to trap a pretty powerful Dark Spirit in a cave. Sounds really interesting. Could this be the same cave I was in? But wait. You wouldn't do that. You would never do something so awful."

Was there anything Ven didn't tell him?

"So what? I trapped the Dark Spirit in the same crevice as you. You're not in there anymore."

"But you didn't know that," he replied, his eyes sparkling. A lustrous black curl fell down his brow. His hair was longer and artfully disheveled, more relaxed than when I'd seen him in the hospital.

"I . . ."

He stepped closer to the bars, "You were going to imprison a destroyer of worlds in there with me. Weren't you?"

I held my ground, grateful for the bars between us, even though they were a false sense of security. "I didn't exactly have a ton of options. It was the only place I could think of. But it's not holding him very well."

"Ah. Great. Next time you want to make me feel horrible for what I did to you, I'll remind you that you almost made us even."

Suddenly, the earth shook violently beneath our feet, and I tumbled forward. I fell into the prisoner's arms, my body bracing for him to convulse. But he didn't so much as flinch. Instead, his hands gripped me tighter and steadied me. Repulsed, I pushed off him with all my might and grasped onto the wooden bars.

When the trembling finally subsided, Maddock said, "Yeah, those happen a lot here. Is that normal?"

"As I said, the crevice isn't holding Erovos very well. He is trying to break free. Hence, the earthquakes we've been experiencing. He is trying to tear the mountain apart to escape the crevice," I replied, backing up and straightening my vest.

"Who is this Erovos guy anyway?" he asked, his eyes scanning my body as if checking for injuries.

"I came here to ask the questions."

"What's with the ears?"

"Stop," I ground out.

"Where's Rowen?"

"You know I could just leave, right?"

"Fine. What do you want to know?" he asked, retreating from the bars.

"How well do you remember what happened in the crevice?"

"You healed every part me, even my mind. I remember everything. Regrettably"

My lip curled. "I'm assuming you're the only one who can touch me because you stole a piece of my Light."

His dark brows furrowed. "Not being able to touch you must be driving Rowen mad. Especially with your bond."

His words pierced through my heart like a jagged lightning bolt. "Don't you dare bring up my bond with Rowen," I seethed as dark clouds gathered overhead. "How do you even know about that?"

He paused before shrugging. "It's pretty obvious you two have something going on."

My bond with Rowen was sacred and not something I would ever want to discuss with the man who'd violated my mind. My blood boiled that he knew about my connection with my soul flame. "How did you end up in the crevice after your accident?"

Maddock worriedly glanced up at the storm brewing overhead before looking back at me. "As my bike shook and I lost control, I knew I was going to die. All I remember thinking is that I deserved to go to hell. So I guess that's where I ended up."

My gut lurched. He had created his own hell. A moment of empathy welled up inside me, but I pushed it down. I would never let him know that I understood the feeling. "What were you going to do with my body once you owned it?"

A painful sound left his lips. "I wasn't thinking clearly. I was desperate and crazed, like a rabid animal foaming at the mouth for you. For your body. Any body."

"Did you enjoy it?"

"Keira," he warned, his angular face looking the most pained I'd ever seen it.

"Did you enjoy taking over my body memory by memory? Tearing apart my mind as you made room for yourself?"

He groaned.

"Did you?"

"Yes!" he shouted. "I did. Every second of it. You were one of the greatest things I've ever felt. But like I said, I was crazed and unwell. I am appalled by my actions—"

"Why are you still here?" I cut him off as my hair and fingertips sizzled with electricity.

"Ask me anything else," he said, nervously eyeing the sky. After being so open and honest, him clamming up like this was suspicious. "You'll only hate me more."

I needed to end this conversation; my emotions were spiraling out of control. "Tell me why you're here or we're done."

Thunder cracked above us.

"I can't. Please. I'll answer anything else," he pleaded.

"This whole act you're putting on, I'm not falling for it." Dry lightning whipped overhead, raising the hairs on my arms. "Goodbye, Maddock. I hope I never see you again."

I turned on my heel and walked away, trying to maintain a calm facade despite the lightning brewing overhead and the growing panic in my chest. The parched ground was like tinder waiting to catch fire. If lightning struck, flames would catch, and take, and spread.

I needed to get away.

As soon as I rounded the corner, I broke into a sprint, desperate to reach the edge of the village where I could finish my panic attack in peace.

·(·(·●·)·)·

I entered the rotating door of the dome, looking like a stray cat covered in twigs, scratches, and dried tears.

"Keira," Rowen said in a relieved exhale. "Are you all right?"

"I am now," I said, taking in the sight of Rowen's shirtless body. His muscles rippled down his stomach, each block of his abs looking like marble. Every inch of him resembled a statue chiseled to perfection. And though his massive body looked as hard as stone, there was a softness in his eyes that welcomed me home.

"You weren't at the training grounds," he said, his eyes worriedly scanning my body.

"I went to see the prisoner," I answered, changing out of my clothes.

Rowen tensed. "You spoke with him alone?"

"I wanted to ask him about that night."

"What did he say?" my soul flame asked as he raked a hand through his hair, his muscles rippling and flexing with the movement. My whole body flushed, first with desire and then with rage. How cruel to have a half-naked god in my bedroom—one who loved me, would die for me—yet couldn't touch me?

It seemed I was suffering from more than one dry spell. Not only was I deprived of water, I was deprived of my soul flame. Being in Rowen's presence, so near yet untouchable, was its own kind of cruel thirst. Much like the glittering ocean in the middle of a drought, they were both beautiful and tempting, yet ultimately off-limits.

I reeled in my thoughts with a deep breath. I couldn't afford another panic attack.

"He acted like he was sorry and was weirdly concerned that you can't touch me. But when I asked him why he was still here, he refused to answer," I said as I changed into a silky chemise and crawled into bed. I was beyond exhausted, cranky, and just downright pissed. I didn't want to think, or fight, and I couldn't fuck. Sleeping was all I could do. "I can't tell what angle he's playing at. But if he wants to rot in a cell, that's fine by me."

"You can still try talking to Takoda," Rowen offered as he crawled into bed beside me.

"Talking leads to thinking," I said, rolling away from him and pulling the plush blankets up to my chin, fighting the tears in my eyes. Rowen could go and talk his little heart out. I wouldn't be participating.

He whispered, "Goodnight, I love you."

"I love you, too," I whispered back. Maddock's smug face was the last thing I saw before sleep consumed me.

16

The next day, Rowen and I headed to the training grounds. Out of habit, I fell into my familiar running stretches.

Before I could even settle into my third pose, Dyani appeared like the flash of a blade you didn't see coming until it was too late. "I want to resume your training," she said, her silver hair down and flowing, accentuating her light brown skin. "Whatever this is," she gestured to my stretch, "it isn't going to help you in combat."

My eyes narrowed, and I contemplated saying no, but I knew turning her down would end any relationship we could ever have. So I met her guarded stare and said, "I accept."

"I'll leave you to it, then," Rowen said as he left the field, and I wondered if he would watch from a distance. He had observed my first lesson with Dyani, and it had been utterly humiliating as she knocked me to the ground again and again. The sting of each fall echoed in my palms, knees, and ego.

"Is this going to be a repeat of last time?" I asked, remaining in the stretch she found so distasteful.

"It was careless of me to start you on your journey and then abandon you. I can't have people thinking this is my work," she said, making a face and gesturing to my whole body. I realized all the training had stopped as everyone turned their attention to my interaction with the Wyn's most fearsome warrior. "I've seen what you can do, and it's atrocious. Most of it is just dumb luck."

"Was it luck when I took you down?" I asked, standing to meet her head-on.

"Watch it."

"Too soon?"

"How about I teach you the proper forms before you start bragging? You look like a youngling with a stick."

I tied my hair back. "Should we pick up where we left off?"

"How about we start at the beginning," she said, tying her own hair into a high ponytail.

"Great. So I'm reverting?"

"I'm not trying to get on Nepta's bad side. These movements technically fall within her parameters of you not overdoing it," she said as she adjusted her red jerkin, and I noticed she wasn't wearing her fighting leathers or weapons. "We need to start at the beginning. It's where we should have started in the first place."

"What's the beginning?" I asked skeptically.

"The Five Phases of the Moon."

"That sounds fun!"

"It's not. It's a life-long and studied discipline."

"Oh. Right."

Even though we were eye to eye, she still somehow managed to look down her sharp nose at me. "Each phase contains a series of movements designed to aid in battle. These exercises will teach you which muscles to strengthen and how to use them properly. Mastering them can be lifesaving."

"Got it."

"No, you don't. But let's begin. The first phase is crescent," she explained, easing into a deep lunge. "The crescent moon teaches us fluidity and smooth transitions when in combat. The second is the waning moon." Her movements gradually changed as she described each phase. "The waning moon teaches us physical conditioning, the working of our muscles both large and small, providing endurance and strength. The third is the waxing moon, which teaches concentration, focus, and breathwork. Fourth is the full moon, adding power to your movements to strengthen forceful kicks, strikes, and attacks," she said as she ended her demonstration with a spinning back kick.

"What is the fifth?" I asked eagerly, admiring the strength and grace in her movements. It was like a dance.

"The new moon," Dyani answered, her body stilled yet became pliant, as if ready for anything. "It represents a blank slate. What lies beyond your sight and senses. You must learn these movements so well that you forget them. Become them. Breathe them. When you are fighting for your life, it must be a natural part of what you are, not something that is reenacted like a play or repeated like a prophecy. It is real life. You must understand this. Your life—and my life—depend on it."

The warrior's words were delivered with such gravity and passion that they infused my spine with steel. "I understand," I said, my gaze never faltering from hers.

"Then are you ready to begin?" she asked, her tone that of a master.

"Let's do it."

Dyani taught me The Five Phases of the Moon, each movement so intricate and nuanced, it would take me forever to memorize them. We ran through each phase several times, then started again, the cycle repeating.

Dyani was as patient as she could be, willing to answer my every question. Was the foot turned inward or outward here?

Was the fist open or closed there? Each time, she answered patiently.

Though the moves were slow, they were agonizing, and I was dripping with sweat by the end of her coaching. Even with my new elven body.

Exhausted and trying to catch my breath, I sat by Dyani, who had barely broken a sweat. I drank the last drops of the precious water from my flask. Though I was grateful for Dyani and her willingness to train me, I couldn't tell whether her motives were altruistic or if she was trying to atone for her brother's sins. Regardless, I had another gripe with her. "Rowen told me you wanted him out of the village while I was gone. Threatened him to a duel."

She scoffed with a shake of her head. "Maybe if I would have been the clear winner, I would have pursued it. But, Keira, he was frightening to battle, and I couldn't beat him. I've never seen anything like it. He's the closest I've come to a true opponent. I knew he was starting to get bad again when he got that look in his eye."

"What look?"

"He used to walk around with an emptiness in his eyes, a hollowness that was painful to witness. Even though he walked around like a soulless shell, he would always help anyone in need without hesitation. He was always the first to volunteer for the least desirable tasks, like cleaning the weapons and dishes, chopping and collecting firewood, dome and path repairs, and plowing the fields. But then he met you, and it was like watching a dormant fire suddenly reignite."

The twin flame within me pulsed with pride.

"Then my brother took you, and it was the worst I'd ever seen him. Before he met you, he was empty, but this time, he was filled with rage—a rage I recognized in myself. When we sparred, Rowen was savage and vicious, but so was I. And I relished it. I can't even tell you how many times we almost killed each other."

I shot her a feral look.

"Sorry. Maybe I shouldn't have said that."

"You think?"

Dyani chuckled, and a smile spread across her stern face. Her features had never softened for me, and the surprising transformation was unexpected.

"I am glad you're back, though I do miss sparring with your soul flame," she said, resting her elbows on her knees.

"So everybody knows he's my soul flame?"

"Please. The way he couldn't take his eyes off you that first day I trained you. He watched me like a hawk, making sure I didn't hurt you." She huffed, flipping her ponytail off her shoulder. "As if I would. Little did he know that I was the one who would have to watch out for you. But really, attempting to make you look like a real warrior will be my new challenge."

I narrowed my eyes, but I was in no position to be picky.

She drank the last few sips from her waterskin, savoring every drop.

Water was no longer flowing steadily towards the village. The black, glass-like forests had spread, drying up the land and air, turning all to a stagnant death.

From the time I'd been gone, the villagers had been put on water rations, using no more than was absolutely necessary. The smallest canteens of water were stretched to their absolute limits. Even the crops were beginning to fail, and I saw the strain on Nepta's face; it was growing more difficult for her to hide. "Too bad your panic attacks can't make it rain again. Only thunderclouds, huh?"

"Does everyone know everything about me?" I asked, throwing my hands up.

"Pretty much." She shrugged. "No one blames you, you know. There is simply no moisture in the air to pull from."

Suddenly, an idea struck me. There had to be water somewhere. Maybe I could bring it here. Somehow.

Realization hit me like a collision of stars.

The Alcreon Light within me was a celestial, gravitational force. I just had to find where there was water to pull from.

When I'd summoned rain in the past, I was furious and crying and not in control. I had no idea what to do. But I had to try something! The land was so dry it was only a matter of time before one of my bolts of light caused serious damage. "I could try pulling water from somewhere else, but I don't have much control, and I'm worried I will hurt the village in the process."

Her eyes tilted to mine, squinting from the sun. "What if you went outside the village?"

My heart lurched. Was she trying to lure me outside the village just like Demil?

Even if she was, she was right. If I couldn't risk hurting the elves within the village, I would have to try outside it.

Was it wise of me to worry, or did I trust Dyani? She seemed to genuinely want to help. But would I be a fool for leaving Nepta's protective borders again?

Rowen appeared in the distance. His body moved toward me with a deliberate gait, each step showcasing the grace and power of his muscles. His arms languidly swayed by his sides, grazing past the holstered weapons strapped to his hips. His green eyes, vivid and locked on me, stood out against his dark hair and rugged scruff.

I reveled that every step he took was to close the distance between us, to get closer to me. "You have a look in your eye," he said as he neared me like an unfolding dream.

A warm glow spread through my chest. He knew me so well. "I have an idea."

"What now, Copeland?" he asked with a knowing smile.

"During the fire, I summoned a rainstorm. And again, when we were stranded in the cave. I needed laith moss to save you from their venom, but the creature wasn't dead. To escape it, I jumped over a geyser. Just as the laith leaped after me, the water erupted and dragged the creature down into the river."

Rowen shot me a concerned glare. I never planned on telling him that part of the story, but here we were. "I asked you if it was dead," he said as he clenched his teeth.

"I said it was nearly dead," I offered with a shrug. "Which technically was true. But there were always drinkable water sources nearby or moisture in the air. Do you know of any places left like that?"

"All our water is sourced from the mountain glaciers, but the last time I checked, the water flow was greatly reduced," Rowen said, sitting to join us. Of course he would know that; he knew this land like the back of his hand, having wandered the forest countless times. "Perhaps we can inspect the main well together," he added, his voice tinged with both hope and caution. "The shift in our weather patterns is alarming, but where one village can suffer from drought, another can be inundated with floods."

"I could help balance it out," I said, feeling optimistic. Just like Althea.

I would do whatever I could to ensure the Wyn didn't suffer. Dyani said no one blamed me, but nearly the entire village shot dark glances my way. I couldn't blame them. I'd caused nothing but problems since the day I arrived. Plus, they had seen my ability to do what this village so desperately needed. It ate away at me that I couldn't protect the elves who had given me so much.

Sitting around chatting about my feelings with Takoda or training with Dyani wouldn't bring water back to the village. I needed action.

Given that the spirits granted me a stronger body, I should be able to wield the Alcreon Light more efficiently . . . I just had to figure out how.

My inability to control my Light hurt everyone; in more ways than I could imagine. Not only was it hurting my soul flame, it was hurting everyone around me.

I needed to get it together. If my touch only brought death, and I wasn't allowed to do anything, the least I could do was use whatever power I had to help the Wyn elves.

I made up my mind. I would leave the safety of Nepta's borders once again. The village was desperate.

17

Today was the day I would get water flowing back to the village. Everyone was thirsty and dehydrated, and we all desperately wanted a proper bath.

"Thank you for doing this with me," I said to Rowen as I threw on a thin linen shirt, a lace-up vest, and leggings.

"We both know you would find a way to go without me, and I would much rather be by your side," he said as we began our half-a-day's journey to the extinct well at the base of the snow-capped mountains. "When the water first ran dry, I searched the land for a potential relocation site. But the more I explored, the more I realized the Wyn village was one of the last safe havens in Luneth. There is nowhere else to go. Though, if I did find refuge, they would have to go without me. I would never leave the only place you would know to go."

My stomach dropped as the ground crunched in a dirge of drought beneath us. Of course he scoured the land while I was away. It was what he did when he was in pain. He wandered. And I was suddenly reminded that I'd been gone for months. A fact I didn't think I would ever get used to.

"Tell me about where we're going."

"I'm taking you to the well I believe will be best for directing water back to the village," Rowen said, sounding nervous as hell.

"I have a very serious question," I replied, wanting to get his mind off the daunting task I planned to do.

"What's that?" he asked seriously.

"Is there a reason you eat like a barbarian?"

He grinned, accepting my offer to *play with me*. "Is there a reason you eat as if it's an art form?" he asked, imitating how I eat with my hands. "Constructing every bite to perfection."

"As an artist, you should not take my art lightly," I teased back. "I am creating a masterpiece with every bite."

"Believe me, I know all about edible art," he said as he looked me up and down. "Every time I draw you, or look at you, it makes my mouth water."

I threw my head back with laughter, allowing the brief reprieve to wash over me. Even though it felt like the world was ending, Rowen and I could escape into each other's company. Our soul flame bond was a comforting light amidst the encroaching darkness.

Just as I was about to make another comeback, my ear twitched, and a flicker of movement caught my eye. "What kind of animals are out here?"

"None too frightening," Rowen said as he patted the assortment of blades attached to his body. A pang of emptiness itched at my thigh. I felt naked without the blade Rowen had gifted me. It was the first weapon that truly felt like an extension of my body, but I had lost it at the Battle of the Crypts.

I would have to find a new blade soon.

Rowen and I continued down the path, sharing our upbringings and favorite memories, keeping the conversation light. I needed to be in a good mindset for what I was about to attempt.

We'd been walking for some time when I saw movement in the bushes again. "Rowen, I think something is following us."

"Not something. Someone," Rowen whispered as he slowly pulled out his blade, and with a speed I could barely register, Rowen hurled his ax into the trees.

I flinched as a yelp rang from within the foliage.

Rowen stormed over and cleared the brush, revealing Maddock pinned to a tree by his shirt sleeve.

Maddock sucked in rapid breaths, his eyes gaping as he took in the ax mere centimeters from his limb. "You almost killed me!"

"No. I didn't," Rowen said, walking through the branches to dislodge the blade from Maddock's shirt. As my soul flame pried the ax from the trunk, Maddock's chest heaved, his eyes never leaving Rowen.

Finally released, Maddock staggered away from the tree. "I really liked this shirt," he said, poking his finger through the tear. "Where are we going anyway?"

I charged up to him, fury boiling in my veins. "*We* aren't going anywhere. I told you I never wanted to see you again."

Maddock ran a hand through his black hair that fell in his eyes. "I know you told me to stay away, but I find I need to be near you."

"Yeah, that's not going to happen because I don't want to be anywhere near you. What part of *I never want to see you again* do you not understand? Stop following us and go get a life," I said as I stormed away.

Maddock followed me back onto the trail. "I just need to make sure you're okay."

"Why are you worried about that?" I asked, whirling around. He shot a glance at Rowen. "Don't look at him. Look at me. Why?"

"Answer her," Rowen demanded. "Make your intentions clear."

"I just . . . I can't explain it. I feel inexplicably drawn to you. Maybe it's the Light we share. Maybe—"

"We don't share it." I glared, a tirade creeping up my throat. "Sharing implies I gave it to you willingly. But we both know that's not what happened."

"Keira, what do I have to do to earn your forgiveness?" he asked, his cherrywood eyes darting back and forth between me and my soul flame. "Forgiveness from both of you."

I squared my shoulders. "Why are you here? What do you really want?"

"All I want to know is that you're safe," he said, stepping up beside Rowen, just a few inches shorter but almost just as wide.

"I'm safe, no thanks to you," I retorted, my fists clenching so tight that my nails dug into my palms. "And to keep it that way, I'd like you to stay as far away from me as possible."

"I don't think I can do that," he replied with a strangled expression, and something in my heart shattered. My sympathy and anger warred. He looked so broken, so alone, but then I remembered what he did to me. The fear I felt as his phantom fingers pulled my mind apart.

Hatred blistered inside of me. "If I ever see you again, I will kill you."

With that, I spun away from him, wondering if I had the guts to follow through with my threat.

⸻ ·⟨ ☾ · ● · ☽ ⟩· ⸻

Now that's Madds was gone, Rowen and I continued our journey in peace.

"Do you really think you could kill him?" he asked, breaking the monotonous sound of our crunching footsteps. "I don't think he is following us anymore, but he seems adamant about being near us."

"If he would just be honest, I might go easier on him. I know he's hiding something."

"I believe you're right. But he appears sincere in wanting to make sure you're safe."

"That makes me even more nervous," I said, brushing my knotted hair out of my face. "But even if he told the truth, I'm not sure I could forgive him for what he did to me. The terror I felt as he overtook my body. The fear that I would never get to see you again, or worse, that I would, but I'd be trapped so deep within my mind that I couldn't speak. Silently screaming inside that it wasn't really me. I don't know if I can ever forgive that."

Rowen's nostrils flared, and his jaw flexed to the point of cracking. "The only thing stopping my blade from carving him up for you is Nepta. It's taking all of my self-control not to beat him to a bloody pulp, but my restraint is hanging by a thread."

"I don't want to talk about him anymore. Let's focus on getting water back to the village. A nice hot bath sounds exquisite."

"I agree," he said, and I reveled in that dangerous grin of his. "That does sound exquisite."

After another hour of walking and sensing no more rustling in the bushes, Rowen said, "Here is the well. It was once filled to the brim with water."

Rowen's knowledge of the land was invaluable, and I thanked the Spirits I had him here with me. I just wished I could lay my fingers upon his beautiful face and feel the coarse scruff on his jaw and the soft press of his lips. His expression turned to steam as his thoughts ventured to where mine lay as well.

Clearing my throat, I realized what Rowen referred to wasn't a well so much as it was a small opening in the ground. I knelt beside it, peering into the massive sinkhole. It was hard to believe this chasm was once filled with water. The land was dry as a bone.

Nepta described me as a gravitational force, much like how the moon compels the tides.

I closed my eyes and took a deep breath, trying to center myself. I focused inward, seeking the water flowing within my own body. Somehow, I knew that to find water in this arid expanse, I would first have to connect with the well inside myself.

Once I latched onto the feeling, I expanded my senses outward, stretching the familiar call across the barren landscape. I concentrated on the elemental beats as a soft light emanated from my fingertips.

I searched for the hidden streams that once nourished the land, but after several attempts, there wasn't even the slightest rumble of water.

My eyes lifted to Rowen. "I need to go deeper. I can't feel anything up here."

His eyes narrowed with apprehension. "I can help lower you, but I am unable to fit through after you," he said, clearly not appreciating the words coming out of his mouth. He may have a narrow waist, but his massive shoulders would never fit through that slight opening. I would barely fit myself.

"Good thing I'm not claustrophobic," I said as Rowen inspected a curtain of drying vines. Finding a rope that met his specifications, he yanked it free and began wrapping it around my hips like a harness. I breathed in through tight nostrils as his hand passed the cord between my thighs. He looped it back up and around, cinching it tight with a tug, and I gasped as he brought me within an inch of his mouth. We were close enough that I could feel strings of electricity zapping between our lips.

"Apparently, I don't have a problem with being tied up either," I said as my mind went wild with images of Rowen, silky vines, and restricting positions. It shocked me how I wasn't immediately turned off by the thought, especially after what happened with Caeryn when he'd abducted me and tied me to his waist. But my trust in Rowen had my mind jumping into realms I'd never considered, and a golden warmth pooled deep in my belly.

Rowen's sensuous mouth ticked up into a wicked grin. "Is this that corruption you were talking about?"

Playing with fire, I leaned in even closer and whispered, "Let's see how this knot holds, and I'll let you know."

He halted my advance with a backward tug on the vine and groaned. "You are going to be the death of me."

I tore my eyes away from his green gaze and lowered to the ground, maneuvering my way through the small opening. Rowen took the brunt of my weight as he lowered me into the sinkhole.

The heat in my veins cooled from the chilled cave walls, but it didn't escape me that the knot held firm.

The well may have a small opening, but as Rowen lowered my toes to the ground, I realized it expanded into an even deeper subterranean cavern. The marble walls swirled and glistened in rivulets of arctic blue, turquoise, and lime. And the eerie sound of dripping water echoed around me.

I wiggled out of my harness, ignoring Rowen's throaty growl as I walked towards the cave wall that had eroded into spiraling shades of aquamarine. I placed my palms on the chilly marble, feeling for any blocked or clogged water. It was there but faint and in the distance.

I lowered my hands to the ground, beseeching whatever water flowed beneath to rise to the surface. The trickle of water was far off, entrenched deep within the earth, and sounded like so little.

I pulled harder, delving deeper into my elemental connection, hoping it would be enough. As the gravitational force within me compelled the water to the surface, the ground beneath my fingers trembled.

That was easy!

Eager now, I pulled harder, the faint water rumbling like a stampede. Satisfied that I had done well, I decided to press my luck—if I wanted to grow stronger, I would have to work with stronger elements.

Suddenly, a column of water shot out from the ground and sprayed my arms and face.

Holy shit, that water was cold, but I smiled anyway. I had summoned water, and now I was going to control it.

I wiped my wet hair from my cheeks as water pooled around my ankles.

"Keira, come up now!" Rowen shouted from above.

I ignored his request as my arms and hands began to glow like liquid moonlight, and I guided the water along to its proper channels. Unexpectedly, a strong current pummeled towards me and almost knocked me off my feet.

I tried releasing my hold on the water, but it was as if I were still pulling it. More water rushed at me and doused me in a whirlpool of my own making.

A thought rounded the dark side of my mind: I was like the moon, compelling the tides, and if I wasn't careful, the waves could rise up and drown me whole.

While I was impressed with how quickly I'd filled the cavern, I knew it was time to go. I waded through the water that was now up to my thighs, reaching for the harness.

"Keira!" Rowen called after me again, but the water answered to a celestial body, a gravitational pull, and I moved my glowing arms to stop the swirling vortex. The onslaught abated, and I thought I was in the clear, but a powerful swell plowed into me and knocked me against the cave wall.

My breath left my lungs as another swell charged up and pulled me under.

What was happening? I thought I could control water. This was yet another example of how I had absolutely no control over any aspect of my life. What a fool I was to think I could command such an elemental force. Guide and direct, yes, but control? Never.

It was as if the land were so parched that my call for water had been met with the necessity of the land. My new body was more powerful than I imagined.

Entirely submerged and swirling within the underground well, I fought to calm the waves, but as I tried to reverse the raging waterwheel, it had the opposite effect and rammed toward my face. Water punched continuously through my nose and mouth while I breaststroked through the water, glowing like a lantern in a lake.

The water charged and swirled me. Filled me. Filled my lungs.

There was no more air.

Stars invaded my vision as I swam, but I didn't know what was up or down. I could be diving farther away from Rowen for all I knew.

How long had it been since my last breath?

Too long. Far too long.

Determination fueled my every stroke, but then my body began to convulse, and I floated in a crystal-clear liquid that reminded me of my time as the Light. It was peaceful yet lonely, and I realized with a jolt of fear that I wasn't ready to return to this tranquility—not yet. The thought of succumbing to the water's embrace filled me with terror.

Fighting my lungs for more time, I searched for Rowen's vine, but my vision was blurring. That rope was my only hope. I couldn't let it slip away.

Suddenly, the loop swayed before me, and with a last desperate heave, I linked my arm through the makeshift harness. But I was too late. The water had claimed me.

I was jerked upward, then pulled through the lip of the well by the scruff of my shirt. Glorious air hit my face, traveled through my hair, and chilled the clothes suctioned to my body. It washed over my nose and lips like a gentle trailing finger, but that was as far as it went. It wasn't entering my lungs.

I chased for the air, begged for it, but my lungs had stopped pulling in oxygen; they were too full of water. All used up.

My body was inert, but my mind was well aware of the fact that I wasn't breathing, and I could feel myself floating away.

Rowen had managed to pull me out without touching me, but as soon as his hands landed on my skin, he was gone. Even in this state, the Light had other plans.

Rowen cried out as he was launched from my body and thrown into the nearest tree with a painful grunt.

He couldn't touch me, but I knew he wouldn't stop trying. He'd likely kill himself attempting to save me.

Hands reached for me again, and I silently pleaded for Rowen to stop before he hurt himself any further, but the touch on my collarbone lingered. Warm fingers brushed against my skin as strands of wet hair were pushed from my face and neck.

"Get your hands off her," Rowen growled in a voice so deep it didn't even sound human in its rage.

But the hand on my shoulder didn't budge.

18

Despite Rowen's warning, the hand remained. "She's not breathing."

"You will let go of her," Rowen said venomously, "if you enjoy your limbs attached to your body."

The grip left me with a sigh. "From the blue tinge of her lips, I'd say it's been some time since her last breath." The voice was Maddock's. That sly bastard must have followed us here even after I told him not to. "What do you plan on doing? You can't touch her, and her time is running out."

"Just let me think," Rowen pleaded desperately.

"She doesn't have time for that. Listen, I know how to help with water in the lungs, but I'm going to have to touch her. Can you handle that, or do you need to look away?"

"If you can save her, then do it."

"You're not going to like it."

"Do it now!" Rowen roared.

Warm lips crashed against mine, forcing breath into my lungs. Two quick puffs of air were pushed down my throat as my nose was pinched tight. Suddenly, Maddock's hands gripped my bodice, and the sound of ripping fabric shattered the deafening silence. He threw my vest off me, baring me in my white undershirt. His palms landed between my breasts, performing chest compressions.

"What are you doing?" Rowen barely choked out.

My body shuddered beneath Maddock's forceful pumps. I tried to remain present, but I could feel myself drifting farther and farther away. "Back off if you want her to live," he snarled before putting his lips back on mine.

The tortured groan that escaped Rowen wasn't lost on me, and my heart ached for his helplessness.

The relentless pressure at my sternum intensified, and a cry formed deep within my chest. I fought to let the cry out, to let Rowen know I was still with him.

Maddock pounded on me with his palms, his attention shifting between my mouth and the space between my breasts.

The cry was working its way up my esophagus, cresting over the curve of my tongue. Almost there, yet so far away.

My awareness was down to a pinprick of light, and it was fading by the second. Desperation raked through me to pull away from the darkness, but its claws were in me too deep. I wanted to scream.

The cry was right behind my teeth. *So close.*

"Breathe, dammit," Maddock grunted as the weight on my chest continued, and it felt like I was about to crack. Everything had gone black. My time left on Luneth was down to seconds.

"The Light," Rowen choked out desperately. "Her Light. You've used it on her before. Do it again!"

Foreign fingers splayed at the swells of my breasts and with a violent pump, a jolt of electricity shot throughout my body. "Come on," someone said, their voice filled with urgency as more Light coursed through me. My back arched painfully off the ground as a lightning bolt surged through me once again.

"Keira. Stay with us," a voice pleaded.

Another thunderclap went through me and light flashed behind my eyelids.

Finally, my cry broke past my lips, but it wasn't a cry at all. It was the water lodged deep within my lungs. It spurted out of my mouth as my eyes flew open, and I gasped, drawing in desperate breaths of air.

Maddock rolled me over to ensure the water didn't fall back down my throat, then settled me against his weight.

In shock and not quite thinking clearly, I reached for Rowen.

Maddock grabbed my wrist and held it still. "Are you insane? You can't touch him. You nearly killed him with that little unconscious blast of yours." His eyes bore into me with a palpable intensity, his chest heaving in exhaustion.

Frozen to the bone and feeling so, so tired, I lifted my blurry gaze to Rowen. He emitted a choked sob of relief when our eyes collided and blood dripped from his nose.

I had done that to him—caused him to bleed. He was lucky to be alive. The thought made me sick to my stomach, but it was Rowen who looked ill as his gaze lowered, locking on Maddock's hands giving me the support he couldn't.

"Your hands and mouth are one thing, but I'll kindly ask you to take your eyes off her," Rowen growled, the tendons in his neck straining. "If I have to ask again, I can assure you I won't be as polite."

Wrapped in Maddock's embrace, I followed his stare down my body.

My bodice was gone, and the thin shirt covering me was practically see-through. It was so soaked, everything was visible: the exact contours of my breasts and the stark contrast of my frozen pink nipples. "I t-t-told you not t-to follow us," I stuttered between weakened breaths as my body shivered uncontrollably. "I-I...said I would k-k-kill you."

"Let me save you now so you can kill me later."

"Hold her up for me," Rowen ordered over my shoulder. "We need to warm her."

Without question, Maddock propped me up within his hold, and I whimpered as my stiff limbs were forced to move. Rowen's hands lowered to my stomach as his black-tinged fingertips gripped the wet fabric around my waist and pulled it up my torso.

Maddock's hands made adjustments on my bare skin while Rowen removed my top. I was too frozen to help, so the men moved and adjusted me like a doll, working together to strip me of my wet clothing.

Rowen's eyes traced over my exposed breasts, his gaze darkening when it came upon Maddock's fingers wrapped firmly around my ribcage.

In one swift tug, Rowen removed his shirt and pulled it over my head. The residual heat from his clothing seeped into my skin, and I hungrily accepted his warmth however I could get it.

Maddock's hands slipped out from underneath Rowen's shirt yet remained on me for support. Suddenly, a surge of heat exploded in my chest, triggering a shock to my system. My frozen blood pumped into motion like sluggish ice, tearing my veins from within. But then, the warmth spread throughout my body like molten gold.

A cry escaped my mouth in pain—or was it pleasure? The warmth disappeared as quickly as it came, leaving only pain, yet the phantom touch of pleasure still rippled through me.

"What's happening to her?" Maddock asked, drawing me in and taking my weight as I fell back and cried out again.

"Fuck," Rowen ground out, his voice strained. "She nearly drowned in glacial waters. I'm trying to warm her through our bond, but I pushed it too fast. We will need to bring her temperature up slowly."

"N-no. Rowen. Don't stop," I gasped, needing my soul flame

to ignite me from within, to touch and kindle the frozen fire inside me. "I'm c-cold."

Rowen's voice broke. "I must, my love. It is sending you into shock."

"She'll never get dry in those pants," Maddock said over my cries.

Rowen huffed in agreement. "Lean back with her."

Maddock obeyed, and even though my body was numb, I felt his heart pounding against my back. Rowen yanked off my boots before his hands flew to my abdomen, undoing the front lacings of my pants. He worked my leggings open, and heat shot to my belly as I ached for his adept fingers to touch the parts of me he was exposing. "Can you lift your hips for me?"

I tried to arch up, but my body was too heavy, too frozen, and I slammed back to the ground with a frustrated groan. The heat Rowen sent through our soul flame bond ignited other parts of me that were starving for warmth. The cold penetrated deeper into my bones, and my flame flickered dangerously.

If Rowen didn't stoke the small fire soon, it would perish. *I* would perish.

A worried conversation transpired over my shoulder. "Lift her for me."

Before I could object, Maddock's arm scooped beneath me, the flat of his palm landing at the base of my spine. He pushed my lower body up in a slow, painful thrust, offering my hips to Rowen.

Rowen carefully tugged my pants and underwear over the slope of my ass, his breath skittering through the gap in my thighs and right to my center. An exhausted moan, laced with aching desire, escaped my lips, and my neck tipped back against Maddock's shoulder. His warm breath fanned across my collarbone as Rowen bared me beneath his powerful, shirtless frame.

"You're doing so good, Keira. We're almost done," he said,

making sure his shirt was low enough on my thighs to keep me covered as he shucked my pants off my ankles.

I whimpered.

This was the most excruciating kind of pain. My soul flame stripping me down yet unable to touch me. To hold me. All the while, I lay braced in the arms of the man I hated.

"Her lips are still too blue," Maddock warned, lowering my bottom to the ground.

"Give me your shirt. You'll need to warm her with your body," Rowen stated with a calm yet pained grimace.

"N-no, please. I'm f-f-fine," I said, rolling away as Maddock loosened his grip to tug off his top. He handed it to Rowen and yanked me back towards him.

"Shut up, Keira, and let me help you," he grunted as he pushed my shirt up and slammed my bare back against his chest. I sucked in a strangled breath as his skin touched mine, and the frozen tundra of my veins sighed in relief. As much as I wanted to, I couldn't deny the heat of his body, yet still, I repelled his touch in every way.

Maddock snaked his hands through the front of my shirt, his knuckles grazing my breasts as he banded his arms across me. A familiar light shivered against me. Not just from my front where Rowen was, but *everywhere*. The thief behind me was forcing my body to bend to his will as he used my stolen gift against me.

Desire flared between my thighs, and I arched my back. "Rowen," I moaned, hating that my body was begging for more than just warmth. "I need you."

A strangled moan vibrated through him. "I know. It's all right. I'm here."

"Please, touch me," I begged, hating the arms that held me. My mind was dizzy, and my body scrambled. The right thoughts weren't wired to the right actions, but there was nothing I could do.

"I can't, my flame. Let Maddock help you," Rowen choked out, and I heard the strike of his blade against a whetstone.

"I'm s-so cold," I stammered, my hips bucking for friction and warmth.

Maddock held me tighter and groaned as if he were the one in pain. "Rowen, I can feel her suffering. Do you need me to . . ."

"Don't even think about it. Rub your hands on her *limbs*. Get her blood flowing," Rowen demanded, and Maddock complied, running his hands all along my body.

My breath hitched as Maddock's palms traced along my arms, chest, and stomach. Though his hands were a meager substitution for what I really needed, I found his touch not entirely unpleasant. In fact, it might have felt *nice*.

I wanted to reject the feeling because I knew it was a stolen emotion. But if I didn't relent to Maddock's help, my organs would shut down, and I would die anyway.

I stopped fighting as Maddock eased me into a comforting lie. I despised that his hands were soothing my desperate need.

My body betrayed me as my eyelids turned heavy.

"You did so good, Keira. You can rest now," Rowen said as a burst of flames danced along my frozen limbs.

Hearing Rowen's command and unable to resist a moment longer, I let myself fully drowse off into Maddock's embrace.

After some time, I heard my soul flame's voice through the crackling fire. "Wipe that smirk off your face, Madds."

"You know I could lay her down the other way, right? Chest to chest. Or completely naked," he said, gripping me tighter as I tried to squirm away, unamused by his suggestion. "They say that works best."

"It would be in your best interest to concentrate on keeping her alive," Rowen said in a menacing growl. "You're holding my only reason for existing in your arms. If she dies, you die. If she loses a single finger or toe due to the chill, I will hold you personally responsible, and you will lose the same in kind. Her fate is your fate."

Maddock's mouth snapped shut. He lifted my wrist to his mouth and blew warm air on my numb fingers.

Rowen wasn't easily provoked, but the anguish in his voice was unmistakable.

Maddock stopped the puffs of air he was peppering along my neck and hands and raised his head. "That pain on your face, it's how I feel every waking moment. It's slowly eating me alive."

"Good," Rowen seethed like a bloodthirsty dragon. "It is no less than what you deserve for your thievery."

"You are just as much to blame for this. How dare you let her enter the crevice all those months ago? What were you thinking? There was a monster inside, waiting for her. Waiting to take her body. If she were mine, I would have never let her out of my sight," Maddock said, running his hands all over my frostbitten flesh. His thumbs grazed against my breasts, hip bones, and thighs. Despite my mind bellowing to resist, my rebellious body curled deeper into his warmth.

"You think I wanted to? She asked me to trust her, and I did. But before she requested that of me, she tried sneaking off to help you."

"Really?" Maddock asked, and I could hear the smile in his voice.

"Yes, but luckily, she isn't as sneaky as she thinks. And in the end, it all worked out for the best, didn't it? Because without you, we both would have died today."

Maddock brushed a strand of my hair behind my ear. "I can only touch her like this because I stole from her, violated her. It's only because of my most heinous actions that I get to feel something this beautiful. She may have only just gotten to know me, but I've known her . . . *felt* her for months. I'm disgusted with myself, and I'll do whatever it takes to make it right. I will return all I stole."

All he stole?

"You will. Because if you don't find a way to give her back what's rightfully and cosmically hers, I will gladly watch as she kills you."

"I know, and I will welcome it."

Satisfied that Rowen would aid and abet me in murder, I let Maddock's warmth seep into my bones and lull me to sleep.

19

I blinked awake and immediately collided with Rowen's verdant gaze. His face was etched with pain, yet his shoulders loosened in relief. "Oh, thank fuck."

My first thought was how I wished I could wipe away the deep smudges under his eyes and the lingering trail of blood from his nose. The second was that I was sweltering, feeling trapped inside an inferno. Even though the sun had barely begun to rise, the heat was unbearable.

A blazing fire licked at my limbs as a massive weight suffocated me. I squirmed, realizing Maddock's arms and legs were draped over me, his bare chest radiating heat everywhere our skin touched.

I was spooning my enemy on the ground in front of the man I loved. But was Maddock my enemy still? My hatred toward him felt less boiling, less all-encompassing.

Though I was grateful he helped save me, we didn't need to cuddle.

Rowen turned to check my clothes drying by the fire. I squirmed and stirred to get Maddock off me. When suddenly, I felt a growing bulge press into my lower back. I shot him a feral look over my shoulder.

"Is it bigger than his?" he asked with a smirk that showed off his perfectly straight teeth.

"Not even close," I said, shoving him away, my strength already returning. "And I was just starting to like you."

Maddock sat upright with a groan. "I'm sorry. I couldn't help it with all your . . . wiggling."

My eyes shot to Rowen. "The water, it's flowing now," I said, changing the subject. I don't think Rowen heard. If he had, Maddock's face would be punched in by now. I imagined my soul flame was in enough pain as it was. We didn't need to address Madds' hard-on. "I was able to control it. For the most part."

"Sure you were. If that's what you want to call it," Maddock remarked beside me, pulling his shirt over his head. "Were you trying to get yourself killed?"

I stood on shaky legs, swimming in Rowen's tunic. The collar was so wide it hung off one of my shoulders, revealing a few of my shimmering scars. "Though the execution was a little rough, the outcome was as intended. Right? Please tell me it worked?" I asked, suddenly afraid I'd failed.

Rowen's face lit with pride, and he nodded in the distance. "Yes, I can hear the creeks flowing again. You were magnificent. Even if you did scare me to death," Rowen said, his eyes leveling with mine before rising to Maddock's. "Thank you for keeping her alive. Though it doesn't make me want to kill you any less."

"Don't mention it," Maddock said, his gaze trailing up Rowen's bare torso. His expression was a mix of admiration and fear until he winced, noticing the mottled scar above my soul flames heart. "So, no one's getting murdered tonight?"

Rowen cocked a thick eyebrow. "That remains to be seen."

"Are my pants dry yet?" I asked. I didn't want to spend

another minute here. I'd done what I set out to do and nearly killed myself in the process. I also didn't want to examine what Maddock had done for me too closely.

"Not yet," Rowen replied, his murderous stare softening only for me, "but your stockings are."

I plopped on a rock and put on my shoes and socks. I may not be able to fully dress, but this was good enough.

"What are you doing?" Maddock asked. "You need more rest. In case you missed it, you died."

"Wouldn't be the first time," I said, my eyes fixed on lacing up my boots. I couldn't bear to look Maddock in the eyes. Even though he helped save me, I wanted to be nowhere near him. Plus, I'd been writhing and begging in his arms, something I would never live down. "I want to get back to the village and take a long, hot bath."

Rowen gathered our things, holstered his ax, and extinguished the fire.

"Rowen?" Maddock asked incredulously, rising to his feet. "You know she still needs rest."

"You'll learn soon enough that once Keira puts her mind to something, she is going to do it," Rowen said, his eyes tipping up to meet mine with a smirk. "If she says she's ready to go, then she's ready to go. Do you want me to tie her to a tree?"

"Yes! That would be preferable," Maddock said as he rubbed his hand down his mouth. "I swear, I'm the only one with any sense around here."

"Sure," Rowen replied, tossing the waterskins to Madds. "Go fill these up for us, will you? There should be a small creek just beyond those trees now."

Maddock caught the flasks and eyed Rowen skeptically. "You won't desert me out here, will you?"

"I think we're far past that," Rowen said, the first rays of sunlight highlighting his bare chest. "Don't you?"

Maddock's sharp features relaxed as his gaze darted between the two of us. "I'll be right back."

Maddock disappeared into the trees, and my eyes shot to Rowen. "Are you all right?" we asked simultaneously and chuckled.

"I'm murderous," Rowen replied. "You?"

"Feeling pretty lethal myself, actually," I said, stepping as close to him as I possibly could. "Thank you for everything you did. That couldn't have been easy."

"I would do it a thousand times over if it meant keeping you alive. When he put his hands and mouth on you, Keira, I don't know, I just had to trust him. Even after everything he did to you, I had to believe he'd save you. He looks at you like he cares. I had to hold onto that."

I glanced into the distance where Madds had passed from sight. "I still don't trust him."

"I know, but what other choice did I have?"

"Good thing it was up to you to make that call. If I'd been able, I would have told him to get the fuck off," I said, itching to run my fingers through Rowen's dark waves.

"Oh, you said that many times," he replied, his breath washing over my face and pebbling my skin. "It is my life's goal to give you everything you desire, but in this, I had to override your wishes. As much as it pained me to see you in another man's arms."

"I wanted it to be you," I whispered. The warmth he awakened in me still begged for his touch. Our lips were an inch apart, our blood pulsing with need and desire. When suddenly, Maddock barged through the bushes like an oaf.

"You ready?" he asked, watching us jump apart as he held the plump waterskins.

I reached for one of the flasks and drank until my belly

bulged. "Yes," I said, wiping the water off my chin. "The sooner I can have a hot bath, the better."

—— ·(·☾·●·☽·)· ——

We made our back to the village in awkward silence, and I found myself sandwiched between the towering men who had worked together to strip, clothe, and save me. I wasn't sure if it looked like I'd had the best or worst night of my life. My hair was a messy halo around my head, I wore no pants, and Rowen's linen shirt barely covered my thighs.

My soul flame was beside me, matching my pace and walking as close to me as he possibly could. He was naked from the waist up, his chest burgeoning with a strength that still amazed me. He had gained so much muscle, and my fingers yearned to explore the new, deeper divots of his body.

I snapped my eyes away from him, wrangling in my thoughts that strayed to what I could find in his pants, what I could stroke, lick, and taste.

Deciding that I would rather be angry than turned on, I slid my eyes to Maddock. He wasn't as tall as Rowen nor as broad, but his lean muscles still promised the strength and agility of a formidable opponent. Despite my lingering hatred toward him, I couldn't deny it was his body that had kept me alive.

Suddenly, my gaze shot upward as a bright light flashed through the dawn. The light was blinding with a tail of white fire. "I've never seen such a big shooting star!" I exclaimed with awe as the light arced overhead. But instead of fading like the last words of a wish, it continued to streak through the sky, barreling closer and closer.

"Me neither," Rowen warily said as he tracked its descent. "That doesn't look like your typical falling star. Look at the speed and brightness. Something is off."

"That's not normal around here?" Maddock asked with clipped paranoia, squinting as the light from the heavens engulfed his gaze.

"No," Rowen replied, his green eyes widening in alarm. "Take cover," he yelled as the ball of light hurtled toward us.

The meteor's impact was brutal and sent shockwaves through the ground. Even though it crashed hundreds of meters away, the force knocked me off my feet. A rising plume of dirt swallowed me whole and cut up my arms and legs.

"Is everyone all right?" Rowen's voice pierced through the ringing in my ears.

"Yes." I coughed, blinking out bits of dust from my eyes.

"Madds?" he called out with concern.

"I'm here," Maddock said, groaning. "That thing nearly killed us. This world is a death trap. Remind me why you moved here again, Keira?"

"Someone I care about happens to live here. Something you wouldn't know anything about," I snapped, still trying to stay angry rather than to feel . . . anything else.

"Yeah, I guess you're right," he said, and it may have been the dirt in my eyes, but I swore Maddock flinched as if my words could hurt him. But that was impossible. This man had no feelings. He was perfectly content to rip my mind apart and slash my memories to pieces.

I stood and dusted off my shirt, redirecting my focus. I raised the crook of my arm to shield my eyes from the smoke.

"What are you two doing?" Maddock asked in shock as Rowen and I made our way to the impact sight.

"Taking a look," I replied for the both of us.

"I'll say it again. I'm the only one with any sense around here," Maddock groaned as he chased after us. "We definitely should not be doing this. Keira, you nearly died. That makes twice today!"

"I told you that's not uncommon," I replied, quickening my pace to reach whatever had fallen to the earth, and a tug pulled at my chest. "Wait. I feel something."

I carefully approached the edge of a massive crater. Deep within the depression, a pyre of ice-white fire flickered through the smoke.

"A meteor," I guessed as Rowen emerged through the lingering whorls of dust.

"Perhaps," Rowen replied, joining me on the precarious ledge. His face was streaked with dirt, but he was otherwise unharmed.

Maddock flanked my other side, his weight sending a small avalanche of rock downward.

The smoke cleared and revealed a massive rock shining as brightly as the moon. It was breathtaking and thrumming with heavenly veins of light and luminous matter. The deep, resonant hum reverberated through the ground and traveled up my legs and into my fingertips. It felt like a piece of my essence had descended to earth, a star truly within my grasp, pulsating with the ethereal energy that seemed to flow within my veins.

"That's incredible," Rowen said. "I can feel the heat from up here."

"Well, this has been lovely. Can we go now?" Maddock asked nervously. "It could be dangerous."

I stepped closer to the edge, my fingers itching to touch the glowing rock as overlapping whispers of time, millennia, and cosmic secrets filled my head.

A strong grip landed on my shoulder, momentarily snapping me out of my trance. "Your eyes," Maddock said with a gasp.

My gaze darted to Rowen. "Keira, your eyes are glowing as bright as the stone."

My throat constricted, and I turned back to the fallen rock. "This is no place for a star," I said, staring into its depths. It was hard to tell where one light ended and the other began. But the meteor slowly flickered out like a dying bulb, fading until it settled into pitch-black obsidian.

"Can I please just get you both home now?" Maddock moaned, more concerned about us than I thought was necessary. "It's been a day, Keira. Rowen didn't take his eyes off you all night. He needs rest. So do you. You were dead for twenty minutes, at least."

My breath caught in my throat. "You performed chest compressions on me for that long?"

"I did," he said, sounding beyond exhausted himself. "Did you think Rowen would let me stop until you started breathing again?"

I glanced between my soul flame and the man who'd pumped air into my lungs. We were all half-dressed, tired, and filthy. And as much as I was sure Rowen hated to admit it, he said, "Madds' is right. We need to leave. There could be more falling debris. It's not safe here."

I reluctantly agreed, and without another word, we all turned from the crater's edge when suddenly, the earth slipped beneath Maddock's foot, and he lost his balance. He stumbled backward, crying out, and an unbidden wave of dread washed over me as I watched him fall.

Rowen's strong hand darted out, catching Maddock by the front of his shirt. Maddock flailed back, but Rowen's grip held firm, balancing him on the precipice of the crater.

Rowen wouldn't even have to push Maddock for him to fall; he would just have to let go. Maddock's eyes widened in terror as he realized his life teetered in Rowen's hands.

The moment stretched on, the two of them locked in a silent battle. I swore I saw a flicker of contemplation cross Rowen's face. It was as if he were considering letting Maddock fall to his death. Their broad chests heaved into each other, their breaths ragged as they awaited Rowen's decision.

Before I could react, Rowen launched Maddock back onto solid ground. The bond thief stumbled and rolled onto his back.

"I thought you were going to let me fall," Maddock panted, raising his head to glance at Rowen over his heaving chest.

"For a moment, I thought I was too," Rowen said, running his hands down his face. "A life for a life. Now we're even."

— ·（ ·（ ● ·）·）· —

We came upon the wooden dwellings, and already, I could hear water flowing throughout the village.

Elves exited their domes to start the day, their pointed ears flexing at the sound of running water. Realization dawned on them as cries of disbelief and joy filled the air. Their celebration drew attention as more villagers gathered to see the commotion. Cheers ran wild as the forest elves sprinted towards the creeks and rivers, jumping in, hugging, and filling their canteens to the brim.

I made eye contact with Dyani from across the way. She dipped her chin, acknowledging what I had done for her village. The warrior turned to nearby elves, her mouth moving with words I couldn't decipher.

Their gazes fell upon me with appreciation, thanking me with smiles and bows.

I nodded back, feeling a bit embarrassed that I still wore Rowen's shirt.

"Looks like the drought is over," Maddock said, smiling at the celebrating elves. He lingered as if he wasn't ready to return to his cell.

"Thank you for your help," I replied, weary to the bone. It

was an awkward goodbye to the man who helped save my life, but I desperately needed to wash this ordeal from my skin.

His eyes pierced mine, and he grinned. "No problem."

Warring emotions overcame me, but I returned his smile before walking away.

Rowen and I headed straight to our private bathing chamber, and I sighed in relief as the stone basin ran full. The cascading waterfalls filled the tub and sprinkled up water like bits of diamonds.

"You go first," Rowen said. "And take your time. You deserve it."

I lowered into the shell bath and moaned. The frigid water had thankfully warmed from the hot springs and there was now enough water to fully submerge myself. I rested my head against the tub and enjoyed the day-lit stars.

After my soak, I felt like a whole new woman.

I wrapped myself in a plush robe as Rowen hopped in after me. He ducked his head under the water and emerged like a god of the sea, whipping his dark curls from his face.

My eyes perused a little longer than they should have, and when I finally walked into the anteroom to finish getting ready, the dying plant wall filled my vision.

Clean, warm, and dry, I felt as if I could do anything. And with newfound confidence, I placed my hands along the withering branches.

I willed the Light within me to flow through my fingertips, hoping to revive the dying foliage. For a moment, a glow enveloped the leaves, and I held my breath as I cradled the delicate life within my hands. It was alive and beautiful, and my heart soared. But then, the ever-present seed of death crept in from the edges and smothered my Light.

"No!" I cried.

I could no longer feel life, only death—it spread its cold tendrils through the branches and leaves and crumbled them to dust. "No! No! No!"

I thought I was getting better.

Despair engulfed me as I realized I'd left the bathing chamber worse than I found it. I had wanted to heal and restore, but instead, I destroyed.

I collapsed to the ground in hopelessness, and nothing could stop my tears as a storm erupted overhead.

Rowen jumped out of the tub and rushed toward me, naked and dripping. "What happened?"

My gaze was stuck on the wall of death. I couldn't see anything else. "I'm surrounded by darkness," I said, my breaths coming in so tight and quick I could barely breathe.

"You've been surrounded by darkness before. You beat it once, you can beat it again," he replied, his eyes filled with sincerity and desperation.

"I don't know how to come back from this."

"Beauty can come out of the darkness. I've seen it. I've seen it with you, Keira. When you first came to this world surrounded by your blight, I couldn't touch you. Call out to you. But I watched you overcome it. And even though I didn't know you, I was so damned proud of you. Watching you fight it alone was agony then, and it's agony now—not being able to touch you. To pleasure you. To hold you. Especially when I see you breaking like this."

I knew it was hard for him to see me this way. It was hard to live through. Especially when all I wanted was to collapse into his arms.

"Find your way back to me," he begged, his knuckles turning white from restraining to touch me.

"I'm trying."

Cheers echoed through the bathing chamber as rain began to fall. Everyone celebrated and laughed while I crashed and burned and destroyed.

20

I slept like the dead, and when I woke at dawn, I was too anxiety-ridden to go back to bed.

I leaned into Rowen's ear, inhaling his earthy scent. "I'm going to train. I will see you later."

He stirred, his voice groggy. "I'll go with you."

"No, sleep. You need it," I whispered, wishing I could press a kiss to his temple. "I love you."

Once dressed and at the training grounds, I went through The Five Phases of the Moon.

The patterns were grueling. Not only was it a physical workout but a mental one as well, and I pushed myself harder than I ever had before.

I focused on perfecting each phase, adjusting my knee here or extending my lunge there. Each time I went through the movements, it brought a deeper level of understanding.

While I practiced, two earthquakes rocked the ground, each one deepening the pit in my stomach. I was nowhere near ready to face Erovos. Since my return, all I had managed to do was get the water flowing back to the village, but I had done it in the sloppiest way imaginable.

Despite the sharp stitch forming in my side, I pushed through the pain and fatigue. Even the earthquakes couldn't stop me. They were a grim reminder of what I was up against.

Sweat trickled down my brow as I struggled with one of the more complex moves.

Everything seemed impossible and insurmountable, but I had to be better and stronger. Failure wasn't an option.

Somehow, I needed to find a way to overcome the darkness threatening the world, but how could I when I couldn't even overcome the darkness within myself? I was wilting from the inside out.

Maybe the key to healing and returning to my soul flame was uncovering the secrets of my past.

Rowen suggested I try mind-mending sessions with Takoda —to face my demons head-on. And perhaps I took his advice a bit too literally because there was one person I was desperate to confront.

I finished with the fourth phase and closed my eyes, searching for the thread I swore I would never touch again. I thought I had buried it deep within my subconscious but imagine my surprise when I found it behind a curtain of denial.

Even now, as I ran my fingers along the shimmering string, the thought of where it would lead, and what I would face on the other end, weighed heavily on the golden lacquer that repaired my broken heart.

I pulled on the thread anyway and landed in a familiar room. My mother's office.

A grin spread across my face. I might suck at everything else at the moment, but at least I was good at traveling.

Even though the room was tall with vaulted ceilings, it was smaller than I remembered, less intimidating.

I scanned the rows of psychology books, notes, and journals, unsure of what I was looking for. My gaze roved over the accolades lining the walls and the couch I was forced to sit on for hours a day, recounting the same story again and again until I was blue in the face.

My eyes widened when they landed on my mother's computer.

I walked to the bay window and sat at her desk. I'd always believed I was bad with technology, but now I understood it was the repressed Light within me. The raw energy lived beneath my skin and could short-circuit any device I touched.

The screen was black, but I quickly nudged the mouse with my finger, and the computer came to life. There were several folders, but the one titled *K.C. - Treatment Plan* caught my eye.

I held my breath and double-clicked the folder, using only the briefest touches to prevent the computer from exploding.

Document after document appeared as my eyes scanned the reports.

Behavioral Concerns: Persistent dissociation, maladaptive daydreaming, difficulty distinguishing dreams from reality. Physical altercations involving students, teachers, and parents, claims of electrical shock. The patient unknowingly self-harms, waking up covered in scratches and blood.

Sleep patterns include sleepwalking, night terrors, overly vivid dreams, and parasomnia.

Cognitive Health: Increased episodes of dissociation.

Treatment History: Daily psychotherapy. Intravenous administration of CereNex18. Drug left noticeable bruises on arms; switched to oral administration—spare sedatives on hand in case of emergency.

Lock on bedroom door. Cameras to monitor sleep.

Removal of beloved items when patient misbehaves.

Medical Analysis: White blood cell count is excessively high with no signs of disease or illness. The cause remains unknown.

CereNex18 is untraceable.

Treatment Prognosis: Over time, the patient experienced fewer episodes. Dreaming subsided after three weeks of treatment. Mental lethargy has increased, but no physical lethargy reported. The patient sleeps through the night and has no memory of sleepwalking or violent episodes. On CereNex18, patient is manageable.

None of the eighteen versions of CereNex passed preclinical testing.

I turned away, unable to bear another word. A silent tear slid down my cheek. I wasn't my mother's child. I was her experiment.

I didn't wipe the tear. Instead, I let it slide down my face, feeling every bit of pain in that single teardrop. As soon as it fell from my chin, I would be free. But in this moment, I would feel it all.

When the tear crashed to the carpet, I spun back to the screen, opened a new email, set the recipient to *all contacts*, and dragged the folder into the window. I couldn't let my parents get away with this.

Just as I was about to hit *send*, a familiar voice halted me in my tracks.

"Oh my God, Keira! Wha . . . Where did you come from?" my mother stuttered as she nearly collapsed against her bookshelf

"I fell through stars, Mama" I said, reciting how I described it as a child—still as true then as it was now.

I stood so she could fully see me.

Her eyes widened like saucers, the whites visible all the way around. "What happened to you? You disappeared from the hospital."

"It's my turn to ask the questions. Tell me everything, or I'm sending my folder to everyone you know," I said, my finger hovering over the send button. "I'm sure you wouldn't want this sensitive information getting leaked. You were always afraid I would destroy the image of Copeland Psychiatry, but you seem to be doing a great job of that on your own."

"I'm just so glad you are safe, my darling," my mother said, running to hug me.

I dodged her embrace. "Don't touch me," I stammered, even though it broke my heart. My mother had never shown such affection, and my inability to run into her arms broke me in two. "It's not safe."

How different my life could have been if I could recall one other instance of a shared embrace.

"I'm so sorry for everything," she said, her voice trembling as if she were about to cry.

My resolve wavered, but I quickly steeled my spine. "Tell me everything," I demanded, my stance and tone making it clear I wasn't leaving here without answers.

"I'm not sure where to begin," my mother said, her strawberry-blonde hair loosening from its clip. "You were always such a strange child," she trailed off as if unsure how to proceed. "I was frightened. For me. But more for you."

"Go on."

"You still don't remember?"

"I deserve to hear it from you," I said, my finger still hovering over the button.

"Very well," my mom replied with a nod. "You would somehow escape out of the house every night. The problem was isolated at first, but then you began displaying symptoms at school. You would hurt other students and teachers. You would tell disturbing stories of a man with orange eyes killing men, forests, and creatures and how we needed to help them. You disturbed everyone—even me. And you would . . . hurt yourself.

"We tried everything before CereNex. We would ground you, punish you, take away your telescope. My, how you cried for that hideous thing. One day we woke to find you covered in blood. We thought you'd been kidnapped, but instead of telling the truth, you would make up outlandish stories. We set up cameras in the house. Some nights you stayed put; others, the footage was too bright to make anything out. It all went away when you were medicated."

"You weren't medicating me. You were poisoning me. I heard Dad say it was enough to drug an elephant and that I'm lucky to be alive."

"You do have some undiagnosed illnesses, but we can figure that out together now. We thought we were protecting you. Can you not see that your delusions run rampant? You never wanted to face the truth, and you still don't."

Her words hit me like a battering ram. "It was you who never faced the truth. I never lied. You just refused to listen. I wasn't ill, I was astral projecting. Walking between worlds."

Something flickered across my mother's face. She eyed my strange clothing and the elongated tips of my ears. "That's impossible. There is no evidence to support that astral projection is real. It's pseudoscience. Unprovable."

"I came here . . ." I choked out, my throat constricting. "I came here to tell you that you kept me from the best thing in my life. You kept me from where I was meant to be, and that nothing will ever keep me from it again. I just came to say goodbye."

This was the most disheveled I'd ever seen her, and her eyes flashed from my hand to my eyes. She fixed the loose strand of her hair and refastened it into her clip. "Would you like to help me prove astral projection is real?"

My eyebrows furrowed. "How?"

It was an unexpected question, but I recovered quickly. She had broken me once, and I wasn't so quick to shatter again. She turned from me and rummaged through a nearby drawer, no longer worried about the email that could ruin her reputation.

"You can start by telling me everything," she said, slowly stepping toward me.

I couldn't tell if my mother was sincere, but there was a flutter in my heart that wanted to give her one last chance. "I would leave my room every night because I was astral projecting to another world—a place that called to me through the stars. Some nights, my body remained in bed while my mind traveled beyond the known universe, beyond my physical constraints. Other nights, more of me would venture out, my entire being on another plane, returning with unexplainable bruises and scratches. I found a new home, Mom, and I don't think I'll be coming back."

Suddenly, a glint of metal flashed in the sunlight. "You need help, my darling," she said, facing me with a syringe in her hand. "This sedative will calm you." Before I could register what she said, I felt a stab of pain. I looked down in horror as a needle protruded from my skin. My eyes widened, a tingling sensation already working its way up my arm. "Let me help you."

I never imagined she could go this far, but as she depressed the solution into my veins, reality hit me like a sledgehammer. I had made a grave mistake in coming here. It was impulsive and stupid.

My body jerked away, but her other hand flew to keep me still. And the second her fingers came in contact with my skin, she jolted off me with a pained shriek.

I shook my head, fighting the effects of whatever sedative she'd given me. I yanked the needle out of my arm and dropped it to the ground, but the damage had been done. At least half the syringe now coursed through my veins.

My limbs grew heavy, and I tried shaking off the drowsiness that crept up my spine.

If I succumbed to the sedative, she would most likely keep me so drugged that I would never be able to return to Luneth. To Rowen.

She would prick me over and over again to get me to comply.

Injecting me until my veins were bruised black and blue. Because I would never give up; I would fight her every step of the way. Even as my strength wavered, my resolve grew stronger —she would never break me again.

I stumbled to the computer as Calliope darted to the half-empty syringe on the carpet. Her gaze wild and her hair a mess.

I could barely keep my eyes open as a thick fog clouded my mind. I wouldn't make it. The pull was too strong, the sedative too powerful. But if I fell asleep now, I would most likely wake up in a padded cell. Who knew what other drugs would be shoved down my throat and forced into my veins.

My vision doubled as my legs gave way beneath me, sending me crashing to my knees. I knocked over the framed awards on her desk, struggling to pull myself up.

With my last ounce of strength, I hit send on the email, hoping it would expose my mother's malpractice. As my body crumbled to the ground, I prayed that the message went through and that Calliope would finally be held accountable for her abuse.

"No!" she screeched, her immaculate hair hanging in front of her face. She retrieved the syringe and rushed towards me.

My eyes closed in exhaustion, but through my drowsiness, all threads home had vanished. *Rowen. Rowen. Rowen,* I pleaded over and over again, fighting against the sleep that was rushing to meet me. I hadn't told anyone where I was going, and the prospect of disappearing without a trace added another layer of guilt to my already weighted body.

My mother raised the needle above me when my golden soul flame bond suddenly appeared like a beacon. Rowen was just on the other side, anchoring me to where I belonged. Yet, the connecting thread was slightly frayed, a strand veering off in a parallel line. Despite the tear that worried me, the weight of our bond felt like a lifeline. And I pulled with all my might.

I felt another stab in my arm, but before my mother could inject the rest of the syringe, my senses tilted, and I fell through space, time, and light.

Traveling between worlds was always a disorienting experience, but this time it was shifted and blurred—a heavy spiral that tugged me towards Rowen. Our soul flame bond was the only constant in the whirl of chaos. But if I didn't concentrate with everything I had, I could end up in any world—in any space *between* worlds.

The two golden threads wrapped around my arms and helped pull me home.

I landed with a hard, ungraceful thud, crying out as I fell on my punctured arm. I moaned, rolling over to release the pressure on my sore limb when my eyes landed on two pairs of worn leather boots.

<h1 style="text-align:center">21</h1>

"Keira!" Rowen yelled as he dropped to my line of sight, his eyes frantically scanning my body. "What happened?" he asked, his beautiful face contorting in panic as his hands flew around me but not on me, and my heart pinched from the loss of his touch.

"You're even pretty when you make that face," I grumbled as I rose to my feet, but my legs buckled, and I fell to the ground. "It's not fair."

"Where are you hurt?"

"My arm," I slurred, trying to shake off the sedation.

Rowen's eyes narrowed further. "Were you hurt in training?" he asked as the veins in his neck strained. "You just fell out of nowhere."

"I traveled to see my m-mother," I said, my eyes two heavy windows.

"Don't just stand there. Help her up," Rowen commanded over his shoulder.

Confused and wondering who he was talking to, I tried lifting my head, but I collapsed in exhaustion. Here was as good a place as any to take a little nap. When suddenly, I was swept off the ground.

"Put me down," I grumbled, squirming in the strong arms that carried me. "I don't need to be carried."

"Keira, you can't even stand." Maddock's chest-rumbling voice vibrated against my cheek.

Of course it was him. Who else would have been able to touch me?

"Wha . . . what are you two doing out here? Together?" I slurred. Either the sedative running through my veins made me see things, or Rowen and Maddock had been out here alone.

"That's not important right now," Rowen said in a panic. "What happened to you?"

"My mom tried to sedate me, and she . . . plunged half the syringe. I stopped her before . . . before . . ." My eyes succumbed to the powerful drug, and I relaxed into Maddock's arms.

"Keira," Rowen yelled.

"She'll be all right. Sedatives won't kill her. It will just make her tired. She will wake soon," Maddock said, and I felt Rowen's nerves calm.

"Remember, her fate is your fate," Rowen ground out, his voice like gravel.

"That makes no sense! I didn't even do this."

Rowen growled.

"No, you're right. It makes perfect sense," Maddock said, his arms tensing beneath me. "I'm ninety-eight percent sure she'll wake up."

"Just carry her to Takoda's," Rowen demanded, not above asking Maddock to provide the assistance he couldn't. "This way."

"Sedatives are a funny thing," Madds replied as he carried me back to the village. "She might not remember she found us together, and we won't have to tell her. Who knows if she heard anything."

"We are telling her," Rowen said sternly. "I won't keep anything from her."

"Tell me what," I asked, fighting to open my eyelids.

"Nothing you need to know right now, my flame. Just go to sleep."

I closed my eyes again as my cheek fell to Maddock's chest, and a deep chuckle rumbled through him. "I've had to subdue her, revive her, and now carry her for you," he mused. "Do you need me to fuck her for you too?"

With a predatory snarl, my soul flame charged Maddock. "I may not be able to touch her, but I can damn well break your bones."

"Yeah," I said sleepily, bolstered in Maddock's strong arms, and I found it immensely irritating that I was comfortable. "Punch him in the face, Rowen."

"Hey! I'm literally carrying your ass," Maddock shouted in my ear.

I shrugged sleepily, not opening my eyes.

"You're lucky you're holding my entire world. It's the only thing preventing me from tearing you limb from limb," my favorite voice said.

"Fine. I'll lay off. Just making some simple observations."

"Make any more simple observations, and I'll bash your teeth in. Besides, you are more than welcome to ask her for a fuck, though I doubt she would be interested. As I recall, she's seen the disappointed look on your partners' faces."

I'd glimpsed into Maddock's life, experienced his memories as if they were my own. And I couldn't shake the image of the beautiful blonde woman who'd thrown a vase at my—his—head upon learning of his many infidelities.

"Good one!" I chirped from my creeping slumber.

I couldn't fathom the pain of depending on someone else to help the one you love. If our situations were reversed, I might have punched someone's teeth in ages ago. But Rowen's control was astounding, whereas mine was slipping away by the second.

I might find comfort in Maddock's arms now, but I still didn't trust him. I knew I should hate him, but I couldn't remember why. I had a million questions on the tip of my tongue when all turned to black, and I succumbed to my mother's sedative.

⸺ ·(· ☾ · ● · ☽ ·)· ⸺

My heavy eyelids slowly blinked open. I was in Takoda's dome of healing, his living medicines hanging from the walls and dangling from the ceiling.

"Keira," Rowen breathed as Maddock let out a relieved exhale.

The sedative sludged through my system, and I was still groggy, but I remembered everything. "What did you want to tell me?" I asked, sitting up too quickly and almost vomiting.

"Careful, you still need rest," Maddock said, helping me sit up.

"No. Tell me. I remember. What is it?"

"Told you she would remember," Rowen said proudly.

"Wouldn't you rather talk about the horrible things your mom just did to you?" Maddock asked, clearly trying to change the subject.

"No," I said, realizing it was the truth. "Those memories no longer serve me."

Madds spun to leave the dome. "I'm going to go and let you two talk about it. I don't want to be here for this."

"Oh no, you're staying," Rowen said, yanking him back down by his arm. "This should be fun."

"What is it?" I asked, rubbing my temples.

Rowen pursed his plump lips and sighed before he said, "Maddock is in love with you."

"Ha. Ha. Hilarious," I said through the dull throb in my skull. "Now, tell me."

"It's true, Keira," he said as Maddock moaned in embarrassment, avoiding eye contact.

I was most definitely still drugged. "Come again?" I asked, dropping my hands into my lap.

I glared at Maddock in confusion, his brown eyes darting back to me. "It's not . . . by choice. It appears that when I invaded your mind—" Rowen glared murderously. "—I went in pretty deep. I dug my claws in as far as they would go, then pushed harder. I saw many of your memories. Saw what you saw and felt what you felt. Your feelings were so powerful, unlike anything I'd ever felt before. There was pain, but there was also silver and gold and love. And when you pushed me out of you, I didn't want to let go. You just felt *so* good. So I gripped tighter. Not only did I take some of the Alcreon Light, but it appears I've also taken a piece of your bond with Rowen." He swallowed hard. "On accident."

"He has felt the power of our soul flame bond, Keira," Rowen said, not moving a single muscle, but I had grown accustomed to spotting the rage just beneath his calm exterior.

So that explained why he'd been able to help me the day I almost drowned and why I felt comfortable in his embrace. It wasn't just stolen emotions. It was a stolen bond.

I pressed my hands to my eyes to clear the lingering fog. "That is . . . weird."

"It's not for a lack of trying *not* to. But what you have is . . . powerful. Better than any drug I've ever taken, and I've damn near tried them all. Better than ecstasy, better than heroin. And a thousand times more addicting. I . . . I find I need to be near you."

My shock faded, the reality of the situation hitting me like a rogue wave.

I shot up from the bed and into Maddock's face, nearly stumbling into the medicine cabinet. He tried to help me, but I pushed him away, nausea creeping up my throat. "How dare you take a piece of my Light, *and* my bond. That is sacred. You've already stolen so much from me. And now this?"

"I know, and I'm so sorry to you both. If I could stop it, I would. I just want to help you now in whatever way I can. That is all I want."

I didn't care what he had to say. Not a single word. I pulled back my fist, anger coursing through me like a riptide. I hadn't been able to intentionally touch anyone for so long that the moment my fist connected with his face, satisfaction rippled through me. And I grinned as his head knocked to the side.

He looked at me in shock, rubbing his jaw. "I know you're mad. But—"

"You have no idea how I feel right now."

"Actually, I do. Maybe not to the full extent. But I hold a piece of your bond within me. I've . . . I've been able to feel you for a while now."

Disgusted, I nearly gagged. "What about your fiancé?" I asked, remembering I'd taken memories from him too.

"I've been dead to her for a while now, since before the accident. She's moved on, and I let myself die there. I'm not going back."

"Well, you can't stay here! I don't want to be anywhere near you. Not even on the same planet as you. We can literally split the universe in half. Stay on your side, and I'll stay on mine."

I punched him again and again. Fury blinded me, but Maddock made no move to evade my onslaught.

"Keira," a voice pulled me back to myself, as it always did and always would. My fist stopped midair. "Are you sure you want to beat him to a bloody pulp?"

"Yes. I really think I do."

"Then continue, my bloodthirsty little soul flame. Exact your revenge."

"I agree," Maddock said. "It's no less than what I deserve."

"You don't get to speak," Rowen snarled, charging up and landing a punch to Maddock's stomach.

Maddock fell to the ground, wheezing. "You've both got quite the aim. A perfect match."

"You weren't there when she fled from the crevice, running as if the Dark Spirit were on her heels. You didn't gather her from the forest floor or hold her as she sobbed her soul out, incoherently repeating that you were *inside her*. You weren't there when she woke three days after you defiled her mind. I was."

"I know. I'm so sorry. I'll do whatever it takes to earn your forgiveness."

"You'll be trying a while," I said, standing over him and glancing at Rowen. "And why were you two alone out there anyway?" I asked.

"I had my suspicions. I was going to beat him senseless. Though it seems you beat me to it."

I wanted to keep punching Maddock's face in, but I couldn't deny we might need him. Especially if he could harness the Alcreon Light and help save Luneth.

"You will find a way to repay us but know this: it might be with your life," I said, knowing it was an awful threat, but I wanted to scare him. Incite the fear in him that he once instilled in me.

"Then my life is yours. Both of yours, however you need it," Maddock said as he stood and walked to the door. "I'll give you two some privacy."

Rowen turned to me, seething.

I wanted to run to him and calm his raging storm. But I

couldn't, and the constant ache of being unable to touch my soul flame was becoming unbearable.

"Keira," Rowen said, pain strangling his voice. "You went to see your mother. Without telling me you were leaving?"

"I know. It was stupid. I wasn't in my right mind," I replied, catching a glimpse of myself in Takoda's mirror. The bags under my eyes were stark against my pale skin, my hair was tangled in knots, and a bandage was wrapped around my arm. I'd been avoiding my reflection, and the sight almost took the breath out of me. I looked bone-weary, as if I carried the weight of the world.

"I can't bear to see you like this—the pain and hurt in your eyes. The guilt." I flinched as his words struck a chord. "I see you hurting, and how I wish I could take that pain away. But I have no such power. I can't even touch you. Can't offer a reassuring hand on the shoulder or a comforting embrace, not even the mind-numbing fuck I've been so desperate to give you since your return."

His words stopped me short.

"Please try talking with Takoda."

"I can't," I barely whispered.

Rowen nodded, but his body deflated, almost too imperceptible to notice. But I did. And it broke my heart.

· (⊂ · ● · ⊃) ·

I needed to get my mind off everything: my thoughts, my feelings, my inability to touch Rowen. I especially didn't want to think about Maddock and how he stole my Light and bond.

I should have suspected, but I was a fool. I let him get too close. I'd even begun to trust him. I was no longer worried about panic attacks but rage attacks.

So when Dyani agreed to train with me today, I gladly accepted.

I walked along the organic pathway to the training grounds when the earth trembled beneath my feet. The earthquake was so powerful that I lost my balance and fell.

A familiar voice echoed down the path as I stood and wiped the dirt from my pants. "Star-touched, are you hurt?" Takoda asked, running up to me. "That was a pretty bad one."

I felt the sharp splinter of guilt. I'd been avoiding him.

Rowen encouraged me to see the healer and talk, but I had decided long ago that therapy wasn't for me. Even Takoda himself had made comments about me visiting him. But going there was just something I couldn't do.

"I'm all right," I said, eying the healer. He wore his tan linen pants, a sage green vest, and an open smile. "What about you?"

"I am all right as well," he replied as he reached for me instinctively before remembering my touch was hazardous. I may as well have a flashing neon sign on my face that said, "Danger. Don't touch."

I dusted myself off, eying for an escape.

"I heard what happened in my dome earlier today. I was just outside, but I thought to give you privacy."

"I'm sorry you had to hear that," I replied awkwardly. Takoda was a dear friend and talking with him had always come so naturally, but now, under the guise of therapy, I completely shut down. "Did Rowen say anything?" I asked, suddenly nervous about how Takoda might see me.

"He worries for you. That much is clear. But we discuss and work on his healing. What you wish for me to know is up to you to tell me."

An idea suddenly struck me. The last time I felt lost, I'd found myself in a sacred ceremony. "Can I go into the Hymma?"

"There are no shortcuts, star-touched, if that's what you're looking for. The Hymma may help with inner reflection. But if your mind is not ready, the answers will fall on un-listening ears, or worse yet, you could go mad searching for something that is right in front of you. It is too dangerous for you to enter the Hymma with the current state of your mind. It is not safe."

I shifted my weight. "Isn't it based on intention?"

"Yes, but also by your mood, your subconscious, and countless other factors. Even what you had for breakfast. Much less everything else you have been through. Your consciousness is interwoven with the threads of the universe. It can easily bend and fray to the whims of the fabric. I'm not saying that you are not strong, that you do not know your own mind," Takoda continued, and I knew a *but* was coming. "But you know firsthand there are many worlds, many realities that you could fall into and not find your way out of. Not to mention, you are susceptible to panic and astral tearing."

"And breaking," I added.

"Keira, we are all a little broken. It is the cracks that let the light in," he replied, his eyes softening. "What is it that is bothering you? Aside from the obvious."

Suddenly, it felt like boulders were collapsing on me, like I was back in the Crystal Crypts. I couldn't speak; the words were trapped behind a stone in my throat. Why couldn't I talk about it? It was as if my heart wanted to, but my mind didn't. Tears pooled in my lower lash line. Having someone take a genuine interest in my health made my voice and hands shake.

How was I to prepare for a battle when I was at war with myself?

"I need . . . I need to meet with Dyani. I will see you around," I stammered before I sped down the trail and didn't look back.

———— ·(·⸨·●·⸩·)· ————

After cleaning up from another training session with Dyani, I returned to Rowen's dome, eager to collapse from exhaustion.

But as I whirled through the rotating door, my gaze fell upon Rowen smiling, standing in the middle of the room with a simple rucksack over his shoulder. "How about a little getaway?" he asked with a wide grin, patting the thin bedroll strapped to the pack.

"Where?" I asked skeptically. I deserved for him to hate me and yell at me or even look at me with disappointment, but there was only love in his gaze.

"It's a surprise. Are you up for it?"

"Why are you being so nice to me? Especially after I almost royally fucked up?"

He readjusted the pack. "Believe me, I have many ideas in mind for punishing you, even though they all ultimately end in your pleasure. So until I'm able to touch you, I thought a night under the stars might help. Give you a little space to think. Breathe."

I swallowed at the thought of my *punishments*. "You think camping is a good idea right now?"

"It couldn't hurt to try."

"The earthquakes are getting worse," I said, brushing loose strands of hair away from my face. "And I'm not improving at all. I'm nowhere near prepared if Erovos escapes."

"That's exactly why we should go. We've tried everything here. Maybe we need a change of scenery with no distractions."

"What if something happens while we're gone?" I asked, pacing the room and biting my nails.

He stalked up to me, commanding my attention and halting my back-and-forth. "Breathe, Copeland. No harm will come to the village. Not tonight. I swear it."

Rowen's words loosened my breathing like an inhale of eucalyptus, and my chest eased. "What about Maddock? You know he will follow us."

"I have him taken care of."

"What did you do to him?" I asked, a tinge of concern lining my voice.

"Don't worry, he's fine. Just heavily threatened," Rowen replied, the rolled-up sleeves of his shirt revealing his muscled forearms.

"We both heavily threaten him every day, and he never listens. What makes this time any different?"

"I offered him some moonstones to help with inner reflection."

"That worked?" I asked in utter shock.

"No. He told me to shove the stones up my ass," Rowen replied with a forced yet amused smile. "Thus began our negotiations, during which he proved quite shrewd."

"Oh my god, please tell me we don't have to endure some candlelit dinner with him," I moaned. I still couldn't bear the thought of looking at him.

Rowen made a face somewhere between a grin and a grimace. "I told him he could train with us."

"Seriously?" I groaned.

"You were pretty spot on with him wanting the candlelit dinner. At least this way, you can kick the shit out of him."

"I don't need an excuse to kick the shit out of him," I said matter-of-factly.

"I know, but what about Dyani?" he asked with a mischievous smirk.

"You're negotiating skills are impressive," I said, immediately perking up at the prospect of Dyani rearranging Maddock's face. I eyed the limited supplies Rowen had packed for our getaway. "I guess we're going camping."

22

———————

The sky stretched out like a canvas as the earth crunched beneath our boots. Takoda once said that everything was connected, from the smallest seed to the most distant star, but as I studied the oil-painted night, its ambivalence appeared endless. For what worries could the cosmos have over rocks and men?

"You'd never think anything was wrong just by looking up," I said, voicing my musings aloud as Rowen and I ventured beyond the village.

"That's the beauty of it," he said with a smirk, our rucksack and supplies for the night strung over his shoulder. "That's why I wanted to bring you here. It has the best views for stargazing."

"Do many people know of this place?" I asked, stepping over a fallen log.

"It's long been abandoned, and I've never shown it to anyone," he said, pushing aside a curtain of branches, inviting me to pass through. "I've only ever come here alone, but now I want to share it with you."

I stepped through the tunnel of trees as a hidden meadow unfolded before me. In the center of the secluded sanctuary, the ruins of a breathtaking temple emerged like a forgotten dream. "What is this?" I asked in an awed whisper.

"These are the ruins of Fleur Uaine. From what I understand, it used to be a lush and thriving garden temple," Rowen said, leading me to a colonnade of arches and thin pillars crafted from white marble. The delicate structure looked as though branches and vines had been coaxed into stone but were now slowly succumbing to time. The overhead awnings were full of weathered gaps and tears. But the intricate carvings upon the stone told tales of maidens dancing amidst lush hanging vines, fountains overflowing with water, and foliage cascading in abundance. The ethereal temple, even now in its forgotten ruin, left me speechless.

"It's beautiful," I breathed, tracing my fingers along the etchings.

"This used to be one of my old sleeping camps," he said as if he hadn't been plagued with misery while searching for this sanctuary. "I found it after I escaped the Crypts the first time."

My soul flame bond tightened painfully in my chest. Rowen's memories weren't even mine, but with our golden connection, they may as well be. I felt his emotions as strongly as my own. It was why I had been so drawn to him and could always feel him near.

An intrusive thought wiggled inside my brain. Had Maddock suddenly felt a swift tug on his heart? Was he questioning why now, in this exact moment, he suffered from a memory he couldn't quite recall?

I wanted to feel empathy, but all I felt was anger. If Madds was experiencing pain from Rowen's past, then it served him right for being a bond stealer.

I shook the thief from my mind as Rowen unfurled our bed and laid it in the center of the ruins.

"This is how you used to sleep?" I asked, lowering myself

onto the thin bedroll. I understood roughing it, but this was something else entirely.

"I came here frequently, especially the nights you stayed in my dome," he said, joining me on our bed for the night. He rested his elbows on his knees and tilted his head toward me. "As you know, I didn't care much about what happened to me. I used to come here to escape myself, but when you arrived, I came here to escape *you*." His gaze met mine, dark and swarming with desire. "My will to keep away from you was weak. I knew if I stayed in the village, nothing would stop me from entering your room and taking you in my bed. I considered all the ways I could have you without anyone knowing. At night, after I was seen leaving you, I would steal my way back through the shadows and quietly open your door. I'd join you on the bed and slowly remove whatever thin bottoms you were wearing. My fingers would inch open your thighs to bare you before me. I would trace and tease you until you woke, and when your eyes shot wide, I'd clamp my palm over your mouth, silencing your screams as I sank my fingers deep inside you and made you come."

Desire flared along my touched-deprived skin, making my mouth water. "That's what I always hoped you would do. Sleeping in your bed without you was agony."

"I believed I was protecting you. Escaping here. Sleeping under the stars is what granted me the strength to stay away. Though when I used to come here, the land was thick and ripe with life, but now . . ." His throat tightened as he looked at the desolate scene, the dead leaves and vines hanging around us. "Most nights, I'd be lucky if I made it to one of my encampments. I would walk circles around the village, waking to find I'd collapsed from exhaustion, sleeping wherever I fell, my gaze always tilted towards the heavens."

My heart twisted thinking of the life he'd led after escaping

Fou. "I know the feeling of using the sky as an escape. It's what I used to do when I was younger."

"You once shared with me how you felt trapped in your old life. How you would look at the stars for hours, taking comfort in the fact that somewhere, something was free. Even if it was only a speck of light in the sky."

"You remember that?"

"I hang onto your every word. I always have."

"Even though so much has happened, I still feel like that trapped girl."

"Keira, you are no longer caged. Look at the stars. Do they look free to you?"

"Yes," I whispered as the pinpricks of light glimmered above. Though my gaze was looking into the past, I knew my eyes were also scanning across prophecies of the future, placed there by the Elder Spirits. One, somewhere, even spoke of me and my return to Luneth. The Synodic Son who would bring life and light back to the dying lands.

"The stars are but a reflection of your eyes. You are free," Rowen said, holding my gaze gently. "Remember your telescope? The one you told me about. You just have to turn the lens inward. See yourself the way the heavens do. The way I do. What must the heavens think of your beautiful soul? Seeing past the flesh and blood, witnessing the living embodiment of itself. Isn't that why we were created? For the universe to see itself through our eyes?"

"That's a comforting thought," I said, genuinely trying to take Rowen's advice and turn the lens inward, to see myself as the heavens might. "You really think this will help?"

"It can't hurt to try," he said with a hopeful smile, lying back on the bedroll and patting the space beside him.

I joined him on our sorry excuse for a bed, already worrying how my back would react to this.

He pulled a blanket from his pack and draped it over our separated bodies. Though the quilt kept me warm, I wished I could curl into him and fill the distance between us. But we remained our usual twelve inches apart, stargazing from within the roofless ruins.

—— ·(·☾· ● ·☽·)· ——

I had doubts about sleeping in the middle of nowhere with barely a blanket, but the views of Fleur Uaine made it all worth it. I could see why Rowen loved this place, and if it weren't for the single crease between his brows, it would appear as if he slept peacefully.

My finger itched to smooth away the worry line, but I kept my hands achingly by my sides.

Eventually, I allowed myself to drift. The rise and fall of Rowen's chest, along with the churning galaxies and shooting stars, eased me into a meditative state.

The threads of the cosmos unraveled before me, and I carefully pushed through the tendrils of light that dangled like vines.

I searched each strand, hoping to find the one that would solve all my problems.

Suddenly, my gaze fell upon a black, void-like string. Its eerie sound hummed within me and pulled on my senses like a powerful magnet.

A mounting pressure grew in my skull, and my bones vibrated. It wasn't until it was too late that I realized it wasn't a single thread at all. It was a net.

The black threads sprang apart and enveloped me, their sinewy tendrils wrapping around my body. There was no time to struggle or react as the threads held me fast and dragged me into oblivion.

Like a butterfly ensnared, I was swept away, and the celestial lights around me vanished.

—— ·(·ℭ·●·)·)· ——

I was somewhere dark. Very dark.

There were no stars or galaxies overhead, no ancient ruins surrounding me, only a dank chill that crept up my spine.

"What is this?" said a voice that leeched the warmth from my body. "A little dreamer come to visit?"

As my eyes adjusted, I realized I'd been here before. I was in the crevice, trapped with the Dark Spirit I'd banished here. Memories of what it took to imprison him flooded back and stole the breath from my lungs.

I needed to get out. *Now.* I would find no answers here, and I was a fool for falling into Erovos' trap.

I searched for the golden thread that would guide me back to Rowen, but the Dark Spirit rushed towards me like a tornado of shadows, and my fingers trembled as I scrambled for my soul flame bond. When I finally managed to grab hold of it, I pulled, but the frayed thread from where Madds had severed our bond took me by surprise, and I ended up yanking it sideways.

Suddenly, the cave opened in a rush of grey stone. Though the dark cave remained behind me, the night sky twinkled before me like a movie screen, revealing two bodies lying side by side. Weathered white arches framed the figures who faced each other without touching.

"Ah, how interesting," Erovos hummed from the dark recesses of the cave. "You are full of surprises, my little light."

I peered closer, immediately recognizing Rowen sleeping on a thin bedroll. A woman lay beside him, her brown hair spilling over her shoulder to reveal one perfectly pointed ear. Even though they weren't touching, envy blazed through my blood.

The woman's lonely fingers reached for Rowen's body, and her skin begged for his warmth.

It took a moment for my eyes to adjust, for my mind to catch up. The silent suffering on her sleeping face mirrored the agony in my soul.

I looked down at my translucent palms, realizing I was in my astral form. It was my body that slept beside the love of my life.

I had meant to pull myself out of the cave, but instead, I'd pulled the cave right to Rowen.

"Rowen," I screamed through the ether, sprinting toward him, but my body rammed into an invisible barrier. He jolted awake and immediately checked me by his side. When he noticed I was unconscious, his eyes darted up, widening in horror as he saw me within the dark cave.

I had opened an astral window, a two-way screen that allowed Rowen to glimpse into my projection—forcing him to watch as Erovos closed in behind me.

Rowen shot up, but what he was seeing was a projection and nothing more, and his hands zapped with electricity as he tried to reach me. "Keira, where are you?" he asked, fear shooting down our bond.

I placed my hand on the astral window. "I'm in . . ."

Before I could answer, Erovos hummed with delight. "So you're bringing this lovely scene to your soul flame. How very talented of you. Yes, let the little lord watch." I whipped around to face the Dark Spirit as he stepped within Rowen's sight. "How did you like her gown? Did she tell you that my shadows caressed every inch of her skin as I dressed her in my darkness?"

Rowen's face twisted in fury, and his fists pounded on the astral screen. "You sick fuck! I'll kill you!"

The orange eyes that haunted me flickered across my face. "I told you I was working on something grand. Now that you're here, would you like to see it?"

"How have you created anything in here?" I asked, his oppressive aura stretching my mind thin.

"I impregnated the earth within this crevice. Even now, my children grow."

I gagged.

"Your powers in sealing this cave are quite impressive. You may have trapped me away from the physical world, but as you know, I've been amassing a great deal of energy for some time. When I'm not striving to tear this mountain apart, I take great pleasure in perfecting my creations," Erovos said, gesturing to three dark figures slowly emerging from an even darker swatch of midnight. "Allow me to introduce my newest creation, the Voro-Kai."

Huge, hulking creatures prowled toward me. Demons made in the likeness of a man but with the tusks and fur of a beast. Their enormous limbs rippled with unnatural muscle, and misted horns curled up from their boar-shaped heads. "Their bodies exist only astrally, but their wounds can cross planes, turning all they have bitten into Voro-Kai."

The pit in my stomach crashed into my spine. I tried to wake up and snap back to my body, but as the demons stalked closer, my limbs went numb.

Was Erovos' plan to get in my head, or could these Voro-kai truly hurt me in my astral form?

"What do you think will happen to her if she dies in this state?" Erovos asked, seeming to read my mind. Curiosity rippled across his face as he turned to Rowen. "I have my guesses, don't you? Will her body slowly shut down beside you? Will she disappear all at once? Or will she be wracked with painful tremors as she dies from the inside out?"

I despised that he was speaking to Rowen, even dared to glance in his direction. He was deliberately antagonizing him to throw me off, to get so deep under my skin that I couldn't think straight. "Don't you dare speak to him," I seethed, clenching my fists so tight they ached. Every poisonous word he spoke to my soul flame fueled my fury.

"Or," the Dark Spirit mused, ignoring me as he continued to speak to Rowen, "should we mentally torment her, ravage her astral body while you watch? See what's left of her when she wakes?"

"You touch her and I will destroy you," Rowen growled, his face a murderous snarl.

Erovos chuckled. "I know my creatures would love to have a taste, and they aren't opposed to sharing."

"Keira!" Rowen roared my name from across the cosmic field, and my frozen limbs rushed with molten rage.

I hated that Erovos' plan was working, that my fury was all-encompassing as he dangled my life in front of Rowen—hated myself even more that I was projecting this scene to him at all. I would let my wrath carry me and do what needed to be done; if not, Rowen would watch me die as I silently laid beside him.

The first demon lunged, its monstrous arms barreling towards me, but I swirled away just in time. My physical body may not be here, but I sure as hell wasn't going to let these fuckers touch me in my astral state.

My peripheral caught Erovos' orange eyes, observing with curiosity as his three Voro-Kai approached me. If I let them surround me, I was as good as dead.

I darted to the nearest cave wall to protect my back. My heartbeat galloped in my throat, and my fear bounced off my skin in a haze of light. There would be no hiding here. My body was lit up like a neon sign.

I reached for my weapon, but my hip was empty.

My heart lurched until I remembered I had other weapons.

The nearest Voro-Kai, a horrifying beast with three tusks, charged at me with a bellowing roar. I raised my palm, willing the Alcreon Light to cooperate as I sent a push of power through my hand. The Light shot through the dark, freezing the beast within a beam of light. I held my arm out, keeping the creature in place as the largest of demons struck down upon my head.

On reflex, I threw my other arm up, creating a barrier of Light between myself and the second demon. Its razor-sharp claws hammered against my blinding shield.

The force from its blow knocked me off balance, causing my hold on the Voro-Kai with three tusks to loosen. The third beast joined in the assault as I held its pack-mate in a stupor of Light. My arms extended out on either side of me, shaking and lowering from the strain of holding back three astral demons.

"Finish her!" Erovos commanded his hatchlings of darkness. They bore down on me with brutal strength, and just like their creator, their black eyes swirled with primordial darkness. Their thick and meaty arms beat against my shield ruthlessly.

One bang, my teeth chattered. Two, three bangs, the force traveled up my arm, putting pressure on my elbow and shoulder. After hit four, five, and six, I fell to one knee, my bones and muscles screaming in pain.

My hold on the demon with three tusks fell, and I immediately shot my arm back up to fortify my shield.

All the horned beasts pounded together, their collective assault hitting me so hard that I was blasted back in an explosion of light.

I skidded across the ground, my hair flying behind me as a barrage of dirt and rocks pummeled around me like shrapnel. The smallest beast charged at me, its battering ram of an arm swinging through the air. I cried out as it connected with my back. The force bruised my lungs and sent me sprawling forward as if I'd been hit by a freight train.

So they could hurt me in my astral form. *Not good.*

I shot to my feet, fighting to pull in my next breath. I couldn't see Rowen anymore, which in equal parts terrified yet relieved me. At least he was safe. The Voro-Kai couldn't get to him through my projection.

All three creatures charged towards me, trapping me against a wall of stone. I was exhausted, my entire body spent and sore, and all of my light sources were depleted. If I didn't think of something soon, they would tear into me with their teeth and tusks, turning me into one of them.

Would I still look like me, or would I thoroughly transform into a Voro-Kai? Would Rowen be able to recognize me? I would take my own life before I ever let my body succumb to Erovos' darkness. I would go to any lengths to ensure Rowen never saw me like that and would never have to make the impossible decision of killing me to put me out of my misery. A decision that would ultimately kill us both.

I scrambled sideways against the stone, begging the Alcreon Light to return. The beasts were inches away, their sharp claws ready to slash me to ribbons. Suddenly, I stumbled back, falling behind a hidden rock wall.

I staggered deeper into the cave, my legs fighting to catch myself. When I raised my head, horror twisted my gut. The crevice yawned wider, revealing a vast expanse of rocky hills and jagged peaks stretching as far as the eye could see. Littered upon the ground in never-ending rows was a sea of demon cocoons.

Their chrysalises were black yet see-through, bubbling and pulsing like external wombs. Through the thin tissue, I could make out demons floating in inky water. Their eyes were closed, yet their bodies twitched and writhed in the dark fluid. Some were fully formed with thick hides and tusks, while others were twisted fetuses, barely recognizable in shape. Yet, no matter their stage of growth, they all seemed as if they could wake at any moment.

My mouth fell open in terror, and a silent scream lodged in

my throat. The sheer scale of what we were facing crashed over me.

Erovos was breeding an army.

All the energy he had taken from the earth through Indrasyl was harnessed into creating an army of astral demons.

The Dark Spirit may be imprisoned, but our destruction would be sealed if his Voro-Kai escaped. And judging by the strength of Erovos' earthquakes, we were edging closer and closer toward war and catastrophe.

My eyes quickly searched for Demil. He'd helped me once, and hopefully, he would help me again. But he was nowhere in sight.

I whipped around to face the beasts, shoving their way through the narrow tunnel. I found myself trapped between the charging demons and sleeping chrysalises. No matter my move, I wasn't making it out of here alive, but I refused to make this hellhole my final view.

I closed my eyes and turned the lens inward, hoping to find one moment of inner peace before I died, but what I saw steeled my spine in silver fire. I was no weakened mare or poisoned girl anymore. I was the wielder and protector of the Alcreon Light, forged in the heat of blazing stars. I was a weapon of celestial force, chosen by the Light itself.

I refused to be overcome.

I released a whisper of a command—a surrender. My skin burning and brightening as if I were pyre-born.

Let them touch me.

My body became engulfed in a heavenly blaze as misted claws reached for me.

The creatures bore down on me, their beastly hands reaching for my skin that crackled like an untouchable star, illuminating the crevice in a blinding glow. As soon as they touched me, the dark creatures screeched, their arms veining with a silver light before disintegrating, melting into smoke and ash as they fell upon me.

I heard laughter echoing from the front of the cave. "Very interesting," Erovos hummed, his voice sending shivers down my spine. I may have trapped him, but his mind was still cunning, and his body was full of power. "So resilient, my little light. I'll find a way to snuff you out yet."

His words reverberated through me like a gravitational promise. When suddenly, Erovos' arms shot out, his cloak unfurling like the wings of a world-eating dragon. His mouth opened wide, his jaw unhinging as he let out a distorted frequency. The air shuddered, the ground lurched, and the crevice shook so violently it felt as if the earth were splitting open from the force of his roar.

I gasped awake, my heart hammering against my ribcage. I thought I had escaped, but before I could catch a breath, strong arms wrapped around me and pulled me tight, trapping me within their grip.

23

————

"Let me go. Let me go," I cried, fighting and kicking with all my strength. I had to escape the arms that held me. I couldn't let myself become a demon.

"Keira, it's me. You're back, you're back," Rowen's voice choked out in relief.

My eyes shot open to my soul flame's face, creased with concern. That ever-present line between his brows was more prominent than ever. "Rowen," I gasped, my chest heaving.

"Thank the spirits," he rasped, his eyes scanning my face. "You weren't waking. My only thought was to get you back to the village in time for Takoda or Madds to wake you."

"I'm so sorry. I didn't mean for you to see that," I said, not realizing I was crying until I tasted the tears on my lips.

"I'm not usually one to feel helpless, but around you, it has become my new normal," he said as his fingers combed through my hair and his palm cradled my face. His thumb gently wiped away my tears as his presence grounded me. "With the way Erovos threatened you, I had to try to get you home. Despite the risks, I grabbed you and ran. As much as the thought of

Maddock's hands on you makes me want to murder . . ." he trailed off as we both realized.

We were touching.

Rowen's hands were on me, touching my bare skin. There was no blood on his nose or a weakened look in his eyes. He'd managed to carry me a few feet from our bedroll, and now here we laid in the dead soil, wrapped in each other's arms.

Our chests heaved, and our breaths collided, yet our touches were timid and hesitant. It was as if we couldn't believe this moment was truly happening.

Carefully, I ran my fingertips up Rowen's arms, my hands looking so small against his rippling muscles. I traced the powerful contours of his shoulders, feeling the wild beat of his pulse before threading my fingers through the lush waves of his hair.

My experience within the crevice had allowed my body to accept the Alcreon Light. I'd turned the lens inward and confronted every part of myself: the dark, the light, and all the shades in between.

I'd escaped Erovos and his astral demons, thinking it was my descent into hell, but the relief of opening my eyes to Rowen's gaze felt like heaven. There was only him. Only now.

He seized my face in his hands and crashed his mouth against mine. His warmth, scent, and taste collided through my senses, weaving through the fabric of my existence. He kissed me long and hard until my lips bruised. His tongue traced and licked and devoured as he worked my mouth open. His kiss was brutal, unforgiving, and savage. But so was mine.

His fingers dug into my skin with delicious pressure, and a moan escaped my lips. "There you are," Rowen breathed at the curve of my neck, sending goosebumps along my skin and tightening my nipples. I clawed at him desperately as my body buzzed to life in his hands. His touch was electric.

Desire rushed through my veins like a stampede of galloping horses—wild, powerful, and unstoppable. I had spent so long taming such feelings that only left me empty and aching. But now that I had Rowen beneath my fingertips, the long-awaited pleasure erupted inside of me and coursed through the depths of my soul like bursting stars.

Our timid touches vanished as they morphed into desperate need—an ancient call for the flames in our souls to reunite.

His hands roamed down my waist and pressed just below my ribs. I arched into his grip, the stars within me pulsing brighter and brighter. His broad hands pinned me down, but I pounced as my barriers shattered, the reins of my control snapping.

I slammed Rowen's back to the ground, and he grunted as I mounted him, my legs opening to straddle his hips. With my palms on his chest, I rubbed myself against the strain in his pants. His thick girth beneath me had me throwing my head back to the heavens. "Rowen," I breathed, about to explode after months of pent-up desire. "I feel you."

"You're about to feel more of me," he growled as his fingers found the exposed flesh of my abdomen, and with breath-stealing efficacy, he ripped open the lacing of my pants.

"Yes," I gasped, a burning desire pooling between my legs as I writhed on top of him, every part of me finally released from its cage. His massive hands guided me over his cock, his tendons straining from his punishing grip. The utterly feral glint in his eye told me his restraint was at its wit's end.

"I think I need to teach you a lesson, Keira. Make it so you'll remember never to pull this shit on me again—make it where I can't touch you," he warned as his eyes and breath went ragged. He sat up, landing his palm on the small of my back to keep me in place while forcing my thighs to open wider around his waist. He pushed my shirt over my breasts and lowered his head to my nipple. He traced his tongue over the pebbled flesh before offering a sharp nip, and I cried out as my core coiled tighter.

He ripped my shirt off, watching the moonlight glint across my heavy breasts as he ground my clit against him. "I'm going to punish you with pleasure. Make you come again and again until you beg me to stop. Each and every one of your orgasms will be mine to control, and I'll wring out every one. When your body can't handle me anymore, and you're begging me to stop, I will give you one more."

I savagely tore at the lacings of his pants and pulled out his glorious cock, already glistening with a drop of precum. "Yes," was all I was able to articulate, desperate to lick the iridescent bead with my tongue. He grabbed me by my waist and shifted me from his lap to the ground. His broad fingers curled into my waistband, pulling my bottoms down until they reached my ankles. He opened my legs as wide as they would go, keeping me spread yet trapped within my clothes. He grabbed the gathered fabric cuffed around my feet and used it as leverage to twist me around in one fluid motion. I landed on my hands and knees with a speed that made me see stars, and I almost choked on an inhale.

He yanked my pants off the rest of the way before tipping my hips up higher to meet him. My blood rushed in my ears, everything was pulsing erratically as I was bared before him in such an animalistic way.

"But first, I'm going to take you hard and fast. And I fear I won't be gentle with you, my flame." His touch trailed up the backs of my thighs before his powerful hands gripped my hips. I jolted as his tongue licked over my clit, up my entrance and backside—the whole slit of me. It was obscene and indecent, and a depraved moan escaped my lips. "Your ass and pussy are blooming so good for me. You will be sore tomorrow, feeling what I did to you with every step you take."

"Yes! Please, yes!" I rasped, my whole body pulsing at his intensity.

I cried out as he drove two broad fingers inside of me, filling me in one slick stroke. He left one palm on my waist as he fucked me with his hand. "Good girl," he rasped deep from the back of his throat. "You're ready for me."

"I've been ready for you for weeks," I whimpered as the cool night air danced along my exposed and dripping pussy. "It's been torture."

"Torture?" He slid his fingers out of me, and I quivered as his cock pushed between my thighs. He lined himself up against my warmth, both of his hands latching onto my hips. There was no more restraint, no more careful control, and he growled as he yanked my waist back toward him, entering me with a soul-shattering thrust. I cried out as he stretched and filled me, my universe narrowing to the joining between my legs. "Torture is realizing you can never be with the love of your life," he said as he pulled out to the tip and then slammed back into me. "Then, by some miracle, she becomes yours, only for her to disappear again." He held me firm as he drove every inch of his cock in and out of me. "And when she finally returns to you, you can't even touch her." My debauched moans filled the starry night as his jarring force rocked my body. "That is torture, Keira."

He gripped my hips tighter and thrust deeper, reaching a place only he had the power to touch, to leave his mark. He was in me to the hilt, as deep as he could go. He squeezed my ass tighter as he dove inside me with another brutal thrust. Again and again.

My palms and knees scraped on the ground as he ruthlessly pumped into me; my head tipped back, and my hips arched up. I was fully exposed and vulnerable to his ministrations as he held me exactly where he wanted me.

His guttural moans brushed up my spine, and I arched my

back further, pleasure spasming through me as he rutted into me with a desperate fury.

His thumb pressed against my empty opening. My eyes shot wide, but I was too pliant and desperate to care. He pressed in deeper. "I told you I would fill your every hole."

My moan was animalistic. "Please," I rasped, needing him with a scorching desire.

Fully claimed, owned, and filled, the dead earth ground into my palms and knees, cutting open my skin as I begged for more.

"Do you need to feel more of me?"

"Yes! Don't stop," I begged as he thrust so deep I swore I could feel him everywhere. "I'm so close."

"Come for me," Rowen grunted out the command as he reached around with his free hand and pressed the tip of his finger against my swollen clit. "Now!"

I obeyed. Spirits did I obey.

An explosion of ecstasy swept through me, yet my climax wasn't just a release or a need satisfied. It was pure deliverance. I cried out as my orgasm consumed me in shuddering waves that reverberated as infinitely inward as they did outward.

My entire body seemed to awaken, every nerve and hidden corner within me sparking and contracting, feeling alive in a way I'd never known.

As the aftershocks of my release subsided, a faint tingling sensation brushed beneath my palms and knees.

When I looked down, I saw tiny tendrils of greenery sprouting between my fingertips. The moss was velvet-soft against my skin, and as my pleasure grew, so did the garden.

Flora broke through the barren soil and twisted up the ancient columns surrounding us.

I was breathless and trembling as Rowen rutted into me from behind, healing me while my blood healed the earth.

Moonlit petals unfurled in glittering waves as Light rippled through the leaves. Saplings morphed into towering trees, their vines draping down around us and brushing against our skin like fireflies. Glowing mushrooms and flowers sprouted as a canopy of wisteria connected the gaps in the ruins. Fleur Uaine seemingly returned to its original glory and encased us in our own personal oasis.

Rowen pulled out of me, but before I could whimper in protest, his calloused hands, that I missed with every fiber of my being, latched onto my waist and flipped me around—my back landing on a soft bed of moss.

"I won't last much longer," he said as he pushed my knees up to my chest, barring me obscenely before him. He folded and unfolded me like origami, bending me to his whims and desires. "You're glorious, Keira," he grunted as he thrust into me once again. I wrapped my arms around his shoulders and my legs around his waist, holding on for dear life as he ground my clit perfectly. And together, we were lost in our thunderous release.

Eons might have passed when Rowen finally pulled out of me with a shudder. He rolled us until we faced each other in the plush nest of our paradise.

Being unable to touch Rowen had been like dying of thirst. I could see the sparkling water in the distance like a taunting mirage, but now, the hidden oasis engulfed me and drowned me in bliss.

I glowed softly from the intensity of my body-high.

After my legs stopped shaking and my breathing returned to normal, a single tear dripped from my eye. Rowen kissed it off my cheek as if it were a drop of ecstasy. "What is it?" he murmured against my cheekbone, lightly stroking me from my shoulder to hip bone.

The newly sprouted forest, vibrant and alive, cushioned my descent back to earth, awakening my senses to the moss and roses surrounding me.

"I feel like myself again," I said, tracing my fingertips along his abs. "I was drowning in a bubble of water, suffocating in plain sight. Everyone tried to help, but it was I who had to swim above the pain. It's still there, might always be there, but at least my chin is above the water. It feels good to finally breathe."

"Keep treading the water, Keira," Rowen whispered as he brushed my hair off to one side and traced his fingertip along the shell of my pointed ear. "And when your legs get tired, I will always be there to help keep you afloat. Tell me you know that."

I leaned forward and gently nibbled his lower lip. "I do."

Rowen smiled, offering me a glimpse of his sharp canines, and I realized he hadn't smiled that wide in ages. "I'm so proud of you. Look at what you did," he marveled as he stroked a low-hanging bulb of light. "You brought Fleur Uaine back to life."

"She's marvelous. I just wish I knew how to use this on a worldwide scale. We can't have sex all over the planet."

"Can't we?" He nudged me playfully, already hardening against my stomach. His face was mesmerizing as the moonlight and shadows danced across his features.

"I mean, we can certainly try," I replied, awestruck by his hard and chiseled beauty.

"Then are you ready for your punishment?" he asked, kissing the shimmering scar tattoo on my collarbone. Then he lowered his mouth to the scar beneath my breast and the one lower on my ribcage. He inched open my thighs and traced my center.

My hungry moan was answer enough.

· (· C · ● · ⊃ ·) · ——

I must have dozed off because I woke to Rowen's head in between my thighs, licking and kissing me. He thrust his tongue inside my walls, and I moaned as I threaded my fingers through his hair.

Rowen had taken punishing me very seriously, making me come for hours. I didn't know how, but he managed to awaken my exhausted body and drown me in pleasure once again.

This man had a skillful tongue.

Rowen claimed me in position after position. I had no idea just how thoroughly my body could be used and claimed.

He'd promised me he would fill me in every way possible, and he had. I was deliciously sore but already aching for more.

All night, he had taken me ruthlessly, forcing me to come again and again. But now he took his time, languidly kissing and making love to me with his tongue.

As Rowen brought me higher and higher, my body coiled tighter and tighter, and I pressed my palms against his broad shoulders. He plunged a finger inside me, and I hissed as the sharp sting morphed into delicious pleasure.

His tongue found the perfect rhythm on my clit as his finger slowly plunged in and out of me.

"Harder," I desperately panted, and Rowen chuckled against me. He slipped in another finger, his gentle ministrations turning into a brutal surrender of my command. He knew I was no fragile thing. "Yes. Yes. I'm going to come for you."

Suddenly, I saw stars upon stars as I came on his tongue, my head tilted toward the sky. I clamped my thighs around him as I rode his head, wanting to keep him there forever as he rolled my clit in his mouth.

"I'm still coming. Don't stop," I moaned as my orgasm stretched on and on. Rowen drew out every second of my release and groaned as if my pleasure were his pleasure. The heavens passed over me, and I finally released my shaking thighs, worried that it had been some time since his last breath.

"Always such a good girl for me," Rowen breathed between

my legs, his lips glistening. Our eye contact was unflinching as he lapped up every morsel of my release.

I arched back as he lowered his mouth to me again, concentrating his tongue on my swollen bundle of nerves, ready to do it all over again.

I let out a delusional giggle as he continued to lick me. I had my doubts about camping, but who knew it could be this fun?

24

———

Rowen and I would never be able to make up for the agonizing months, days, and seconds of being apart, but we certainly tried. We couldn't keep our hands off each other as we journeyed back to the village.

Rowen scooped me up in his arms and spun me around until we were dizzy with laughter. We walked a bit more before he hitched me up his body by the backs of my thighs and held me against him. I wrapped my legs around his narrow waist and languidly claimed his mouth.

Our kisses ranged from sweet and tender to fervent and passionate. But no matter the kiss, my heart raced each time his lips moved against mine, and I would lose all sense of time.

We weren't even halfway home before he pressed me up against a tree and ripped off my clothes with an urgency that stole the breath from my lungs. "Spirits, you feel so good and tight," Rowen moaned into my neck as he took me hard and fast against the trunk. "I'll never get enough of you, Copeland. Never."

The bark bit into my back as our shared release echoed throughout the forest.

With all the distractions, our journey back home took longer than anticipated. We were intoxicated by the thrill of each other's touch.

It was near sunset when we reached the village, and our haven unfolded in the golden-hour light. The forest bungalows stood gracefully amongst the trees, connected by intricate walkways and bridges that seemed to float above the ground. Wooden carvings and natural grass sculptures seamlessly blended into the village, combining art with the everyday lives of the elven community.

The enchanting village was a sight for sore eyes, and while I felt a wave of familiarity and comfort, a profound realization washed over me.

I wasn't coming home; I was already walking beside it.

My sense of belonging was no longer tied to a place but a person—my person. As long as I was with Rowen, anywhere and everywhere could feel like home.

The thought made me smile, but my grin quickly faded as I saw Maddock and Sabra waiting just outside the village. They spotted us immediately and sprinted towards us.

"Where's Ven?" I asked, my heart lurching with dread. I would never forgive myself if anything happened to him while I was away. "Are you okay?"

"Don't worry, everyone is fine," Maddock assured me, though it looked like he was running on fumes. Rowen was my home, but Maddock held a piece of that sanctuary, and I couldn't help but feel relieved we were back in his presence.

"Thank the Spirits," I said as relief flooded through me. I relaxed into Rowen and landed a palm on his chest. "Why is Sabra with you?"

Maddock's onyx-black hair was wild, tousled from repeatedly running his hands through it, a clear indication he'd gotten no rest at all. "Ven knows I get . . . lonely and sends Sabra to keep me company."

"That kid is too sweet for his own good," I said, dropping to the ground and offering my hand to the majestic white wolf. Her tail went wild as she closed the distance between us and licked my hand.

Tears welled in my eyes as I threw my arms around her thick mane and buried my nose in her fur. Not being able to touch people for so long had been isolating, but I hadn't realized just how deeply it affected me until I embraced Sabra.

Rowen joined me on the ground, and together, we lavished Sabra with love and attention. Her mouth curved into a panting smile, and her paw batted at us for more.

Eventually, we stood, and I wiped a tear from my eye. Rowen stepped closer, wrapping his arm around my shoulders as he kissed my temple.

Maddock had been eerily quiet as his sharp eyes traced over our flushed skin, disheveled hair, and unkempt clothes. "You can touch her now," he said to Rowen, and a part of me wished we'd tidied up a bit better. Our all-nighter was plain as day, and I felt a flash of regret for taunting it so obviously in Madds' face. "What happened? The bond has been going haywire."

"I can touch my soul flame. Is that so shocking?" Rowen asked.

"I—No. It's just . . ." his eyes darted all over my body. "Did you have to be so rough with her?" he asked, his brows furrowing. "Her mouth is swollen, and her arms and chest are covered in marks. And that's just what I can see."

My jaw dropped as I struggled to keep my composure. "Don't presume to think that I didn't want or ask for it."

"He's a big man who doesn't know his own strength. And who knows what you're asking him to do?"

"That is none of your business," I seethed, stepping up to his chest.

Maddock matched my affront, his eyes burning. "It is my business," he shot back, but Rowen quickly put a halting hand on his chest.

"Watch it, Madds," Rowen warned in a low growl.

Maddock eyed us both, his chest heaving. "I can feel *everything* between you two," he continued. "Why do you think I'm still here? Because I want to be? No. It's because I have to be. It's agonizing, the bond keeping me trapped. I've tried to leave, but I can't. If I go too far, it starts to feel like I'm in the crevice again. Anguish and loneliness swallowing me up. If I knew how to give you back your Light and bond, I would."

"That would be nice," I said, my voice laced with bitterness, and I realized Rowen was acting as a barrier between us. "But this is all your fault, you know. We didn't ask for this."

Maddock's face twisted in pain. "And you think I did? You think I wanted to be an intruder to your bond? To feel the strength of your love and emotions and know that it's not meant for me?"

"Enough. You two," Rowen said calmly. Too calmly. "Madds, just give us an update on the village."

"There was a violent earthquake," he replied, his eyes bruised from lack of sleep. "It took everything in me not to find you two, but I gave my word that I wouldn't interrupt. Even though no one was sure what happened or if Erovos escaped."

The high I'd been riding came crashing down. It had been nice to forget, to be pleasured beyond the point of comprehension. Rowen had taken my mind and body to a place where I'd been able to forget. But now, reality slammed back into me like a battering ram. Erovos and his army of astral demons were growing, and it wouldn't be long until they escaped.

"He is still trapped," I said, my tongue drying in my mouth. "But we need to gather the Summit first thing in the morning."

"I'll leave you to it, then," Maddock said, his tone cold and detached, his eyes sorrowful as he retreated from us. "You know where to find me."

Before I could stop him, the air rippled with a gentle pulse. Then, piece by piece and layer by layer, Madds started to fade. It was as if he broke himself down into fragments of light, his body becoming translucent until he vanished altogether.

For a moment, the world felt emptier, less complete, but I knew he was reforming in his jail cell, building himself back up until he was whole again.

Watching him astral travel was incredible. Even though I had the same ability, experiencing it and witnessing it were two entirely different things.

As I watched Madds disappear, a pit formed in my stomach. For the first time, the thought of him willingly returning to his cell bothered me.

I shot a glance at Rowen, and he sighed. "You used to do that to me all the time. Not fun, is it?"

"I thought you said I vanished in an instant?"

"Sometimes you would, but other times you would slowly fade away, depending on how much of yourself you brought to me. Why do you think that is?"

Suddenly, another piece of my strange ability fell into place. "Growing up, and when I first began appearing to you, I had no control over how much I traveled," I said, my voice filling with confidence as I finally had the words to articulate my experiences. "Some nights, layers of my being were on Luneth while my physical body remained on Earth. I would sleepwalk and sleep-run, my body moving through the night as my mind wandered into a different realm. I'd been breaking myself down into layers of light to walk between worlds. It's no wonder why I was always so disoriented."

"I remember you telling me you thought you were going mad. You were convinced I wasn't real," Rowen said, his eyebrow cocking up mischievously. My eyes danced across the strong planes of his face, lingering on the hollow contours at his temples and cheeks and the enticing curve of his lower lip. It was no wonder I believed I had conjured this man. He was perfect for me in every way, as if I'd crafted him myself.

Reflexively, I lifted my hand to his face and ran my fingernails through the rough texture of his scruff.

"Are these the famous beard scratchies?" he hummed, deep and low.

"They are," I replied with a wry grin. "It's also a test to make sure you're still real."

He smiled as he placed his palm over my hand, still tracing the sharp angles of his jaw. "If me pleasuring you all night can't convince you I'm real, then nothing can."

I chuckled. "Hmm. You might have to show me again."

"Again? My greedy, little flame," he purred with a delicious smile that met his eyes. "When we are no longer out in the open for anyone to see just how well you take me, your wish shall be my command."

A flush raised to my cheeks, but curiosity got the better of me. "Did you ever doubt if I was real?"

"You were the realest thing I'd ever felt, but for a moment, I started to believe you. I hadn't felt real in so long that I started to question my own existence. Had I really died the day Fou plunged her dagger into my heart? Was I a lost and wandering phantom? Or were you a sylph? A being of light and air and nothing more? But the more you appeared to me, the more my body and soul came back to life."

The flame in my chest swelled. "Science and rationale told me that you couldn't be real, even though every fiber of my being demanded that you were."

"When did you know," he asked, his voice a grated whisper, "that I wasn't a figment of your imagination?"

"It wasn't until Graem bruised me that day in the clearing that I knew you were real. That it was all real," I answered, my fingers unable to stop caressing him.

His eyes darkened. "That was one of the days you slowly flickered away from me. Every time you disappeared, I thought it was the last I'd ever see of you. You've been giving me heart attacks since day one."

"I'm sorry," I said, my gaze lifting to his through my eyelashes.

"Never apologize for appearing to me," he said, taking my hand to his mouth and brushing my knuckles with his lips. "You were so young when this all started. With no one to help you, no one who understood what was happening to you. Navigating your beautiful gift all on your own . . . it must have been terrifying."

"It was, but knowing you were there, real or not, made it all worth it," I said, remembering when I'd stretched myself so thin, I'd astrally torn myself—half of me stuck on Luneth while the other half lay comatose in a hospital bed, and how Rowen had helped me pull myself back together. "You've always been my anchor, my tether home."

Rowen's thumb traced soothing circles on the back of my hand. "We've come a long way, haven't we? From thinking we were both losing our minds to realizing we were just two lost souls connected by an unbreakable bond, drawing us together."

"All the disorientation, the unexplained injuries, and the restless nights brought me closer to you, to Luneth," I whispered, my voice thick with emotion, realizing that everything I had ever searched for had been searching for me, too.

Before I ever knew Rowen or possessed the power of the Alcreon Light, I was just a small girl with the ability to astral travel. Were these connections the reason the Elder Spirits chose me as their vessel? It was hard to say, but as remarkable as it all was, I didn't have the time or luxury to dwell on the marvels of astral traveling. We had much bigger concerns. "What if when Erovos escapes, he comes straight here?"

"We'll meet with the Summit, and we will come up with a plan," Rowen said with a reassuring squeeze of my hand. "We will be ready."

⸺ ·(·☾ ·●· ☽·)· ⸺

Rowen's hand in mine was a steadying force as we walked to our dome, Sabra trotting beside us. "I'm surprised how easy you went on Maddock," I said, still seething that he had accused Rowen of being too rough with me.

My soul flame sighed, his expression thoughtful. "Keira. I pity him. I don't have to imagine his pain because I've experienced it myself. Before I knew we were soul flames, I felt our connection, the irresistible pull drawing us together. But I had to fight it—fight the bond that stretched across galaxies to bring you to me. I resisted you to keep you safe, and it was sheer agony. I know precisely what Maddock is going through, and considering everything, he's holding himself together quite commendably."

As Rowen spoke, the depths of Maddock's torment became clear. My own hatred and anger had blinded me from understanding. He was isolated from everyone by an invisible barrier, just as I had been.

"I guess I could go a little easier on him," I said, rounding the corner to our bungalow. "But he just makes it so hard to—"

Before I could finish my thought, a deep, strangled cry pierced the air behind us.

I spun towards the tree line, my gaze landing in the direction of the crevice.

Alvar, the war captain, emerged from the shadows, limping with his arm tight by his side. "Sabra, get Takoda!" I said with growing alarm, pointing to the healer's dome before charging toward the warrior. I stole a glance to ensure the wolf was on her way, her form dashing like a lightning bolt.

"What happened?" Rowen asked, worry in his voice as he swiftly dove under Alvar's good arm to help carry him.

"We were attacked," the captain ground out, his breath coming in short and labored. Blood streaked his face and matted his silver buzzcut. His warrior leathers and linen undershirt hung in tatters around his massive frame. "We were patrolling the area around the crevice when the earth shook, and a demon slipped through the cracks. My soldiers fought bravely, but the creature cut right through our weapons. It's unlike anything I've ever seen. Simply using its claws and teeth."

My gut sank as I peered at the war captain. "Where are you wounded?"

"My ankle is twisted, and I have a few cuts and bruises, but my arm is the worst," Alvar said through a pained grimace. His body swayed with fatigue as Takoda and Sabra ran up to us. "We tried to fight them, but our weapons were useless against them."

"Help me lower him. Gently," Takoda said, his tone calm yet urgent.

"Were you bitten or scratched?" I asked, trying to keep my voice steady as Rowen helped him to the ground.

Alvar winced. "What? Why does that matter?"

"Bitten or scratched?" I repeated more firmly as Takoda peeled back the shredded layers of his clothes and armor, revealing the extent of his injury.

The wound was unlike anything I'd ever seen. It was as if a shadow had been spliced into his skin, painfully and with jagged edges that seeped into his bloodstream. Even now, I could see the blackened veins spiderwebbing up his left arm.

"Bitten," the captain grunted, his voice strained.

My heart stopped.

"I have never treated anything like this," Takoda said, his eyes narrowing in concern as he applied a shimmering paste around the raw flesh. "We need to stop the darkness from spreading, but the noxlily salve is not working."

"Listen to me," I said, panic welling in my chest. "He was bitten by a Voro-Kai. They are Erovos' newest demons. There is no stopping it. It will spread until he becomes one of them."

Alvar's face paled, his eyes flashing with horror. "The two other warriors . . . I thought they were dead."

"They might be turned," I said solemnly, wishing any other outcome for the brave soldiers.

"How do you know this?" the healer asked, his eyes widening in alarm.

"I just returned from battling them," I said, recalling their grotesque faces and boar-ish tusks. "Rowen was there. He saw the whole thing. He can attest."

Rowen's eyes were heavy with sorrow. "It is true."

"My arm," Alvar said, his voice weak yet resolute. "Take it. Quickly, before it spreads."

"Alvar, let me try to save it," I choked out, knowing the risks. If I did try to heal him, I might accidentally latch onto the parts of him that were dying, and like the flower in the bathing suite, I would only kill him faster. But I had to try. I couldn't let the war captain lose his arm.

"You have no mastery over the Light," the war captain grunted, pain etched on his face. "We've all seen what you've done around the village. You are still a weakened mare in my eyes. I can't take the risk."

"Alvar," Takoda said, his expression torn between concern and duty. "I can see the dark veins. They have yet to reach your heart, but it is spreading. If you're sure, I will need to get everything prepared."

"I'm sure," he grunted, his face hardening in determination.

"No!" I pleaded.

"Alvar, don't be proud," Rowen said as Takoda readied the tools from his medicine bag. "Not with this."

Alvar's battle-worn face twisted as he yelled, "Do it!"

The air was thick with tension, and I held my breath as Takoda readied his knife.

The blade pressed into his skin, and Alvar let out a guttural cry, tears streaking down his dirt-smeared face.

"Stop!" I screamed, and Takoda's hand stilled. "I'm not giving you a choice. Weakened mare or not, I'm going to save your arm," I said, reaching for his hand, his dark veins bulging.

The second I latched onto his hand, darkness choked up my throat and blinded me. The death I'd been running from clogged up my veins and cut off my airways. It was overwhelming. Suffocating. Alvar was as good as dead. We all were.

"Keira, your eyes are pitch black," Rowen yelled beside me, but I could barely hear him over Alvar's screams and the shadows whirling around my mind. "You're absorbing the darkness!"

The thread of death tangled around me, its tendrils heavy and rotting, constricting my throat. What was the point of living if everything was already dying? Why was I even here at all?

Consciousness felt like too heavy a burden to bear. I didn't want it anymore.

"You must stop her," Takoda cried, his voice filled with panic. "She will become one of them in Alvar's place if she doesn't let go."

"No. Give her a chance. She can do this," Rowen demanded firmly before his voice echoed in my ear. "Keira, find the light."

"Why?" I wanted to scream, and maybe I did. The darkness was going to find me one day anyway. Why not just end it all now?

"Because I need you. I need you to choose to come back."

Suddenly, Nepta's words rang through me: *You must choose which beast to nourish, the one who heals or the one who destroys.* Her words made it sound like a choice.

But did I? Have a choice?

I could focus on all that was dying or dead, but neither of those scenarios anchored me in the present or allowed me to admire the beauty of the now.

The weight threatened to pull me under as glimpses of the dark cave and slumbering demons flashed before me. Dark figures twisted and churned in their cocoons, but I was one of them. *No,* I was all of them—a part of their hive mind.

Images of my face appeared over and over again in the shared mind, thousands of times and from every angle. Their mind focused on one task and one task only.

Find. Find. Find.

Take. Take. Take.

Ours. Ours. Ours.

The cave echoed with their chilling, sleeping chant. Their collective consciousness was searching for me. A whole sleeping army was seeing my face, dreaming of destroying any obstacle in their way to bite into my skin and tear through my flesh. I saw them lifting my limp, bloody body in their arms, reverently, as if delivering me like a precious offering to Erovos.

Once that mission was complete, they would have full reign to unleash their terror unto the world.

"Keira!" I heard Rowen and Takoda scream my name.

Instead of falling into the darkness, I pulled back, desperately searching until I found the vibrant thread of Alvar's life. I waded through endless strands that conglomerated together like sticky spider webs. If I didn't find it soon, the war captain would be lost to the hive mind.

I batted away at the thick ropes that caught on my limbs and slowed me down. When suddenly, in the sea of dark webbing, I saw a bright strand.

There it was! The thread of Alvar's life. It was strong, resilient, and beautiful. But turning. And fast.

With a concentrated effort, I summoned a gentle blast of Light, incinerating the darkness within Alvar. I flushed out the blight that would have turned him into a Voro-Kai—a being that would hunt me to the ends of the earth.

Slowly, my vision returned, and my veins faded from black to silver, a familiar, comforting glow emanating from my body. I dropped his arm, our veins shimmering as we both blinked back to our bodies.

Rowen and Takoda sagged with relief, their tension melting away.

"You did it, star-touched," Takoda said, awe etched on his long, slender face.

Rowen wrapped his hand around the base of my skull and pulled me in until our foreheads touched. His warmth and strength brought me back to my senses.

Alvar flexed his arm and rolled it at the socket, his eyes wide with wonder. "Thank you, he whispered, his hazy stare filled with gratitude. "I was wrong. You are no weakened mare. You are the Alcreon Daughter, and you have saved my life."

I offered him a weak smile before I glanced up, realizing we had attracted a crowd of worried villagers. Their faces were a mix of fear and relief, solidifying how real this war had become. So far, the Wyn elves had been shielded from the impending darkness. But now it had crossed through their front door.

Terror churned in my gut like acid. There was officially nowhere left to hide.

25

The Summit gathered at the Sacred Vale, each member in their usual chairs, including Alvar. He looked exhausted but determined, his arm cleared of the blight. Others who were not part of the Summit also joined. Everyone needed to be here for this, including Maddock. I'd gone to his cell and told him he could come if he kept a low profile. Nepta had called off his security detail since he helped bring water back to the village, but still, I didn't want to push it.

Everyone gathered around the stone table, its smooth surface reflecting the anxious faces of those assembled. Among us was Dyani. Her nostrils flared, and her chest heaved beneath her jerkin, betraying the turmoil within.

I had just returned from where her brother was last seen, but during my time in the crevice, I hadn't seen Demil. It pained me that I didn't bring better news for her, for everyone. At least the roaring waterfalls had returned.

Once everyone settled, I took a deep breath and recounted the harrowing events of the last twenty-four hours. I explained how I'd fallen into Erovos' trap and faced his new breed of demons. I described the earth-shaking tremor that had allowed a demon to slip through the crevice, attacking our scout party and nearly transforming our war captain into a Voro-Kai.

"While I battled the demons," I continued, choking down the tremor in my voice. "I discovered a slumbering Voro-Kai army waiting to mature."

"The Voro-Kai?" Driskell, Nepta's second in command, questioned in disbelief.

"It is true, and a miracle I escaped with my life," Alvar said as murmurs of shock rippled through the crowd. "Our weapons would slice and cut their hide, but it did little to stop or slow them. We didn't stand a chance."

"They are astral demons, but the horrors they inflict crossover into our dimension," I confirmed as the Vale fell silent.

"These astral demons are shades upon the earth," Driskell said, his expression filled with horror. "If they escape, there are no weapons to stop them, nothing to prevent the darkness from consuming us all, and—"

"Driskell," Nepta interjected firmly, raising a withered hand to silence him. "My child, what else did you learn?"

"While I was in there, I gained control of my powers," I said, shifting my gaze from the second-in-command to Nepta. "They couldn't touch me when I was aglow with the Alcreon Light."

Driskell's face lit up. "Of course!" he exclaimed, a broad smile lifting his features. "You are our weapon. We need to learn how to harness your power and use you." A chill ran down my spine, and my nerves tightened. The thought of facing the Voro-Kai again, and possibly losing myself while in my astral form, filled me with dread. "The Synodic Prophecy may yet come to pass. You will bring light and life back to the dying lands."

Rowen's powerful grip found my hand under the table. "Keira Copeland, the bearer of the Alcreon Light, will not be referred to as an object that needs to be used," he said with utter disdain.

"It is true. She is a powerful woman, not a tool for us to wield as we please," Alvar said, shocking us all. Especially me.

"To make matters worse," Takoda said, his expression drawn. "One bite from these creatures will turn you into a Voro-Kai. It nearly spread to Alvar's heart before Keira incinerated the blight."

"Can anything be done to safeguard ourselves from such an affliction?" Nepta asked the healer, calm as a raging undertow. "There must be some cure you know of, Takoda."

"There are no precautions of which I know," Takoda replied regretfully.

A heavy silence fell over the Sacred Vale. Nepta's discomfort was palpable, yet she didn't shift in her seat. Her composure was a masterclass in restraint, power, and poise, and I made a mental note to school my body and face to betray nothing, just as she did.

"Driskell is right," I said, meeting the eyes of those around me. "The only defense against the Voro-Kai resides in my veins, a force that I alone wield." Even now, it pulsed within me as if it agreed. "I am a weapon."

"See?" Driskell beamed. "She understands her place. We can use her to draw out the army, gather them all in one place, and destroy them."

"We will not lay her out like a piece of meat. Besides, relying on one weapon to defeat an entire army is a poor strategy," Rowen continued as he scanned the faces around the table, his gaze connecting with each person in turn, and I saw the commanding war general he had once been.

"If the dark army escapes the crevice, they will indeed be starved, trampling these lands until nothing is left," Alvar said, the scar on his chin white and prominent.

"How many of these darkened wombs did you see?" Nepta asked, her aged voice unwavering.

I recalled the endless rows of dark chrysalises, the horrifying sight seared into my memory. "Not all of them have reached full maturity, but I'd say thousands upon thousands," I admitted, my voice trembling. The terror I felt wasn't for myself. It was for the Wyn people, the inhabitants of Luneth, and the countless distant worlds that would be threatened if we failed to stop them.

The crowd stiffened in horror, but no gasp left a single mouth.

"It is . . . it is beyond our numbers," Alvar pushed the words out, his face paling as he gripped his blades. The war captain's gaze was distant, as if his eyes could already see the outcome of this war. "Three of us alone could not defeat one of them."

"What happened to the demon you fought?" I asked.

"It escaped," he replied with pain in his eyes. "There was no destroying it."

"I will search for it, along with the other warriors," Rowen said, and fear gripped my spine at the thought of him seeking out Erovos' demons.

"What about my brother?" Dyani asked, her muscular shoulders squaring with fierce intensity.

My soul flame's gaze shot to Dyani, two emotions warring in his eyes. He respected the warrior, but the man in question had been responsible for my three-month disappearance. "I will search for Demil, too."

Dyani appeared surprised yet impressed, and I noticed she was wearing silver armbands in honor of her twin. "I will go with you."

"Me too," I agreed. "I can't let you go without a weapon."

My soul flame's eyes met mine. "If the Voro-Kai's weakness is the Alcreon Light, maybe there is a way for you to infuse our weapons with it. You can't be everywhere at once."

"I'll try," I said, even though I had never attempted such a thing.

Rowen nodded before turning his attention back to the crowd. "We need to establish a multi-faceted strategy. Some of us will need to search for allies to aid us in this war. Others need to fortify our position here, preparing defensive wards and barriers."

"A reminder of the prophecy might do us all some good," Driskell said, clearing his throat to recite what he'd likely spent years studying, working to decipher every word. "*The lost light of Luneth shall return to its synodic beginning when the first six stars align with the stones of shattered ruin. Through blood, bone, and crystal, the marked son,* or sun, depending on your translation, *will breathe life anew unto the deadened lands of darkness.* Keira is clearly The Marked. She bears the ears of the Ancients, and her body is covered in Alcreon Light tattoos."

I wanted to wrap my arms around myself. I didn't appreciate how much attention Driskell paid to my body, but I schooled my expression, just like Nepta.

"There's more to the prophecy," I said, not betraying a single emotion. "*Shall the lost light fall unto those who feast, darkness will reign an unending beast. Worlds have fallen and so they shall remain as a Sylvan door opens to a universe unrestrained.*"

Driskell's eyes nearly bugged out of his head. "It . . . it could mean—"

"It *means*," I cut in. "Erovos will return to the Sylvan Mother Tree to finish what he started. But who's to say if that's before or after he ravages the world with his astral demons."

"I will return to monitor the crevice," Alvar volunteered, and despite his recent brush with death, every scar on his body spoke to his bravery. "If he or any of his demons escape, I will know about it, and track wherever they head."

Rowen nodded, his commanding tone never faltering. "They

will try to overpower us with their numbers. We cannot let that happen. We must find allies."

"Indeed," Nepta said, her muted eyes landing on every soul. "This is not our fight alone. The Wyn may have been the protectors of the Alcreon Light, but now this fight affects us all."

"It will take armies to defeat what I saw in that crevice. What about the Stonefist Giants?"

"They have retreated far into the mountains. If you ever did manage to find them, you would have another war on your hands," Nepta replied, her mouth forming a thin line.

"What about the souls we freed from the Crystal Crypts?" Dyani asked, one white eyebrow shooting up. "This is their world, too, and a favor is owed."

I hated the thought of putting all those who suffered beneath the rule of Aliphoura through more trauma, but we'd need every ally we could find.

"The people have scattered to the winds," Alvar remarked with a wave of his hand.

"I knew many of the people trapped within the Crypts. Most of them were from Viltarran," Rowen said as his eyes filled with longing. The pride he held for his destroyed citydom was palpable. "If we could find them, I know they would be willing to fight."

Suddenly, a warm glow flashed in the darkest part of my memory, and I gasped. "Rayal, a woman who helped me while I was imprisoned in the Crypts, mentioned help amongst friends." How could I have forgotten Rayal? She'd smuggled food into my cell, beaming like the sun in the dark prison I thought would be my grave. Even the memory of her smile warmed my skin.

"We know nothing of these people," Driskell replied in a frustrated but weary exhale.

"There was a symbol on the necklace she wore," I added,

remembering Rayal's fingers gliding along the smooth metal at her throat. "It was a curved line with two circles resembling suns."

Nepta stiffened, her face turning to Driskell. "That symbol, it is the mark of the desert elves. If the woman you met bore that symbol, her people may be hidden but watching."

"The desert elves," Driskell whispered as if it were a sacred fable not to be mentioned above a murmur. "No one has seen or heard from them in decades. They have made themselves impossible to find."

Alvar nodded. "They could be invaluable allies if found."

"She told me a way to find them," I replied, searching for the words she had spoken right before she left my cell. "*If you should survive this and ever find yourself where sun casts upon sun and your shadow greets mine, know that you are amongst friends.*"

"That's about as helpful as a luminorb in the broad light of day," Alvar muttered, looking around the table as if chuffed with his observation.

"It is something," Takoda disagreed, as he appeared to wrack his brain with where such a convergence could lay.

"Sun casts upon sun," I mused aloud. "A reflection?"

"Perhaps," Nepta said thoughtfully.

"Another world?" Rowen offered.

"Also possible."

"A prophecy of another son?" Alvar chimed in.

"We know not where to even start with such a puzzle," Driskell said, throwing his arms up in exasperation, his long sleeves billowing around him. "I decipher stars, not riddles. But in the meantime, I will send correspondence to nearby villages and citydoms to aid us in battle."

"Until we can seek help from others, there is much to do," Nepta said as she began delegating rules and responsibilities with precision. "We face a great challenge, but our strength lies in our unity."

The Vale buzzed with renewed purpose as strategies, roles, and tactics for the upcoming battle were discussed. A glimmer of hope swept over us all, yet doubt lingered in my mind: would it all be enough against the sea of demons headed our way?

While others strategized and planned, I remained where I sat, repeating Rayal's words over and over again, hoping to unlock some hidden meaning.

With any luck, we wouldn't have to face the Voro-Kai army alone. We would find a way to tip the scales back in our favor.

———— ·(·C · ● · Ɔ ·)· ————

I followed the village healer out of the Sacred Vale, my pace quickening to catch him. As the stars and forest canopy hovered above me, I jogged across the floating stone steps.

"Takoda," I called, touching his bare shoulder. "I need to go to the Hymma." My tone left no room for question. I wasn't asking. "I have to find the desert elves. We can't do this without them."

"I know." He nodded, his long hair billowing in the moonlight like tinsel. "This war is much bigger than us. I shall prepare it for you tomorrow night."

I blinked in surprise. I hadn't expected him to agree so quickly. "Thank you," I said with deep appreciation. A few elves from the war council passed by, their eyes flickering with curiosity. "I'm stronger now. More in control," I continued, recalling the insight I'd gained in the crevice. But doubt gnawed at me. Was my mind in a solid enough place to enter the Hymma?

Takoda placed a reassuring hand on my arm, and I almost cried because I could feel the care in his healing hands. "I'm saying that while you have grown, you must tread carefully. The

Hymma is not just a place; it embodies your very essence. As within, so without."

The moment had finally come; what I had been avoiding all this time—talking to someone about my feelings.

My heart raced, and my palms turned clammy.

"And I know you, star-touched. You don't give up easily. If you can't find the answer, I know you will go deeper, crossing through doors that are hard to return from. You need to know when to stop. I've seen it many times: elves who have gone too far and never recovered from what they saw inside the Hymma. Some are not ready to face their own mind or how deep it can go."

"I'll be careful," I said, trying to sound confident. He might change his mind if he sensed even the slightest quiver in my voice.

"The decision is up to you. It always has been. But if you would like to talk beforehand, I am willing to listen," he offered gently. "Regardless of what you decide, the Hymma will be ready for you."

When I'd talked in the past, I was deemed a liar and forced to say things I didn't want to. Anxiety crept up my throat, and I swallowed hard, trying to push it down.

"Just say you'll think about it," he said, his umber eyes locking onto mine with such understanding that I almost unraveled right in front of him. He gave me a gentle squeeze on my arm before continuing down the watery pathway.

"I will," I whispered, though I wasn't sure he heard me or if I would think about it. I'd been against it for so long.

I made my way back to the Vale, searching for Rowen and Madds. The floating stone steps felt both solid and precarious beneath me, like an omen of my journey ahead.

The moonlight danced across the surface of the returned water, and I found Rowen and Maddock standing where the steps morphed into land. Both of their eyes lit up when they saw me—forest green and solid earth. "What did Takoda say?" Rowen asked, his smile warm and encouraging.

"He agreed to prepare the Hymma for me tomorrow."

Maddock slid his hands in his pockets. His head was down, but his gaze tilted to mine through his brows. "Ven told me you nearly lost your mind in that thing. Are you sure you want to go in there again?"

"Seriously?" I asked, throwing my arms up in the air. "Is there anything Ven didn't tell you?"

He gave me a wicked smirk. "Tell me another secret, and I'll let you know."

I side-eyed him. "Not happening."

"Just ignore him," Rowen said, jerking his chin at Maddock. "I do."

"Oh, you mean ignore the man who gives unsolicited advice while wearing a prison uniform?" I quipped. "He's kind of hard to ignore."

"Hey, I like my outfit. It's nice quality. And I look good."

I rolled my eyes. The off-white linen pants and shirt he wore were indeed nice quality. The Wyn crafted everything with meticulous care, making each piece one-of-a-kind. The earthy, frayed fabric draped off his lean body effortlessly.

He did look good now that I thought about it, and damn him for making me think about it. "You're right. The prison look does suit you."

Rowen smirked. "Don't encourage him. His ego is already big enough to eclipse us all."

I laughed, shaking my head. I would have Pia and Xala, the ladies who put my wardrobe together, lend Maddock a helping hand. Looking good or not, he was still wearing a prison uniform. And if I truly thought about it, I didn't want someone who shared a piece of my bond stuck in a cell. "I'll see if I can find you some proper clothes and maybe a better place to sleep if you don't push it."

Maddock smiled as if I had just given him the world. "Finally, some appreciation."

Rowen chuckled, then turned his attention back to me, running his knuckles along the back of my arm. "Do you want to try a Hymma joining?"

I shook my head. "Takoda said our emotions affect the Hymma. You might sway the results of where I go. It's something I need to do alone. I can feel it."

"The last time you said that, you ended up hitching this guy to our wagon," he replied, jabbing his thumb at Madds.

"I'll be careful," I said for the second time today. My panic attacks no longer resulted in lightning storms, death, and shocking people, which was a relief, but the impending war still weighed heavily on my shoulders.

Did the fate of Luneth truly rest on the state of my mental health? I prayed to the spirits that it didn't because if it did, my mind might drag us all down with it.

26

The next morning, after breakfast and a quick chat with Pia and Xala, I went straight to work on Rowen's plan. He was hopeful that I could infuse our weapons with the Alcreon Light. But after trying short blades, long swords, and arrows, I was no closer to strengthening our weapons against the Voro-Kai.

"It's not working," I said, dropping the knife to the table. We were in one of the weapon storerooms filled to the brim with pointy objects. The dome was bathed in the afternoon sun. The golden rays bared down through the wooden structure and onto my brow. A breeze had yet to pick up, and I was hot, frustrated, and tired.

The weight of the situation threatened to collapse my ribcage, just like the Crypts I dreamt about each night. The war, the prophecies, and the threats from Erovos loomed closer and closer.

"I'm sorry I didn't have time to discuss this plan with you first," Rowen said, sensing my stress. "The idea just came to me, and I had to get Driskell off your back. He was about to start making plans regarding your body and how to wield it. I had to sway the conversation and keep you in control."

"It was a great plan, in theory," I said, charging the Light into Rowen's ax, but the steel heated and glowed briefly before dying out. "The Light goes in for a few seconds but then dissipates. It won't hold. None of these materials are strong enough."

After trying twenty different blades made from varying metals and using different strategies, I finally gave up, slumping in exhaustion.

"You look like shit," Maddock said, appearing in front of me, wearing new clothes. Pia and Xala had done an excellent job dressing him in brown pants and a loose, blue linen shirt that brought out the warmth in his eyes.

He ran a hand through his jet-black hair, sweeping back the strands that had fallen into his face. He swung a leg over the bench and joined me at the table.

A piece of my agitated bond settled as Maddock appeared in the room,

"I've never felt better," I said sarcastically, rubbing my temples.

"I thought my new clothes would make you happy. Pia and Xala have excellent taste," he said, modeling his new outfit for me.

"You do clean up nice. Although the incarcerated look was growing on me," I chuckled half-heartedly.

His eyes traced my face before roving over the piles of weapons. "Why don't I give it a try?"

"You?" I asked incredulously. "My Light is your Light. If I can't do it, you can't do it." Rowen shot me a stare, and I remembered I said I would go easier on him. I swept my hand over the broad array of weapons. "Be my guest."

"Careful," Rowen said, leaning against a weapon rack with casual yet deadly grace. "She's competitive."

Madds picked up a small blade and looked at me with a cocky grin that made a single dimple appear on his left cheek.

His broad hands became aglow, and my eyes widened. Watching Maddock wield the power he had stolen from me was marvelous yet jarring.

The metal went alight and held and then dulled back to normal.

I let out a breath, shocked he'd been able to hold the light longer than me.

I couldn't let him hold the record for the longest-lit weapon. So with a newfound fire, I doubled my efforts.

Madds and I kept our techniques to ourselves as we battled to be the first to make an Alcreon Light blade. Sweat dripped from our brows as we tried method after method with no luck.

Rowen straightened his posture. "We will find another way. Or do you two want to keep battling it out?"

"Yes," we replied at the same time.

Rowen shrugged with a smirk and leaned back against the rack. "Then carry on."

·〔· ● ·〕· ——

Just as Takoda promised, he awaited me at the Hymma.

I had chosen not to speak with him beforehand, but if the healer was disappointed, he didn't let it show.

I'd assured him I was strong enough to face what lay ahead. But what if I was wrong? A Voro-Kai demon had already slipped through the crack in the mountain, leaching into our world like a poisonous weed. The thought of more slowly escaping until Erovos tore the mountain apart was unbearable, especially without proper weapons to defend ourselves.

Each day, the clock ticked louder, and the war drums echoed closer.

I walked toward the Hymma, the geodesic dome reflecting the outside world panel by panel. At this distance, it appeared as no more than a mirage, a strange ripple against the rich forest landscape.

The last time I'd been in the Hymma, half of my body lived on Luneth while the other half laid comatose on Earth. I was weak, poisoned, and astrally torn.

Now, the mirror reflected a different image back at me.

I strode toward the Hymma with strong, determined steps. My hair was twisted down my back in a single braid, my dark pants fit snugly and laced up either hip, and my dark blue vest came to a point at my navel.

Rowen and Maddock flanked me on either side. The man on my right, his presence like warm wood and sharp steel, had been in the Hymma with me, while the other, like stolen silver and gold, had slept next to my motionless body in the hospital.

They offered their support, reminding me that though the journey in the Hymma was mine to make, I was not alone.

"Remember, no earthly possession may enter here," Takoda said reassuringly. "Set the intention and have it be so."

"I will," I said, glancing over my shoulder as Takoda averted his eyes. "Maddock, look away."

"Why? Are you getting naked?" he asked sarcastically.

"Do as she says," Rowen said, gripping his shoulders and spinning him around until his back was to me.

Shock lanced through his voice. "She is getting naked!"

"After the well, I told you if you ever laid your eyes on her like that again, I would rip you limb from limb," Rowen said without a shred of jest.

"Why did we bring him again?" I asked, unlacing my top. Takoda had busied himself, walking around and checking the Hymma.

Madds remained turned from me. "It's not like I haven't seen it before."

"I might just rip you limb from limb for your tongue,"

Rowen remarked, his eyes boring into the back of Maddock's head, but then quickly darting back to me as I slid my bodice off my shoulders.

I removed everything, my eyes never leaving Rowen's as I stripped down to my bare skin. My soul flame's gaze heated my flesh as the cool air kissed my naked body.

"See you soon," I said, turning and stepping beyond the moon-encrusted doorway. I took a deep breath, feeling the ancient energy of the Hymma becoming one with my body.

Takoda's words rang through me like a guiding melody.

My intention was set.

I sat cross-legged on the ground and attuned myself to my breath.

I hadn't realized it my first time here, but the Hymma was an introspective ceremony, like stepping into the room of your mind. The splashes of color and inverting shapes that existed behind my eyelids came to life around me. It was a reflection of the stardust that danced in my mind—a whole universe within me.

The lights pushed and pressed against the black cloak of consciousness.

As I started to float away from my body, my mind began to feel adrift, as if it had nowhere to land.

The last time, I'd been so weak that I hadn't noticed how odd the sensation was. I had been without a body before, and I didn't want to repeat the experience.

It would have been easy to give way to panic, but I needed to remain calm. I couldn't let my fears influence my time here. I promised Takoda I would be careful.

I intended to find the desert elves, but it felt like I waded through the sea of my mind, finding no real answers. The glimmering lights and otherworldly landscapes blurred together with no clear direction. Frustration gnawed at me, but I brushed it aside, knowing such an emotion would hinder my progress.

After what felt like ages of wandering—and maybe it had been—I felt a gentle golden ripple through my chest.

My soul flame bond!

I quickly reeled myself in, like smoke returning to a candle's flame. I opened my eyes to the familiar weight of my body, grateful to be back in it. I exited the Hymma, blinking against the light.

Rowen was immediately there and quickly wrapped me in a robe. "Is everything okay?" I asked anxiously.

"You've been in there for hours," Maddock said as Rowen tied the garment around my waist.

Rowen cinched it tight, his fingers lingering on the tie. "We grew worried."

"I felt you calling to me," I said, rubbing my chest, still feeling the aftermath of his glow.

Takoda answered, his eyes searching me, "I had him call you back."

I glanced between the three men, understanding their concern. It felt like I had run a mental marathon. "I didn't realize how much time had passed. It's . . . it's different in there."

"Did you find anything?"

"No," I replied, my eyes locking with the healer's. "I need to go back in."

Takoda shook his head. "It is too taxing on the mind. I understand these are dire times, so you will be permitted entrance every other day."

Annoyance flared within me. "We don't have that kind of time," I urged, light-headed and exhausted. Even though Takoda was right, I wanted to charge right back into the Hymma and spend as much time in there as I could until I found some helpful information.

"Your sanity and Light are more important than losing your-self," Takoda said, his eyes soft with understanding but rimmed with authority. "We need you for when the battle arises. Erovos and the Voro-Kai escaping could happen any day. You are too valuable. If we lose you, we lose everything. You promised me that you would be careful. Please."

"Every other day then," I agreed, letting his orders sink in. On the days I didn't go in the Hymma, I could focus on training with Dyani or looking for a solution with the weapons. And while I felt overwhelmed with tasks that had no clear solution, I was grateful for the support I had helping me.

27

———————

The following day, Rowen walked me to the edge of the training grounds before his session with Takoda. The sound of clanging weapons filled the air. The energy was intense and focused as the warriors honed their skills for the upcoming battle.

Rowen kissed me on the lips, a simple gesture that had been missing from our lives for so long. Though it was quick and sweet, my knees went weak. I would never get over something as simple as a peck from him. "Have fun today," he said, kissing me again, but before he could pull away, my grip found the front of his shirt, and I yanked him back toward me.

He chuckled against my lips, and I took the opportunity to stroke my tongue against his mouth. He moaned into me. "Spirits, you make it hard to leave you."

"Then don't," I said, not letting go of his forest green shirt.

"Oh, I will be coming back for you," he murmured at my temple, his beard scratching deliciously against my skin.

I grinned, releasing him from my clutches. "Good, because I have plans for you."

His voice turned to a low gravel. "I think it is I that has plans for you."

As much as I wanted to cancel the day and retreat to the bedroom, I knew how important his sessions with Takoda were. Even though I wouldn't attend myself, I wanted to show support. "So much has been going on, I haven't had a chance to ask you how it's going with Takoda," I said, not quite ready to let him out of my sight.

"I'm finding the mind-mending sessions helpful. As you know, I have memories that are . . . hard to forget. Thought patterns I am trying to break," he said, rubbing the scar over his heart. The knife wound was entirely healed, yet every now and again, it flared with phantom pain.

"It makes me want to snap Fou's neck all over again," I seethed, wishing I could dive into the lush forest of his eyes and battle the ghosts that still haunted him.

"Always so bloodthirsty when it comes to protecting me," he said with a grin, tracing his thumb over my lip. "It's adorable."

"What thought patterns are you trying to break?" I asked, tilting my head back to meet his gaze. "How can I help?"

He pressed his hand against my chest, right where my heart galloped at his touch. He shifted higher, his palm widening to encircle my throat.

Though his touch was light, a spike of fear and adrenaline shot through me.

"It is that look that haunts me," he breathed, leaning in close to trace his nose along my jawline. I released a shuddered moan, exposing more of my throat to him.

"You won't hurt me," I said as my whole body flushed.

Rowen pressed his thumb to my quickening pulse. "Your body believes otherwise. Your pulse quickens like a hunted deer."

Even though I could barely think straight, I suddenly knew what haunted him. "That night in the cave, you weren't yourself," I said, remembering his fevered hallucinations induced by laith venom. He'd thought I was Fou, and he had tried to strangle me.

"It torments me how I hurt you," he said, his voice a tortured moan. He used his hold on my neck to tilt my gaze to his. "I could have killed you."

"But you didn't," I whispered, my pulse quickening beneath his fingertips. He could easily withhold my next breath if he wanted to, press a little harder or squeeze a little tighter to make me see stars. My body told him that I would like it, that I trusted him.

His breath fanned across my collarbones and erupted goosebumps on my skin. "I've touched one other this way . . . this coarsely. I hate that this memory is hers. I want you to claim my every thought, you to own every experience this body can have."

"Then let me take it, Rowen. Let this memory be mine," I said as his forearm rested between the rise and fall of my breasts. "Be coarse with me."

The growl he emitted sent a rush through my blood as he backed me up and caged me against a tree, his hand still collared around my throat.

His lips crashed onto mine, easing my mouth open with his tongue. He applied the most delicious pressure on my throat as he deepened the kiss, stealing my breath in more ways than one.

He nudged his knee between my legs, forcing them apart as he pressed up at the apex of my thighs. I moaned as he pushed me to my tiptoes, causing my weight to center on my clit. I was pliant and buzzing as his kiss untethered me from my body, my thoughts, my worries. He pinned me in place as he rocked his knee against me and squeezed my neck just a little tighter.

He tilted my head to the side and lowered his mouth to bite and nip at the curve of my neck. "Tell me," he rasped against my skin. "Who do I belong to?"

"Me," I panted as a whirlwind fluttered in my head. "You belong to me."

I moaned, arching into him. I couldn't care less that his fingers were wrapped around my throat or that I was high-centered on his knee in broad daylight where anyone could see.

"I told you to be careful with her," a voice said, snaking through my senses and jolting me back to my body.

Still pressed to the tree, I blinked out of my daze to find Maddock staring at me with his arms crossed and his eyes narrowed. He was dressed in dark, fitted trousers and a loose, clay-red shirt.

Pia and Xala had worked their magic yet again. The subdued and earthy colors enhanced his high-contrast features.

Rowen chuckled. His hand left me with a trailing touch down my chest as he gently lowered me to my feet. "Be careful with her while you train and see how she likes it."

"I'm training with you today?" he asked, his voice hitching with excitement.

I reined in my ragged breathing. "You did hold up your end of the bargain."

His eyes narrowed suspiciously. "Why are you being nice to me? I'm scared."

Rowen kissed my temple. "That's my cue to leave. Try not to beat each other to a pulp," he said as he turned to leave, and I watched his back muscles shift in the most riveting way beneath his shirt.

"Are you really going to let me train with you?" he asked, his voice not quite clearing the euphoric buzz in my head, but the subject matter did.

My gaze shot to his. "Erovos could escape at any moment. You need to be prepared just like the rest of us. I think we can put the past behind us, don't you? A world eater on the verge of escaping seems a little more pressing. Besides, you earned this fair and square," I said, understanding what Rowen had meant about going easier on Madds. Before I knew Rowen and I were soul flames, I'd felt the intensity of our connection through my whole body, and I'd had to fight it. "And thank you for holding up your end of the deal. That must have been hard."

I knew the struggles Maddock faced, and while I wished he would disappear, a part of me needed him beside me. My feelings toward him may be stolen, but there was nothing I could do about that now. I needed to keep the host of my Light and bond safe.

"Well, all right then," Maddock said with a faint smirk as we walked to the weapon rack and selected our weapons.

Dyani approached us, her strides confident and assertive. "So you've finally decided to join us, Madds?"

"Yes, even though I'm scared of you," he said, holding a short blade. "You weren't very nice to me the first time we met."

Dyani rolled her eyes and landed her palm on her hip. "I only *threatened* to torture and kill you. I could have done far worse."

"See?" he said, looking at me to defend him. "She's terrifying."

Dyani's expression softened despite keeping her tone and body language staunch. "You will want to learn how to use your opponent's strength against them. It's how I am able to defeat those who are bigger than me," she said, her chin raised high.

I frowned, glancing between her and Maddock, "How come he doesn't have to start at the beginning?"

Dyani gave a short laugh. "We don't have that kind of time. Besides, haven't you seen him watching from the trees, learning? Plus, by how he holds the blade, I can tell he's done this before. Unlike you, who looks like—"

"—Like a youngling with a stick. I know, I know," I interrupted with a sigh. "Let's just get on with it."

Our coach hid a smile as she continued her instruction, "The knife is an extension of your arm, an extension of you. It's a simple, beautiful object; but in the right hands, it can fell armies."

Dyani performed a series of quick attacks with her blades. Her precision and power still amazed me.

Maddock and I mimicked her movements, exchanging glances. We were both determined to master the skill before the other.

"Attack me," Dyani said to Maddock, just as she said to me my first day.

Madds obliged, and she dodged his attack, mimicking a blow to his middle. "You're dead."

"How did you do that?" he asked at the same time I said. "Hey, why didn't you knock him to the ground?"

Dyani ignored my complaint. "You are too stiff, Madds. Relax and let the blade become a part of you."

Her quick eyes turned to me. "Now, you. Show me what you got."

She darted towards me, and I blocked her blow for blow. Barely. "You are stronger than you used to be," she said, her sharp gaze lingering on my elongated ears and the other subtle changes in my body. "But it is clear that you do not trust your instincts. Or the blade in your hand."

I took up another blade, testing its weight and balance, but something still felt off. I tried another and then another. "I guess I don't trust any of these."

"A poor warrior blames her weapons," Dyani said, her stare as unyielding as the metal in her hand.

"Yeah, yeah. What does it take to get a compliment around here?"

We continued training under her watchful eyes, but despite everyone's focus, a part of me couldn't help but think that our efforts might be in vain. All these weapons were useless against the Voro-Kai. Yet doing nothing wasn't an option either. We had to prepare, even if the odds were impossible to beat.

I pushed the useless thoughts aside and continued to work on my drills, incorporating the Five Phases of the Moon. I tried to make my movements precise and fluid as Dyani and Madds focused on disarming techniques.

Dyani flicked the blade out of Maddock's hand, and he froze, eyes wide as he stood dumbfounded.

"Do not stop. Think quickly. On the battlefield, if your weapon gets knocked out of your hand, your enemy will not stop to wait for you," she ground out, gesturing for him to do something. Anything.

Maddock's eyes slowly sharpened with understanding. He frantically glanced around and picked up the nearest rock, lifting it as if it were a sword.

"Good," Dyani said. "Use whatever you can as a weapon."

Something about how Maddock held the rock made me remember, like a wish granted by a shooting star.

I grinned.

There might be hope for us yet.

28

"The shooting star we saw crash to the earth in silver flames. It might contain a metal we can use against the Voro-Kai," I said to Rowen, Maddock, and Dyani after practice. "It's already infused with Light. Or at least it was."

I couldn't believe I'd forgotten about the meteor that had nearly crushed me to death.

Dyani's eyes widened. "That sounds like an Ever-burn star. My mother used to tell Demil and me about them when we were younglings. She said she had only ever seen one in her lifetime."

"What's an Ever-burn star?" Madds and I asked in unison, exchanging an unamused stare.

"Ever-burns are extremely rare," Dyani began, her voice taking on a reverent tone as she shared her mother's memories. "When they fall to the earth, they do not diminish or die. They burn forever—a bright light that never fades."

"That sounds exactly like what we need," I said, hope flaring within my chest. "But this one slowly flickered out. You've never heard of that happening?"

Dyani's sharp eyes flared with concern. "No. That should not happen. Ever-burns are supposed to be eternal."

"Let's get Nepta's opinion," Rowen said, his hand on the small of my back. "She might have come across something like this before."

Dyani nodded in agreement. "Nepta's knowledge is vast. If there is an explanation, she'll find it."

I took a deep breath, trying to calm my whirl of emotions. I knew it was a long shot, but maybe, just maybe, this meteor was the solution we were so desperately seeking.

As we walked the short distance to the crater, Nepta followed, her slender knuckles curled around her crescent moon staff. She'd forgone wearing her quartz headdress, leaving her fine, silver hair in a low, elegant bun.

Two master bladesmiths accompanied us, their faces eager yet curious, ready to examine the fallen star.

Nepta's steps were slow and measured, but her presence was commanding as if the very earth responded to her authority. I'd witnessed the Elven-head create a portal and had even traveled through it after the Battle of the Crypts. Yet now, she walked beside us, her movements deliberate.

"Why didn't you create a portal to the crater?" I asked, hoping it wasn't a foolish question. The scope of her powers interested me, especially since they were so different from mine.

"I can only travel to places I know, or that I can feel a direct path to," she said, her wise, rheumy gaze turning to me. "This crater? I have never been there, so I cannot simply arrive there. I must have a connection to a place. Unlike you, I cannot appear out of thin air."

"That makes sense," I replied with a small laugh. I admired how knowledgeable she was regarding her abilities, but I also felt a twinge of envy. Every day, I learned something new about mine.

Nepta smiled softly. "I didn't learn it all overnight," she said as if she sensed where my mind had gone. We brought up the rear of our party, her staff tapping rhythmically against the ground. Ahead, Rowen led the way, followed by Maddock and the bladesmiths. "Many believe energy to be limitless, but that is far from the truth. It is reciprocal with rules and limitations. It is not always about the power one has, but how one wields it. There is always an exchange."

"Where does it come from?"

"It should come from your own inner well of energy. If you do not have enough, you can always ask the earth or spirits to aid you. Anyone can tap into this power, but it must be used with reverence. Elves have always had a deep understanding of the earth, but there are those who do not understand it is a give-and-take relationship."

Her connection with the earth and heavens was intrinsic and powerful. Unlike Erovos, she didn't steal energy for her own gain but asked for it reverently. "Have the spirits ever said no?"

"Sometimes I ask, and the spirits say no. When they do, I must respect their decision. Those like Erovos, Caeryn, and Aliphoura disregard this sacred connection, taking by force and any means necessary. Look at the devastation that follows when they do," she said, her free arm sweeping over the dead and barren forest we now walked through.

I nodded, recalling my own experience. "When I summoned the water, I didn't understand that even if you ask, and the spirits agree, they can give you more than what you asked for."

"Ah, yes," she replied, quiet approval lighting her face. "The balance can easily tip the other way. You are gaining insight every day. And I thank you for risking your life to bring water back to my village."

Her words stayed with me as we continued to the crater. Even though I was certain her abilities could rival those of Erovos, there were boundaries she would not cross. Knowing when to hold back and when to honor the energy around you was a power in itself.

The pale-yellow sun had lowered in the sky when we finally reached the crater. It was even bigger than I remembered, especially in the daylight. The sheer impact left me awestruck.

"This stone called to you?" Nepta asked, her gaze piercing as we stared down the crater's edge. Though its silvery glow had flickered out, the meteor seemed to hum with energy.

"It felt . . . like a part of me, as if it knew I was here," I replied, feeling the weight of her question.

"And almost killed us in the process," Maddock said with tension in his jaw.

"Dyani said it sounded like an Ever-burn star, but it was only aglow for a few minutes," I added. "Have you ever heard of that?"

Nepta's eyes closed, her senses focusing intently on the stone. "Ever-burns do not simply fall to the earth by accident. They have a reason for appearing. They are meant to be eternal. That it has flickered out is yet another bad omen. It could be the same corruption that drains life from our world."

The bladesmiths exchanged glances, their interest piqued. Bailon, the older and more experienced of the two, said, "We will take a sample to be sure."

Nepta nodded, and the two elves carefully descended into the crater. From our vantage point, we watched them navigate the rocky terrain, eventually reaching the black-and-silver rock that towered over them.

They ran their experienced hands over the smooth surface of the stone, testing its texture, murmuring to each other as they worked.

The sound of metal striking metal echoed up the crater walls. With precision and tools, they carefully chiseled off a fragment of the Ever-burn star. Leer, the younger elve with short, brown hair and boyish charm, helped Bailon wrap a piece of the star in a protective cloth. We all waited with bated breath as they made their way back up.

"It appears to have all the right qualities for a good blade," Bailon said, carrying the wrapped star fragment under one of his well-muscled arms.

"I've never seen anything like it," remarked Leer, his face filled with awe.

"If it forges as well as it looks, we might have a chance of making many weapons in a short amount of time," Bailon said, his exceptionally thick brows shooting up in excitement. "I have worked with countless materials, but none such as this."

"Do you think it will work?" I asked the older smith.

Bailon's deep-set eyes mirrored my cautious hope. "It is hard to say."

"Can you have a few pieces ready by tomorrow?" Rowen asked, standing beside me, his eyes locking with mine as the strong column of his throat bobbed. "There is no way to know if these blades will work unless we find the escaped Voro-Kai."

Leer's youthful face hardened with determination, and a spark of purpose lit his hazel eyes. "We will work through the night. One of the missing warriors is my friend. I would like to see him found and put to rest."

My gut lurched at his words. Not even our war captain and two seasoned warriors had been able to defeat a single Voro-Kai. And now we faced the brutal task of potentially searching for three. The thought of hunting down the demon sent terror and panic through my very soul, but he was right. We needed to know if this metal could stand against the Voro-Kai.

"We have much to do," Nepta said, swirling the top of her

crescent moon staff before her. A circle of shimmering light appeared, revealing the familiar sight of the Wyn village on the other side. "When I know the destination, I can get us there faster." Her sharp eyes shot to mine, and I could have sworn she winked at me. "Space is but a cloth. Once folded, the two destinations meet, making from here to there mere touch points."

I stepped through her portal, feeling the borrowed energy shift around me. The earth had accepted Nepta's request, and in one step, I traveled across hours of land. I emerged on the other side, marveling at how my and Nepta's abilities differed.

As the smiths left to begin their work, the suffocating weight of terror eased, just a little. In its place, a sliver of hope settled in.

Rowen's broad hand landed on my shoulder. "We need rest. We have a long day ahead of us tomorrow."

"Am I—" Maddock said, but Rowen cut him off with a knowing look.

"Yes. You're coming," my soul flame said, his voice steady. "You carry Keira's Light. We may need your help more than we'd like to admit."

"Let's hope this Ever-burn thingy is what you've all been searching for," Maddock said, grinning as he gave Rowen a pat on the shoulder.

I nodded in agreement, unable to say a word. The enormity of our situation pressed down on me and stole my breath.

If the meteorite proved successful, the real work had yet to begin.

— ·⟨·☾·●·☽·⟩· —

I spent the next day in the Hymma, searching tirelessly for any sign of the desert elves or the symbol on Rayal's necklace. I passed through doorway after doorway within the maze of my mind but found nothing.

Mentally exhausted, I left the Hymma and dressed.

A sense of failure coated my skin like crackling mud. It irritated and chafed. But no matter how hard I tried to find our salvation, I came up empty-handed. It was as if there were a barrier keeping me from finding Rayal.

I needed a few minutes to gather myself before returning to the village.

The mirrored walls of the Hymma reflected my face, and I traced the changes in my appearance. I began at my pointed ears, bejeweled with shimmering studs, and then the freckles of light scattered across my nose like constellations. Finally, I gazed into my irises, the Alcreon Light brimming in my eyes with the energy of the stars.

What ancient knowledge and long-forgotten secrets had yet to emerge from the nooks and crannies of my mind? The answers I sought seemed so close yet so far away.

A frown tugged at my lips. We were running out of time.

Suddenly, Rowen appeared in the reflection, his towering frame striding toward me. The night mist whirled around him, reminiscent of the times I had astral-projected to him in my sleep, thinking him no more than a hallucination.

My full attention turned from my reflection to the man whose presence washed over me like a spring rain.

Usually, his strong arms swung freely by his side, but tonight, he kept one hand hidden behind his back.

"Is it my turn to ask what you're hiding behind your back?" I asked, remembering when I'd hidden my woven basket from him, tucking it behind me so he wouldn't see my jumbled creation.

Rowen chuckled, the sound rippling over me in healing vibrations. "Go on. Ask me."

I squared my shoulders and steeled my face, doing my best Rowen impression. "Show me," I said, lowering my voice to what

I hoped sounded like a velvet threat. "Or I'll make you show me."

The devilish grin that spread across his face made me break character, and a wry smile pulled at my lips. "As you wish," he said, flourishing his arm out from behind him.

A gasp escaped my lips.

He held a stunning weapon, unlike anything I had ever seen. The metal looked like it had been forged from the night sky.

Rowen bowed as he presented the sword to me with both hands.

My grip settled perfectly around the hilt, between a diamond-shaped pommel and an intricately flared crossguard. The blade itself tapered into a long, deadly point.

Wide-eyed, I drew the weapon before me. It was elegant, threatening, and felt like an empty chalice begging to be filled.

I sent a pulse of Light through the metal, and the sword came to life in my hand. The meteorite glowed brilliantly, casting rings of light around my wrist and forearm, humming with simmering energy.

We waited with bated breath, hoping the Light would hold. And it did.

"It's breathtaking," I whispered, watching the blade gleam like liquid starlight. "It's like it was made for me."

"That's because it was," Rowen said, his green eyes rimmed with silver. He pulled out a piece of parchment from his pocket, unfolding it to reveal a sketch of the blade in my hand. "I designed it just for you, taking your height, weight, stature, and fighting style into account. It's not too heavy or bulky so you can remain light on your feet."

I beheld the sketch in awe. It was identical to the weapon I held in my hand.

I'd chosen blades that were too big for me in the past, and

Rowen ensured I would never make that mistake again. "It's perfect. How did you even—"

"I've been working on the design for a while. Ever since I saw you fight the Voro-Kai weaponless. When I realized you held no blade, my whole life flashed before my eyes. It was the most horrifying thing I've ever witnessed. I showed the design to Bailon and asked if he could forge it for you. He agreed and did a masterful job. See how it's perfectly balanced; the pommel providing the exact counterweight," Rowen explained, his voice growing with excitement. "It will give you more control. And these two prongs act as hand guards."

"It's spectacular," I said as tears welled in my eyes. The blade felt as sturdy as the trees yet as swift as a shooting star.

Rowen had poured so much love and effort into designing my weapon. He must have spent countless hours constructing the perfect blade for me, tailoring it to my every need. He had given me a blade before; one I had loved but lost during the Battle of the Crypts. "The old blade you gave me, it would zing in my hand. Just like this."

"I didn't know it then, but your old blade must have had fragments of Ever-burn in it. Though nowhere near the amount this blade contains," Rowen said, eyeing the weapon he'd designed with pride. "See how it's infinitely light yet looks heavy? This is no ordinary metal."

He was right. It was a piece of an Ever-burn star, flowing with Alcreon Light. But more than that, it was designed by him. In a way, his hand would see me through every battle.

"It will be fierce to behold you wielding this weapon, Keira. It is uniquely yours."

I lifted my new blade, marveling at the craftsmanship. Even though it was made with haste, it was flawless. The bladesmiths were truly masters of their craft. It fit like an extension of my arm.

I ran my fingers over the cool metal, noticing a mark etched into the alloy. It was a small, delicate symbol with interweaving loops that seemed to have no beginning or end.

"What does this mean?" I asked, tracing my finger over the mark.

"It is the symbol of resilience. It is one of the first things I learned about you. I thought it only fitting that such a mark lay on your weapon. A desired quality for the mettle of your heart and the metal of your blade."

My heart nearly burst out of my chest. Rowen didn't just know me; he truly saw me, every facet of my being, no matter how bright or shadowed. I had never felt more seen. What Rowen had designed for me was nothing short of magnificent.

"What would you like to name it?" he asked, interest sparking his eyes.

My mind immediately thought of my favorite galaxy. I'd spent hours gazing at it, not only as a faint smudge in the sky, but also in greater detail through my telescope. It was easy to find once you located the Andromeda constellation. "One of my favorite lights in the sky. M31."

"Did you say Mithrion?" he asked, raising a questioning eyebrow.

I couldn't help but laugh. "Close enough," I said, arcing my new blade through the air, watching trails of Light ripple around me. "Mithrion."

A proud smile beamed from Rowen's face. "It is fitting."

I stepped into his aura, which was thick, heady, and welcoming. "I love it. Thank you," I whispered, rising up on my tiptoes to kiss him. He groaned softly as I ran my tongue along the seam of his lips. "And I love you."

His hands gripped my hips and tugged me closer, his touch searing. "If I said I love you, too, it would be a lie."

I tried to pull back, but his grip on my waist kept me caged in his embrace. I raised Mithrion to his throat, waiting for an explanation.

"It would be a lie because what I feel for you runs far deeper than love," he said, his voice as steady as his pulse beneath my blade. "You're the first star that appears in my night sky, and the first ray of dawn in the morning. You're the flame that withstands the rain, and the lightning that brightens my storms." His voice dipped into a lower tone. "You are the light that guided me out of my darkness."

My heart skipped a beat. "If I'm the light, what does that make you?" I asked, lowering Mithrion from his throat.

"I am your ground. Your earth. Your safe place to land, to breathe. To be."

"My rock," I said, wrapping my hands behind his neck.

"Yes, now let's see what you can do with that blade of yours," he said, a spark of excitement flashing in his eyes.

A thrill coursed through me as I worked on the Phases of the Moon. Mithrion's added weight felt inherent and needed, especially now that I could integrate her into the movements. My steps were precise and fluid, each strike flowing seamlessly into the next as Mithrion and I became one.

Dyani insisted that poor form couldn't be blamed on a weapon but having one tailored to my every need definitely helped. I moved through the phases, correcting and adjusting each stance as I went. Auras of white light reflected up my arm as I swiped and parried, casting elliptical rings that pulsed around me.

The next move was a challenge. My feet normally got twisted up when transitioning from the spin into the downward slash, but determination flared in my veins. I built up the momentum as I concentrated on the footwork. I whirled around in a fierce and powerful spin, using all my strength to slash the weapon down.

Suddenly, a clash of metal rang through the night as a shockwave reverberated up my arm.

Something had caught my blade.

I glanced up, meeting Rowen's eyes over our locked weapons. "Remember when I said you didn't have a predilection for combat?" he asked with a crooked smirk, his white teeth shining in the darkness.

Without missing a beat, I swung my blade out and around, freeing my weapon to strike again. "I do," I replied, exhilarated by his impromptu cut-in.

He parried. "I was wrong," he said, the moon casting pools of light on the sharp angles of his cheeks. "You look fierce. Absolutely remarkable."

"Thanks," I replied, and for a moment, we were locked together again. A curl of his brown hair fell into his face, momentarily distracting me before I twisted and struck again, keeping him on the defense.

He blocked me easily, then sidestepped and lunged. "I know something that will make you look even better."

"What's that?" I asked, spinning away and blocking his strike.

"This," he said as he nicked the lace of my bodice.

My eyes opened wide in shock. "What are you doing?"

"I thought it was obvious," he said as three deft swipes landed my vest on the ground. "I'm trying to get you naked."

29

The area around the mirrored dome was dark, isolated, and surrounded by trees, offering privacy to those who participated in the Hymma.

I smirked and slashed Mithrion through the air, cutting open Rowen's shirt. The fabric billowed open to reveal his chest and the defined lines of his abdomen.

A wicked grin lit up his face, the moon highlighting his roguish beauty. My momentary distraction left him room to parry, and in one skillful motion that I couldn't deflect, he cut open my undershirt. My breath hitched as the tip of his blade whispered over my skin, exposing a strip of flesh down to my navel.

I rotated away from him to get his sleeve, but he flicked his blade up and caught hold of my shirt, stripping it off me as I spun. I swirled back on him, facing him naked from the waist up. Cool air met my flushed skin and pebbled my nipples.

"So glorious," he hummed, his eyes dancing across my breasts. "Such pretty pink nipples that beg to be sucked."

It was my turn to seize his distraction. I flicked my knife forward and cut off one of his sleeves. I felt a moment of pride before I looked down and realized he had already sliced open the panels of my pants.

"Hey!" I exclaimed, annoyed that he was beating me. I thrust my blade at him again, but his ax caught on the prong of my crossguard. He spun me around and slammed my back against his chest, our weapons locked above us. His chest heaved behind me as his erection dug into my back.

Before I could counter, his free hand dove into the waistband of my pants, and I jolted as his finger tapped my clit through my underwear. He tapped me again, then pressed, and a needy sound escaped my mouth as he circled my bundle of nerves.

He chuckled as I moaned and rested my head against his shoulder.

His finger inched aside the fabric of my panties, feeling just how damp and aroused I was. "Always so wet for me," he hummed in approval, his breath skirting along the curve of my neck.

I cried out as he drove two fingers inside of me.

My breasts turned heavy, and tension tightened in my core. "Look at yourself in the mirror. See how you writhe on my fingers?"

My eyes flitted up, and the image of our tangled bodies reflected on the Hymma walls. Rowen was behind me, holding me in place as he pumped his fingers inside me. My face was flushed, my body breathless and needy.

He was right. I was writhing.

Both of our gazes were fixated on our reflection as he pumped harder and faster. Tension built in my core, and I moaned uncontrollably.

"Watch as I make you come," he whispered in my ear just as a violent spasm rocked my body.

His touch was deliberate, unforgiving, and extracting every ounce of my pleasure as I came on his hand.

He laughed. "My, how easily you let me win when my fingers are deep inside of you."

I blinked my half-lidded eyes. Oh. That's right. We were in the middle of sparring; my blade was still in my hand.

I wanted to claim victory, especially because it was Mithrion's first fight.

"Who said I let you win?" I replied, kicking back and hitting him in the shin. He grunted and released me, his hand sliding out of my pants.

I spun around, and we collided like two celestial bodies.

Slowly, we finished stripping each other naked, and in the end, it was hard to say who won.

·(·☽·●·☾·)·

"It is one of the lithest materials I have ever worked with," Bailon said the next morning with enthusiasm, heat radiating from the forge. The building was a breathtaking blend of nature and elven craftsmanship. Tools and anvils with intricate designs lined the hearths and fire pits. Even though the space was open, the smell of metal, fire, and sweat filled the air. "It appears to be a type of crystal. Easy to manipulate yet strong and balanced. It is quite remarkable."

"And there's this," I said, brandishing Mithrion. The room fell into quiet astonishment as the bladesmiths realized the crystal could hold Light. The room collectively gasped, gazing wide-eyed as the blade cast an ethereal glow upon their faces.

"It is an Ever-burn star! It just needed a little help," Leer said with awe as the Light held strong, thrumming with a celestial pulse.

"It must have been sent from the Elder Spirits," Bailon added, wiping the sweat from his brow after a long day at the forge. "For the Synodic Son."

His eyes immediately shot to mine, his face reddening in embarrassment. "Oh, forgive me, my lady. You are no son." His eyes flickered over me. "But are you The Marked?"

"Master!" Leer exclaimed in horror. "That question is most inappropriate."

"It's all right," I assured him, showing the silver scar tattoos on my arms. "I have these. Though I'm not sure if that qualifies me as The Marked."

"That's a good enough sign for me," Bailon replied, grinning as he proudly pulled out a few more blades, each shining like the depths of a black sea.

Just as I took another weapon and pulsed the Alcreon Light through it, Maddock entered the forge.

"Very cool," he said, the Alcreon Light glistening on his face.

"Try one," I said, passing him a blade. A sparkle ignited in Madds' eyes, as if asking for his help truly moved him.

His large hand wrapped around the hilt, and with a small blast of Light, the weapon came to life in his grip.

We grinned, then Maddock and I each ignited one more blade with the celestial brilliance.

"Now, we need to test them," Rowen said, his voice solemn.

Five weapons had been forged overnight—a feat from the master bladesmiths. Each one was placed on the table, except for the one strapped to my thigh, their edges gleaming with an ethereal glow. Rowen took the largest.

Bailon placed the sample rock on the table and said, "Even a little goes a long way. The metal flattens out nicely. We can make a few more while you are away."

Maddock quickly charged the stagnant rock with Light. "Here you go," he said, looking pleased that he had been able to help again.

Rowen glanced between Bailon and Leer. "Thank you," he

said, the Light shining in his emerald eyes. "These are magnificent. A true testament to your skill."

"They are amazing," I agreed, though mine was my favorite.

"The Alcreon Light certainly adds a celestial flare," Leer said, offering me an approving nod.

Maddock inspected the newly forged weapons on the table and grabbed the one that spoke to him. "There are two left. I know one is for Dyani, but who else will be joining us on this perilous quest?

"We told Dyani to pick the fifth," I said, trusting her explicitly.

"Now that you know your warriors, please find Enrin and end his suffering," Leer urged, his voice heavy with emotion, and I briefly wondered if they were more than friends. "I would like to know his blue eyes have closed in peace."

Rowen gripped Leer's shoulder, a firm promise in his gaze. "We will. I promise we will."

——— ·(·☾·●·☽·)· ———

Rowen, Dyani, Maddock, and I prepared for our mission in the weapon storeroom. The space was filled with gleaming blades, piles of fighting leathers, and various combat accessories. Rowen grabbed some extra rope, supplies, and bandages and stuffed them into his rucksack. We slowly built the armor over our arms and chests.

We were all quiet, focusing on the mission ahead.

As Rowen slipped a fighting leather through my arm, he glanced at Dyani. "Who did you ask to be our fifth?"

Dyani flipped her ponytail off her shoulder. "Minroe."

"The little one you spar with?" he asked, tightening the strap on my shoulder.

She huffed, straightening the silver bands on her arms. "Don't let her hear you say that. She's more vicious than I am."

"She's late," Rowen said, unamused, as his hands roved over my body, adjusting my straps with deft precision.

"She'll be here."

Rowen tightened my thigh strap and slipped my newly forged blade into the holster, ensuring it was secure. "I haven't seen you spar with her in a while. Everything all right between you two?"

Dyani rolled her eyes. "All you need to know is that I trust her with my life. She may be small, but she's absolutely lethal."

Rowen started to check and tighten my leathers again, but I stopped him, placing my hand over his. "They're good, Rowen. Any tighter, and I won't be able to breathe."

He paused, catching himself, and flashed me a grin. "Apologies, my flame. You look incredible."

I couldn't help but smile back, helping to ease the tension. "I feel like a badass," I said, patting the illuminated star blade at my thigh.

Rowen's gaze trailed up my body with heat, admiration, and pride. "You are a badass."

A clattering sound echoed from the corner of the room, drawing our attention. "Hey, am I wearing these right?" Maddock asked, turning around and looking like a jumbled mess of straps.

A silent beat lingered in the air. "No," we all said in unison before laughter filled the room.

I'd given Madds a hard time in the past, and rightfully so, but I had to admit, I was glad he was here to help ease the tension.

All three of us helped Madds fix his leathers when the door suddenly slammed open. All our gazes shot to Minroe, standing in the threshold, fully dressed and ready for battle.

If she found it strange that all our hands were on her former prisoner, she didn't mention it.

The last time I'd seen her, she let me pass unlawfully to visit Maddock. We'd essentially committed a crime together, but now, striding toward the center of the room, she acted as if that never happened. She picked up the last remaining blade and inspected it with an appreciating nod. She shoved it into her holster and said, "Let's get this over with."

Minroe barely looked at Dyani, offering only the briefest nod. Dyani returned an equally awkward chin dip, and I shot her a questioning stare. Every time I had seen them together, Dyani's face would light up with joy. Now, it was withdrawn, forming an emotion that, if I hadn't been watching so closely, I might have missed—heartbreak.

"Thank you for coming," Dyani said, twisting and securing a tendril of hair behind her pointed ear.

Minroe's slight features worked so well with her pixie cut, and her light green eyes pierced through thick lines of kohl. "Don't act like I wouldn't do this for you or the missing soldiers," she said, her voice and stare even sharper than Dyani's. "Just because we didn't work out . . . romantically doesn't mean I don't care about you. Someone has to have your back."

Rowen cleared his throat. "Let's be on our way, then, shall we?"

━━━ ·(·C· ● ·)·)· ━━━

"Alvar has been tracking the Voro-Kai's movements," Dyani said, her new silver blade shining at her hip. "He reported three demons traveling in a pack near Eldemar River."

We traveled the dark path, each carrying our Ever-burn blades. As we neared the river, Rowen and Minroe inspected the ground, searching for tracks.

"What happened to you two?" I asked Dyani in a quiet whisper.

"You think we're friends now?" Dyani asked, resting against a tree.

She wanted the question to sting, but it was clearly hiding a deeper pain. I knew the art of deflecting all too well. "You know you want to be."

Dyani sighed and pushed off the tree. "She wanted me to train less. She said I was devoting too much time to the sword. She needed more of my attention, more of me, but training was the only thing that helped me forget the pain of losing my brother, or at least lessened it. I couldn't give her what she asked for."

The suffering in her voice mirrored Rowen's when he told me how the two of them would spar all day. They would drive each other to the brink of exhaustion, nearly killing each other to keep from thinking of what they'd lost.

"You were grieving," I said, glancing at Rowen wading through the dense underbrush. His hawk-like eyes were precise and sharp as he searched for the demon's trail. I was beyond grateful Rowen had never given up on me, never pressured me, or given me ultimatums. I felt the tug on my chest—a bond so powerful it echoed across the stars. "That was a lot to ask."

A twitch pulled at her thin lips. "Maybe so, but we all can't have a soul flame like you," she said, watching me watch my soul flame.

My eyes darted back to the warrior. "Why not?"

"Not all of us are destined for such a love. Some of us have to battle the world alone. Even if we think we have someone, they eventually let us down or abandon us. Unlike you and Rowen, your bond directly reflects the first soul flames: Donis and Althea. No matter how far apart you are, you'll always find a way back to each other. Like the sea and the sky."

"You deserve it, Dyani. Everyone does," I said with my whole chest. I had once believed I was incapable of love, that I couldn't give what others asked of me. "When it's real, they won't have to ask. You'll give it willingly."

She offered a small, sad smile, but it was the realest, most genuine smile she had ever given me.

Before I could reply, Rowen's voice cut through the trees. "We found a trail," he said, standing up from his crouch. His eyes met mine, and our connecting flames offered me a spark of warmth. Then, my eyes immediately darted to Maddock, and I felt the tear in the bond. Madds' eyes were already on me, and he flashed me a smile, but I glanced away, hating that my bond with Rowen was torn in the first place. And I walked past him.

We followed the trail, the sun rising higher and higher in the sky.

Finally, we approached the pack of Voro-Kai demons, rummaging through what looked like the Wyn's soldier camp.

We crouched low in the bushes. I tried to steady my breathing, but the thought of facing another astral demon made my blood curdle.

I had battled three of these creatures in my astral form and barely escaped with my life. Even from a distance, their presence sent a shiver down my spine.

The largest boar-like creature was covered in dark fur that bristled as it moved. My heart stopped as I noticed the two other Voro-Kai. Their fur was patchy and short, and filthy clothes clung to their bodies in scraps.

I gagged as a wave of nausea hit me, and I clamped my hand over my mouth. These weren't just any demons—they were the Wyn warriors who had been bitten.

Their bodies rippled with unnatural muscle from their necks and arms, and they'd grown at least three feet, causing their beautiful, one-of-a-kind clothing to hang like grotesque tapestries.

They appeared fully transformed, twisted beyond recognition. Though I hadn't known the two warriors personally, my heart sank as I tried—and failed—to find any semblance of their faces beneath the tusks, fur, and horns.

The sight was straight out of a nightmare, one that I would never forget.

We crouched low in the bush, Rowen ensuring we remained downwind. But one of the demon's eyes flickered, its nostrils flaring as it sniffed the air. Its gaze darted, and I noticed its eyes were completely black—a chilling reminder of the power Erovos used to create these astral abominations.

The Voro-Kai huffed through its boar-like snout, signaling the others to snap to attention. But the transformed warriors were *made,* not born, and I noticed their movements were more hesitant, more elven. And when their eyes darted, a flicker of humanity remained. The whites around their eyes were still visible, though they were beginning to blotch with darkness.

Was there still time to reverse the process?

"Let me try to save them," I whispered, my mouth bone-dry.

"Keira . . ." Rowen breathed, a slight hitch in his voice.

My stare remained unwavering. I refused to give in to the overwhelming odds. "There might still be a chance."

Maddock turned to me, his eyes soft yet worried. "Keira, I don't think—"

"No!" I hissed, cutting him off. "I have to try. We need to lure one away so I can attempt to save it like I did with Alvar."

Rowen's jaw clenched, his eyes darting between the demons and me. His face was etched with concern, but he knew once my mind was made up, I wouldn't back down. Finally, he gave a nod. "We'll draw one out. Be ready." Rowen pulled a rope out of his rucksack and quickly tied it to the hilt of his blade.

"We don't know if the bitten are venomous and can turn others, but we have to assume they can," I said in a calm whisper. "So remember, stay away from their teeth."

"What about you?" Maddock asked worriedly, shifting his weight to stare me in the eye. A twig snapped and echoed through the air.

I winced.

Suddenly, three sets of demon eyes shot toward where we lay hidden in the brush. One black as night, the other two still eerily elven.

A savage snarl emanated in our direction, and in a sudden heart-stopping rush, they charged upon us.

30

———

My plan to get one of the bitten alone flew right out the window. The five of us charged out of the bushes, attempting to meet the astral demons head-on.

Rowen immediately went for the largest of the three, the true Voro-Kai.

Dyani and Minroe took on the second largest, working together like a well-oiled machine. They practiced together daily, learning the intricacies of each other's fighting styles. And it showed.

My heart lurched at how close they were to the demon's talons and boar-like tusks, but Maddock and I had our own demon to worry about. Rowen and Dyani were among the fiercest warriors in Luneth; I couldn't afford to worry about them now, and they wouldn't want me to. They would want my full attention on surviving.

"Don't hurt him," I shouted at Dyani and Minroe. "There might be a chance I can save him."

The Voro-Kai slashed at Dyani's midsection, and she leaped back. "No problem," she yelled sarcastically, her eyes focused.

"Just keep him distracted," I shouted back, determination burning within me as I sprinted toward the demon with hints of blue in its eyes.

Enrin! Leer's friend.

I approached the turning warrior, my arms up in a surrendering plea. "Enrin," I shouted, trying to reach his humanity. "Do you remember who you are?"

I desperately hoped the blue eyes would snap back to life, but he lunged at me with a deadly swipe.

"*Find,*" he hissed and swiped again.

My gut dropped. He had become a part of the hive mind.

I quickly unleashed my Light, trapping Enrin within my beam, but he was far stronger than the demons I had fought in the crevice. My arm trembled as I struggled to keep him steady. Suddenly, the creature's massive leg kicked back and hit Maddock square in the stomach. "Madds!" I screamed as he flew back and landed on the ground with a painful thud.

Guilt assailed me. Asking everyone to avoid killing the demons put us all in danger of being hurt—or worse, bitten. I needed to hurry. I only had a moment to see Maddock trying to get back on his feet. "Don't let him go," he wheezed.

My gaze shot back to Enrin. He was pinned within my beam of Light, but I would have to touch him if I were going to heal him. My hand passed through my shimmering Light with ease, and my fingers wrapped around the fur-covered wrist of the Wyn warrior.

"*Ours. Ours. Ours.*"

I closed my eyes and searched for Enrin's thread of life—any remnants of who he had been before, but despair rammed against me like a brick wall. It had been easy to find with Alvar, but now, the transformation was too far along.

I waded through the thick, black poison, but there was no

blight to cleanse. The venom ran deeper into the blood, bone, and skin. It was fully integrated into the host.

My stomach dropped through the earth as I realized there was nothing left to separate, nothing left to save. Enrin was gone.

We were too late.

A grunt from Rowen snapped my attention back to the battle. He masterfully evaded each strike of the demon's claws as he grabbed the rope tied to his blade.

At first, I was confused, but I realized he had transformed the blade into a whip-like weapon capable of slicing from a distance.

He brandished the makeshift weapon with ease as he spun the rope in a wheel and hurled the blade through the air. The edge cut the demon's hide as black blood oozed from its shoulder. Rowen pulled his arm back, and the star-blade returned to him. He spun around, looping the rope around his middle to regain control of the line before sending it flying back to the demon.

The Voro-Kai screeched in pain as Rowen lanced it again. Its ear-splitting wail caused the other two demons to rear in panic.

My eyes flew back to the demon I was holding. It thrashed and snapped its maws at me savagely. Tears streamed down my face as I realized there was nothing I could do. We were too late for these brave warriors who had risked their lives, their souls. Everything. There was no recovery for them, only mercy.

"It's too late," I cried out, despair engulfing me. The least I could do was make sure they found peace. Rowen had taught me how to strike vital organs, a lesson that would guide me as I made Enrin's death as swift as possible.

I thrust my star blade upward, slipping it between the demon's ribs, angling it toward the heart, or what was left of it.

The demon let out a gargled breath, stilled, and then collapsed to the ground.

I only had a moment to register that the Ever-burn blade had worked, that it was a viable weapon against the Voro-Kai. When suddenly, the once-brave warrior erupted into specks of light.

I could only hope the shimmering fragments made their way back to the heavens, where Enrin truly belonged.

The other two Voro-Kai, having witnessed the destruction of its own, erupted into a lethal frenzy. And the larger one cracked Rowen upside the head.

Bile rose up my throat and choked me as the demon grabbed my soul flame's head and wrenched it to the side.

The beast bared its fangs and lowered them to Rowen's neck.

—— ·(·☾·●·☽·)· ——

Terror engulfed me as ropes of inky drool dripped onto Rowen's shoulder.

"Over here!" I screamed.

Its head snapped up. "*Ours,*" it hissed, recognizing me instantly. Erovos had fed it images of my face since its inception. I knew it wanted me.

The demon dropped Rowen and stalked towards me.

I raised my hand to unleash a beam of Light, but someone beat me to it. Maddock had returned to his feet. He was hunched over in pain with his arm outstretched, but he hadn't hit the beast, only angered it, and the Voro-Kai turned its attention to Madds.

I traveled to the other side of the clearing. "Hey! Over here!" I shouted again, waving my arms.

The demon's nostrils flared, its eyes darting for me. It thrashed its head in confusion and wailed.

I traveled to another side of the clearing and called out again, wanting to disorient the beast. I stepped back, about to hit it with my Light, when my foot collapsed through a rotten log. I cried out as wood spliced through my calf.

The demon's eyes locked on mine as it bounded toward me.

I tried to travel, but the pain kept me rooted in place, and I couldn't pull my foot from the log, the splinters were in too deep. A wetness trickled down my ankle and the beast's nostrils flared at the scent of my blood, its eyes going wild.

"Keira, watch out!" Rowen roared and threw his whip-like blade in a straight, smooth motion. The blade lodged in the Voro-Kai's shoulder, and the demon bellowed. With its free hand, it grabbed the rope and pulled with unimaginable force, sending Rowen hurtling through the air.

"Rowen," I screamed as he was flung from my line of sight.

"Keira, run!" Maddock pleaded through the chaos.

"I'm stuck!" I shouted, desperately trying to pry my foot free, but the more I pulled, the more the jagged wood cut into my skin. Even if I could run, I would never leave them to face the Voro-Kai alone. I'd spent my whole life running, but here, I would stand my ground and fight beside the bravest warriors I'd ever known.

Dyani and Minroe still fought their demon. Minroe, small and nimble as she was, ran and dropped to her knees. She slid between the Voro-Kai's legs, winding the rope through its ankles. When she emerged from the other side, she threw the rope to her sparring partner. Dyani caught it and ran around the creature in the opposite direction, tangling its legs. And with a swift tug, the beast toppled to the ground.

The bitten roared in frustration as it scented my blood, too, its eyes snapping to mine. Its guttural snarls sent bolts of fear up my spine as it dragged its massive body toward me inch by inch.

"The heart!" I yelled to the former lovers. My pulse pounded in my ears as the beast writhed closer, wrenching its head and dragging itself toward me despite its wounds. Its eyes locked on me, black, hungry, and primordial.

Dyani cartwheeled over the tied demon to straddle it and plunged her Ever-burn blade into its heart. Silver motes engulfed her as I whipped around, not even able to wipe the tears from my eyes. There was still one more demon to face.

I gripped Mithrion tighter.

The beast swarmed my vision as it stood to its full height, baring its razor-sharp teeth. I raised my star-blade, but before I could strike, Rowen's rope snapped around its neck. He pulled back, stopping the beast mere inches from my face.

"*Take.*"

Minroe darted low to the ground, slamming her blade into its foot as Dyani grabbed hold of its arm, straining to pull it back from me. It took all three of Luneth's fiercest warriors to hold the Voro-Kai at bay.

"Do it, Keira," Rowen grunted, his body straining as he held back the demon. His muscles flexed and glistened with sweat as his heels dug into the ground.

My face reflected in its pitch-black eyes. I was close enough that, for a chilling moment, I could see Erovos watching me through the creature's eyes.

"You're looking well, little light," the creature warbled in a disturbing mix of speech and growls. "So well that I can practically taste you. It's making my mouth water."

Revulsion twisted my face. "We're ready for you, you sick fuck," I seethed, channeling my rage as I gripped my blade tighter. Mithrion glowed and surged with Light, growing brighter as if in direct response to the darkness before me.

The beast's black eyes dipped to my blade, and my grip tightened on the hilt. The swirl of first-light extended and glowed up my arm in refracting halos. "You may have pretty weapons, but you have nowhere near the numbers to defeat my brood."

Before Erovos could utter another word through his shadow beast, I plunged Mithrion deep into its chest. The beast erupted into black motes that whirled around me as a high-pitched shriek punctured my eardrums and drilled into my skull.

31

Rowen darted to me and pried the wood from my ankle. He gently lowered me to the ground, his eyes trailing over my body. His rough palms cupped my face as he checked my eyes. "Just your leg, my flame?"

I bit back the pain and nodded, glancing at the blood seeping through my leggings.

Rowen carefully folded up my pant leg, and I sucked in a breath through my teeth. His fingers trailed down my calf and ankle, gently examining my injury. There were three nasty puncture wounds and countless scratches. He pulled a tin of noxlily salve from his rucksack and applied the medicine over my mangled skin.

My wounds mended before my very eyes as the shimmering ointment worked its magic.

Rowen passed the tin around, and I glanced at the exhausted warriors. Dyani and Minroe appeared banged up and bruised while Maddock clutched his side.

"Madds?" I asked, hoping he wasn't hurt.

"One kick, and I was down for the count. I felt worthless," Madds gasped, holding his side. "That thing only seemed to care about Keira."

"That was your first battle. You'll get better," Rowen assured as he lowered my pant leg and helped me stand. "But Takoda needs to look at you."

"I'm fine. I just had the wind knocked out of me," he said, waving off his injury.

Dyani's chest heaved as she shot us all a worried look. "It took all of us to defeat that . . . thing."

"The odds are not good," Minroe chimed in. "How many more will escape before we can stop them?" she asked, her dark kohl smudged around her eyes.

"At least we learned how to defeat them. You have to pierce them through the heart. The bitten return to the heavens, where they can hopefully find peace. While the Voro-Kai disintegrates into dust and smoke."

"Thank the spirits, the star-blades work. Now we just need a thousand more," Dyani said, wiping the blood from her weapon.

She was right. "I need to go to the meteor and infuse it with Light. The production of weapons needs to start as soon as possible," I said, testing the weight on my leg.

"Are you good, Madds?" Rowen asked, all our chests heaving.

"I think so," he grunted, standing upright and offering me a wink.

"Good. Keira, take Maddock with you."

"You take Maddock," I countered.

"Are you fighting over who gets to keep me?" Maddock said excitedly, a grin spreading across his face. "It's just like my childhood."

"Please," Rowen said, his eyes softening as his broad hands gripped my shoulders. "You will need to infuse the Ever-burn with your Light. That is no small task. Let Madds help you."

I nodded. "Fine. I'll keep him, but please be safe."

"I will," he promised.

I didn't want to leave Rowen, especially after such a vicious battle, but reality was setting in like a chill in my lungs. It was a half-day's journey back to the village on foot. If Maddock and I astral traveled, we could save precious time.

"I'll see you tonight," I promised, knowing it was the smartest decision.

Rowen stepped toward me and pulled me in for a kiss. I tasted the sweat and blood upon his face, a reminder of how close we'd come to losing each other today. I wished I could revel in his kiss forever, vanish in the plume of his scent, but time was of the essence. "I hate to leave you," I murmured against his lips, and as I pulled back, I noticed Rowen's hands were rubbed raw from the rope, and his knuckles and wrists were marred with lesions and blood. "You're hurt."

"It is nothing. I will take care of it," Rowen said before turning to Madds. "Remember, her fate is your fate,"

"Yes, I remember," Madds said with an eye roll. "Vividly."

"Please be careful," I begged again, hating the thought of splitting up, but we were out of options. I turned to Madds and grabbed his hand. "Whatever you do, don't let go. We need to travel together. I don't have time for you to get lost."

"Got it, sparky," Maddock said easily, shooting me another wink.

I glared at him.

"What?" he questioned with a shrug. "I can't very well call you *my flame.*"

"Absolutely not," I shot back.

"See? So 'sparky' is better."

I closed my eyes and tried to breathe in through my nose. "Believe me. It's not."

Rowen, who had been watching us, slid his gaze to Maddock. "Take care of her," Rowen said, holding his stare with such gravity that it sent a chill down my spine.

"You know I'm not going to let anything hurt her," he replied, matching Rowen's tone.

"I swear to the Spirits if anything happens to her . . ." he said, his words laced with warning.

My eyes widened at the severity of his voice. When I first came to live with the Wyn elves, Nepta had appointed Rowen as my bodyguard—a role he accepted and would sacrifice his life for. The trust he had in Maddock to let him take over was nothing short of a miracle.

"Nothing will happen to her," Maddock swore, never breaking eye contact with Rowen, his joking tone nowhere to be found. "You know how strong she is."

"I do," my soul flame said before his emerald eyes shot to me with gleaming intensity. "If he bothers you in any way, remember the three most sensitive kill-points I taught you."

I smirked. "I will."

Maddock squeezed my hand. His palm was warm and encompassed mine, and an odd mixture of security and guilt raced through my emotions.

I didn't want to be alone with Maddock or be nice to him. It was easier to be cruel than acknowledge he held a piece of my soul flame bond, and that my feelings for Rowen were now attached to this man who had followed me across the universe.

"Pay attention and stay close," I said, glancing at him over my shoulder. "You ready?"

He nodded, and together, our bodies became less corporal, but I could still feel his hand in mine—a grounding sensation in such an ethereal journey. And layer by layer of light, we began to astral travel.

The threads of the cosmos unfurled around us, an interwoven tapestry of light and energy.

Maddock walked through the dangling vines, his eyes wide

and reflecting the shimmering strands around us. We were on the astral plane. Together.

"So this is how you do it?" he asked in awe, his fingers hovering over the threads.

"Yeah. Don't you?"

He huffed a laugh, his angular brown eyes lit with stardust. "Not even close. I just feel where I want to go, and I go there. This is way cooler, though. Like stepping into another dimension."

I grinned, pride welling inside me, and with Maddock's hand in mine, we traveled through the stars, the world around us shifting and swirling.

I had never traveled with anyone before. The feeling was unsettling, yet the shared experience blossomed into something unspoken between us.

But what happens on the astral field stays on the astral field.

I found the thread to the crater and pulled, clutching Maddock's hand. And as slowly as disintegrating light, we traveled to the Ever-burn star.

· (· ☽ · ● · ☾ ·) ·

We appeared within the massive depression of the earth, standing at the foot of the Ever-burn star.

I dropped Madds' hand and gazed at the meteorite.

Why it had flickered out was still a mystery. I just hoped Maddock and I had enough strength to charge such a massive rock.

I placed my hands on the meteor, and Madds followed suit.

The smooth surface was cold beneath my palms, and deep within the rock, like a song muffled through the ocean, I felt the Alcreon Light. "The Light is in there," I said, excitement coursing through me. "It has just retreated."

His eyes widened. "I feel it, too."

"On the count of three," I said, looking at him over my shoulder. His gaze met mine with a steely determination, and he nodded. "One, two, three."

In perfect unison, we unleashed our Light, coaxing the retreated glow to burn bright once again. When we had tried this in the weapons room, our wills had been clashing and fighting against each other. Here and now, our Light harmonized as one, working together to infuse the Ever-burn back to her rightful glory.

Light blinded me as I poured my strength, willpower, and Light into the dormant star, rekindling what had dimmed.

Sweat dripped from my brow as we worked to awaken the Ever-burn star. "Keep pushing," I ground out, straining against the resistance. The Light had retreated deep within the meteor, and I focused on channeling everything I had to resuscitate the star. It was resisting, protecting itself from the darkness that engulfed this world. But I pushed harder, feeling a timid flicker of trust.

"*You* keep pushing," Maddock gritted through his teeth. He mirrored my effort, fierce and focused. Seeing him care so much about a plight that wasn't even his made my chest burn, urging me to dig deeper.

The stronger my resolve, the brighter it glowed, and suddenly, the meteor blazed to life, flooding the night in a radiant shower of Light.

Suddenly, everything was aglow. I could barely see, but then my eyes adjusted and I could only make out Maddock's face, smiling. I returned the smile, realizing what we had accomplished. Together.

Without warning, Madds wrapped me in a hug, tight enough for me to lose my breath. His arm slid firmly around me, one palm resting on my lower back as the other swept up my neck, his fingers tangling in my hair. For a heartbeat, I leaned in and actually let myself be held by the man I hated. I might have even hugged him back.

Feeling me give in, he squeezed tighter.

When he didn't put me down, I pulled away and cleared my throat.

Madds held my closed palm and tugged me a little closer. His breath washed over my face and hit my flushed skin like a cool cloud. I hated that my body and bond betrayed me.

"Good job," I said curtly.

"Thanks. You too."

I swayed on my feet. "I'm exhausted. I think I need a minute."

"Me too," he replied, and we sat with our backs against the glowing Ever-burn star.

"So," I said after a while with my elbows on my knees. "I know you wish you could leave, and that the bond is keeping you here, but do you miss Earth? Will you go back once . . . once we figure out how to give me my bond back?"

He rested his head against the meteor and tilted his eyes to the swirling galaxies above. "After seeing a sky like this, who could ever go back?"

"That's one thing we agree on."

He kept his gaze on the heavens. "My parents cared more about the family business than anything else. Everything we did was to maintain the perfect image. It was exhausting. And it was a lie. My whole life was mapped out before I was even born. Even my engagement was arranged."

My heart lurched.

When Maddock possessed my body, he'd glimpsed into my memories, but I had seen his too, and I remembered flashing through his revolving door of women.

"That's awful, and I know you were in pain. I felt it. But that's no excuse for how you treated her. You slept with other women," I said, revulsion creeping up my throat.

"She wasn't exactly faithful herself, and I know that's not a good excuse," he replied with a sigh. "When I was in the crevice, I was in never-ending agony, but I didn't regret. I *longed*. Now, I regret almost everything I've ever done. I died a disappointment to my friends, parents, and fiancée. I never cared about the family business as much as they did. Even when I tried—really tried—it was never enough."

A lump rose in my throat when I realized how much we had in common, how deeply our stories reflected each other's. "I know the feeling. My parents had a company with an image to protect as well. I was a stain upon that image. One they tried to scrub clean no matter how much it rubbed me raw."

"Your parents weren't kind to you," Maddock said, his eyes shifting from the heavens to me, his gaze piercing. "Even in your memories I could see that. They stole your life from you."

A pang hit me in my chest. "If your life was all preplanned, they stole yours too."

He nodded. "I tried to follow the path my father laid out for me, but I even failed at that, and it felt like my life was over. It was then I realized how much I had lost myself along the way. That's when I got on my bike. I knew it wasn't smart, but I was broken."

The lump in my throat grew.

"I thought my life was over, and I had such little regard for it anyway. My time in the crevice showed me just how alive I was. How everything I thought was important in life really wasn't. I had it all backwards. Was it like that for you?"

I hesitated, unsure how much I wanted to divulge to Maddock, but something in his eyes made me want to open up.

"No. It was the opposite. I knew there was more to life, more to love. I just didn't know how to reach it. It all felt so far beyond my grasp, that to even hope for it felt like a form of self-torture."

"We're two sides of the same coin," he said, a look of shared understanding on his face. "Yet somehow, we both ended up here. Despite everything, and I'm so damn thankful for that. Thankful for you."

I hadn't realized he was holding my hand, his thumb gently tracing circles on my skin. My chest fluttered with warmth, but I immediately jolted away.

I had wanted to open up, but not like this—not enough for him to slip through my cracks and use our connection against me.

My sacred bond felt ripped out of my chest, and suddenly, I wanted nothing more than to be wrapped in my soul flame's arms.

I took what I felt and pushed it down my bond to Rowen, letting him know I was thinking about him.

I stood up quickly and dusted off my pants. "We better get back to the village."

⸺ ·(·☾·●·☽·)· ⸺

We returned to the Wyn village in a swift, silent journey, taking no time to marvel at the shimmering strands of life. I kept my gaze forward, ready for this night to be over.

I sure as hell didn't want to spend any more time with my bond stealer.

Weary from how much energy I'd expended and nervous that Rowen hadn't made it back yet, I picked at my nails. Our connection told me he was alive, his flame flickering strong and steady within my chest. It was a quiet comfort, yet I still found myself biting my nails down to the quick, tearing until they bled.

Maddock grabbed my wrist, his touch stalling my breath. "Easy," he murmured, giving my hand a gentle squeeze. "He's all right, Keira. If you bite down on those anymore, you won't have any fingers left. And that worries me greatly. Rowen said whatever happens to you happens to me. And I would really like to keep my hands in one piece. So cool it. He's fine."

His eyes perused my face, and his intense stare caused unwanted heat to rise in my cheeks. I cleared my throat and ripped my hand away, annoyed that Madds could feel Rowen in any capacity. "I know, I feel him too," I retorted, sending Rowen another wave of warmth down the bond.

Suddenly, Nepta appeared at the edge of the clearing, her arms welcoming and her face anxious yet hopeful.

I let out a relieved breath.

"What news?" she asked, her senses telling her where we stood.

"The blades worked," I said, patting Mithrion at my thigh. "And we brought the Ever-burn star back to life. She glows. Beautifully."

"Thank the spirits," Nepta exhaled, a breath that felt years in the making. "And the warriors?"

"Returned to the heavens," I said solemnly, the heaviness in my heart reflected in the tone of my voice.

Nepta's eyes closed, her head dipping in pained understanding. A moment of silence followed for the slain warriors. "What else?" she asked, sensing the tension that rippled off my body like smoke.

"Erovos is watching through his demons. The Voro-Kai saw everything," Maddock said, his voice low and filled with respect. He had never spoken directly to Nepta, and it hit me how much this had become his fight as well.

"The Dark Spirit knows we have weapons, yet not enough soldiers to defeat him," I added, disdain filling my voice. The fact that the Dark Spirit knew anything about our plans enraged me beyond belief.

"What is found out is too late to take back," Nepta said. "But not all is bleak. We learned the weapons worked against the Voro-Kai."

"It was only five blades," Madds said, his voice raising to a heated tone. "We will need more than that to defeat those motherfuckers." My gaze shot to Madds in shock, and he cleared his throat. "I'm sorry. Please forgive my crude language, your majesty."

"That's not her title," I ground out in embarrassment.

A smirk lifted her wrinkled lips. "No harm. I quite like the sound of it."

Madds continued unfazed, "We need everyone armed and ready for what's coming. Those Voro-Kai are nasty beasts."

My fingers tightened on Mithrion. I'd seen the amount of demons we needed to destroy. "We're going to need a bigger forge."

A heaviness sat between us, not one of devastation, but one of silent decision-making. Nepta raised her gaze, a woman capable of turning our plans into action. "I will have Bailon and Leer expand the forge to meet the demand."

A new wave of hope and determination washed over me. The Voro-Kai may have tasted our metal, but they had yet to taste our ire.

This war was just getting started.

— ·(·(C · ● ·) ·)· —

Rowen still hadn't returned. My nerves were a twisted jumble in my stomach, but the flame belonging to Rowen flickered in my chest. I knew he was safe; I could feel it through our bond.

I sent him another little flare down our connection, smiling as I recalled the groans he'd made while we stripped each other bare with our blades.

To pass the time, I worked on the Phases of the Moon. This late at night, the training grounds were empty, and I had the place to myself. Sweat dripped down my face, but I didn't let it deter me. With Mithrion in my hand, a renewed sense of purpose fueled me. Our movements were synchronized and symbiotic, as if we were training for battle together.

She was a new blade, but already, she had tasted blood. Astral demon blood. She was created in a time of war; I couldn't expect anything less.

The motions became mediative, allowing my mind to sharpen yet flow in time with the blade. I worked meticulously on the forms, yet with every thrust and slash, I tried to incorporate the fifth and final phase: the New Moon. But that defeated the purpose entirely. I needed to learn so I could forget.

Suddenly, I sensed eyes on me, a predatory stare that gave me goosebumps.

Rowen was watching.

He appeared impressed by my physical prowess. I also noticed that he was aroused. Very aroused. His thick cock jutted against his pants. "Does this do something for you?" I asked with a smirk, pushing my ass out a little more than necessary on the next move.

His voice turned low and guttural. "It very much does. You've been pushing your desire down our bond all night."

My jaw dropped as if I were surprised. "I thought I was sending you sweet nothings."

"Definitely not. Do you know how difficult it is to hike with a cock that aches for you?"

"No," I said, cocking one eyebrow at him, lowering into a very deep and suggestive lunge. "Tell me."

"It makes me want to take you. Right here and now."

I strapped Mithrion to my thigh and stepped up to the incredible man who taught me love and inner strength, hope and belonging. He gazed down at me, and I smirked up at him as I lowered to my knees.

"Keira, what are you doing?" he rasped as I unbuttoned his pants and pulled out his cock.

"I thought it was obvious," I replied, wrapping my hand around the thick base of his erection. "I'm going to put you in my mouth."

I parted my lips and flicked my tongue onto the plump head of his erection, and his hips jerked. "Spirits," he groaned, tilting his head back, his eyes falling closed.

I wrapped my mouth around him and stroked him with my tongue. He threaded his fingers through my tangled waves, guiding my mouth further down his length. My cheeks hollowed out as he hit the back of my throat, my lips nowhere close to meeting my hand.

His grip on my hair tightened as I sucked him in leisurely pulls, taking my time.

I worked my wrist and mouth together, pumping him deeper into my throat. I gagged but didn't stop, loving the hard, velvety texture of him in my mouth.

His ragged groan made me smile around his girth.

His hips picked up speed, and my free hand shot to his hip to keep me steady as he thrust into me, and I gagged again.

"Breathe through your nose, Copeland. It will help you take more of me." I did as he said and braced my other hand on his hip, trying to open my throat even more. "That's it. Take me."

I sucked him harder and deeper.

"Fuck," he grunted as he pumped into my mouth, and my eyes watered. "I won't last much longer."

My nails dug into his ass, letting him know I was ready for

him. His cock twitched against my tongue as his earthy taste spilled into my mouth, and I hungrily took everything he gave me.

His spasms eventually slowed, and his grip on my hair loosened. He gently cradled my face and tilted my head up, bringing me to my feet. He claimed my mouth and kept me steady as my knees went weak.

He pulled back and gazed into my eyes. "Keira, you are perfect."

Rowen and I stood under the cover of darkness, little rays of moonlight shooting through the leaves and reflecting on our skin.

Rowen's hand played with mine, his face one of sated bliss. Suddenly, his brow darkened. "You're bleeding," he said as he inspected my fingers.

"It wasn't Madds," I replied quickly, then my face flushed with shame. My self-inflicted wounds had tried to heal, but the constant picking kept them raw and sore. "I . . . I did that."

He kissed the tender flesh around my nails and thumb. "Please don't hurt yourself. These hands are far too precious."

"Sometimes I don't even realize I'm doing it."

"Then I will just have to find ways to keep your hands busy," Rowen murmured, taking my thumb in his mouth. Heat blazed through my blood and shot to my core as his tongue pressed against the pad of my finger. I slipped my thumb free, gently pulling down his bottom lip. His mouth softened open with a groan, and I closed the distance between us, capturing his lips in a soul-deep kiss.

Rowen pulled me closer and squeezed me tight. His scent enveloped me, and his taste fed a hunger that could never be satisfied.

Such moments of simple bliss were few and far between, but

I drank in every second, savoring the reprieve from the darkness. We held onto each other as if our lives depended on it, unwilling to let shadows find us.

And just for a few moments, nothing could pierce our stolen bubble of peace.

32

Nepta wasted no time in expanding the forge. The once meager yet elegant space had multiplied in size. The changes were hastily made to accommodate the upcoming work, but I still marveled at how quickly it had been assembled.

Anyone with even the faintest idea of how to work a hammer was called to help, and the volunteers were many. One team was dedicated to cutting the Ever-burn meteor into manageable bricks while the other processed the pieces at the forge, shaping them into all manner of weapons.

Nepta stood in the center of the operation, her crescent moon staff maintaining a constant portal between the forge and the Ever-burn site. Her lined face was deep in concentration, and sweat dripped from her brow. Her shimmering portal churned as chunks of the celestial stone were transported to the village.

The newly expanded forge buzzed with activity, working like a well-oiled machine under both Nepta and Bailon's instruction.

Several stations were set up with basins of water, blazing hearths, and tool racks filled with tongs, hammers, and chisels.

The air was full of steam, heat, and the sound of clanging metal. Each strike sounded like a countdown to war.

The scale of work was unimaginable. We needed to create armies worth of weapons in a matter of days. Every elve moved with urgency and determination as they worked with the gleaming metal. Flames flickered across their faces as our rebellion sparked to life.

"We gathered every able-bodied elve to help with the weaponry," Bailon said, wiping the sweat from his brow with the back of his gloved hand. His eyes were bloodshot, and his face was worn with exhaustion. "We have streamlined the process as much as possible, but many here are new to the craft. Though we are teaching and producing simultaneously, I believe our results are promising."

My gaze swept over the racks and workbenches filling with knives and swords. The weapons gleamed with Light, and though Bailon felt optimistic about production, the cache of weapons seemed dwarfed by the brood of demons in the crevice. The weapons weren't needed for just one army—but two. The one I still hoped to raise with the desert elves.

Rowen's deep voice cut through the symphony of hammer strikes and hissing steam. "You are doing great work, Bailon. We will need more arrows and spears, long-range weapons that can be used at a distance."

He pulled out a worn leather book, its pages filled with weapon designs.

Bailon's bloodshot eyes studied Rowen's sketches. "These are excellent designs. We can make them quickly enough, faster perhaps if we streamline this section right here," he said, pointing to the notebook.

I could see Rowen's strategic mind turning. "Yes," he said as their heads bowed over Rowen's drawings, working together to make the most efficient designs. "That will work with the light-weight tips I designed for speed and distance."

As they flipped through the pages, Rowen made corrections with his charcoal pencil. After a few more suggestions, my soul flame closed the book and clasped a firm hand on Bailon's shoulder. "Go and get some rest. I will take over for a few hours."

"That will be much appreciated," he said, his voice heavy with fatigue. He gave a grateful nod before he removed his apron and gloves, hanging them on a nearby hook. Though the dark threat looming over us made it hard to rest, Bailon trusted Rowen to keep the hearth fires burning.

As the master bladesmith left the forge, Rowen took his place at one of the stations, his hands gripping the tools with familiarity. "You ready to learn how to forge a blade?"

"Are you sure I won't get in the way?" I asked, eyeing the blazing hearths, dancing flames, and splashing oil.

"You heard Bailon," he said with a widening smirk. "We need everyone able to wield a hammer. Plus, it will keep you from biting your fingers. And who knows, maybe you will find a hidden talent."

I looked at the pre-cut bricks of Ever-burn waiting to be shaped into our salvation. I took a deep breath and stepped beside Rowen, picking up the nearest hammer. "Let's see if I'm a natural."

After I put on the protective gear, Rowen walked me through the process step by step. "Grab the metal with the tongs and place it in the forge. Yes, like that," he encouraged as I followed his instructions. "You want to leave it there until the steel glows yellow."

I held the tongs with a firm grasp. "I like when you talk me through it," I said with a side smirk, remembering other activities he had *talked* me through.

"Eyes on the steel, Copeland. Now, remove the metal and place it on the anvil."

I jumped back to attention. "Yes, sir," I replied, carefully following his directions.

"Start with a corner and hammer it into a point. Focus on tapering both sides," he instructed as I worked the blade, starting at the tip and hammering my way down, shaping it into a knife. "Good girl. Now, flip it over and work the other side."

"I love it when you talk dirty to me."

Rowen breathed in through his nose, trying to stay focused. "Plunge it into the water to quench it," he continued, and I stifled a laugh. "Once the steel has cooled and returned to its normal color, place it back in the forge, and repeat the process three times."

I did as he said, and what started as clumsy apprehension turned into something more. Something cathartic. I fell into a rhythm, hammering out all the hurt, trauma, and wounds of my past. The heat of my ire matched the temperature of the blade, and with each pound of the mallet, I sharpened my resolve.

The tighter I held onto the hammer, the more I was letting go. The grip I'd held onto my anxieties and depression would now be the grip with which I handled this tool. I was strengthening my mental weapon as I forged a physical one.

My arms ached from the movements, and at this point, I wasn't sure what was sweat and what was tears. It all hurt as I healed some part of me.

On and on, the hammers fell as the forge filled with the sounds of creation. The flames rose higher, the metal sizzled, and water spilled and splashed.

It was a cathartic release that I hadn't known I needed.

Rowen guided me as I worked, his watchful eyes flicking from my face to the blade. The molten silver gleamed in his eyes with pride.

As I continued to shape the steel, I forged something deep within my bones. Something that was stronger than any weapon and more balanced than any blade. I strengthened myself.

···(·(·●·)·)····

A week passed in a busy blur. The constant cycle of war planning, discussing, and re-planning was exhausting—not to mention the Hymma journeys and grueling training with Dyani.

Each day, the tremors grew stronger, more violent. It was clear Erovos was biding his time, waiting until every last demon was fully formed to emerge from the crevice.

There was no scenario where Erovos wasn't planning on conquering this world and all others to come. He had a clear-cut plan, one that he had been preparing for who knew how long. All while we scrambled to keep up.

I looked at the shining blades piling higher on the racks and tables. The Wyn had worked tirelessly to create these weapons. I had to find the desert elves soon. Putting a warrior with every blade was paramount to our war plans. We needed more soldiers.

Despite all the action and constant distractions, there was something I couldn't shake. Something I was missing. Despite all the progress I seemed to have made, I was no closer to discovering the whereabouts of the desert elves.

Every day I failed to find them felt like another boulder piling on my chest.

My heart lurched as I realized there was one final thing to try. One last path I had refused to walk down. It was so glaringly obvious, yet I avoided it like the plague, hoping I would never have to confront it. But I had exhausted all other avenues. Only one thing remained.

The time had come to talk to Takoda, to try his mind-mending therapy.

The thought alone filled me with fear, but I had to try. The fate of our futures depended on it.

⸻ ·(☾ · ● · ☽)· ⸻

The walk to Takoda's dome was heavy and filled with trepidation. With each step, my lungs grew tighter, and my palms dampened. I'd resisted speaking with the healer for so long, grasping onto some form of independence, or was it stubbornness? I refused to face the fact that I might need more help, that all answers weren't within me, or maybe they were, but I couldn't hear them within my own echo chamber.

If it were pride, there was no place for it in a world hanging on by a thread.

My hands trembled as I reached to knock, but just before my knuckles met the latticed wood, the circular door opened, and Rowen stood in the threshold.

"Are you all right? Is everything okay?" he asked, his eyes wide with concern. I thought he would be finished with his mind-mending therapy by now, but they must have gone over.

"Yes. Everything is fine. I came by to see if Takoda had any time for me today," I replied, nervously stroking the laces of my vest.

Rowen's expression softened as his gaze caressed mine.

Takoda peered his head through the door. "For you, startouched, always. Please come in," he said as he held the door open for me, his eyes kind and never judging.

Taking a deep breath, I walked past Rowen, my gaze never leaving him. "I love you."

"I know," he replied as I crossed the threshold, and I realized I'd never entered Takoda's dome willingly. I'd always been

290

carried in here while I was unconscious. Somehow, taking the steps for myself filled me with a sense of strength.

The healer's dome was overflowing with living plants, herbs, and natural medicines. Vines trickled down, and dried plants hovered above. I took in a deep breath, letting the scents fill my lungs. I was finally facing what I could no longer ignore.

"Um," I said, wringing my hands. "Where should I sit?"

"You can sit anywhere you like," Takoda said, waving his hand around the room in invitation.

Sitting on the bedroll where I'd been a patient didn't feel right. There were chairs and stools I could choose instead, but the act of sitting down to speak sent a fresh wave of anxiety up my spine.

I wasn't afraid of Takoda by any means, but I'd sworn off lying on a couch and gushing my feelings to anyone ever again, but the time had come. And I trusted Takoda with my life.

"Should we go for a walk instead?" the healer asked, somehow sensing my apprehension of sitting down.

I released a heavy breath. "That would be nice."

⸱⟨⟨⸱●⸱⟩⟩⸱

We walked the organic pathways that slowly came back to life from the renewed water.

"I'm glad the water is running," I said to the healer, unsure what else to say.

"It is not just the water that returns life. It is also you," Takoda replied, noting the glowing flowers that bloomed as I walked by.

"I . . . I might bring life, but I've also brought death. And . . . and I almost killed everyone in the Crypts," I said, tears burning in my eyes. I hadn't said it out loud—hadn't even really known that was what was affecting me until the words poured out.

"How can I ever forgive myself for almost killing thousands of people?" I confessed as I let the tears fall; now that they had started, it was too late to stop.

"In the Crypts, when I tried to hit the false queen with my Light, I missed. I swore I wanted to strike her directly, but instead, my blast hit the ceiling and caused a cave-in. I almost killed everyone."

Takoda walked beside me, matching my pace. "The spirits could have guided your hand, knowing what was best," he said, his kind umber eyes sparkling with understanding. "Did you ever suspect it might have been the gentle brush of an Elder Spirit? That you were meant to bring the Crystal Crypts down? To *save* everyone trapped within?"

I let out a hiccup. Why hadn't I thought of that?

The shame had been too thick and heavy to think through. My guilt had shut out any form of rationale.

I had accepted the Elder Spirits help before. The giant, foxlike guardian who had saved me from being ripped and clawed to death in the mangroves. And again when they reforged me as an Ancient Elve.

It made so much sense. The Elder Spirits had been helping me all along the way.

"The Crypts weren't meant to be escaped," I barely whispered.

"But you escaped them. Along with freeing everyone imprisoned within their clutches."

"I was meant to destroy the Crypts?"

"I believe you were," Takoda said, stopping his strides to face me. "If you had only hit The False Queen, who knows how the outcome would have differed. There might have been no weakening the wall for Nepta to blast through, or there would have been no rumblings to show her your exact location. Or her followers might have turned on you. You didn't miss, Keira. You hit exactly what you were meant to."

The heavy burden I'd been carrying lifted off me like a weighted cloak, and I took in a breath of guilt-free air. I should have known talking with Takoda would be nothing like talking with my mother.

After one session I wasn't fully healed, but at least I had taken the first step. "Sometimes, I wonder if I'm enough for all this."

"I've seen your abilities with the noxlilies—you revived an extinct plant by bathing it in a celestial light. You infused seeds of light into barren lands, causing rapid growth and acceleration. Not to mention the vegetation that sprang from the blood-soaked soles of your footprints. I suspected your abilities were limited to light and creation. But the night of the fire, I saw you summon a rainstorm. You called upon lightning and rain. And you ended a drought. You are a force to be reckoned with. Never forget that."

"Thank you, Takoda, for everything. For not pressuring me when maybe you should have." I half-laughed and half-cried.

"You cannot force balance. It must be found on its own. I trusted you to know your mind, and you did. You listened to yourself; that is what matters." His long, silver hair blew across his youthful face, making him appear ageless.

"I need to go to the Hymma now."

Takoda nodded, his eyes shimmering as if he felt the shift in my demeanor. "Get your soul flame, and it will be ready for you."

I made my way to the Hymma, feeling stronger and more present than ever. My head was clear in what felt like the first time in forever.

Rowen followed beside me, taking my clothes as I undressed. I removed everything. Even my favorite part—the starlit weapon sheathed at my thigh.

After speaking with Takoda, I felt like I could face anything. Go through any door.

I know the healer said one could lose their mind in the introspective ceremony, and I could see why; you could easily find a doorway to yourself that once you walked through it would be hard to turn back.

I entered the Hymma and sat cross-legged on the ground. I took a deep breath and closed my eyes.

Suddenly, a tunnel of indigo light appeared before me, whispering for me to enter. It was as if it had always been there, just waiting for me to see it. How had I ever missed it?

Fear cemented down my spine, bonding me in place. What if I went through and couldn't find my way back?

Realization hit me like an avalanche. I had already experienced my greatest fears. Yet I hadn't crumbled under the weight of that fear but used it as stepping stones and grip hooks to climb above it—over it—then down the other side, able to look back upon what seemed an insurmountable feat.

I'd walk through any door and ask any question if it meant saving this world. My home.

My golden tether to Rowen would hold strong. No matter how deep I went, there would always be a trail back to his arms.

Steeling my spine and setting my jaw, I walked through the tunnel of my inner eye.

I thought the information I sought would involve winding through corridors after corridor like a labyrinth. But it wasn't a maze at all; it was a core with rows of concentric rings.

I studied the dark and light patterns swirling all around me.

Was I inside a tree?

My fingers traced over the thick years of heavy rainfall and slim seasons of drought. My touch hitched at the scars from millennia-old fires.

This tree was old. Very, *very* old.

The distinct and ancient circles of wood spiraled around me, the imprints similar to the whorls of a thumbprint.

As I expanded my awareness, I recoiled as I was met with branch death and decay. The parts of the tree that were still healthy curled in on themselves, furling deeper into its first ring for protection. I tried another direction, and another, flinching at all the dead edges around me. The only way was down, deep into the roots.

The roots extended into smaller threads stretching farther than I could fathom. Interwoven white fibers that extended into a vast underground network. Who knew such a universe existed within the ground, connecting the world just under our feet?

But the unseen world was weak and dimming, already with roots curling up into themselves like wounded tentacles. It was a travesty, witnessing the death of what kept the forest alive and healthy.

Suddenly, a hum vibrated through my fingertips, through me, and I shivered as strange yet extraordinary images flashed before my eyes.

Lost Light, you have returned.

I jumped as the sound echoed through my being. The ancient voice reverberated as if I were a harp and it was pulling the strings within me to communicate. The dissonance and lack of harmony was apparent, because this tree was in pain. It was dying.

"Who are you?" I asked gently.

My name is Indrasyl. I am the Sylvan Mother Tree of this earth. And you are the one written in the stars? The one who shall return light and life back to the dying lands?

Relief bloomed within me like a field of wildflowers. Indrasyl was alive! But the joy was fleeting. She was very sick.

"Yes. Though I'm not sure how," I replied to the ancient tree. "How do I heal you? And Luneth?"

A sacrifice is required. I felt her hum through me. *The blood and bone of The Marked.*

"How much do you need?" I asked, my voice barely above a whisper.

I think you know, Lightling.

A piece of me collapsed in on itself. Any hope lingering in my chest shattered like a stained-glass window. The broken shards lacerated my breath in my lungs.

"You need all of me?"

As it's written in the heavens. Yes. She pulsed around my astral body. *I can tell you much of this earth, of its bounty and of its droughts. Of its fires and floods. But this darkness is unlike anything my roots have ever known.*

Trees know sickness and death; such is the way of life. We nurse where we must and retreat where we must. But an unnatural darkness has entered our roots, a rot we cannot escape, and it is spreading. The earth is dying. I am dying.

"I won't let that happen," I cried out. Her sorrow was my sorrow as I intertwined with her roots.

Through your blood and bone, we can become one to heal this earth.

Sorrow punched down my throat.

This saddens you. Why?

"I . . . I have people I love. One very much so, and the thought of leaving him—"

Somewhere deep in the rings of time, you will always be together.

"That isn't good enough!" I screamed, sorrow turning into rage. "We haven't had enough time together. There's always been something keeping us apart. This, right now, was supposed to be our time. There must be another way."

I am afraid it is already too late. My time grows shorter yet. Even now it is taking what little strength I have to communicate with you. If you wish to save this earth and all who inhabit it, you must give everything. If you love this man, this is how you save him.

An unimaginable pain erupted in my chest. It was as if my ribs had splintered open and pierced my heart.

Rowen wouldn't let me do it. If he knew, he would find another way or die trying. He would let the world burn before he'd let any more harm come to me. Or, and the thought tasted like rust in my mouth, he would follow me no matter where I went, in life and in death.

"War is at our doorstep. Even if I sacrifice myself, what's to stop the darkness from spreading? I've seen the army headed our way. They will fell and uproot every tree to get what they want."

You must seek help before we become one.

"Where?"

I do not know.

I wanted to scream and tear my hair out.

This was a lose-lose situation. No matter what I did, there was no scenario in which we prevailed. Erovos would win.

No one had come to our aid, and we were unable to locate Rayal and her people.

Suddenly, an idea struck.

"You know this earth. Do your roots extend to all?"

Yes, my arms are all-encompassing, holding this planet together.

In my mind's eye, I imagined Rayal's necklace, the one she stroked with reverence. There was a symbol upon it, a graceful line, sweeping over and under two circles. "Have you seen this symbol before? Do you know the people who wear such a sigil?"

I do not, Lightling. I am sorry.

If there had been little hope before, it was now squashed. It was utterly and entirely hopeless.

A phrase came to mind: Rayal's parting words from deep in the Crypts. "If you should survive and ever find yourself where sun casts upon sun and your shadow greets mine, know that you are amongst friends."

Sun upon sun?

"Yes! Do you know where that is?"

Not well, for it is dry, and my roots there are very small.

"Where is it?" I implored.

It is hard to remember.

"Please," I begged. "It's our only hope."

You must mean the Eye of the Sun

"Yes. Yes! Where is it?"

I grow weaker yet.

"Try!"

Suddenly, I was yanked down, deep within the earth. There was no time to fight or claw my way out because before I knew it, I was surging forward, flying through Indrasyl's roots like an electrical current—or at least some part of me did. My body still sat on the floor in the Hymma.

Indrasyl guided me through the vast underground system. It was a marvel. A hidden world with endless webs that glowed in my mind like a galaxy. All interconnected.

I only received fleeting snippets as the Sylvan Mother Tree projected me through her roots. The terrain changed and shifted around me as she avoided thin or frail pathways, some already wilted and dead.

I kept charging forward in bursts of light when I slammed into a barrier, halting my traveling.

What the hell? I'd never stopped mid-flight.

My awareness shifted upward, wondering what could have blocked my path.

Towering above me was a stone archway—a breathtaking marvel of rock and time. It stretched impossibly high and loomed over me like a cathedral.

An arch! The marking on Rayal's choker was an arch.

I tried to step through again, but I was met with resistance as if I'd run into a glass door. Upon further inspection, I realized a thin mist emanated from the arch like a veil. It was made of dust, golden specks, and a gentle pulsating wind. It reflected on the sand, decorating the ground in a dance of shadows and light.

Was this some sort of protection ward? I knew Rayal was on the other side, but I couldn't get to her, no matter how hard I pushed within the rootways.

It appeared that whatever I had to do, I had to be in my corporal state to pass through. But I had no idea where this arch was!

Suddenly, I felt a ripping—a tearing—like all the seams of a tapestry were being pulled apart. Millions of shrieks echoed within me as Indrasyl rushed me back to my body in waves of pain.

The earth quakes and trembles as the Dark Spirit rips open the world.

"Hold on a little longer," I desperately begged, clinging to Indrasyl's presence.

I shall try.

She sounded so weak and fragile.

"We're coming," I said to the tree who hopefully had turned the tides of the war.

My astral self returned to my body, and my gut lurched as Indrasyl's pain lingered. I opened my eyes and staggered out of the Hymma.

Rowen scanned me worriedly and helped steady me. "What did you see?" he asked, handing me my clothes.

His presence was a double-edged sword, one that offered me strength yet sharpened the ache in my chest and cracked my heart open. I dressed as quickly as I could, allowing the act to hide the pain and anguish that flooded through me. It was an anguish I couldn't afford to show. Too much hung in the balance.

Althea and Donis, the first soul flames, had found a way to leave this world together. I wasn't that strong. I couldn't ask that of Rowen. I'd never want to.

I would try everything within my power to save Luneth without sacrificing myself. If I could find the desert elves and convince them to help, perhaps I wouldn't have to face that impossible choice.

Rowen didn't need to know because I had every intention of finding another way.

I wanted to collapse into my soul flame's embrace, sob into his strong chest as his encompassing arms held me and I told him what Indrasyl had asked of me. But there was no need for us both to suffer. I would protect him from this pain because I was determined to find another way to save us all.

"The Eye of the Sun," I said, offering Rowen a smile to keep from crying. "We are looking for an archway."

My gaze brimmed with equal parts hope and dread.

Even though I'd found our salvation, I might not survive this war. And if my death were part of the prophecy, I would simply have to rewrite the stars.

34

Urgency snapped at my heels. There wasn't a moment to lose. Rowen and I sprinted home to gather supplies and fill our waterskins. Though it was late, we didn't dare waste another minute. We darted through the village to alert Nepta of what I'd seen. Rowen pounded on her door, her dome no more lavish or exquisite than the rest of the village.

After several urgent knocks, she opened the door, her cobalt robe draped around her in an embroidered plume. Her fine, silver hair was loose and cascaded down her back as her withered hand rested on the doorway. "Yes?" she questioned calmly.

"I need to find the desert elves, convince them to help us, and hopefully bring back an army," I said, rushing to get the words out as I quickly recalled what happened in the Hymma. "Nepta, I need to leave immediately. Indrasyl showed me the way. In the Hymma ceremony, I somehow connected with the Sylvan Mother Tree. And with what little strength she has left, she showed me the way to the Eye of the Sun, but she's fading fast."

"This news comes swiftly on the wings of the night. Much needed and right before the dawn," she replied, and even though we had woken her before sunrise, it looked like she hadn't been sleeping. "What is your plan?"

"We haven't exactly figured out the logistics," Rowen admitted, his hand on the small of my back, casting circles to calm my breathing. "She can't go alone to a foreign city. If the desert elves know what is happening, they've either chosen to ignore it or believe such a blight could never reach them. Either way, what could convince them?"

"Perhaps witnesses," Nepta said, peering her head around me to call out into the darkness. "I know you are there."

Dyani stepped forward, surprising me. I didn't know she'd followed us. "We saw you running through the village. Figured it must be important," she remarked, almost embarrassed she'd been caught.

"'We'?" I asked, my eyes scanning the darkness behind her.

Maddock emerged from the shadows, his broad shoulders rippling through his shirt, his thick thighs filling out his pants. He'd gotten bigger since I'd first met him. "Were you really going to leave in the middle of the night without telling anyone?" he asked.

"Always lurking behind trees," I said, pinching the bridge of my nose. "Wait. Are you two . . .?" My gaze shot back and forth between them, a slight pang of jealousy twisting in my gut.

"Ew. No. You know he is not my type," Dyani said, brushing her hair off her shoulder, her eyes colliding with Maddock. "No offense."

"None taken." He shrugged. "We were just training. And you think you can hide things from me?" he asked, tapping his chest, indicating the stolen bond. For a moment, I froze, and my heart stalled. Had he felt my anguish, the pain I'd tried to push away when Indrasyl told me what I had to do?

I had so many questions but now was not the time to ask them.

"Time is of the essence," Nepta continued as she walked down the steps of her dome, muscle memory leading the way.

The moonlight illuminated the forest, casting a line of silver along the treetops. "I'm coming with you," Dyani said, her arm cuffs shining as brightly as the steel strapped to her body.

"Dyani, thank you, but this is dangerous. I don't even know if I can get us there."

The warrior unsheathed her blades and lowered to one knee, silencing my protest. "I offer you my blades, Alcreon Light," she replied, her sharp eyes unfaltering. "Do you accept them or deny them?"

My breath caught in my throat, and my eyes burned at the depth of her loyalty. "I accept your blades," I nodded with gratitude.

"Good," she said, standing upright. "I would've had to hurt you had you declined such an offer. And you will get us there. I believe in you."

"Well, if she's going, then I'm going," Maddock said, stalking up to us. "Don't fight me on this one, sparky. Rowen, tell her."

"The more protection you have, the better. We know very little about the desert elves. They may not take kindly to being disturbed."

I didn't have time to argue. Indrasyl needed me. Luneth needed me. "Fine, but only because we don't have time to argue."

"You have two minutes to get provisions," Rowen said, and our tagalongs darted off.

"Can you get us there?" I asked Nepta worriedly.

"I know little of this 'Eye of the Sun,' but I'll call upon the spirits and ask them to allow you to guide this portal. Focus on where you must go. Hesitate, or let your mind wander, and you could all be lost."

"No pressure," I said, shooting Rowen a glance.

"I regret I cannot leave," the Elven-head replied, and though hope shone faintly in her eyes, fatigue lingered in the subtle movements of her face. "My protection wards are connected to me, and it's nearly taking all my strength to keep them up. We cannot risk any stray Voro-Kai entering the village. You must go without me." Her hand rested on my shoulder. "I cannot leave my people, but when you speak to the desert elves, you speak for us all." Her voice carried both the weight of unspoken fear and immeasurable trust.

"Thank you for believing in me," I said, honored that she viewed me as an extension of her and her kin.

"No need for all that," the Elven-head said as Dyani and Maddock returned with their supplies.

Nepta raised her hands and summoned a portal of pulsing blue light.

I gathered my strength, both physical and mental, hoping what Rayal said was true—that if I did manage to find her, I would be amongst friends.

I approached Nepta's shimmering portal, feeling Rowen, Maddock, and Dyani close behind. Whatever Nepta had asked of the spirits, I prayed they accepted.

I emptied my mind of everything except for one thing: the arch.

Indrasyl showed me the Eye of the Sun—or at least I hoped she had. She was a dying tree who had admitted to having memory issues. She might have led me to the wrong place, but I couldn't think too hard about that now. Instead, I focused on that arch as if my life depended on it. I stepped through Nepta's portal, hoping it would land us somewhere close.

The air changed in an instant as a bright light blinded me. I felt the environment shift from a forest filled with sap, salt, and evergreens to a dry and arid landscape.

My eyes adjusted to the harsh light, revealing a sea of golden sand. Heat like a furnace washed over my skin. The sun was bright and blistering, with no shade or protection anywhere in sight. Sand billowed across the dunes in a hazy glow, making it hard to tell the distance and height of anything. It all felt like an illusion.

"I don't see an arch. Do you see an arch?" Maddock's voice held an edge of panic as he spun around, looking in all directions.

"Keira," Rowen said calmly, the desert wind making his shirt billow around him. "Where are we?"

I spun back around, looking for Nepta's portal, but it had vanished. "We should be at the Eye of the Sun."

Dyani shielded her eyes from the harsh light. "What exactly were you thinking when you stepped through?"

"I was thinking of the arch," I said, trying to remain calm.

"What else?" Dyani ground out.

My heart stuttered in my chest. "Oh no."

Oh no, oh no, oh no.

The memory struck me. My last thought had been one I didn't even realize. "I may have thought, *land us somewhere close.*"

Dyani dropped her hand and closed her eyes, breathing slowly as if refraining from stabbing me.

"We're lost, aren't we?" Maddock asked, voicing the thoughts I tried to keep at bay.

"We're not lost," Rowen said, the pools of his green eyes the only oasis in sight. We stood in a circle of fresh footprints with no trail leading in or out. It was as if we had simply dropped out of the sky. "You heard Keira. She said we are close."

"*Close* is relative," Dyani pointed out. "Especially to the spirits! For all we know, their idea of being close could mean on an entirely different planet."

I stood in the sea of golden sand and closed my eyes, trying to feel the way Indrasyl had shown me.

"We're still on Luneth," I said, praying to the Elder Spirits that I was right. The arch was an imposing presence, one I'd felt down to my core. "I projected through the Mother Tree's roots to see the arch, so I've technically been there before. Plus, the sand looks familiar."

"Did you hear that everyone? The sand looks familiar," Maddock said sarcastically throwing his arms up in the air. "Let's just follow the sand then, shall we?"

He turned to take an exaggerated step, but as soon as his foot landed, the sand beneath him gave way. Maddock disappeared as the ground collapsed, his startled cry echoing after him.

Panic struck me like lightning. Without thinking, only reacting, I dove after him. It was pure instinct to protect the piece of the bond he had stolen from me. Who knew what would happen if he died carrying a piece of my soul flame bond?

Suddenly, I was rolling down a dune, choking as dirt flew up my nose and into my mouth. I tried to reach for something, anything, but I kept tumbling down the collapsing mountain of sand.

Just as it seemed like I would fall forever, I hit a sharp bump, and my stomach lurched as I flew through the air. I was weightless for a split second before I landed on something soft yet firm and rippling. Whatever it was, I was grateful it had broken my fall.

A groan rumbled underneath me, and I realized I'd landed on Maddock. "This . . . isn't how I pictured you on top of me," he muffled, and if my eyes weren't so full of dirt, I would have rolled them.

Dazed and shaken, I lifted my head, squinting from the sand in my eyes, but my gaze kept rising, up and up. I had to tilt my head all the way back to take in the red-and-copper rock that arced like a rainbow.

My breath hitched. I was staring into the Eye of the Sun.

Sprawled out on top of Maddock, I offered Indrasyl a silent prayer of thanks. She was fighting back against Erovos the only way she could.

"Keira!" Rowen and Dyani shouted as they ran down the hill after us.

"I'm okay," I said as Rowen's hands slipped around my waist and lifted me off Madds.

Once he placed me on my feet, I dusted off my pants, though I had a feeling sand had already found its way into every nook and cranny of my body.

"This is incredible," Maddock said in awe. "I knew we weren't lost."

"Yeah, so glad you remained calm," Dyani said dryly, offering Madds her arm. He clasped her wrist as the warrior rolled her eyes and helped him to his feet.

"We're here," I breathed, my gaze locking on the arch that represented everything I'd been searching for.

The stone arced over me like a sculpture, and I marveled at nature's artistry, using only wind and time as tools. As I stepped closer, I noticed the cascading sheet of golden mist, or was it swirling sand? Whatever it was, it stopped me dead in my tracks, just like when I'd been in Indrasyl's roots. I peeked around the arch, but the sand stretched on forever.

It must be a portal.

I might be able to astral project through, but the sentient mist seemed to promise death, dehydration, and a slow descent into madness if I tried.

The grave warnings were enough to have me sprinting in the opposite direction, but I'd come too far to give up now.

I planted my feet and stood my ground as determination surged through me. "Now, how do we get through?"

35

"You mean you don't know?" Maddock asked incredulously. I ignored him and took another step toward the shimmering curtain, but as I did, the sun blazed into my eyes. But how was that possible? The sun was behind me. "Be careful," he urged.

A shadow stretched out towards me from the opposite side of the mist, a sun beaming behind their back.

My heart leaped in my chest. "*Sun casts upon sun!* This has to be the right place."

The shadow didn't share my enthusiasm or mirror my movements. It made no move to invite me in at all.

"And your shadow greets mine. But how?" I mused aloud. I had no clue what the desert elves deemed an appropriate greeting.

I turned back to everyone and shrugged my shoulders. "I think I need to greet the shadow," I whisper-yelled. "Any clues?"

"Try waving," Maddock offered enthusiastically.

Feeling ridiculous but having no better idea, I waved. The shadow before me remained unchanged as I waved like an idiot.

I whipped around and hissed, "I knew that wouldn't work."

"Try the old Wyn greeting," Dyani said, planting her fist on her heart and bowing.

I did as she showed, but the shadow remained impassive as ever.

"Perhaps the bow of a lord or lady," Rowen offered, giving a courtly nod with a slight raising of his hand. Though sweat beaded on his brow and a rogue curl fell into his eyes, he exuded an innate grace that was palpable and caused a fluttering in my stomach.

"Well, that looked official," Maddock said with a crooked smile.

"And here I thought you were a fearsome warrior," Dyani added, fighting a grin herself. "Speaking of. Try this! It's a warrior greeting meant to show respect to your opponent."

"And when have you ever done that?" Rowen asked with a skeptical lift of his brow. "The most you offer is a swift kick to the groin or an elbow to the ribs."

"You're lucky it's not a fist to the nose," Dyani countered, crossing her arms over her chest. "I'm showing respect by not marring that pretty face of yours, though it does nothing for me." She shrugged. "Take the greeting you get."

"As long as I remember to dodge it," Rowen responded with a smirk.

Though I knew it was a long shot, I tried their suggestions.

I tried all manner of greetings, but nothing worked. The shadow only appeared when I was right at the veil of sand. Anytime I stepped away, the dark silhouette disappeared.

After several frustrating attempts, I walked around the entirety of the arch, scanning the stone for any markings or notches that would allow us entry.

Having circled the soaring marvel several times over, with no clues revealed, I plopped down in front of the colossal curve.

I gazed into the arch for what felt like hours, trying to

uncover its secrets. I stared into the abyss, feeling like it was staring back, taunting me.

The others had grown quiet, their joking at an end, allowing me space to think.

The sun beat down on us incessantly, burning our skin and drying our lips. My frustration mounted as time ticked by.

I astral projected in place, sending tendrils of myself toward the curtain of mist to see if I could communicate with it. But the air was thick with the portal's energy. "There must be wards up. I can't project through it."

"Me either," Maddock said, his linen shirt sticking to his body, his eyes squinting from the relentless glare.

"I have to be close to figuring it out," I insisted, trying to emit confidence. There had to be a way through. Rayal and Indrasyl wouldn't have sent me on a fool's errand. But the mystery of how to enter pressed down on me like the desert heat.

"I hope you're right," Dyani said, shooting me a glance. "I am a forest elf not meant for this blasted desert. I can feel myself wilting."

"Did Rayal make any movements as she told you the riddle?" Rowen asked after taking a swig of water.

My body recoiled. The memory he asked me to unlock remained in a place I never wanted to revisit. But I drew a deep breath and closed my eyes anyway. It was like stepping into a grave as I brought myself back to the deep, dark cell of the Crystal Crypts.

Rayal's bright but terrified eyes shone across my memory as I replayed our conversation word for word, seeing if I missed any clues.

Rayal spoke the riddle, "If you should survive and ever find yourself where sun casts upon sun and your shadow greets mine, know that you are amongst friends."

My eyes flew open. I remembered! While she spoke the words, she grabbed my hand and made a gesture—a greeting!

I shot to my feet, hope flittering in my chest like a delicate butterfly. The whispers behind me fell silent as I stepped to the curtain of mist again. Three bodies shuffled behind me, flanking me and holding their breath.

The shadow met me at the veil, its dark silhouette the only constant against the swirling haze.

Keeping my voice steady, I repeated Rayal's words aloud, extending my arm with my palm facing the sky. My shadow reached to the stranger beyond the veil, and slowly, the body on the other side mirrored the motion, stretching their arm back toward me.

The shadows aligned through the archway as the air cracked and whipped with energy. Before I could comprehend what was happening, a hand circled my wrist, and I was yanked through the curtain of sand.

The falling golden particles separated for me as I entered the land of the desert elves, the sun in my face, blinding me.

36

"Welcome to Hara'dune, friend," came the rich, deep voice of the man who held my hand. "My name is Thaydril, Keeper of the Eye of the Sun. And who might you be?"

I blinked several times as a large man appeared through the bright sun flares. I could barely see a thing, but even on this side of the arch, it looked like we were in the middle of nowhere. "My name is Keira," I said, straightening my shoulders. "I come on behalf of Nepta, the Elven-head of the Wyn village. We all do."

I waited for the others to introduce themselves, but my heart dropped into my stomach when no one spoke. I spun around, hoping to see familiar faces, but through the archway, there was only shimmering dust.

I tensed, concerned for their safety but also my sudden vulnerability.

I was alone.

The Keeper came into focus, his warm, brown skin radiant against the white fabric sweeping around his frame. His head was completely shaved, accentuating the sharp peaks of his ears that dripped with gold jewelry. Chains cascaded from his lobes to his body, wrapping around his bare shoulders like decorative armor

He looked me up and down, his eyes landing on my ears. "How very interesting."

"Where are they?" I demanded, ripping my hand away.

"Only your shadow spoke to mine," he replied, sounding slightly intrigued. Two guards in gold breastplates were behind him, their curved swords at the ready. "One immediately jumped in after you. The other two followed after that. I do believe they are now wandering in an infinite desert storm."

"No!" I cried, darting towards him, but the guards grabbed me by my arms.

"You know the sacred laws. Release her," Thaydril said, and the guards shot each other questioning stares. "She greeted us as a friend. She is to be treated as such."

The guards released me reluctantly but stayed nearby.

"My offer of friendship was an extension of theirs as well; they seek the same," I pleaded, meeting the Keeper's eyes, which shimmered under golden eyeshadow. "Please. Let them through."

"Very well." Thaydril sighed and shoved his arm into the veil. He seemed to rummage around for a moment before he pulled Rowen through the curtain of dust. My soul flame was coughing and covered in sand. Unlike me, he hadn't been given the courtesy of a smooth crossing.

We scanned each other worriedly before our eyes met in relief, and I quickly tipped my eyes to the guards. Rowen shook his hair, dust flying from his loose curls as he followed my gesture, quickly noting the armed soldiers as well.

"Rayal invited us here," I explained, returning my attention back to Thaydril. I hoped the elves recognized the name and, more importantly, that the woman who had snuck food into my cell, made it home safely. "The people behind me helped rescue her from the Crypts."

Thaydril's eyes lingered on Rowen, his lips curling into a mischievous grin. "My apologies, beautiful," he purred, his eyes practically undressing my soul flame. "Allow me to welcome you to Hara'dune. And perhaps a private greeting later in my chambers?"

"I am honored," Rowen said, placing his hand on the small of my back. "But I must decline."

I pulled Rowen closer; the need to claim my soul flame was a physical force I couldn't ignore. "He's *mine*."

"Ah, my apologies. I see now that he is spoken for," Thaydril said, his amber eyes sparkling. "All the beautiful ones always are."

"Your warm welcome into Hara'dune is much appreciated," Rowen replied, his courtly demeanor radiating off him in full force.

Thaydril sighed and cupped his cheek with his palm. "And so polite. What a shame."

His admiring stare never left Rowen, and despite the need to play nice, a low growl rumbled from my chest; my elven body vibrating in a way I'd never felt.

"You can retract your claws, little lioness. I won't take him from you."

My retort was on the tip of my tongue, but Rowen rubbed my back. It was a gentle reminder that we didn't know this man and were at his mercy.

"There are two more," I ground out, my tone laced with agitation.

"Yes. Yes," the Keeper said impatiently and dove his arm back into the veil.

He pulled Dyani through the gate in a burst of sand. "What

the spirits' was that?" She coughed, placing her hands on her knees.

Maddock was pulled through immediately after. "Well, that was awful," he choked out, shaking out his clothes and hair. "What took so long?"

Thaydril's gaze immediately snapped to Maddock, scanning him with the same appreciative stare as Rowen. "Hello, gorgeous—"

"He's spoken for, too," I said, the protective growl making its way up my throat again.

The guardian chuckled and shook his head. "My, don't you have all the pretty ones," he replied, his eyes darting between Rowen and Maddock. He stared longingly as if savoring a delicacy just out of reach. "Aren't you lucky."

Maddock looked at me with a confused smile that I brushed off with a shrug. He and Dyani were at my sides, and I released a small breath of relief that they were safe.

"What business have you with the princess?" Thaydril asked, inspecting the gold polish on his nails.

My heart hiccupped. "The princess?"

Rayal was royalty? She'd never told me, but then again, I guess she'd never had the chance. During our first and only encounter, we'd been prisoners together in the Crystal Crypts. The few moments we'd shared were under duress, with guards threatening our every move. "Y-yes," I said, quickly changing my tone to an authoritative one, standing straighter despite my dirt and sweat-slicked appearance. "She is expecting us."

"We have no news of this," the blond guard with pale skin said, tightening his grip on his scimitar.

"We can't just allow them into the city," the other replied, his hazel eyes peeking through the cloth around his head and mouth.

"That's precisely the point of the secret greeting," Thaydril replied, rolling his eyes. "What would the king say if he knew you spurned his niece's guests?"

The guards relaxed their shoulders but only slightly. "Very well, but we will report this to King Aedris immediately."

"Now that that's dealt with. Let us be on our way, shall we?" He turned his sleek head, sweeping his robe around him in a grand flourish. The two guards marched to our flank, their eyes narrowing in suspicion. Even though we were allowed entrance, my nerves were taut and on edge. It appeared Thaydril didn't appreciate the hovering soldiers.

"How well do you know Rayal?" I asked, trudging after our guide, who seemed to glide above the sand.

"Quite well, I would say," he replied without breaking his stride. "For she is my cousin."

"Your cousin?" I repeated in surprise.

"Indeed," he said, glancing over his decorated shoulder. "Though leaving Hara'dune has been forbidden for some time now, my cousin left to find the false queen. Tales of her supposed benevolence and how she helped struggling villages reached us even behind our protection wards. Now that Rayal has returned, we have learned the truth of the queen's deceit. It was a lie to trap villages within her crypts and use their energy, siphoning their life force in a daily offering hour. And from what I hear, Aliphoura's body was never found."

Rowen tensed beside me at the mention of his former lover's name.

I knew Rowen had attended mind-mending sessions to heal from the torment Aliphoura had caused him. My heart crushed in on itself to see how her shadow still lingered over him. "How long have you been the Keeper of the Eye of the Sun?" I asked, steering the conversation into safer territory.

"It has been my life's work," he said before languidly

motioning to the guards trailing behind us. "Though only recently have I acquired such . . . dedicated chaperones."

"What happened?" Maddock asked, struggling to keep up through the shifting sands.

"The new king is paranoid and has forbidden guests. I'm to report any suspicious activity, but you know the ancient greeting —it's a law the king himself cannot override. We are never to turn away a friend, no matter the circumstances. Not even these two could argue with that," he said, his eyes glinting with satisfaction as they flicked towards the guards. "I would say it's a punishment having to watch over me. Not a very riveting position as you might imagine. Though, it was quite entertaining watching you try to remember the greeting."

"You saw us struggling at the gate and did nothing?" Dyani asked, her hands resting on her sheathed blades.

"I'm under very strict rules not to interfere. Punishable by death. I trust you understand," Thaydril replied smoothly, nodding to her blades. "The ancient laws that allowed you entry are the same ones that are preventing us from searching your bags and confiscating your weapons. A friendship's greeting is not to be met with bad faith."

"Thank you for honoring the sacred greeting," I said quickly, sensing he was choosing his words carefully in front of the guards who followed us with stony expressions.

"Of course," he said with a flourish of his arm. "And welcome to the oasis of Hara'dune."

As we followed him into the light, it took my eyes a moment to adjust, but as my vision focused, the sight left me speechless.

A city emerged from the sides of a colossal slot canyon. The walls towered in layers of red, pink, and orange rock that curved in unbelievable patterns against the bright blue sky. The cliffs, buttes, and mesas weren't just natural formations, they were the foundations of homes, buildings, and grand halls.

The mountainside was alive with the architecture of the desert elves.

My eyes opened wide, taking it all in. The whole city stood stock-still in an undulating swirl of red rock.

My knowledge of oases was limited, but I had a feeling it should be greener than this. The vegetation was brown and brittle, and the towering palm trees had wilted ferns and shriveled fruit.

Thaydril led us deeper into the heart of the copper city, his robe trailing behind him like a billowing curtain. Pillars rose above us, topped with massive statues resembling hawks in flight. Their enormous wings extended out like canopies, casting marvelous shade over the city. The statues were sculpted with such detail that it looked like they could take off at any moment.

"The Sunshades were once majestic hawks that flew over the city," Thaydril commented, noticing where my gaze lingered. "They were great friends to the desert elves, granting us blessèd shade during the day as they hovered in the sky. They left these lands long ago, but these stones were erected in their image."

"They're incredible," I remarked, enjoying the reprieve from the relentless sun.

"This way," Thaydril said as we entered a vibrant desert market. The air swirled with the scents of warm stone, pottery, and dyed fabric. Though crowded, the market appeared to have seen better days. The colorful tents were faded and tattered. The stalls were filled with jewelry, tools, and handcrafted knick-knacks. No fresh fruits, food, or water in sight.

Vendors approached and tempted us to purchase their wares. If I were allowed the luxury, I would've perused the shops until my feet ached, but there were more pressing matters.

The desert elves moved gracefully, yet their demeanor appeared skittish and nervous. They wore light, gauzy fabrics, sweeping shawls, colorful scarves, and headwraps.

There was something about their expressions that hinted at distress.

"This is clearly your first time in Hara'dune," Thaydril commented, noting the look of wonder in my eyes.

"It is," I said, not wanting to blink and miss a single detail.

"This place is giving me the creeps," Maddock whispered, noticing the look of despair I had seen as well.

"Not our finest hour," Thaydril agreed, confirming my suspicions.

"Nor is it anyone's," Dyani said, striding alongside Maddock. "Many villages and citydoms are struggling—"

"No one here is struggling," interrupted the guard with sun-bleached hair.

"Of course not," Thaydril said, rolling his eyes before gesturing to the structure towering above the city. "Behold one of Hara'dune's most impressive landmarks: the palace. It is said we have the most stunning sunrises on the planet. Our princess loves watching it from her balcony surrounded by birdsong."

"Sounds like the princess has it made," Maddock said, his neck tipping back to admire the palace.

I wasn't so sure. Rayal said if I found her city, I would be amongst friends, but so far, our visit felt . . . off.

Thaydril shifted his attention to me. "As you can imagine, not many know the ancient greeting. This is the most excitement I've had in a while, and you brought so many gorgeous treats with you," he said, eyeing Maddock.

Jealousy shot to my belly as his eyes languidly perused over him.

Suddenly, a lake came into view, its blue water sparkling like a diamond in the desert. Though it was beautiful, it was nearly empty.

More guards surrounded the lake, their gold armor, curved

blades, and watchful eyes glinted in the light. It looked as if they were protecting the water. But from what?

My unease grew with every step deeper into Hara-dune.

A young elve in tattered clothes darted from the crowd and tugged on my pant leg.

"Water," the small voice said as he pointed to my canteen.

"Do you want some?" I asked, my eyes widening at how frail and dirty he was. And it hit me why the guards were standing by the water—the oasis was suffering from drought.

My throat dried. I knew the feeling all too well.

I unclipped my waterskin from my hip and offered it to the young elve. His pale skin was dirt-stained, and as he voraciously drank my water, rivulets of mud dripped from his chin.

The guards noticed the young elve and marched toward us. The youngling's eyes flashed to the soldiers in terror. He took a few more desperate gulps before handing me back my canteen and darting away.

"Are you okay?" Rowen asked, wrapping a comforting arm around my shoulder.

"I'm fine, but they aren't," I replied, gesturing to the elves of all sizes, colors, and ages, aimlessly wandering. The city was grand and beautiful, but the inhabitants were suffering.

"Why can't they drink from the lake?" Rowen asked, nodding his bearded chin to the well.

"It's low, but there's still water in it. Surely that's better than letting your younglings die of thirst," Dyani agreed, her face pinched with disgust.

"To speak ill against King Aedris' laws is grounds for imprisonment," said the guard with hazel eyes. "His family must have gone through their rations. The new king sees to it that everyone is cared for."

My fists balled in frustration. I'd been here thirty seconds and knew that wasn't true.

There was a new king, and he was lying to his people, pulling the wool over their eyes to shield them from what was happening to Luneth. No wonder the borders were closed and Thaydril had chaperones.

I wanted to scream and cry and summon a rainstorm or find water deep within the earth to pull to the surface, but when I reached for my power, it was so faint I could barely feel it.

This was not good, but I had to remind myself why we were here. Defeating Erovos was the first step to restoring Luneth. I had to focus all my attention on convincing the desert elves to join our battle.

The sound of grinding stone startled me out of my thoughts as my gaze snapped skyward. The hawk statues folded their wings into their bodies, revealing the sparkling cosmos overhead.

The sun had set since we'd ventured into Hara'dune, and the desert landscape offered a whole new sensation to the comets and galaxies overhead.

"How do they do that?" I asked, pointing to the stone Sunshades.

"The desert elves can command sand and stone," he replied. "How else do you think we erected this marvelous city?"

"Similar to how we command wood and vegetation," Dyani added, her sharp eyes calculating.

"Fascinating," I said, my neck aching from tilting my head back. The deep connection between the elves and nature never ceased to amaze me.

"I will show you to your quarters," Thaydril said, his painted toenails peeking out from his robes.

"You said you were taking us to Rayal?" I questioned, my brows furrowing.

"I said to 'follow me,' and you did so without question," he replied, and my jaw dropped. I knew to be more precise with wording. A carefully crafted sentence had saved me many times.

"But—"

"You're lucky they don't throw you in the cells. You all look filthy and unfit to meet the princess," he continued. It was clear he was placating to the guards, walking a fine line from being thrown into prison himself. "And you should know, you can't just summon royalty."

"We don't have time for formalities! It's urgent that I speak with her."

"Look, I'm sure you're used to getting your way," he said, his eyes darting to Rowen and Maddock. "But those big, silver eyes won't work on me. There is a way to how things work around here. I will show you to your rooms now."

"I'm not ready to go back to any cells just yet," Maddock said, resting his hand on my shoulder.

"Viewing our quarters would be lovely," Dyani agreed, giving me a look. "When might we be granted an audience with the princess?"

"I will see if I can arrange something tomorrow. For now, this should keep you comfortable. How many rooms will you be needing?" Thaydril asked as he directed us to a mesa rising above the desert. A multi-story building with pillars and arched windows was carved into the smooth stone.

"Three, please," Rowen said. "If you can spare the room."

"Of course," he replied, leading us through the stone doorway, up several flights of stairs, and down a long corridor. The Keeper motioned to three handcrafted doors at the end of the hall. "I hope you find them to your liking. Only the best for Rayal's friends."

Maddock picked the first door, and Dyani the second. Rowen opened the third door for us.

It wasn't dark or damp but unexpectedly inviting. There

were no constructed walls or ceilings, just raw stone elaborately chiseled away into intricate designs. The room extended into a breathtaking balcony, overlooking the dunes rippling like the sea. The gold sand appeared indigo under the night sky.

Brass lanterns hung around the room at varying heights, casting a warm and pulsating mosaic of light. Woven rugs and cushions covered the floors, and billowing curtains hung from the ceiling, offering a luxurious feel amidst all the hard stone. Our room perfectly incorporated the beauty of the desert along with modern comforts.

"It's breathtaking, thank you," I said, trying to remain calm even though my nerves were screaming at me to do something, anything but just sit here and wait.

"It is much appreciated," Rowen said, his watchful eyes studying the room.

"You're very welcome," Thaydril said with a bow of his head. "Keep your lanterns lit. It's said to be a very dark night."

Once the door closed, I turned to Rowen, his expression as suspicious as mine. "What the fuck is going on here?"

37

Rowen and I sat at the mosaic table in our quarters, picking at the tray of food Thaydril had delivered. The desert air blew in through the balcony, swaying the gauzy curtains against our bare arms.

We had basins of water in the room to wash up with, but how could I use any of that to clean? Not when children were going thirsty.

"We don't have time for this," I said, barely able to stomach the flatbreads and dried desert fruits. "Erovos could escape at any moment, and we aren't prepared."

"I know, but take in this small victory. You found the desert elves," Rowen said, brushing a lock of my hair behind my ear. "Yesterday, that felt impossible."

"I know, but I feel like nothing is happening fast enough," I admitted, biting into a cactus berry. My hand froze at my mouth as our door slowly opened. Rowen and I exchanged looks, our hands instinctively reaching for our weapons.

We braced ourselves for the worst when Dyani emerged through the threshold.

I let out a relieved breath and loosened my grip on Mithrion. "What are you doing here?"

"Have you tried traveling?"

"Yes, but I can't do it inside the city."

Dyani and Rowen exchanged worried glances.

"I don't have a good feeling about this place," the warrior said in a low voice. "Thaydril seems to be out of favor with the new king. The guards were breathing down our necks, and now they are blocking the front entrance." She handed me a small scroll of paper. "But look what he slipped in my food."

I unspooled the note and read the elegant calligraphy.

When you come to a dead end,

whisper A'Anhara to the stones

and a way up they will send.

"Dinner and a poem?" I asked skeptically.

Dyani rolled her eyes and snatched the scroll from my hands. "It's a clue. He also managed to tell us which room is Rayal's."

"It faces the sunrise," I remembered, perking up.

"And there will be birds," Rowen added, keeping his voice quiet. "Her balcony will most likely have an aviary."

"Exactly," Dyani said, resting her hand on her hip. "It must have something to do with their mastery over stone."

I jolted upright. "We can meet with the princess tonight!" Thaydril had given us clues to find Rayal, and though my heart leaped, a seed of worry took root. If the princess was out of favor with the king, how could she help convince him to join our war?

"How? The door is guarded. Remember?"

I glanced over my shoulder. "Yes, but the balcony's not."

"All right," the warrior said as she grabbed a dried fruit and plopped it in her mouth. "Let's go."

"What about Maddock?" I asked, grabbing my boots to put them back on.

Dyani huffed a laugh. "I just checked on him. He's out and snoring like a baby. Plus, this mission requires a light touch, not a bumbling oaf. I think it would be best if you and I went alone."

I shot a glance at Rowen, who looked deep in thought. "What do you think?" I asked, tying up the laces to my boots.

"If you think I'm going to let you—"

"Let her?" Dyani snapped before he could finish his sentence, her tone feral. "She doesn't need your permission. Nor do I need a whole lecture about keeping her safe. You know I've got her."

"If you'd let me finish," Rowen said, resting his palm on his knee, his posture relaxed in front of the predator before him. "I was going to say: if you think I'm going to let you have all the fun, you're sorely mistaken. I know you are both quite capable of taking care of yourselves."

I laughed as I adjusted Mithrion.

My soul flame continued, "I think it's a good idea. Though waiting for you will drive me mad. I'll gather more information and map out the city while you two ladies handle things."

Dyani stared blankly, struck silent for perhaps the first time. Her shocked stare made me laugh again.

She blinked a few times and said, "That's actually a good idea, Damascus."

"I know." He smiled. "Now, am I allowed to say be careful?"

"No, that's for me to say," I teased as I kissed him, placing my hand on his rugged jaw.

Dyani groaned in disgust. "Can you not?"

Rowen ignored her gripe and grabbed the collar of my vest, pulling me closer toward him. "Seriously, be careful," he said as he kissed me again.

"I will," I replied, my heart lurching. I would be careful—at least for tonight.

I hadn't forgotten what Indrasyl asked of me. It was written in the stars for me to give my life.

But I refused for that to be true. To reject the heavens wasn't something that could be done quietly or cautiously. It would have to be bold, precise, and loud. I would have to grab the heavens by the horns, shake the sky with all my might, and rearrange the stars.

— ·(·C · ● · Ɔ ·)· —

We stood at the balcony's edge as Rowen rummaged through his pack for rope. I leaned over the railing, calculating the distance to be at least three stories high.

Dyani's gaze followed mine, her throat bobbing with a gulp. "On second thought, you can go alone."

"Are you afraid of heights?" I asked in surprise, taking in her white-knuckled grip on the railing.

"No," the fierce warrior shot back. "I just don't like looking down from high places."

"Right." I grinned as she shot me a glare that was sharper than steel. "That's totally different."

As Rowen wrapped the rope snuggly around my hips, he peered at me through his thick lashes. "We're getting quite good at this," he said with a smirk.

I returned his smile, recalling when he'd used a vine to lower me into a well. "I seem to remember promising that if the knot held, we could try it again sometime."

"There is still time," he said, his voice low. The desert wind wrapped around us, stirring the loose strands of my hair around my face.

My heart clenched. I knew our time left was fleeting, but I had to stay focused. This was the only way to ensure we got more time together. "Until then," he continued, "I'll imagine all the ways I can put these knot-tying abilities to good use."

"Ew," Dyani hissed from the darkness. "Not the time!"

I stifled a laugh as Rowen threaded the rope through the carved railing, his hands expertly creating a pulley system. I climbed over the balustrade and held onto the railing from the other side.

"I love you," I said softly, taking his mouth in a fierce and fleeting kiss.

"I love you, too," he murmured, his fingers tangling and fisting my hair.

Rowen reluctantly released me and pulled back, planting his stance with the rope in his hands.

I nodded that I was ready, and Rowan gave me slack to walk backward down the wall.

Once my feet hit the sand and I stepped out of the harness, Rowen reeled the harness back up for Dyani. As he readied the warrior, I glanced around to make sure we hadn't been spotted. Thaydril's comment about a dark night made sense now. There was no moon. It would be easier to sneak through the city of sandstone.

Moments later, I heard Dyani muttering curses as Rowen lowered her in the night.

She dropped to the sand, and we walked around the mesa, sticking to the darkness as best we could. Our movements were swift when darting through the shadows, and thankfully, we slipped between the patrolling guards without notice.

We faced the palace, scanning the balconies that would embrace the sunrise. My eyesight had improved with my new elven body, and the stars offered just enough visibility to aid my search. "There," I whispered, pointing to the balcony filled with intricately carved aviaries.

"It had to be the highest one, didn't it?" Dyani said, crouching low beside me.

The sand muffled our footsteps as we approached the palace made of red rock, but the place was surrounded by Hara'dune soldiers.

Suddenly, a soldier jolted and turned to his companion. "Did you hear that?"

My heart stopped, and I clutched Mithrion's hilt. We'd wrapped our star blades in ripped curtains so they wouldn't give away our positions. But how had they heard us?

The other guard nodded and drew his blade.

Me and Dyani made eye contact, a silent conversation that there would be no witnesses to our midnight rendezvous. The other guards drew their scimitars, and in unison the whole line of soldiers took off running in the opposite direction.

Dyani and I exchanged glances as the wall was left unattended. I silently prayed to the spirits that whatever they heard, it wasn't Rowen.

We approached the smooth wall. "A'Anhara," I whispered, and suddenly, blocks of stone were pushed from the rock, starting low and rising higher and higher. It was a hidden staircase!

I turned to Dyani in awe, but she looked like she was going to be sick. "What?" I asked. "This is easy."

"No, it's not," she whisper-hissed. "There are no rails."

"Just don't look down," I assured, patting her shoulder.

The staircase was precarious. One wrong step and we would plummet to the sand, but we kept climbing.

We landed silently on Rayal's balcony, careful not to wake the birds sleeping within the massive aviary. There were many different kinds, all slumbering with their wings tucked comfortably to their bodies. I realized some only had one wing or half a beak, or bandages around their bodies and legs.

The birds appeared to be in rehabilitation.

A few of them rustled their wings as we passed, but for the most part, they remained unbothered as we walked through the billowing curtains.

The scent of jasmine wafted from the room that I prayed was Rayal's. When suddenly, Dyani was yanked away from me. A flash of steel appeared as my companion was whipped around and held at knifepoint. A familiar face peered over Dyani's shoulder, her grip firm as she held a letter opener to the warrior's throat.

"Who are you? And what do you want?" Rayal demanded, her tone sharper than the blade she held. "Make another move, and I'll slit her throat."

"Rayal, it's me—Keira. From the Crypts," I rushed to say, feeling awful that we had scared her.

Rayal's citrine eyes met mine and her blade fell to her side. "By the spirits. How?" she asked, her voice filled with relief and utter shock.

Dyani released a breath and stumbled away, rubbing her throat. With shocked eyes, she looked Rayal up and down, her chest heaving. "You are exceptionally quiet," Dyani said, sounding impressed. "And fast. For a princess."

"You think princesses don't train?" she asked, bringing the tip of her makeshift blade back to Dyani's throat. Her warm brown skin, similar to Thaydril's, gleamed in the moonlight. Despite being barefoot in a silk crop top and pants, she stood like a princess—like a warrior.

"Maybe," Dyani admitted, her eyes never wavering from Rayal as she brought her finger to the edge of the letter opener and slowly pushed it away. "But you've certainly changed my mind. Though if you want to skewer me, you should use something a little sharper."

Rayal was as strong as the stone used to build her city, but still, she allowed her hand to be guided to her side by Dyani. She twirled the letter opener and tucked it into her pajama pants, their eye contact painfully intimate. "All my weapons have been taken from me. This is all I could find."

I cleared my throat, and both of their eyes shot to me as if they suddenly remembered my presence.

"I found the Eye of the Sun, and Thaydril told us what room was yours," I said as we steered ourselves deeper into the shadows.

"I have only seen my cousin a few times by the way of the staircase," Rayal said softly. "We've been kept apart, both of us heavily guarded."

Since I'd seen her, she'd pierced the center of her bottom lip with a delicate golden hoop. Her dark hair was lighter, streaked with caramel highlights from the sun.

As I studied her, she studied me. "You are changed. Last I saw you, you were human, and now you resemble the Ancients," she said at last, reaching up to tuck my hair behind my ear. "I told you your power could be changed and altered but never taken. How did this happen?"

"Erovos," I answered, though the name left a rancid taste in my mouth. "He broke me down until I was nothing but the Alcreon Light, and the Elder Spirits built me back up in an elven body. It was the only way I could . . . come back."

"The Dark Spirit?" Rayal confirmed, her eyes going wide. "I heard whisperings of his name in the Crystal Crypts. The False Queen mimicked his power by siphoning energy from life. It is he who is—"

"Who is destroying Luneth," I finished, my voice steady yet urgent.

"He is amassing an army of astral demons," Dyani said, squaring her shoulders to the princess. "I have seen and battled them myself. They are waging war on Luneth, and I have pledged my blades to the Synodic Daughter."

I'd never heard her call me that, and the changed title struck me. It carried a weight of purpose to reclaim and heal what had been lost. It made this mission all the more dire.

"That is fortunate for her. I saw you in the Crypts when you were battling the false queen's men. You are quite a skilled fighter," Rayal said.

I could have sworn Dyani's cheeks flushed. "Will you pledge yours?" she asked, gesturing to the letter opener in her pocket.

"If only it were up to me," she responded, downtrodden. "I've barely been outside my room and balcony since I returned. You helped me escape one prison only to return to another."

"You said we would be amongst friends?" I asked in confusion.

"It was true at the time," she replied as tears filled her lower lash line. "Or would be true if my father was still alive. When we were saved from the Crystal Crypts, I came home to find he had returned to the Eternal Sun Stone. He died of a broken heart when I never returned."

"I'm so sorry," I said as her loss pinched my heart. It was hard losing a parent, no matter the circumstances.

"Thank you. My father was frail and old. He lasted longer than he should have. But I couldn't wait around for him to die, leaving no hope or future for his people. Lake Imperial was drying up faster than the rains could fill it. He didn't want to alarm his subjects and cause pandemonium. So, I left quietly to find hope. The throne was mine to inherit. I had a legacy to protect. I never thought I would be gone for nearly a sun's turn."

Urgency burned me from the inside out. "What do you mean *had* a legacy? What happened?"

Her nostrils flared. "While I was imprisoned in the Crypts, my step-uncle Aedris claimed the throne."

The loss of her father saddened me, but the loss of her throne and her ability to provide for her people enraged me. "But you're back now. Can't you claim it?"

"Aedris is ruling with fear and an iron fist. I'm afraid there isn't much more I can do," she said, her eyes boring into me. "I left to find hope. And I did. I found you. You can heal this earth and, in turn, my people. Their safety is more important than any title."

"Tell me how to help," I beseeched.

She grabbed my hand and held it in hers. "You must convince them of what I already know. You must bleed for them."

My heart thumped against my chest, and I glanced at Dyani. "W-what?"

"The blood-soaked soles of your feet brought the dying land back to life. I heard your Elven-head speak of it after she blasted open the Crypts. How the plant life led her to you—to all of us trapped beneath the ground. As everyone escaped, word spread of what you had done. The world is waiting for you."

"I will find a way to tell them," I said, willing to scream it from the canyon tops if I had to.

"No," she replied, shaking her head. "You mustn't tell them. You must *show* them."

"My powers don't work here," I confessed, gripping her hand in mine.

Rayal's eyes were knowing. "The charms my uncle has on the city are strong. But nothing is stronger than blood. I know you have already bled so much, but I must humbly ask you to bleed once more. Open your veins for my people."

Before I could react, she pulled her letter opener and sliced it across my palm. "Ow," I cried, trying to pull my hand away.

"Princess?" we heard a voice call out from beyond her door. "Are you well?"

"I am well, thank you!" she called back as she held my hand firmly and pressed it to a nearby plant. Silver light bloomed in the darkness and illuminated our faces. The wilted edges of her succulent sprang to life. "Your blood is your power," she whispered in awe, letting me go.

"Good to know," I said, clutching my closed fist to my body. Dyani's eyes widened in shock. She had only ever heard of my power, and seen its aftermath, but never witnessed it in action.

"Princess?" the voice called again, shaking us out of our stupor.

"You must go," Rayal urged, pure terror in her eyes. "I can speak with my uncle. Because Thaydril led you to me, I might be able to help. Otherwise, Aedris would have kept me in the dark. Wait for him to summon you."

"What should I say to him?"

"If you don't open the door, we will bust it down," another voice boomed.

"I'm coming!" she yelled over her shoulder before meeting my gaze. "My uncle will be intrigued with you. He enjoys shiny things. Keep him interested. He loves a challenge, but only if he knows he can win. Now, you must go!"

I couldn't help it. I threw my arms around the princess and hugged her. "You came to me and brought me hope when I thought there was none. Your kindness saved me. I'll do whatever I can to help you now."

Her arms gripped me tight before we both let go.

I wished I could talk to her all night. We still had so much to discuss, but our time had been cut short once again.

Dyani and I quickly left the princess's chambers and hurried down the staircase precariously hanging off the palace walls.

I quickly turned back and whispered the secret word to the stones. The rock pushed back into the wall with barely a sound.

And just like the disappearing steps, we vanished into the night like we had never been there at all.

⸻ ·(·C · ● · ꓚ ·)· ⸻

By the time we arrived back at our quarters, Rowen was waiting on the balcony, and my heart burst with relief. As soon as he spotted us, he lowered the rope.

"You go first," I said to Dyani, helping her climb into the harness. Rowen pulled her up as the sun began to rise, gently blushing the day with its fire.

My foot tapped impatiently. The sun grew brighter and brighter. Finally, the harness was lowered to me. As I slipped into the straps, Dyani hopped over to her balcony, and with a flash of her ponytail, she disappeared into her room.

The second my feet landed on the balcony, Rowen pulled me into a fierce embrace.

I remained in his hold as I told him everything.

His fingers dug into my arms. "Our suspicions are correct. It is not safe here."

"Did you see something while you were out?" I asked, my gaze dancing across his face.

He nodded. "There is much unrest. A skirmish broke out while I was scoping the city."

I clutched him tighter. "Are you all right?"

"Don't worry, I stuck to the shadows. No one saw me."

"What happened?"

He sighed. "Several elves tried stealing water from the oasis. They managed to fill several canteens before they were caught. Keira, the guards executed them on the spot. We need to be careful. We are in extremely dangerous territory."

My stomach dropped. It was so much worse than I thought.

"Soldiers guarded the palace, but they left their stations. The skirmish must have been the reason they abandoned their post."

Suddenly, a knock sounded at the door.

"Go," I urged Rowen as he tried to help me out of the harness. "I got it," I said, quickly untangling the rope from myself and the railing.

Before Rowen opened the door, he turned to me to make sure I was ready.

I nodded and slowed my breathing.

Rowen pushed open the double doors, and standing in our doorway was an entourage of desert elves.

38

The Keeper of the Eye of the Sun batted his lashes at me; his eyelids painted pink like ripe cactus blossoms. He was dressed in a bright yellow kaftan with a hood over his bald head. As suspected, he was flanked by guards and other elves I couldn't quite make out.

"Can we see Rayal?" I asked, joining Rowen at the threshold, trying my best to make it look like I'd gotten a good night's rest —that I hadn't heard the horrendous news of elves being murdered in the streets for trying to survive.

"It seems an audience has already been requested," he replied, eyeing us with a knowing look. "The princess was informed of your presence and would greatly like to meet you."

"How lovely," I said, trying my best to sound calm, keeping up with the pretenses for the guards.

Thaydril scanned me up and down, noticing I still wore my rumpled clothes from last night. "You cannot meet the princess looking like this. You must change."

The Keeper of the arch clapped his hands, and a rush of desert elves swept into the room, their arms filled with garments, accessories, and platters of food.

"Really, this isn't necessary—"

"Of course it is," Thaydril cut in. "You must look presentable."

Suddenly, Rowen and I were yanked behind a screen. My hair was tugged at from all angles, and my clothes were stripped from my body.

Beside me, the same was happening to Rowen. Women ran their fingers through his hair and unbuttoned his shirt. We made eye contact as our transformations began, agreeing to remain compliant.

There was no way Thaydril was going to let us out of this.

I sighed and allowed myself to be fussed over. Time was slipping through our fingers faster than an hourglass, and the sooner we looked presentable, the sooner I could meet with the king.

Thaydril sauntered over to one of the guards and began twirling his curly hair within his finger. "Hello, beautiful. As you can see, things are about to get quite hectic in here, and you and your men will only get in the way. Would you be a love and guard us from the other side of the door?"

The soldier stiffened, uncomfortable by how close and personal Thaydril was getting with him. He cleared his throat, his eyes widening in alarm as he saw the amount of clothes and beauty products.

"We will be just outside the door," he said, nodding to his troops to follow him out of the room.

"Finally, some privacy," Thaydril groaned. "As beautiful as they are, they are quite the nuisance."

Stripped down to our undergarments, we were ushered into two copper tubs placed side by side. Water was dumped on us as we were scrubbed clean, and I cringed as I was doused in the very thing the elves needed to survive.

"Do we really need to do this?" I asked again, wincing as two young ladies dried me and sat me on a stool to brush the knots from my hair.

"We do," Thaydril replied, his tone leaving no room for negotiation. "The king can take one look at you and banish you from the city before you've even had a chance to speak. Let your looks get you through the door so your words can convince him to listen."

"That's ridiculous. He should listen regardless. The elves in his streets are dying."

Thaydril winced. "Maybe don't start with that. If that's all you got, we're in trouble. You'll need to be a bit more convincing, I'm afraid."

"What are you suggesting she do?" Rowen murmured, his eyes looking like green fire as an elve with heavy freckles applied lotions and perfumes to my body.

"Nothing too extreme," the Keeper replied, fishing through what looked to be a makeup bag. "But trust me, you'll thank me when the king actually lets you close enough to listen."

Nerves twisted my gut, but I had no choice but to trust the man who'd already helped us so much. "Why are you helping us?"

"My cousin saw long before anyone else what was happening to the lands of Luneth," Thaydril said, picking up a stick of kohl and applying it to my eyes. "I believed her without question. I knew who you were instantly, but I could not let on. If the guards suspected, they would have alerted the king. Rayal spoke of you when she returned home. It is why I trust you. It is why I am going through all this trouble to make you look presentable. The king wouldn't look twice at you in your bedraggled state."

"Watch it," Rowen said. "That is my soul flame you're talking to."

"If she's your soul flame, a little flirting with the king

shouldn't threaten you. Now, be quiet. This is the hardest part," he said as he dragged the kohl to the outer corner of my eye.

I wasn't convinced this was necessary, but with no other choice, I stilled and tried not to move a muscle as Thaydril painted my eyes.

· (· ☾ · ● · ☽ ·) ·

Thaydril wrangled Maddock and Dyani into our room, staring at us like a proud mother hen. "I must say, this is some of my best work."

Rowen and Maddock wore loose pants and scarf-like shirts that folded around their shoulders in layers of light material. Dyani was dressed similarly, but over her pants, she wore a wrap-around skirt. Her arms were bare except for the silver armbands she wore in memory of Demil.

"I think I missed a few things," Maddock said, standing in desert elve attire, looking fresh, clean, and rested. "I woke up to women undressing and bathing me."

"Not a bad way to wake up. Though it would be better if we could keep our blades," Dyani said, her hands fidgeting without being able to rest upon her weapons.

"I'm sorry you aren't able to take your blades with you today, but they will be returned to you after you meet with the princess and king," the Keeper replied, smoothing a strand of my hair and adjusting my makeup. It was as if my appearance was cause for greater concern than the drought.

I already felt naked without Mithrion, but what Thaydril had chosen for me to wear wasn't helping. I was clad in sheer tulle.

The dress was light and airy with a structured silhouette and internal corset. The fabric draped down my body in varying lengths; some pieces were long enough to trail behind me as I walked, while others barely reached my upper thigh. There was at least one slit that ran all the way up to my hipbone.

"Why do I look like a human sacrifice?" I asked Thaydril, gazing at everyone else who was fully dressed.

"It can't hurt to look . . . appetizing," he replied, gazing at me from head to toe as if pleased with his work.

Rowen's gaze traced along my body like the gentle trail of his blade. My skin erupted with goosebumps as his jaw and temples flexed. The look was equal parts desire and fury. A desire to banish everyone from the room and take me against the stone wall, and a fury that I was wrapped like a present for another man.

Rayal said I would need to bleed for the king, and it didn't escape me that red was starkest against white.

⸻ ·(·C·●·)·)· ⸻

The Keeper of the Eye of the Sun led us to a towering stone wall lined with guards. Even though a cloth covered their mouths and noses, their eyes and blades were piercing.

"They are here to see the princess," Thaydril said, his confident demeanor unchanging. "She is expecting us."

The guards separated, allowing us to pass through the stone wall that parted with ease. We entered a drawing room that emanated wealth. Gold and maroon tiles spiraled upward along the lined columns in mesmerizing patterns while teal tiles covered the floor, giving the illusion we walked upon an oasis. Wide doorways were framed with gauzy curtains that draped down and swayed in time with the desert breeze, and the ceiling was decorated with gilded suns, resembling the emblem on Rayal's choker.

Though the city was hot and dry, the drawing room

remained cool, and I realized it was due to a constant stream of misters placed throughout the area.

My nails dug into my skin, creating half-moons on my palms.

Why would the king be blasting misters when elves on the streets were begging for water? He must be hoarding all the resources for himself.

Thaydril led us to a seated area where couches, settees, and cushions laid around the room. Plants filled the space, lending a vibrant green that was missed from the city that claimed to be an oasis. I could only guess how much water it took to keep these plants alive and thriving.

The palace was in pristine condition, nothing like the city we had walked through.

Suddenly, Rayal appeared out of a swaying curtain, followed by even more guards. Her hair was a blend of braided and curly textures that surrounded her face and fell to her hips. Gold makeup, bangles, and hair jewelry shone vibrantly against her rich brown skin. She wore a light-weight marigold dress that twisted down her chest and flowed elegantly to the floor. She was decorated from head to toe in regal opulence.

She was truly a princess—no. A queen.

A queen robbed of her throne.

My eyes darted to Dyani, but her gaze was locked on the princess, and she folded at the waist to bow.

"Welcome, friends," Rayal said, her gaze welcoming yet snapping to Dyani before finding me again. The memory of her bright eyes had comforted me, but as I gazed upon her face, her spark had faded. As if she too were exhausted by the lies and appearances her step-uncle maintained.

When I was locked away in the Crypts, Rayal snuck into my cell and gave me not only food, but hope. Hope in a place I thought would be my grave. She had saved me in more ways than one.

And now it was my turn to return the favor.

The palace was gold and glimmering, and if I weren't standing within it, talking with the princess, I would have thought it a beautiful mirage. "Thank you," I said, offering her as much strength through my eyes as possible. I remembered to keep up the ruse in front of the guards and added, "You have no idea how good it is to see you."

She smiled and walked to Rowen and Dyani. "I remember you both from the Crypts," she said with an appreciative nod. "Thank you both for helping save me and all the souls trapped within."

"It was my honor," Rowen said with a slight half bow.

Her eyes perused my soul flame with a calculating stare, almost as if she were sizing him up for something. "I do recall your valiant efforts in the Crypts. The Alcreon Light is lucky to have you," she said before her gaze turned to Maddock. "But you. I don't recall."

He bowed. "I'm afraid I was trapped in another prison, Your Highness. Keira saved me from a dark hell as well."

Her eyes shot to mine questioningly. "He is attached to you?"

"He is," I said, and for the first time, bitterness didn't coat the words. Maybe I was finally coming to accept Maddock.

Dyani cleared her throat. "Sun casts upon sun? That's quite the riddle."

Rayal's eyes wandered to the warrior, a moment of lingering perusal before finding my eyes. A faint breeze blew through the courtroom and swayed my dress against my bare skin.

"It is a doorway that reflects the outside world. But my cousin is the expert on all matters concerning the Eye of the Sun," she said casually, walking to the Keeper of the Arch. The cousins embraced.

"It is good to see you. You are looking well," Thaydril said, kissing both of Rayal's dewy cheeks.

Rayal's smile appeared, bright and genuine, and for the first time, I noticed she had matching dimples on either side of her grin. "As do you, cousin."

"A doorway, you say?" Dyani asked, repeating Rayal's words.

"Of course," Thaydril replied, stepping away from the princess. "The Eye of the Sun can be a door that leads anywhere."

"Anywhere?" Rowen asked with a calculating look in his eye.

"Anywhere," Thaydril confirmed with a mischievous smirk. "At the king's behest, of course."

"Yes, of course," Rowen agreed, looking so comfortable and assured in his surroundings. It was a gift he had, to appear as if every space were made for him as if he owned every room he entered. His commanding presence was hard to ignore and exuded off him in a predatory elegance.

"The king awaits you at the Sun Dial," the Keeper said, turning to face me.

"One last thing," Rayal announced, pulling something out of the pocket of her dress. She ran up to me and placed a hooded veil over my head, pulling the sheer fabric down to cover my eyes and nose. Only my lips and chin remained uncovered.

"I can barely see!" I exclaimed, tilting my head back.

"It's covering up all my makeup," Thaydril complained.

"You look beautiful," Rayal said, straightening the veil. "And mysterious."

I took a deep breath through my nose and straightened my spine. I was a wolf in sheep's clothing—a seemingly innocent mare ready to bare her teeth to the unsuspecting king.

⸻ ·⊂·❍·⊃· ⸻

Thaydril and Rayal walked us through the palace in a procession that felt equal parts like a parade and a death march.

I was to meet with the king and prove the worth of my blood. I had to convince a ruler of a city to come out of hiding and aid us in battle. It was no small request, but with the number of guards I'd seen, they had plenty of soldiers who could help us defeat Erovos.

The elves of Hara'dune might feel safe behind their arch, but the darkness seeping into the world would eventually find them. I just had to make them see that . . . if they didn't already. How could they not? Children were begging for water in the streets.

I was terrified to meet King Aedris. How could I convince him to join our battle after he had hidden himself away and ignored all the signs of a dying earth?

It was as Rayal said—I would have to bleed for him.

I shivered as I thought about cutting myself again. The mark from Rayal's cut was already healing, but the memory of the blunt blade ripping me open made my skin crawl.

My gaze shot back up as we were led through a long, stone tunnel that opened up into an expansive courtyard. There was a circular dais, engraved with lines and symbols I couldn't decipher. Directly in the center of the platform was a massive upright pointer in the shape of a triangle. The inclined edge of the pointer cast a shadow onto the dais, and I realized I was standing on a giant sundial.

One side of the dial had colosseum-style seating, filled to the brim with elves, and on the other, stood a massive spherical sculpture made of concentric rings.

"Step to the gnomon, Alcreon Light Bearer," said a commanding voice that could only belong to King Aedris. My eyes snapped to the pointer of the dial—the gnomon—which also happened to be the throne. He gestured to the center of the sundial, where he sat on a chair of solid gold. "I cannot cut you open from way back there."

39

———

Every muscle in my body rejected his words, and bile crept up my throat. I wished I could summon a lightning storm. Instead, I had to willingly approach the king like a gentle breeze.

What else could I do? I needed his help. Desperately. Countless lives depended on it. There was no way we could defeat Erovos and his army alone.

I took my first step toward the king, my bare leg slipping through the slit of my sheer dress. Rowen grabbed my hand from behind, offering a squeeze before our fingers trailed away with my next step.

"What is she doing?" Maddock asked, concern etched on his face. Rowen put a hand to his chest, warning him with a look. Madds stared at me questioningly, but I snapped my head to the gnomon. I couldn't look back.

Rayal told me to keep the king intrigued, but I figured the dress and veil were doing most of the work.

I walked toward Aedris with determined steps, feeling like a bride at some fucked up wedding. He waited for me to approach, sitting far too comfortably on a throne that didn't belong to him.

348

Dirt clawed at my throat, and the sun beat down on my brow. I'd had to stand and be judged by a council before. However, this time, I would be palpated and gutted like an animal.

At least now, I knew the power I carried within my veins, and I let it radiate through me like a crown of stardust and dignity.

The king rose to meet me, and though I could barely see him, his curiosity was palpable. My heartbeat pounded in my ears, and my breath came in short, shallow bursts. Was he going to cut me right now?

He raised his hands, and I braced myself, expecting to feel the cold sting of a blade against my neck. Instead, he merely grabbed the edges of my veil and pulled it back over my head, letting the fabric fall to my feet.

I lifted my gaze to one of the most striking men I'd ever seen. He was tall, muscular, and beautiful, with a golden crown resting atop his greying hair.

His tan skin glistened against his white-and-gold robes, and a well-kept beard framed his strong features. I was close enough now that I could see the pale blue color of his eyes dancing across my face.

His voice boomed and echoed across the courtyard. "So you are the prophesied one my niece speaks of."

"I am," I said, my voice low yet unshaken. "Funny though, I've never heard of you. It must be because you hide behind an arch while the rest of the world suffers."

The king barked out a laugh, his near-translucent eyes trailing up every inch of my body. His gaze lingered on my ears where the Light peeked through like star-studded jewels.

I recognized the predatory stare. It was the same look Harlan, Demil, and Erovos had given me. Even Aliphoura and Maddock at times.

I was told that the Alcreon Light revealed one of two natures: one that sought to protect, while the other, to possess.

My senses sharpened on instinct because the king fell into the latter category. Though he would soon learn I was anything but prey.

"The world has taken many violent turns," he finally answered. "We protect ourselves behind the arch to escape all that. What happens beyond its threshold is of little concern to us."

"How can you say that?" I asked incredulously. "It has already affected you. Elves are suffering in your streets. You are running out of water."

His posture didn't flinch. "The water running a little low has been known to happen on occasion. It is no cause for concern."

"It may seem like a small drought that will eventually pass, but can't you feel the air? It's different. No healing rain will come to save you, and your circumstances will only worsen." My chest heaved as I tried to plead my case. "A world eater is slowly sucking Luneth dry, and it's only a matter of time before he and his astral demons find you. No one is safe. Not even a king holed up in a palace."

"What an imagination you have," he said with a flippant chuckle.

"Erovos has an army ready to end this world. One bite from his demons will turn you into a Voro-Kai—a soulless monster out for blood and destruction."

The crowd gasped and murmured amongst themselves.

The king's stare snapped to his subjects and then back to me. "Is this what you came here for? To spread terror with your fear-mongering? If that is all, you may go now. Your mission is accomplished."

"That's not all," I replied, raising my chin. "I've come to ask for your army's aid in battle."

His stare regarded me with amusement and perhaps respect. "We've heard tales of the Marked Son. My niece made certain we all knew the prophecy. But you are no son," he said, his eyes roving over every inch of my skin. "And far from what anyone expected."

"Expectations don't matter now. I'm the one standing here," I replied, reining in my breathing. "Your army must use the arch to reach the Wyn village. That's where our forces are stationed and where skilled bladesmiths are forging the only weapons capable of defeating the Voro-Kai. If you won't help us, at least take some blades and arrows to defend yourselves when they eventually come for you."

Aedris was slow and deliberate with his words. "The former heir to the throne was quick to believe these fables. I, on the other hand, require more convincing. As I'm sure you understand."

I held my chin firm, knowing what he was about to ask of me.

"Are you ready to bleed?" he asked, his eyes darting to my pounding pulse.

"For the ruler of Hara'dune? Of course," I replied, keeping my voice steady despite the tornado of nerves raging within me. I couldn't push him too hard. Not yet.

He nodded off to the side, and an attendant ran to the center of the dial. His pale skin and red hair caught the sunlight as he placed a dried potted plant between us. The elve bowed to the king and retreated without a word.

Aedris grabbed my wrist slowly, allowing me time to withdraw, but I didn't budge. I wouldn't give him the satisfaction.

"Tales of your blood have certainly spread," he announced as he retrieved a knife from his robes. The pounding vein in my neck raced with my heartbeat.

He placed the tip of his blade on my pointer finger. I sucked in a sharp breath as he applied more pressure, and a bloom of blood sprouted on my finger,

Before I could drop the blood on the dried plant, Aedris plopped my finger into his mouth and sucked. Hard.

Disgust roiled through me as his tongue stroked the pad of my finger.

The ring of his unnaturally bright eyes shrank, and his pupils widened. He didn't stop me as I pulled my finger from his lips, fighting the urge to wipe his saliva on my dress.

"You certainly taste of the stars. Sweet and mouthwatering. But is it enough for me to lend you my army?"

"Take more, and let's find out," I said in a sultry murmur, gesturing to the dead bush between us.

"Very well then," he replied, reaching out for me once again.

Giving him my hand after he'd consumed a drop of my blood without consent was an act of the utmost control. I plastered on a grin and gave him my hand, wishing I could blast him with my Light.

Aedris' pupils continued to shrink as whatever effect my blood had on him worked its way through his system. I really hoped it didn't have ecstasy-inducing properties, but I feared that wasn't the case. Even Erovos knew that if he tasted me, he wouldn't be able to stop. And something told me Aedris didn't have nearly the self-control as an ancient spirit.

He held my wrist tight as he dragged the blade across my palm, a line of crimson seeping to the surface.

It hurt like hell, but I kept my face impassive as he tilted my hand and allowed my blood to drop onto the dead weeds between us.

And just as I knew it would, buds of green and white began pushing through the soil, fighting and searching for the light of life. As if watching a time-lapse, the sprouts grew until a small, thriving cactus plant emerged from the dead soil.

Though I was familiar, Aedris and the crowd were not, and they gasped when they realized what was happening. My eyes shot to Rowen for the first time since I'd been up on the dial, and his gaze flashed with worry as he watched Aedris' face. My stare shot back to Aedris, his expression turning from astounded wonder to pure, unadulterated desire.

It was at that moment I knew I was in danger.

"Keira," Rowen roared, but before I could react, the king grabbed me from behind my knee and hiked my leg up onto his hip. The folds of my dress fell down either side of my thigh as he pressed me closer to his chest. My hands landed on the tops of his shoulders as I fought to reclaim my balance.

Suddenly, I felt the sharp tip of his blade on the inside of my thigh, right at my femoral artery.

Fear choked up my throat. One slip, and I could bleed out in minutes. Aedris seemed to be thinking along the same lines.

"What is to keep me from draining you right here?" he asked with crazed eyes. Rowen, Dyani, and Maddock charged toward me, but the guards leaped into action with their curved blades.

My heart seized in terror. Though they were exceptional fighters, they were unarmed against the desert elves. It wouldn't be a fair fight.

I raised my hand and motioned for them to stop. Maddock and Dyani hesitated, looking to Rowen. My soul flame heeded my command and froze within the guard's hold, but I could tell by the raging fire in his eyes and the heaving of his chest that it was taking all of his strength not to fight his way to me.

My pulse rang in my ears as Aedris' grip tightened on my leg, the blade pressing deeper into my skin.

"It's a whole world in need, not just the city you've recently come to rule. Draining me for your own gain would certainly help the elves of Hara'dune," I said as he pressed harder, drawing a nick of blood that seeped down my thigh. "But my blood is not a long-term solution." I tried to remain as calm as possible, considering my leg was wrapped around a man who threatened to exsanguinate me.

"I will have saved my people," he said, nodding to the crowd, my leg still hitched at his hip. "With the help of your body."

Despite the mayhem, my eyes remained calm and fixed on Aedris. "You will have given them a false hope, turned to ash as swiftly as a burning bush."

"This is most inappropriate," Rayal shouted with an authority that reminded me of Nepta. I prayed the desert elves realized she was the true ruler of their city—their queen who'd been unjustly pushed to the sidelines. If they couldn't see, I would just have to remind them.

Aedris' grip on my knee tightened before reason suddenly flashed through his eyes. He released me with a shrug and straightened his sash around his shoulder.

"I'm told you brought down an entire cavern. I see the wildness in your eyes. If I agree to help you, you would need to pledge your body to me," he stated matter-of-factly, his hand gesturing from my feet to the top of my head. "You are a weapon—a dangerous one at that. And as the greatest sovereign of Luneth, it is only fitting that the greatest weapon should be under my command. You in exchange for my troops."

My heart plunged into my stomach like a boulder, and my face paled at his proposal.

"Absolutely not," Rowen roared behind me.

I couldn't turn around to look at him. I knew his face would crumble my resolve, and we were out of options. "What are the terms of this pledge?" I asked, not stepping down or backing up a single step.

"Keira, don't," Dyani snapped. "Do not entertain this."

Aedris bent down and plucked the small pink succulent from the revived plant. "Your body would be pledged to me in times of war as well as in times of peace," he said, looking up from the cactus flower. "And love."

I nearly gagged at the insinuation but quickly swallowed my emotions as the negotiation for my body began.

"You're right," I said, though the lie tasted like dirt. "It does make sense for the greatest city to possess the strongest weapon. I never thought about it that way."

The king's shocked expression quickly morphed into triumph. "I'm happy to hear that you are seeing reason."

"I could hand myself over," I said, speaking as if I were still in control despite my vulnerable position. "But what would be the fun in that? It seems like you like a little challenge. Let's discuss a plan for a worldwide solution." I leaned closer to him, though my body was repulsed. "I'm sure we could come to an agreement," I countered, trying to tamp down the rapid heaving of my chest. I kept my face a stoic mask, one I'd learned from Nepta.

"No," was his casual reply.

So much for negotiations. It appeared he wasn't willing to budge. And as much as we needed his armies, the price wouldn't —couldn't—be my body.

"Then it's a no for me as well. Which is a shame. I looked forward to working with the mightiest ruler of Luneth," I replied, remembering Rayal said her uncle loved a challenge so long as he was winning. "Thank you for your hospitality. We will be leaving now."

"It appears we are at an impasse," he said, grabbing my wrist and turning me back towards him. "Although," he mused, and my pulse ratcheted up once again, "you did mention a challenge." His eyes glinted, tracing up and down my body. "If you win, my help is granted in whatever way you need."

He knew we were desperate for his help, and the mischievous glint in his eye told me he was enjoying this.

"And if I lose?"

"You will be mine in whatever way I see fit," he said, his unnaturally bright eyes roving down my body with lust. "And maybe you could convince me to send troops."

"What is the trial?" I asked.

"You will have to agree before I disclose such information."

It was a risk worth taking, though I knew the emerald eyes watching from the crowd would disagree. I could feel Rowen's emotions through our bond, begging me to refuse. "Decide quickly. The sun is already beginning to set."

"If I win, your army will fight by my side. If I lose," I said, stepping closer to him and trailing my hands along his muscled arms. I blinked up at him through my lashes. "My body shall belong to the true and mighty ruler of Hara'dune. Those are the terms. Do you accept?"

"I accept," Aedris grinned, and the air crackled with the energy of our deal.

My fate was sealed.

He placed his hand on the small of my back and directed me toward the giant sculpture of rings. "This is an armillary sphere, an instrument used to track the movement of the heavens. It can map the past, present, and some believe the future. The central globe represents Luneth, while the neat and tidy rings depict the entirety of the cosmos. The trial is to activate the four celestial runes and make it to the center globe before nightfall catches your heels."

Oh. That didn't seem so hard. The armillary sphere was massive, but it looked like a pretty straight shot to the center. But that couldn't be all, could it? If I appeared too confident, Aedris might rescind on our deal.

I ignored the pull of Rowen's presence—a presence so strong, it had pulled me across galaxies. Across worlds.

If I thought about our soul flame bond right now, it would knock me off my game. "I should also mention, no one has been able to activate it for some time. Though that should be no problem for you and your abilities."

"Let's just go," I ground out, softening my knees into a runner's stance.

"Very well," Aedris said with a confident air. He waved his ringed fingers over the armillary sphere. "Your time begins . . . now."

40

I sprinted toward the celestial globe and ran up the staircase to the center ring.

The giant metal hoops were smooth and slippery, and my sandals had absolutely no grip. I would have to watch my step as I worked my way through the skeletal sphere.

My eyes darted for the first marker, scanning for divots or protrusions of any kind, but there were none to be seen.

I jogged around to the other side, the rings hovering around me like a giant ribcage. Finally, I spotted a diamond-shaped marker engraved into the golden surface. Upon further inspection, I noticed it was a sun rune.

I had no idea what I was supposed to do. Aedris had been sparse with his information, and I'd failed to ask the right questions. If my abilities weren't suppressed, I would blast it with my Light. But my time to solve this sphere was running out. The sun was setting fast.

My fists balled in frustration, and a sharp pain flared in my hand.

My blood!

I placed my sliced palm on the symbol, praying to the spirits that it worked. I had no other ideas, but as soon as my blood touched the rune, Light entered the engraving in a shimmering blaze.

I let out a relieved sigh. Now that I knew what to do, I would have enough time to find and activate the markers before sunset.

Suddenly, the ring beneath me shifted, threatening to throw me off balance. I braced myself as the armillary sphere detached from the staircase and rose from the ground. It kept rising until it completely hovered in the air.

Then, the rings around me began to shift, and my stomach dropped as the hoops groaned and whirred to life.

I had no idea it moved! And Aedris had conveniently with-held that information.

The ring I stood on spun faster as it tilted up to begin its horizontal rotation. If I didn't move, I would slide right off the sphere as it spun.

I bolted up, searching for the second rune. I scanned the map of the heavens with my heart in my throat. The crowd roared in my ears and clashed against the violent beat of my pulse.

My eyes darted frantically as the ring beneath me tilted more and more. The second marker flashed as it rotated by, but it was spinning vertically around me. I'd have to jump onto the ring as it descended into a horizontal turn, with only a split-second window to land the jump.

It didn't escape my notice that Aedris hadn't allowed me time to prepare. Or even change. I was wearing the worst outfit possible.

I quickly kicked off the slippery sandals and held the panels of my dress in my fists.

My muscles tightened in anticipation; one wrong step and I would plummet to the ground. I inhaled a deep breath as the rings aligned, praying muscle memory from my track days kicked in. I hadn't known just how much I was running for my life back then. And today would be no different, aside from the fact that I wasn't running for my sole survival but for everyone else's. I knew what would happen without Aedris' army, and it would be a massacre.

I pushed off my dominant leg and launched myself into the air. The moment of weightlessness struck terror into my soul. It seemed to last forever as I hovered high above the desert city.

It wasn't until both of my feet landed on the precarious platform that I could breathe again. I landed in a crouch and used the position to launch myself into a sprint. There would be enough time to catch the third marker as it spun back around. But suddenly, I was yanked back violently, my wrist taking the brunt of my fall. I felt something snap, and I cried out in pain.

I went to stand, careful not to put pressure on my wrist, but I was yanked back again.

I shot my gaze backward.

When I'd jumped, the convergence of metal on metal caught my dress. The rings slowly pulled me towards the joint that would crush me to death.

I desperately clawed at the ground, scrambling to escape, but my fingertips found no purchase on the smooth metal surface.

The audience gasped in horror as I was sucked back by the train of my dress. Not wasting another second, I viciously tore at the fabric, ripping it past my knees. I was free, and the cloth vanished from sight as it was sucked through the hinge of the rotating gears.

I dashed to the second marker without thinking, only acting on the adrenaline pumping through my veins. It was a rune of the moon, and I quickly lit it as I had done the first. My blood touched the symbol, and it sparked to life as if it recognized me.

The rings picked up speed, and the sound of the spinning wheels whooshed around me like a wind turbine. My hair blew in my face as I shot up, searching for the next marker. It was above me and already circling to disappear out of sight.

I barely had enough time to catch the next ring as its axis changed. I jumped onto it without falling or catching my dress, and I grinned. I was finally getting the hang of it!

The crowd let out another collective gasp, and I barely turned around in time to see a ring flying right at me. I ducked, narrowly missing being decapitated.

This was a steel trap of death!

I sprinted towards the third marker, my body veering to hug the innermost lane of the ring. I dropped to the ground and quickly lit the marker, this one engraved with a series of planets.

The rings began to spin faster and faster, and terror sat in my throat like a stone. I removed the heavy thought, needing to be as light on my feet as possible. The sun was setting by the second, the bright light lessening as it curved back behind the earth, but I still had one last marker to find.

I ran around the ring, searching for the final marker. I couldn't see it anywhere. I jumped to another shifting platform, and there it was! Placed on the center orb of the armillary sphere.

I raced against the sun for the final rune.

I waited for the ring to pass and timed my jump, but with a gust of wind and the axis shifting, I lost my center of balance and slipped off the edge of the ring.

My fingers barely caught the smooth lip as my legs dangled beneath me, and I swore I heard someone scream my name.

My arms were on fire as my legs searched for a foothold that wasn't there. The wind rushed around me and threatened to sweep me off the celestial globe. My wrist screamed out in pain, but I couldn't let go. I wouldn't survive a fall from this height.

With trembling arms and a shaking wrist, I screamed as I pulled myself up. I wanted to lay back and kiss the ring, but I didn't have time. My body shook with adrenaline as I darted up and sprinted to the final marker.

As I placed my bloody palm on the final rune, silver-white light surged through the structure, alighting the whole armillary sphere in runes. A mixture of silver and gold light shot out of the globe in a beam of intertwining moonlight and sunshine.

I made it. I won!

My chest heaved as relief coursed through me, and the sphere stopped spinning. It lowered to the ground and halted in a plume of dust.

As I made my way down the staircase, clutching the railing for support, Aedris appeared through the sand, striding confidently toward me. He didn't look furious or upset. He looked happy.

"You lost," he said with a smug grin.

"No, I didn't," I shot back, exhaustion threatening to overcome me. "I lit all the markers before the sunset."

"Your heel hit the shadow, I'm afraid. You have failed, Alcreon Light Bearer," he said, walking toward me. "Though you did put on an impressive show."

"Wait. No. That's not—"

"You are mine now," he said, pulling a gold collar from his robes. He must have had that all along! He'd never meant for me to win, and now he would collar me like a dog. "This is just for precaution. It is imbued with the power of our deal."

Two of his guards snatched me off the staircase and held me before the king. Their fingers dug into my flesh and bruised my skin.

Aedris stepped up to me and brushed my hair away from my neck. "You will be my greatest treasure—a celestial light collared for me to command in whatever way I choose." He encircled the choker around my throat, and the cold bite of the metal raised the hairs on the back of my neck.

Familiar voices erupted in fury.

I slammed my eyes shut as disgust bubbled inside of me. "We had a deal," I gritted out as he latched the collar around my neck.

"We did," he said, and I could hear the grin in his voice. "And you were foolish enough to pledge your body to me. There are so many possibilities. I'm not sure where to begin."

A small smile spread on my face, and my eyes flashed open. "I pledged myself to the true ruler of Hara'dune. And that's not you, is it?"

Aedris' hands fumbled as the latch wouldn't take. It was not him to whom I pledged myself, and when he realized what I'd done, his eyes widened in outrage. "How dare you utter such accusations!"

I raised my voice for all to hear. "Rayal is the true descendant of the throne. And you stole it from her. She is the rightful queen of Hara'dune."

The crowd emitted a unified gasp, looking to their leader.

"That is not true," he answered, the veins in his forehead looking like they were about to explode. "I wear the crown!" He acted like a petulant child unable to play with his favorite toy. "You have defied the great king of Hara'dune and are therefore sentenced to a life of labor in the sand pits."

Elves shouted from the crowd. "Usurper!"

"False King!"

"Liar!"

"Tyrant!"

Aedris' eyes widened in terror. "Guards! Attack the treasonists!"

Terror clogged up my throat, but I'd done what I could. These elves knew who their true ruler was. And in a unified fury, they charged the sundial.

41

———————

As the stampede of elves rushed toward Aedris, the guards dropped me and formed a protective circle around the king.

"Attack!" Aedris screamed at his soldiers.

A stray elbow caught me in the face, and my head snapped back as stars clouded my vision. Warmth pooled under my nose as droplets of blood fell onto my white dress.

I hadn't meant to get entangled in a revolt, not when a bigger war marched closer every day. Yet here I was, standing directly in the middle of a revolution.

I swayed on my feet as Rowen and Maddock charged through the dust like two beautiful titans. They consumed my narrowing vision as they sprinted toward me.

Rowen caught me just before I fell. His emotions poured over me in desperate waves, a raging tempest that was easy to read as he noted the blood on my face and the gold collar at my feet. Whereas Maddock was barely containing himself. It looked as if he wanted to touch and examine me for himself.

Convinced that I was mostly unharmed, Rowen gathered me in his embrace.

Even though a battle erupted around us, I wanted to break

364

down and cry in his arms. "I failed," I said, holding onto him so tight that my fingers bunched the fabric of his shirt. Maddock hugged me from the back, offering me more comfort as he kissed my head.

I'd believed that somehow Hara'dune would help us defeat Erovos and save Indrasyl. But without their help, there was no other choice. I would have to . . .

"No, Keira. You were perfect. It's not over yet," he murmured against me.

Two sets of arms held me and stroked me as a battle raged around us.

Rowen said he wouldn't survive if he lost me again, so how could I go through with Indrasyl's plan, knowing it would kill us both?

I wished I could give him a reason to keep living without me.

Suddenly, Dyani, Rayal, and Thaydril cut their way through the commotion. The guards were armed, and the rioting elves were armed only with anger.

"You must go," Rayal urged. "While there is pandemonium. If you are here when the dust settles, Aedris will throw you into the sand pits."

"I'll kill him," Rowen snarled, kicking the collar away from me. "For making her bleed."

"I'll be right behind you," Maddock agreed, his hands still on me.

The princess shook her head. "He is too heavily guarded. You must go."

"Come with me," Thaydril agreed through the chaos. "I will open the arch for you and take you home."

I grabbed Rowen's corded arm. "Our role here is done," I said, knowing there was nothing more we could do. "We need to focus on the battle ahead."

"Can you run?" he asked, his eyes trailing down my body.

Barefoot and clad in a ripped dress that billowed around me like the ghost of my hopes, I nodded. Rowen and Maddock helped me to my feet, and without another word, we sprinted into the fray, weaving through the uprising growing more violent by the second.

One of the guards grabbed Rayal by the arm. "You're not going anywhere," he growled, handling and yanking her roughly.

Dyani pounced from the crowd like a mountain cat. "Get your hands off her," she snarled and punched him square in the face. The guard howled in pain as his hands flew to his bloody nose.

Rayal shot her eyes to Dyani. "I could have done that."

"I know, but I've wanted to do that since we got here," the warrior replied, her silver ponytail billowing in the wind.

The princess grinned.

"Quickly," Thaydril called as he led the way back through the city. We cut through the empty streets and passed the drying lake. The acrid taste of failure coated my tongue as my bare feet pounded against the ground. I may have lost this battle, but I still had a war to win.

The giant arch finally came into view, towering like a marvel with its shimmering curtain of sand.

We were all out of breath and clutching our sides.

Thaydril's eyes found me, his chest heaving. "The arch will take you home."

"Our weapons," Dyani reminded him, patting her empty hips. "You said we would get them back."

Thaydril rolled his eyes with a heavy sigh. "I'll be right back." His yellow cape flourished behind him as he darted through the arch.

"Come with us," I said, turning to Rayal.

"I cannot leave now," the princess replied, shaking her head.

"Not when you have planted the seed of my reign. I wish I could thank you properly, but we don't have much time, and there is something you must know."

"What is it?" I asked as her golden stare turned to Rowen.

"Have you ever considered reuniting Viltarran?"

Rowen's eyes widened in shock. "I have. Several times, but I hold no claim."

"What if you did?" the princess asked. And suddenly, Erovos' words rang through me like a gong. He had called Rowen a lord.

Was Viltarran rightfully his? The land where he had grown up and lived a struggled life with his mother—a scullery maid who sacrificed everything to love and protect him? The very land his lord and father figure had charged him with protecting?

Rowen's sharp, green eyes narrowed, shooting me a glance. "What do you mean?" he asked the princess carefully.

"What if you have a true and binding title?"

"That's impossible," Rowen said, his strong jaw flexing. "Aliphoura murdered her father before he could bequeath it to anyone."

"As you well know, I was a prisoner in Aliphoura's crypts, but that doesn't mean I stayed put. I explored her underground kingdom as much as I could. It was how I smuggled in food for Keira," Rayal said, her eyes flashing with the dark memory. "I searched for a way out or any other weaknesses the queen might have. I found her private quarters once. It was a depraved place, filled with toys and torture devices."

She shook off the memory and reached into her dress pocket, pulling out a folded piece of paper. "This is for you."

With a questioning look, Rowen took the parchment from her outstretched hand and unfolded the letter.

I waited with bated breath as Rowen read the writing. His eyes snapped to mine. "It says I am the true ruler of Viltarran."

My mouth dropped, and my broken heart filled with joy.

This was exactly what I was looking for! A reason for Rowen to live.

"I went through Aliphoura's desk. My father was a king, so I know all about hidden compartments, and in one of the drawers was this: Lord Leones' final will and testament," Rayal said, gesturing to the scroll in Rowen's hands. "It says that you, Rowen Damascus, are the rightful heir of Viltarran. I caught her speaking of you many times. Her goal was always to get you back. Her plan was to abduct Keira and use her as leverage to get you to do whatever she wanted, even impregnate herself with your heir. Any question of her claim would be silenced through your child. She would have succeeded had it not been for Keira's cave-in."

I almost vomited. What a depraved plan. The night Rowen had exchanged his body for mine, Fou made it clear she was going to rape him. But to bring a child into the world in that way was despicable.

I had torn down her entire kingdom to ensure he escaped such a fate.

"It does look like Lord Leones' handwriting," Rowen confirmed as he gripped the paper like a letter from home.

"Can you rebuild Viltarran? Reunite your people?" I asked, staring at his severe yet striking beauty. He was born for this role. His powerful aura was undeniable and exuded from his every pore.

"I will certainly try," he said, his throat bobbing from choked-up emotion.

Realization shredded my soul as the blood drained from my face. He would try without me.

"Keira, what's wrong?" Rowen asked, his thick brows creasing.

Oh no. I couldn't risk Rowen feeling my agony through our bond. Instead, I shoved all the hurt, anger, and fury away from our connection. I thought I was in the clear when Madds suddenly doubled over and grunted as if he'd been punched in the gut.

Rowen's gaze shot to Maddock. "Madds?" He asked, concern engulfing his voice, but the thief of my Light and bond stared at me, his nostrils flaring.

"It's nothing," he replied, his hooded eyes snapping to Rowen.

"Erovos called you a lord," I said, taking the attention away from Maddock, who looked like he was about to be sick. "Even he knows you are the rightful heir of Viltarran."

Rowen faltered and lowered the letter. "I don't know if I can do it."

"You can," I said, grabbing his hands that held the scroll. "I know your strength and compassion; your integrity and ability to care for others. I've seen your sketches and heard the love in your voice when you speak of where you came from. You could restore it all and make a better future for your people."

"A future?" he asked as if remembering a dream from another lifetime. He'd been in survival mode for so long, living each day on the brink of life and death. There was hardly a moment to contemplate what lay beyond the war. "Leones made comments, but I never thought he was serious. And I told him I didn't want it."

"Those who do not seek power are those who deserve it most," Rayal said, her eyes softening at Rowen's confession. "Look at the false queen and my step-uncle, going to any lengths to rule, much to the detriment of their people. Their laws hurt everyone but themselves, and they line their pockets no matter the cost paid in blood and lives. Those who can easily gain such power are the ones who should never have it."

Thaydril shot back through the curtain of sand, carrying our weapons. "Here you go," he said as we grabbed our rightful pieces. A sense of completeness washed over me as Mithrion returned to my grip.

In the distance, the sound of rioting grew closer.

Thaydril parted the curtain of sand with a practiced motion. Nestled through the arch like a painting was a lush forest, brimming with greenery, mist, and morning dew.

A Hara'dune sunset blazed at my back while a Wyn sunrise flickered on my face.

"Time to go," Thaydril said urgently.

"Good luck with your war," the princess said, her eyes filled with regret. "I wish to the spirits I could help you."

Dyani took the princess's hand and bowed, placing a kiss upon her wrist. "I hope to see you again one day," she said before backing into her forest.

"Yes, would love that," Maddock said, following after her. "As long as there is no sand involved."

Thaydril kept the connection between forest and desert open as I stepped through the arch.

"Keira," Rowen said, grabbing my hand to stop me. The way he said my name made my heart drop into my stomach. His dark expression was tortured yet set with determination. "I need to find what's left of Viltarran. I can unite my people now. The warriors I once commanded under Lord Leones' rule might help us. We need more numbers." He turned to the man who first welcomed us into Hara'dune. "Thaydril, can you help me get there?"

The Keeper of the Arch noted my look of utter shock, then pivoted to Rowen and nodded. "I can, but we must hurry."

"I can't bear to be away from you," Rowen said as he stood on golden sand and I upon moss. "You are my reason for living, the oxygen that keeps me breathing, and the fire that keeps me fighting. But I must—"

"I know," I said, our bodies standing a world apart yet

clutching each other through the Eye of the Sun. "And I need to be here."

"I will come back with help. I promise you," he said before kissing me with an intensity that stole the breath from my lungs.

He pulled his lips from mine, the shadows in his eyes darkening. It looked as though he were pulling away from life itself. His green gaze shot to Maddock with a frightening intensity. "Take care of her."

"You know I will," Madds promised, his voice deep and resounding.

"Okay. It's really time to go," Thaydril urged, glancing over his shoulder at the approaching guards.

Rowen clutched my cheek and wiped a tear with his thumb. I didn't even know I was crying. "I will bring armies to your feet," he whispered to me. "Let's get through this war, and I will rule cities with you, make a better world with you, and worship you like the goddess you are."

For a heartbeat, I thought about telling him everything, but then, the Earth shook as I'd never felt it shake before. The ground trembled like the world was ripping apart.

"Erovos!" I cried, my and Rowen's eyes locking onto each other. "He'll go back to Indrasyl!"

"I can't hold the portal," Thaydril grunted as streams of dirt and rock fell between us.

"Give me two days. I'll meet you there," Rowen called through the diminishing connection. "I love you."

"I love you, too," I called back, wanting to yank him back to me and never let go.

Erovos' earthquake was too much to fight, and with a strained groan, Thaydril lost control of the arch.

Maddock pulled me back as Rowen, my soul flame, my rock, my everything, disappeared in a crashing avalanche of sand.

42

——————

I stood silent and unmoving. My body numb and ears ringing.

There was no way Erovos and his army hadn't escaped the crevice with that quake.

"Keira." I heard my name, but it was a muffled call. The loss of Rowen by my side hit me like a crashing meteor. I might never see him again. He swore he would come back to me, but what if he was too late?

All my hopes hinged on the desert elves helping us. Yes, Rowen had gone to find another army, but realistically, how many soldiers could he find? Viltarran was destroyed; its people scattered to the winds. It would take months, maybe even years, to reunite his people.

Indrasyl said our joining was the only way to save Rowen—to save everyone. I had foolishly believed I would find another way. But I had officially run out of time.

"Keira!" someone shouted again, knocking me out of my stupor.

"I think Erovos just escaped," Dyani said, standing in her beloved forest yet looking like a desert elve. "I'll go get Nepta."

The warrior sprinted away, leaving me alone with Maddock.

"What the fuck was that?" Maddock demanded from my periphery.

"I don't know what you're talking about," I said stoically, staring at where Rowen had disappeared.

"Like hell you don't," Madds seethed, grabbing me by the shoulders and spinning me to face him. "You're hiding something from Rowen and pushing it all to me. And it hurts like hell."

"I'm not," was all I could pathetically say.

He shook me by my shoulders. "What the fuck are you hiding?"

"Nothing."

He huffed a laugh. "You're a terrible liar. I hope you know what you're doing."

He dropped his arms from me, and with the loss of his touch, I felt more alone than ever.

I staggered on my bare feet as the flood of adrenaline faded. My body was shutting down. I hadn't slept in over twenty-four hours, my wrist was sprained, and I'd been elbowed in the face. But I couldn't rest; there was too much to do.

I took a wobbly step, but Madds blocked my path. "Where are you going?"

"Following Dyani," I pointed after her.

"Oh no, you're not."

"And why's that?" I asked, beyond exhausted.

"You need rest," he said, his warm gaze dipping up and down my body. "You are covered in blood and bruises, and you look like you are about to collapse."

"Dyani isn't resting, and neither is Rowen," I replied, my heart clenching as I pictured Rowen scouring the land for his people. Exhausted or not.

"In case you missed it, they weren't the ones attempting an impossible challenge in the sky. That bastard king cut you and tried to collar you," he said, his jaw twitching, and his eyes raging. "I've never felt so fucking terrified and helpless as when I watched you on that sphere."

"Well, I failed. Time to move on to the next plan," I said, turning my back to him.

He grabbed my wrist, the one that wasn't screaming in agony, and spun me back around. "Rowen told me to take care of you, and that's exactly what I plan on doing. You need rest and healing."

"I'm fine," I lied.

His face twisted in agitation. "No, you're not. Now, go to bed, or I'll put you to bed."

My jaw dropped. "You can't tell me what to do. I need to help."

"Why does it always have to be you, Keira? Why are you the one who has to be everything for everyone?" he asked, his hands clutching me, holding me as if he never wanted to let go. "Dyani is perfectly capable of relaying what happened in Hara'dune by herself."

"I have to—"

"Don't make me throw you over my shoulder," he threatened with an unyielding expression, looking nothing like the man I once saw in a coma. "You know I will."

I shouldn't have poked the bear, but I was too tired to care. I wrenched free of his grasp and stared him down. "You don't have the balls."

Suddenly, his hands were on me, and I was thrown over his shoulder. "Okay, okay, okay," I said, banging my good fist on his well-muscled back. "I'll walk."

"Too late," he said, holding me like I was a sack of potatoes.

"Put me down," I demanded, kicking my legs.

Maddock banded an arm across the backs of my thighs, holding me still. "Fight anymore, and I'll spank you. Your ass is in the perfect position, and I don't think Rowen will mind if it's for your own good."

I immediately went lax.

"Atta, girl." He chuckled, then adjusted me more comfortably over his shoulder. My cheeks burned in outrage, but I was too tired to keep fighting.

His smug smile radiated off him as he carried me to my and Rowen's dome.

— ·(·☾·●·☽·)· —

Maddock opened the door with his foot, carried me into the room, and plopped me on the bed. I bounced before I stilled in a pile of tight silk.

"I'm going to get Takoda. Don't move," he ordered before turning to go.

"Wait," I said, the boning of my dress pinching into my ribs.

He spun around with a dangerous look in his eyes. "Are you going to fight me on this, too? Do I need to tie you to the bed?"

"It's not that," I shot back, reaching to undo the dress, but the lacing was between my shoulder blades.

"What is it then?"

"I . . . I can't get out of this dress," I said through gritted teeth. I hated asking him for anything, but I only had one good hand.

His face softened, realizing the dress I wore was filthy, torn, and covered in my blood. "Oh. Here, let me help you."

I scooted off the bed and gave him my back. Maddock cleared his throat as he swept my hair off to the side. After a moment, I peered over my shoulder. "Everything okay?"

"There are a million knots back here," he said in shock. "Wait, hold on." He grabbed his Ever-burn blade and severed the laces in one fell swoop. My eyes shot open as I clutched the top of the dress to keep it from falling.

"Was that necessary?" I asked, breathing comfortably for the first time in what felt like ages.

"The dress was already ruined," he said, his voice suddenly deep and gravelly. His breath washed against the curve of my neck, and his knuckles brushed against my back. I sucked in a sharp breath as he traced his fingertips down the length of my spine.

His touch was nothing like Rowen's, yet there were tendrils of my soul flame bond that ran through his veins and ignited my skin.

The fact that he was here and Rowen wasn't made my blood boil. It was so wrong. If Madds didn't leave, he could use the stolen bond against me—against my body, and my skin would cave at the familiarity. "You need to go," I said, my chest heaving.

He backed away from me, his fingers slowly trailing away from my skin. "I'll go get Takoda," he said, clearing his throat again.

Once I was sure Maddock had left the dome, I changed into a slip and crashed onto the bed. Rowen's woodsy scent encompassed me like an infinite forest. I rolled onto his side of the bed and clutched the sheets smelling of him.

I curled deeper into his scent as tears burned my eyes, but I was too tired and numb to even cry.

·(·C·●·⊃·)·

I woke to the familiar rustle of branches overhead and comforting light-leaks through the dome. The momentary calm vanished as panic set in. I darted my hand to the other side of the bed, hoping Rowen had returned, but his side of the mattress remained cold and vacant.

Emptiness expanded in my chest like a balloon.

"Star-touched," a well-known voice said, and my eyes flicked up to Takoda.

"You're a sight for sore eyes," I said in a relieved exhale. This wasn't the first time I'd woken up with the healer tending to me while I slept. But it may be the last.

"As are you," he said with a gentle grin. "Always coming home with bumps and bruises. Nothing a few of your noxlily petals can't heal."

"Thank you," I said, sitting up to hug him. My hands encompassed the healer's lean frame, and I realized my wrist had been wrapped and my bruises tended to. I raised my hand to my face and felt the caked blood had also been cleaned.

"Maddock came to retrieve me," Takoda explained, packing away some of his medicinal powders. "You were already asleep when I arrived."

My gaze immediately shot up to the warm brown eyes watching me from across the room. His jet-black hair was in a state of disarray, as if he'd run his hands through it repeatedly.

My body stiffened under the sheets. He'd watched me sleep in the bed Rowen had claimed me in, over and over again in every way. Heart. Flame. Body. And soul.

Madds shouldn't be here.

"You can go now," I said curtly to Maddock. He may have tucked me in and fetched the healer, but I hadn't forgotten how he'd thrown me over his shoulder and threatened to spank me.

"Do you see the thanks I get?" he asked Takoda incredulously, throwing his arms in the air. He gave me one last smoldering look before darting out of the dome.

My eyes shot to the healer whose long, white hair and tan skin were striking against his dark green vest. "Everyone knows everything?" I asked, my voice taut with emotion.

"Yes, but do not fear," he replied, giving my hand a comforting squeeze. "We have been preparing for this. Our warriors are ready, and Nepta deployed them this morning. They march toward Erovos' brood."

"And Rowen?" I asked, fear clogging up my throat. I had no idea if he was alone or hurt. The only thing that reassured me he was alive was the steady flicker of our twin flames.

"He seeks the army of his people," Takoda said, his eyes coursing with an undercurrent of worry. "Change quickly and meet me at the Vale. There is something you should know."

43

———

Dressed in leggings and a pale blue vest with Mithrion strapped to my thigh, I entered the Sacred Vale. The watery pathway once intimidated me, but now I marched with determined steps.

Takoda pulled out a chair for me at the white quartz table where Alvar, Driskell, and Nepta sat. Dyani and Maddock weren't a part of the Summit, but they had been invited and stood nearby. My gaze flickered to the shattered Alcreon Stone floating above us before darting back to Nepta.

"Erovos' army is marching toward Indrasyl as you predicted. In the Lirien Valley," the Elven-head announced, sensing my eyes on her. "It is clear they mean to leave this world and carry on to the next. No doubt Erovos and his newborns are starved. Rowen's calculations of two days was correct. At the rate they are traveling, they will be there by morning."

My gaze shot across the table to Driskell. At the last Summit gathering, he said he would send correspondence to find help. "Did anyone agree to join us?"

Driskell frowned, his eyes glancing around the table.

Nepta answered for him. "Driskell beseeched other villages to aid us. Had other citydoms agreed, we would have outnumbered the demons ten to one. But only one thousand souls agreed to join our battle. Even now, they march with the Wyn warriors to Indrasyl. Everyone else regretfully declined, stating: the sooner this evil leaves our world, the better."

Shock engulfed me. "How is that possible? There won't be anything left. Erovos will make sure of it. He will use Indrasyl one final time, and there will be no coming back from that. If the Sylvan Mother Tree of this world dies, we will slowly succumb to floods, famine, and drought." My chest heaved in frustration. Why was no one willing to see the dire state of Luneth? It was like shouting into the void.

"Be that as it may, it is only we who will stop this cosmic darkness from spreading. I deployed our brave soldiers just after dawn, as soon as Alvar confirmed the crevice had been opened. Our forces are headed to the Lirien Valley, armed and transporting the Ever-burn weapons."

The war captain cleared his throat, his eyes glistening with terror while his body stood still as stone. "I was there when the mountain broke apart, keeping watch. The dark creatures poured out of the crevice like a plague, clawing over each other, scrambling and fighting for release. It was a nightmare to witness. I stayed hidden, thank the spirits, and counted every last demon that escaped." He shifted his arm as if reliving how he'd almost lost it. His dark eyes turned graver still, and his voice tightened. "They are ten thousand strong. Our warriors cap at seventeen hundred."

A chill ran down my spine. We were vastly outnumbered, and I feared the Wyn warriors marched to their destruction. "I have to get to the Mother Tree before they do," I said, not with fear but with pure determination. "I can astral project there and arrive before anyone else."

Nepta's sharp stare nearly sliced me in two. "With no army? No protection? And without your soul flame? We know Erovos can travel through dark tunnels. What if he is already there, waiting for you? What is to keep him from killing you the moment you arrive? Without an army to shield you, you will be vulnerable. We cannot be careless with you."

Her words rang true, and I nodded. It was hard to stay still when my body begged to jump into action. "Why can't you portal in the army? Why make them march?"

Nepta's half-moon staff rested in her hand, and her fingers tightened around the tool that helped her navigate the world. "My portals are not nearly big enough to transport an entire army. It would expend too much energy and take days. Not even Erovos is portaling in his army. He must be saving his strength for battle."

"Both armies will approach the Lirien Valley from the south, though they are ahead of us," the war captain said. His face was taut, accentuating the white scar on his chin. "By the time our forces arrive, the Voro-Kai will stand between us and Indrasyl. We will have to make a path to the tree. If you project there, you will have no protection. We must keep you surrounded at all times."

"Nepta relayed that you spoke with the Sylvan Mother Tree," Driskell said, his eyes gleaming with interest. "How very fascinating. What exactly did she say?"

All heads whipped to me, and my tongue turned bone-dry in my mouth.

"You know the prophecy better than anyone," I replied, meeting his stare head-on. "*Through blood and bone.* Seems pretty specific to me. I need to be there. You wanted to figure out how to use me as a weapon, well, that's how it's done."

"We need you on the front lines," the Reader of the Stars argued. "Are we meant to die while you speak to a tree?"

Alvar raised a silencing hand. "I am the war strategist,

Driskell. I do not counsel you on how to read the stars. Leave the battle planning to me."

Driskell huffed and folded his arms within his robes.

"Yes, it's important to destroy Erovos' army," I added, "but it is equally important to repair the damage he's caused to the earth. The Wyn village might be healing, but the rest of the world is suffering. Indrasyl's roots extend to everything. With her reach and my Light, we can try to heal Luneth."

I left out the part where I would become one with the tree. They didn't need to know that. I would wait until the last possible second, hoping beyond hope that Rowen found his army.

"What's to say you will be successful?" Driskell asked, his blunt statement taking me by surprise. "You see why I have pause. You failed to acquire the Hara'dune elves."

The failure hung from my neck like an albatross.

"That wasn't her fault," Dyani interjected, wearing her usual fighting leathers and henna-red jerkin. "The king was never going to help us."

"We must make do with the army we have," Nepta said, her voice steady despite the discouraging numbers.

"Rowen is searching for more soldiers," Takoda pointed out, offering a sliver of optimism. "Let us not forget that."

"Even if Rowen found every soldier from Viltarran, it would never make up the difference," Driskell said, his head, and the crystals hanging from his hair, dipped low.

The shift around the Vale was palpable.

My fingers flexed, reaching for the calloused hand that always found mine, but Rowen's reassuring touch was nowhere to be found. I balled my fists and took a deep breath, searching my own inner well for strength. My soul flame offered me a grounding presence, but it was always to support and uplift the strength he knew I had.

I wouldn't let Driskell have the final word.

I lifted my chin and met the eyes of everyone at the table. "Rowen, the lord of Viltarran, will bring help." The members of the Summit exchanged glances, letting my words sink in. "And you have me. I won't let us fail." Maddock shot me a sharp, questioning look, but I continued. "Erovos wants to bleed this world dry and move on to the next. He means to leave a trail of floating husks in space, but as long as we fight, there is still a chance we can defeat him."

"Here, here," Alvar said, flashing me a proud smile. "At dawn, Nepta will portal us to the edge of the Lirien Valley."

"And then what?" Dyani asked, placing her palm on the table.

"We march to the tree, and under no circumstances are we to engage first," he replied, leaning forward in his chair. "We need to draw the army away from the tree. This will allow a smaller team to slip around undetected, getting Keira to Indrasyl safely."

"Those demons foam at the mouth when they see her," Maddock said, shifting on his feet as all eyes turned to him. "If we want to lure them away, they will have to see her first."

"As bait?" Dyani asked incredulously. "You know Rowen would never go for that."

"We don't have much of a choice," Alvar said with a frown. "We will keep her hidden, and when the time is right, we will reveal her presence. The goal is to tempt the demons to charge recklessly towards us. Hopefully, this will serve as a distraction."

My hopes had been dashed more than I could count. But one last time, I prayed the spirits heard me. "Let's hope Rowen arrives with the help we need."

Not just to bolster our forces but so that I could see him one last time.

◦ ⟨ ⟨ ● ⟩ ⟩ ◦

It was the night before battle, and I was a nervous wreck. I paced the dome, picking at the skin around my nails and thumb. I needed to fuck my soul flame to release this pent-up frustration, but I'd left him in a desert halfway around the world.

I knew Thaydril would help him get to Viltarran, which wasn't far from the Wyn village, but with my aching heart and throbbing core, it might as well be oceans away.

Not having Rowen by my side on the eve of battle left my nerves shredded and raw. It felt like I was hacked in half. We already had so little time together, and now, we were separated by obligation and duty. The only thing that gave me the slightest bit of comfort was gripping Mithrion until my knuckles ached. Rowen designed every dip, point, and curve of my star blade; its weight a reminder that he would always be with me.

I knew I needed to sleep, but my mind wouldn't stop racing. My thoughts were haunted with images of people dying or turning into Voro-Kai.

It was too quiet. Each and every one of my heartbeats was like a countdown to war, terror, and pain.

I strode out the door, unable to stand the sound of my pulse for one more second. The moon and floating luminorbs lit a winding pathway to the beach, and my bare feet followed it without question.

I dropped onto a sandbank overlooking the ocean and towering sea stacks. The waves were violent, almost as if they sensed the looming battle ahead, but I welcomed the tumultuous tides. They were the only things big enough to drown out the horrific thoughts in my head.

Above me, the sky lazily rotated in a glittering dance—a stark contrast to the ocean and turmoil within me. I inhaled deeply, letting the cool, salty air fill my lungs. I held the breath as Rowen's absence, the looming battle ahead, and my certain future pressed down on me. The slow exhale allowed me to shrug, just a little, to readjust the weight of the world on my shoulders.

I shivered as the chilly ocean air washed over my skin. I'd changed into a pale blue night slip that hugged my every curve yet did little in the way of providing warmth.

I ran my hands up and down my arms when a thick blanket was wrapped around my shoulders, trapping my hair within the fabric. The broad palms gave a firm yet welcoming squeeze, and a familiar warmth seeped into my skin.

I whipped my head around, my heart leaping in anticipation.

"Are you okay?" Maddock asked behind me, and my heart dropped. I blinked up to his large frame that eclipsed the stars in the perfect shape of his body.

"I needed to get some quiet. It was too loud in my dome," I said, digging my toes into the sand.

"Yeah. Same," he said, gesturing to my side. "May I join you?"

I nodded, and he plopped down next to me on the sand. His arm settled against mine, offering me more warmth and protection from the cold.

"You ready to tell me what's going on? Why you've been acting strange?"

I wrapped the shawl tighter around my shoulders. "Is war not a good enough reason to act strange?"

His angular eyes narrowed. "It's more than that, I think."

"I'm just stressed, tired, and without my other half."

"Keira, you can tell me anything. You know that, right? I would never tell anyone."

The sincerity on his face made my bond hum. It wasn't his bond, or at this point, maybe it was. He placed his palm on my hand, his touch sending a bolt of electricity through my skin.

"What is it, Keira? You're scaring me. I'll imagine the worst if you don't tell me."

My bottom lip trembled. "It is the worst," I barely whispered, unable to look him in the eye.

"What do you mean? Does it have to do with Rowen being a lord, or what happens after?"

Something in me crashed like sea stacks falling into the sea. "There won't be an after for me," I said, my eyes finally meeting his.

"Keira, what do you mean?" he asked carefully, his smooth jaw clenching.

"I spoke with Indrasyl in the Hymma. She said . . . she said, I will have to give all of me. But no one can know. They won't let me go if they know."

Fury rippled through him. "N-no. There has to be another way."

"I thought I could rewrite the stars," I said, looking back at the ocean. "But I can't. Indrasyl was clear."

He hooked his finger on my chin and pulled my gaze back to his. "What does she know? You aren't some sacrificial lamb that gets to walk willingly to the altar. You did it at Hara'dune, and you're doing it again now. And how many other times I wonder. It's not your job."

I blinked back tears. "Yes, it is."

"It's a job you didn't sign up for. It isn't fair," he yelled, squeezing my chin tighter.

"It's not," I agreed with a wince, and he dropped his hand from me.

"Rowen doesn't know, and you don't want him to. That's why you've been pushing all your pain to me."

"I didn't do it on purpose," I said, my mind flashing to Rowen and our last moments together. They were fleeting, but there was no mistaking how his face lit up at the prospect of creating a better world with me. It had given him light at the end of the tunnel. Something I hadn't seen myself or even thought long enough to imagine.

I couldn't bear to tell Rowen there would be no future with me. It would break me and make me question everything I had to do.

Maddock's eyebrows furrowed. "You can't expect me not to tell him."

"It's not just for the Wyn village or Luneth, but Earth too. That's where Erovos means to go next. If you tell Rowen, he won't let me do what needs to be done."

"And you think I will?" he demanded, pouncing toward me. I fell back onto my wrists as the blanket slipped off my shoulders. His narrow hips slid between my knees.

My eyes narrowed. "If you say anything, I'll kill you."

His gaze darted to my mouth, then to my peaked nipples beneath the slip. His gaze snapped back to mine, and he chuckled a dark, humorless laugh. "You've threatened to murder me more times than I can count. It's adorable at this point."

The air stilled around us. "Maddock, please," I barely whispered. "It's my last wish." Something on my face must have told him how much I needed to do this. "Swear to me you won't tell him."

"Keira, he already knows something is up. He's not stupid. He can sense it."

"Just swear to me," I said, ignoring how his hips would only have to lower an inch to line up with mine. "If you do, I'll finally forgive you."

He hesitated, his eyes shocked and wide. "I swear," he finally said, his whole body poised over mine.

I smiled, but it was hollow, and I placed my hand on his cheek. "Thank you. I appreciate it. Just promise you'll be there for Rowen afterward. Don't let him do anything stupid."

"Like what you're doing now? What if I already promised Rowen not to let you do anything stupid?"

I smiled and patted his cheek. "Mine trumps his," I said, gently pushing him off me.

"If I promise not to tell him, you'll really forgive me for what happened in the crevice?" Maddock asked, kneeling before me. Our breaths were heavy and mingled as the weight of my confession thickened in the air.

For a moment, I wanted to tell him that I had forgiven him long ago. But I couldn't bring myself to say the words. "We'll see if you keep your promise."

A small, sad smile pulled at his lips. "All I have ever wanted is your forgiveness."

I got up and handed him the blanket. "It's difficult to forgive someone you hate."

His eyes trailed up my body that glistened like a pearl in the moonlight. "You expect me to just let you walk away, knowing what you will do tomorrow? I could chase you down, tie you up, and lock you away. Guard the door and miss out on the battle myself. The last time we fought, I was worthless. At least this time, I would be doing some good by keeping you safe. You'd hate me for it, but you already hate me anyway."

"You would never be able to catch me," I said, pivoting on my heel.

I walked away from my bond and Light stealer. I'd threatened to kill and hate him for all of time, but as I left him on the beach, I realized I'd confessed my darkest secret to him.

I turned back to the man I'd first met in a coma. He'd been a shell of a human, but now, he was vibrant and warm and bursting with life. "You know, you're making it harder for me to hate you."

44

———

I'd finally made it to bed, or at least that was my last memory. I'd tossed and turned in the sheets, wishing I were beside Rowen, but now, I walked through a city of elegantly carved marble. Intricate archways, spires, and turrets soared above me and stretched up the craggy mountainside. Every wall and balcony dripped with ivy, and the sound of running water trickled in the distance.

It was foreign yet somehow familiar. Almost as if the place I remembered had been rebuilt with love, care, and a deep appreciation for the surrounding mountains.

My breath caught in my chest when I realized.

It was Rowen's home! The place he drew over and over again in his sketchbooks.

I walked through Viltarran. Or at least an improved version of it. But how could that be? Aliphoura destroyed it years ago.

The stars glittered above, casting a silver glow along the cobblestone path. I crossed a bridge that arched over a river winding through the city.

My feet eventually led me to a grand stone castle encased in moss and glowing blossoms.

I slipped through the entrance, wearing nothing but my nightgown. I passed through great halls, dining rooms, and libraries filled with books. An awareness spread through my body. It was as if I intimately knew these halls, somehow aware of every passageway and alcove. As if Rowen and I had stolen kisses and touches within the hidden shadows.

A set of massive double doors called to me as a faint light glowed from within. My hand hovered over the iron handle before I pushed inside.

I gasped as a throne room stretched out before me. Pillars resembling trees lined the chamber, their stone branches extending up into an elaborate, vaulted ceiling. Wrought-iron windows spanned the walls, letting in fractals of moonlight that danced throughout the room. Vines and greenery cascaded from every surface, and the hall shimmered in shades of emerald, onyx, and silver. My eyes snapped to the matching thrones upon the dais. They were equal in every way and spoke of a shared power that made the flame in my chest thrum.

Suddenly, a presence that warmed my blood yet pebbled my skin came up behind me.

"Lady Damascus," said a voice like sin and smoke. Hands trailed up the flares of my hips and locked around my waist. "Shouldn't you be sleeping?"

I rested my head against his shoulder and smiled. "Shouldn't you? And when did I agree to take your last name?"

His hands tightened around me, and his mouth dipped to the curve of my neck. "Even in my dreams, you fight me," he said, his lips dancing across my sensitive skin.

"This is what you dream of?" I asked, melting under his touch.

"It is," he barely ground out, his hands gathering my slip over my ass. He moaned as he toyed with the edges of my underwear and slid them down my legs. "I dream of making you my wife and taking you in our throne room."

The flame in my chest burst, exposing a soul-deep desire to be his wife and his undoing. "I would need a ring," I said coolly, belying my burning body and pounding heart.

He spun me around to face him. His sharp and honed features danced across my face as if I were a star-filled sky. He was naked from the waist up, looking like he'd been chiseled from marble. His abs and lateral muscles rippled down to the V-shaped lines that disappeared into his pants.

We were both barefoot and tousled as if we'd wandered in from our sleep.

"I will give you a ring that rivals the stars," he swore as he reached overhead and plucked a small vine from above us. He took my hand and wound the ivy around my finger, tying it off at the ends to secure it. "But for now, this will have to do."

I didn't think a heart could grow any bigger or love any more, but the look on Rowen's face spoke of forever—in this life and beyond. "It's perfect," I said, tears welling in my eyes as I made one for him.

He admired the twisted vine around his finger, his smile so big I could see the peaks of his canines. "I've never been happier in my life."

"Me either," I said, rising up on my tiptoes to kiss him. His tongue darted between my lips as our arms and bodies crashed into an embrace. We held each other as if we had all the time in the world, not a few hours before battle. Our lips collided, and our tongues starved for each other's taste. "By the spirits, you feel so real," he groaned, his fingers digging into my hips hard enough to bruise. "I've dreamt of Viltarran often, how I would improve and change it, but your presence is altering the details. You're making it better, more alive, as if you've added pieces of yourself. As if we are sharing this dream and creating it together."

I had astral projected into Rowen's dream. *Our* dream. It was of the future we wished to create. Together.

"Where are you?" I asked, suddenly remembering our bodies weren't really here. Which was crazy because I felt him underneath my fingertips, pulsing with life and strength. And desire.

"I'm sleeping on the ground at our war camp. But I don't want to talk about that right now. Not when I have you like this," he said, grabbing the backs of my thighs and lifting me in the air. Honoring his request, I wrapped my legs around his narrow hips and planted kisses along his face and jaw. He walked me up onto the dais and placed me on one of the elaborately carved chairs. "I want to worship you on your throne. I may be a lord in title, but I am nothing without you. You are my lady, my goddess. My wife."

He dropped to his knees and spread my legs apart. "And I shall worship you," he said, his head of dark hair dipped to my core. His tongue darted out to lick my slit, and I jolted at the contact. My arms gripped the high-back seat of the throne to keep me steady.

His tongue licked in broad, torturous strokes, and I arched further into the chair. He passionately kissed my core, his hands gripping my thighs to keep them apart.

I squirmed in desperate need as his tongue pushed inside my entrance. "Please!" I begged, needing him to make me come.

He chuckled against me before honing in and concentrating on my clit.

My belly clenched. "Don't stop. I'm so close. Yes. Ye—"

Rowen pulled away, and my eyes shot open as he abandoned my body on a pinnacle with no release. I made a frustrated noise.

"I forgot to ask," he said with an utterly wicked grin, his lips glistening with my desire.

"And what's that?" I panted impatiently.

"Will you marry me?"

I sucked in a sharp breath, wondering if I had suddenly gone insane.

I was on another plain of existence, in a throne room, holding onto a chair for dear life with my drenched and aching pussy bared to my soul flame. It was obscene, delicious, and depraved. I loved this selfless and loyal man—with everything that I was—every speck of dust and starlight that made me *me*.

Kneeling at my feet, he patiently waited for my answer. His loving smile flickered before me, like a reel of memories from a million different lifetimes and worlds. In each and every one, he was mine, and I was his.

A choked laugh erupted from my chest. "Yes. For as many stars as there are in the sky, yes. Now, please, make me come!"

Spurred on by my answer, he dove to my clit again, flicking his tongue against me with a masterful speed and accuracy. It felt like my heart was going to beat out of my chest. I could barely breathe.

My core spun tighter and tighter until I came on his tongue.

My release was cosmic, astral, and out of this world. If I weren't already having an out-of-body experience, I would be now. Or maybe I was having an out-of-body experience within an out-of-body experience.

The all-encompassing euphoria made me weightless. The only thing keeping me from drifting into space was Rowen's tongue on my clit, tethering me to my body—to my pleasure.

Stars were born, erupted, and re-birthed as Rowen wrung out every last second of my climax, his tongue lapping and caressing me.

When I finally returned to my senses, I opened my eyes to

see Rowen staring at me. My arousal coated his mouth and the throne room chair. "So beautiful when you come undone for me," he said with a wild hunger in his eyes.

In a pleasured daze, I sat up and undid the lacing of his pants. His proud cock jutted out, the tip gleaming like a single star. I went to lick him, but he hoisted me up as if I weighed nothing. I wrapped my legs around him and shivered as his solid shaft grazed against my drenched core.

He sat on the other throne, keeping me straddled around him. I reached between us and wrapped my hand around his width. I lined him up against my entrance and slowly lowered myself on his cock.

He moaned and kicked his head back, the tendons in his throat flexing as I adjusted to his size.

Once I was lowered to the hilt, I rocked my hips against him. He sat up and put his mouth to my nipple, kissing me through the fabric of my slip.

Spirits! He felt so good and real.

My pussy clenched around his cock, and Rowen growled as he yanked my nightgown down, exposing my breasts to the moonlit throne room.

He captured my nipple in his mouth and stroked my hardened peak. I sank my hands into his thick hair, grinding him harder.

"No matter what happens, always remember this," I breathed, my throat constricting.

"Yes, Keira," he moaned, diving his lips to my neck and collarbones.

I pumped my hips faster. "Promise me, no matter what happens, you will rebuild Viltarran."

"I will," he panted as he grabbed my ass and helped me bounce on his cock. The delicious sensation nearly split me in two.

"I love you," I said as another climax consumed my body.

"I love you," he grunted as his cock twitched inside of me. Jets of warmth shot into me and made my pulsing core contract even harder.

He roared my name, sitting on his throne like the lord he was to his people and the king he was to me. My name reverberated throughout the chamber as if it would echo through eternity, letting every subject know I was his queen, his goddess. His.

Our breaths tangled, and our foreheads touched as we came down from our shared high. I grabbed his bearded face as he held me in place, his cock still inside of me, pulsing.

His chest heaved, and his eyes narrowed. "What did you mean by 'no matter what happens'?"

"The future isn't certain," I said, kissing his lips. "All we ever have is here and now."

"I won't let anything happen to you. And when this is all over, I will properly wed you and make you my wife."

I could feel myself drifting. "I love you so much."

"I know," he said, his words echoing around me as we slipped through each other's fingers and disappeared in a plume of sparkling mist.

— ·(·☾·●·☽·)· —

I woke at dawn, my thighs coated in slick.

I raised my left hand, and around my finger, like a promise of eternity, sat an ivy ring.

I didn't know how I could feel such joy and sorrow simultaneously. The dichotomy threatened to rip me apart. All I could do now was focus on the impending battle.

I crawled out of bed, my movements deliberate and concise as I dressed in black and dark plum fighting gear. The protective leggings and vest hugged my body and were reinforced with thicker panels of material. I strapped Mithrion to my thigh and adjusted my forearm guards. Every part of me was buckled in and secure in the lightweight gear, ideal for swift and untouchable movements.

I didn't have time to comb my hair, so I quickly twisted and pinned my wild waves away from my face.

Dressed as a soldier from head to toe, I steeled my spine and took a deep breath. I shut off all my emotions as I walked out into the crisp morning air.

My feet carried me to the Vale, where Nepta, Dyani, and Maddock were gathered and dressed in similar war attire. Starblades gleamed at everyone's side, their hands resting on the weapons forged for this very battle.

I made eye contact with Maddock. His severe stare held mine as if he contemplated revealing my plan. Eventually, he dipped his chin without a word. It was a simple gesture, one that told me my secret was safe with him.

My gaze darted to Dyani. She'd pulled her hair back into her signature ponytail and donned her silver armbands. At first, it was hard seeing her wear the cuffs. They were identical to her brother's, but now, I couldn't imagine her without them.

"Alvar and Takoda have already been sent through," Nepta said, breaking the deafening silence. "Driskell remains here with a small battalion in case . . . in case the worst should happen." She paused, needing a moment before she continued. "I will take us to the war camp at the edge of the Lirien Valley. It is five hundred paces from Indrasyl and protected by the raised ridges. There, we will make our final preparations before we march."

The air was heavy and crackled with nerves, but we all nodded, accepting our fates as Nepta summoned her small portal. And in a determined line, we stepped through the shimmering blue light.

One second, I was in the Sacred Vale surrounded by waterfalls and the shattered Alcreon Stone; the next, I stood between rows of lightweight canvas tents.

The war camp was a whirlwind of running soldiers, shouting generals, and clanking weapons. I padded along the muddy ground as warriors inspected their armor, and archers fletched their arrows. Those who weren't trained fighters were gathering water and setting up supply lines.

I noticed Takoda from across the way, preparing a shelter for wounded warriors. Medical plants and rags lined the tent, and his tall, lean frame ground up fresh noxlilies.

Wyn warriors were at transport carts filled with the newly forged weapons. They helped hand them out to soldiers I'd never seen, wearing thick, metal armor.

"Keira!" My name shattered through the wartime cacophony, and I turned to see my soul flame exiting a tent with a man I didn't recognize.

I had just been with Rowen on the astral plane but seeing him in the flesh still sent a shockwave through my system. He looked like a lord dressed in silver-black armor—Viltarran armor.

He closed the distance between us and gathered me into a fierce embrace.

He released me, and my eyes swept over his commanding form. He wore a breastplate and gorget, with gauntlets on his arms and greaves on his legs. A glowing Ever-burn sword and a few star-blade axes were strapped to his side. I counted at least ten weapons on his body, and that was just what I could see.

He was power incarnate, and a flush hit my skin as I recalled how he'd handled my body in the throne room.

I glanced at his hand, and sure enough, a matching ring of ivy was wrapped around his finger. Our eyes locked and simmered with an unspoken understanding of our shared dream.

"You found help," I said, dipping my chin to the man approaching his flank. He was shorter than Rowen, but even through his armor, I could tell he was broad and muscular. He had wavy, reddish-brown hair, a strong jaw, and a wide smile.

Rowen snaked an arm around my waist and pulled me close.

"This is Callum," Rowen said, addressing the smiling man beside him. "He was one of my best men in Viltarran."

I nodded in greeting but kept my guard up, wondering if he was one of the soldiers who'd followed Aliphoura without question. Had he been one of the guards transporting me to and from my cell in the Crystal Crypts? Had he stood by while I was nearly beaten to death?

Rowen sensed my tension and said, "He escaped Aliphoura's imprisonment. He has been a ranger for the last few years."

Callum turned his dazzling stare to me. "When I heard Rowen had been murdered, I fled. I knew that bitch was up to no good. For a while, I couldn't believe Rowen was gone. I went searching for him, but he was too well hidden, and I assumed he was truly dead. Imagine when I found him wandering the ruins of Viltarran looking like a ghost. Nearly shit my pants."

Rowen chuckled and patted him on the back. "Callum has been locating survivors from the Crypts. A small settlement is forming there, going through the wreckage and building temporary homes." His tone turned more serious. "But, Keira, you should know that most of the warriors I recruited fought for Aliphoura."

My jaw locked. I hadn't had time to consider how their help would make me feel. Grateful? Apprehensive? Worried? "They have sworn their allegiance to us?" I asked, knowing we weren't in a position to be picky.

Rowen nodded. "They fight for you now."

I swallowed the lump in my throat and met Callum's

piercing blue eyes. "Thank you for helping us. I wish we could have met under different circumstances."

"I feel like I already know you. What you did in the Crypts has been told around campfires," he admitted, flashing his straight teeth. "And Rowen? He hasn't been able to shut up about you. Your name and Light encouraged us as we pieced Viltarran back together. Without you, my people, *our* people, would have never escaped."

I never knew my blast of Light in the Crypts was such a guiding force. I'd been afraid for so long that they would all hate me for almost killing them in a cave-in. The thought choked me up. "How many warriors were you able to find?"

"Five hundred willing men and women," Rowen replied, his gaze flashing to mine. His commanding stance didn't falter, but the look in his eyes told me it was fewer than he'd hoped.

"I know it doesn't seem like much, especially with what we are up against, but these warriors are some of the bravest souls I know," Callum said, his hand resting on the hilt of an Ever-burn blade. "And loyal to a fault. Even though some fear they will be imprisoned for their time with Aliphoura."

"We will grant them amnesty," I said, feeling in my bones it was the right thing to do. "Everyone deserves a fresh start, especially if we survive this war."

Rowen beamed at me as Callum elbowed him. "You got a good one, brother. Not bad on the eyes, either."

"Thank you again for your allegiance," I replied with a small smile. "If you'll excuse us now."

"Of course." Callum bowed, then swiftly turned on his heel.

Rowen gathered me in his arms as the war camp bustled around us. "Are you ready?" he asked, his hands trailing up and down my back.

I threaded my fingers behind his neck and met his gaze. "I'm ready to kick some demon ass."

He smirked, his eyes sweeping over my body in admiration. "Spirits, you are so fucking strong and beautiful," he whispered, then palmed the back of my skull and pulled me in against his armor. He claimed my mouth, my body, my soul, right in the middle of the war camp. He kissed me with abandon, unashamed to express his love for me in front of his army.

The flame in my chest erupted and filled my veins with fire.

He breathed me in like he was drowning, and my kiss was the only thing pumping air into his lungs, keeping him alive. It was just a moment, a stolen fragment of time, one that we might never get again.

He groaned into my mouth and then pulled away as if it were the hardest thing he'd ever done.

He raised his chin. "It's time," he commanded like the true and rightful leader he was. "Fall in line!"

· (· C · ● ·) ·) ·

I stood before the army with Rowen and Alvar. Our small but mighty forces were aligned in perfect formation.

The front lines were formed by soldiers skilled with spears and shields, and in my opinion, the bravest of us all. Behind them were archers, their bows and Ever-burn arrows strapped to their backs. Farther back were those tasked with pushing the weapon carts filled with bundled arrows and spare blades. We had flanking formations on either side, utilizing the warriors who excelled at hand-to-hand combat.

"Remember," Alvar shouted, his face, clothes, and shield covered in past battle scars. "We draw the army out. Under no circumstances do we engage first. Then, once we lure the enemy away, we wedge a path to get Keira to the tree."

The Wyn and Viltarran soldiers nodded, conveying they understood the mission. Everyone knew what they were marching towards, yet here they stood, ready and willing to fight for Luneth.

"The odds are against us," Alvar continued, voicing our concerns, and the gathered warriors slouched imperceptibly at his words.

I stepped in front of the war captain. "But this battle isn't about numbers," I cut in, speaking to every soldier. "One of you is worth ten Voro-Kai. They are driven by a single thought: destruction. But we? We fight for something much greater." I let everyone see the Light in my eyes and the glow emanating from my palms. Gasps rippled among them, and the atmosphere shifted. "We fight for everyone we love, for the forest, the future, and the spirits. We have more to lose but so much more to fight for."

"We fight for the Light of Luneth!" Rowen roared beside me, pounding his fist on his breastplate while the other lifted his star blade in the air.

"We fight for the Light of Luneth!" the army chanted back, raising their glowing weapons like a sea of rebellious stars.

Our unified voices sounded so much more than twenty-two hundred strong. We sounded like an army determined to defeat the ender of worlds.

45

We marched the five hundred paces to Indrasyl, and I fell back into the second line, waiting for Alvar's signal to reveal myself.

I heard Erovos' demons before I saw them. They grunted and growled in a deadly cacophony that shook the earth.

The closer we walked to Indrasyl, the darker and more desolate the Lirien Valley became. No birds or any living things were in sight, and my throat closed as I thought of the beautiful starwings who once thrived here but were now extinct.

I gulped, glancing up at the sky. It was morning, yet the clouds were so dense they completely blotted out the sun.

Indrasyl finally came into view, stretching above the Voro-Kai like a dark tower. Her twisted branches and blighted bark no longer saddened me. It enraged me. A fury rose beneath my skin and urged the Light in me to thrash and swell.

The grotesque demons surrounding her made me want to explode like a supernova. Nothing had ever looked more wrong. She was sick, dying, and encircled by those who meant to destroy her. I prayed she was still alive, somewhere deep inside, holding out for hope.

When my gaze lowered to the Voro-Kai, my blood froze.

Though I had seen the horde before—mere fetuses in murky cocoons—they were now mature beasts of darkness, equipped with fangs, tusks, and jagged claws.

Rowen halted our army with a closed fist.

The Voro-Kai were the only thing standing between me and the salvation of worlds.

You'd think there would be a calm before the storm, but there wasn't. Instead, the air whirled with tension and dread. I could barely breathe as my inner tornado built into a swirling vortex. Even my tongue tingled with notes of metal and ash. It was as if I could already taste the impending bloodshed.

I glanced at Rowen, committing every line of his beautiful face to memory.

He drew my left hand to his lips and kissed me just below the ivy ring. "No one will touch you. Your path will be clear, Keira. I will get you to Indrasyl, even if it's with my last breath," he said like an unbreakable vow. Little did he know it was a vow to my last breath, not his.

Suddenly, an emptiness ached in my chest. "Where is Maddock?" I asked, realizing he was nowhere to be seen.

Rowen and Dyani looked around, but it was as if he had vanished into thin air.

"Have you seen Maddock?" Dyani hissed to the soldiers beside her.

A Wyn soldier with obsidian skin and dark green eyes spoke up. "I saw him leave just after we fell in line. He said the Light Bearer asked him to get her another weapon."

My voice went numb. "I never asked him for anything."

"He's gone?" Dyani asked, not hiding the disgust in her voice. Her grip tightened on her blades. She must have grabbed another Ever-burn, one for each hand.

My knees went weak, and I nearly sank to the ground. "He told me he didn't want to fight again. That he felt worthless," I barely whispered. I should have told him he wasn't worthless, not to me, but I was too concerned with my own problems to notice he had no intention of fighting this battle.

Dyani scoffed in disgust. "He deserted us."

The words didn't sound right. Not after everything he'd promised. But as I desperately searched for his warm eyes, the truth plunged into my gut like a sinking ship.

I should have known he would leave, but that didn't stop the sting of betrayal any less.

"I'm so sorry," Rowen said, squeezing my shoulder. "He's gone."

"I couldn't care less," I said quickly, biting my lower lip to keep it from trembling.

The words weren't true.

I cared.

I cared with every fiber of my being. Or what was left of it. He went like a thief in the night with my Light and soul flame bond. He'd driven his hand into my ribcage, grabbed onto vital organs without a care in the world, and wrenched them from my chest.

The gaping hole bled and convulsed, but I couldn't think of the wound he'd created, healed, and ripped open again. It hurt too much.

I had confided in him, telling him what I needed to do. And still, he left me.

Maddock was a deserter whose cowardice would outlive me. Once I was gone, Rowen would seek a way to exact revenge; maybe he would hunt him down and kill him. That was if I succeeded.

I locked my knees and faced the enemy ahead. "Let the coward go. We have a battle to win."

·(·C·●·)·)·

Neither the rattle in my bones nor the breaking of my heart was enough to drown out the sea of demons grunting, *"Take. Take. Take."*

Despite the deathly chant, Mithrion was a comforting weight in my hand.

I glanced at the soldiers around me. I couldn't ask for braver souls to die beside, unlike Maddock, who was a coward through and through. I hated that I had ever grown to like him or call him a friend, but the worst part was that I had started to trust him.

Alvar was about to signal for me to show myself when suddenly, a single demon emerged from the line, hunched and hulking.

What was Erovos' plan in sending out one Voro-Kai? We weren't stupid enough to charge one demon. We needed to lure them farther away from the tree. They were still too close!

My eyes narrowed, searching for the world eater, but he was nowhere to be seen.

Suddenly, a scream pierced through the grey sky. It was a wailing unlike anything I'd ever heard, and it was coming from our side of the battlefield.

My eyes darted back to the lone astral demon when a flash of silver bounced off its bulging arms, and my breath caught in my throat.

Silver cuffs encircled the Voro-Kai's wrists, their design unmistakable. They were the exact same cuffs Demil wore the day he helped Erovos kidnap me.

A chill slithered down my spine. One bite from a Voro-Kai could turn you, but had Demil been turned? Or had his cuffs been stolen off his body like a sick war prize?

It could be a coincidence, but when it came to Erovos, there was no such thing as coincidences, and when the Voro-Kai raised its boar-shaped head, terror gripped me like a steel claw.

Yellow eyes peered at me—Demil's eyes.

The wailing persisted, and I realized it was Dyani. She'd recognized her twin within the twisted demon face.

Demil raised his blade as a bleeding darkness swarmed his irises. The silver circlets that once sat high on his arms were now snug around his wrists from how much he'd grown.

Suddenly, a slash of white bolted from our ranks.

"Dyani, no!" I screamed as she charged across the field toward her brother. "It's a trap."

"Hold the line!" Alvar screamed as Dyani continued to run, losing us precious ground.

I wanted to chase after her, but as I took my first step, Rowen pulled me back to keep me hidden. "If we charge, she dies."

I knew he was right. Dyani was too close to the opposing forces. If we charged, the Voro-Kai army would swarm her, and no matter how skilled a warrior she was, no one could survive that. She had a better chance of beating her brother one-on-one.

I fell back in line, though the dread twisting my gut did not lessen. We all remained rooted in terror as the siblings collided on the battlefield.

Demil slashed at his twin, but she ducked just in time, narrowly missing a blade to the chest.

She spun back around, but his yellow eyes were fixed on her dual blades. "Demil, it's me, your sister," Dyani coaxed, tucking her swords within their sheaths. "You don't have to do this. We can find a way to fix you."

My heart seized. There was no cure for a Voro-Kai bite this far along.

Demil grunted, banging his chest with his monstrous arms.

"Please, brother. Remember me. I promised Mother I would keep you safe." The pleading in her voice broke my heart.

Sadness seemed to engulf his eyes, which still looked so human on the face of a demon. Suddenly, Demil attacked, barreling his blade on his twin sister, but Dyani had always been faster, and in a move that was so swift, I almost didn't see it, she pulled her knives out and blocked him with a cross-blade formation.

"Demil, please," she grunted, holding up both her arms as Demil pressed down on her with his blade—his Wyn warrior blade. "Remember who you are, my brother."

He released his weapon and struck again, but Dyani deflected the blow.

"Kill her!" Erovos shrieked in a tone that made everyone cover their ears. His voice rang out like it was everywhere, in all our heads.

As if on cue, the last traces of humanity vanished from Demil's eyes. Now a mindless demon, he brutally attacked his sister. Blow by blow, she defended herself, but only just. Dyani was fighting for her life.

The siblings crashed like thunder, and sparks rained down upon them as Ever-burn crystal met steel. Dyani had always been a better fighter, but now, Demil was twice his original size. His body bulged with unnatural muscle and brute demon strength.

They were evenly matched.

Demil beat down on his twin in a barrage of hits.

My heart was in my throat as Dyani blocked each violent swing, but her arms were beginning to shake. She was tiring.

Then, the demon hit Dyani so hard she lost her footing and opened up her side. Demil struck her unguarded ribcage, and a cry warbled up my throat. But Dyani twisted away at the last second. She dropped to the ground and swept her leg out in a precise semi-circle, kicking his legs out from under him. Her brother staggered and crashed into the mud.

It was just like the first day I'd seen them sparring on the training grounds. Demil must have remembered, too, because something flashed in his eyes, and the darkness receded.

"Sister," he grunted. "I'm so sorry."

"I'm here. Everything is going to be all right," Dyani wept, dropping to the ground to gather her brother in her arms.

"Please, end this."

"I can't," she sobbed.

His voice was different as he tried to speak around the tusks. "I beg you."

"No!"

"Mother wouldn't want this for me."

"I can't!" she cried again.

"Do it! Please."

With a gut-wrenching scream, Dyani bore her star blade down on her twin. His guttural scream echoed through the air as his body shook and slowly disintegrated into motes of starlight.

Dyani's gaze darted up to the Voro-Kai army, savagery burning in her feline eyes.

"Dyani, come back!" I screamed, but my plea fell on deaf ears.

The formidable warrior stood as the light bounced off her hair and star blades. Her chest heaved as she lost herself to her grief.

With pain etched on her face and a cry on her lips, she sprinted into the army of darkness.

I raced after her without hesitation. Our strategy to lure the Voro-Kai away from Indrasyl was shot to hell, but I would never make Dyani face the demon army alone. And neither would Rowen. Together, we ran across the barren field to join our friend in battle.

"Attack!" Alvar roared as ten thousand demons launched into a thundering stampede.

The Wyn and Viltarran soldiers obeyed. The ground trembled beneath my feet as we ran towards a head-on collision.

The brave warriors charging beside me had a chance of surviving.

But I? I charged toward certain death.

· (· ☾ · ● · ☽ ·) ·

The tide of darkness enveloped me. Shimmering blades crashed against talons and tusks as a canopy of arrows whizzed overhead. Blood sprayed past me, staining my comrades and the earth in red and black ichor.

I battled through the chaos, carving Mithrion through the air in exacting strikes.

Adrenaline heightened my senses as I took in my surroundings.

Takoda's healing hands were deadly as he unleashed a flurry of arrows. His gaze shifted slightly with each pull of his bowstring, his eyes locking onto target after target.

Rowen hurled an ax from each hand, hitting two different demons. Empty-handed, he reached behind his back and unleashed two more weapons. He swiped and slashed, losing a blade in the skull of a Voro-Kai.

Another demon lunged at Rowen's unprotected side.

Terror and Light surged through me as Mithrion hummed in my hand. I spun in a tight circle and sank my blade into the beast's heart. It disintegrated into a fine, black mist beneath my fingertips.

Rowen spun to me with a shocked yet impressed expression. "Thanks. Now, don't move," he said as he pulled his ax out of the skull of the first demon and launched it over my shoulder.

I whirled around just in time to see a Voro-Kai right behind me, stopped dead in its tracks with an ax lodged in its chest.

I pulled the star blade from its ribcage, ignoring the nause-ating squelch. I didn't even have a moment to breathe before we were caught in another swarm of astral demons.

The plan had gone up in flames. It was pure and utter chaos.

I had never been in battle; could scarcely imagine the terror it would bring. But now, I didn't have to envision it. I was living it. And the reality was far worse than any nightmare.

As I gouged a demon in the eye, I prayed Dyani was still alive. I had completely lost sight of her after she disappeared within the wave of demons.

My eyes caught on Nepta. When the Elven-head walked, her movements were careful and unhurried, but as she fought, her motions were swift, lethal, and precise. She wielded her moon staff in one hand, opening the ground to catch and close around the heels of the Voro-Kai. With their hooves trapped within the earth, she plunged her Ever-burn blade into their black hearts.

Bodies battled and fell around me as screams reverberated in my ears. Suddenly, a demon with a contorted face lunged at me, its claws aiming to slice me in half.

Instinct took over, forged from hours on the training grounds. I lifted Mithrion and blocked the blow, feeling the reverberating impact all the way to my teeth. I gritted as I held the enemy inches from my face. The sound of sharp talons on metal made my skin crawl.

The Voro-Kai's other arm reached up to swipe me, but I quickly ducked, swirling my blade around until it connected with the Voro-Kai's legs, cutting it at the knees. The demon crumpled to the ground with a screeching hiss.

I glanced up as Alvar caught my vision. His brutal force was mesmerizing as he felled demon after demon. Where Rowen was fluid and versatile, and Dyani was swift and agile, Alvar was punishing, blunt, and aggressive. His scarred face and white hair were already coated in black blood.

"Drive a wedge to the tree!" Rowen yelled as he fought one of the biggest Voro-Kai I'd ever seen. It towered over my soul flame in bulging mounds of muscle and hair. "Keira, run!"

Four nearby soldiers obeyed Rowen's command, joining my flank. Their blades swiped and pierced through thick demon hide as they helped me clear a path to Indrasyl. Dread clawed at me to be separated from my soul flame, but the mission was clear: get to Indrasyl.

I sprinted toward the Sylvan Mother Tree, slicing and blasting my way through a tunnel of demons. My mind became a blank slate as I drove my blade while unleashing blasts of Light from my palm—as I became deadly.

Disintegrating forms erupted around me like smoke bombs and clouded my vision. Thankfully, Mithrion's bright aura led the way.

I tumbled out of the plume, tired, aching, and braced for the next wave of demons. But as I raised my gaze, I realized my path was clear. Indrasyl's hollow trunk was begging to embrace me.

I dashed toward her when suddenly, an entity of darkness spilled from a tear in space and blocked my path.

"Erovos," I hissed, staggering to a halt. "Finally decided to show up?"

His cloak billowed around his pale hands and bare feet. His eyes locked on me, forever churning like the pits of hell. "I was going to quietly abandon this world and leave you to die. However, your meager forces are an irritant I can't ignore. It's pathetic what you have shown up with, and honestly, it's quite insulting. Now I shall destroy you like the pests you are."

His jaw unhinged, and his mouth opened unnaturally wide as he concentrated on the soldiers behind me. And just like that day fifteen years ago, when I'd witnessed him murder a man he thought was the Synodic Son, I watched Erovos drain the life out of the soldiers around me. Their bodies froze mid-fight, and they tore at their skin as it shrink-wrapped to their bones.

My face twisted in horror as their bodies withered and wasted away. Everything that made them beautiful, strong, and brave was siphoned away in an instant. The light left their eyes long before they crumbled to the ground.

Each of their energies was a vibrant and unique hue, but as soon as their auras came in contact with Erovos' skin, they turned into murky darkness.

Their stolen energy crackled around the world eater as his veins turned black, and without hesitation, he ricocheted the power back, hurling it at a group of charging warriors. Their comrades' life force was used against them as they hurtled through the air. One slammed into the trunk of a tree. His body went limp, and he never stood back up.

"You sick fuck!" I shrieked as I charged at the embodiment of a black hole. He side-stepped me easily and swept me up into his black cloak, spinning me around until I faced the battlefield.

He grabbed my chin in his bony grasp and wrenched my face forward. "Watch," he commanded.

I couldn't move. My arms were pinned by my sides as my eyes helplessly darted across the battleground, witnessing horror after horror.

Alvar cried out as a demon slashed his leg, and he fell to one knee. He struck out his sword, blocking the demons that charged him. He was barely hanging on.

Dyani was nowhere in sight, and Nepta was fighting to stay on her feet.

The scent of sweat, iron, and blood filled my nostrils as the battle unfolded into the unthinkable.

We were losing.

I found Rowen, expecting to see my beautiful warrior on his

feet, tearing down the enemy. But instead, I saw him on the ground, a Voro-Kai slashing down upon his chest.

Rowen rolled away at the last second but was kicked violently in the stomach. He flew through the air and landed in a painful thud. Before he could stand, he was kicked again. He couldn't get up; the Voro-Kai was keeping him pinned down.

My body struggled, kicked, and erupted in Light, but I couldn't escape Erovos' gravitational hold. I was going to watch Rowen die—the love of my life—so inherent and unstoppable that I'd crossed the thermals of space to find him.

My eyes darted for Callum, Dyani, or anyone to help him, but everyone else was in the same dire position: fighting for their lives. Who knew how Maddock could have shifted the tides of war. I hated him even more.

Rowen's eyes flashed to me trapped within Erovos' grasp. His expression was so beyond broken, it was sorry. So, very sorry. His tortured gaze apologized that I would have to watch as his life ended. It was something I would never wish on my greatest enemy.

Deadly claws flexed, aiming at Rowen's heart.

My throat was raw from screaming. It wasn't supposed to end like this.

"Watch your precious lord die," Erovos whispered in my ear. "Look at his face. He knows you will be next and that there is nothing he can do to stop it. His love for you is quite beautiful, really."

I began to travel to Rowen, but I couldn't. Erovos' fingers dug into me like pins on a butterfly's wings, keeping me in place.

If I couldn't get to Rowen physically, then I would astrally. I started to project, my body going limp, but Erovos violently shook me back to myself.

"Don't you dare leave this body or I will snap your neck. I know you'd rather witness your love die than have him watch as

I kill you and give your body to the Voro-Kai. And I would. I would make him watch it all. Then, I'd slowly torture him," he cooed in my ear as his frigid breath skittered along my skin. "Let him have the swift death."

"Don't touch him!" I screamed, thrashing in his hold.

My body shook uncontrollably. I couldn't run, I couldn't astral project. My blood and bones were useless. The only thing I could do was squeeze Mithrion tighter in my grip.

Suddenly, an idea struck!

Erovos had to feel me in my body, but that didn't mean I couldn't split myself in two—be in two places at once. I'd separated before, though not intentionally, and I'd never controlled both forms simultaneously. But I had to try!

I found the thread of my existence shimmering with the Elder Spirit's first-light. It looked so precious and fragile, but I had no time to second guess how this might affect me.

I pulled at the frayed edges, tearing myself apart. My head felt like it was splitting in half; the pressure was unimaginable, but I gritted my teeth and kept pulling until I snapped like a rubber band.

At first, nothing happened, but then I stepped away from my body as if it were as simple as stepping out of a coat. I was the bow and the shooting arrow all at once.

My awareness shifted in two, doubling the horrors of war.

I blinked as my realities flashed before me. One helplessly watched as Rowen dodged a barrage of blows while the other ran towards him.

Explosions of shadow, light, and debris burst around me as I charged across the battlefield. Dead and wounded soldiers littered the ground. Most were unmoving while others writhed in pain, and some, I suspected, were already turning from Voro-Kai bites.

My gaze shot forward as my body moved on its own accord, habitual from hours at the training grounds.

The Voro-Kai had one of its hooves on Rowen's chest, holding him down for the final blow.

I ran between them; it was the only thing I could do. The Voro-Kai's talons would cut right through my spectral form and kill Rowen, but I couldn't stop. I threw myself between them and raised my Ever-burn blade.

A jarring force clashed against me, and both sets of my eyes widened as I realized I'd blocked the demon's strike midair.

I'd carried Mithrion across the threshold of reality. One part of me held her within Erovos' cloak while the other blocked the attack that saved Rowen's life.

I knew my blade was remarkable, but I had no idea it could cross the plane's of reality; just like me.

I existed in a faded, glowing version of myself, yet my fury was in full force. I pushed my blade until the beast's claws met my hand guard, then I whirled out from under the Voro-Kai's weight. Power charged through my limbs and into the extension of Mithrion as I stabbed the demon's chest.

The beast roared and staggered back, but I followed, my grip steady on the hilt. Fetid breath washed over me as I drove the blade in deeper, and as soon as the tip punctured its heart, the beast disappeared in a plume of smoke.

Before I had time to look at Rowen, I painfully slammed back into my body.

Erovos realized what I had done, and his long nails dug into my skin. "You think you're clever?" he snarled. "Look around you. Your army is dying. You are losing. My Voro-Kai are overwhelming you."

What he said was true. I had saved Rowen from one Voro-Kai only for him to be attacked by another. For every ten demons slaughtered, one hundred more took their place.

The claws of darkness hovered and closed in, burying us alive.

I knew I wouldn't survive this battle, but now, it looked like none of us would. Both Wyn and Viltarran blood would stain this earth forever.

— ·(·❮·●·❯·)· —

Suddenly, a blinding light pierced my eyes.

Was this how it ended? In red-hot flames?

The air here was cold and dead, and I closed my eyelids, welcoming the lick of flames on my skin.

If it was all to end in fire, I hoped the scorched earth would one day beget new life, but first, we would all have to burn.

46

———

The flames weren't scalding. They were warm and comforting.

My eyes opened in confusion.

It wasn't a world-ending fire as I had suspected. It was the sun: bright, vibrant, and full of life. But how? The sun never reached here. Erovos made sure of that.

I squinted through the blinding glow, and as my eyes adjusted, a giant, red arch appeared through the rays of light.

The Eye of the Sun!

I peered closer, not believing my eyes. Was I already dead, returning to the Eternal Sun Stone?

But I wasn't the only one who was stunned. The entire battlefield twisted in shock at the colossal arch.

A choked sob erupted from my throat as thousands of Haradune soldiers marched through the haze, gleaming in golden armor. The Eye of the Sun framed the cerulean sky and never-ending dunes like a painting, stark against the barren and bloody battlefield.

The sun was shining through the arch, which meant it was the evening here, but the sky was so shrouded in a grey haze, it was impossible to tell.

I almost broke down when I realized we'd been battling all day. And just as all hope was extinguished and we bravely faced our deaths, reinforcements and daylight broke through the clouds.

Rayal led the charge, dressed in armor that looked molded to her body as if she'd been dipped in gold. She'd pulled her braids into one long twist down her back, revealing every strong and determined plane of her face. She must have taken control of her city, now leading her warriors in a cavalry charge.

"Grab an Ever-burn weapon!" Alvar commanded, gesturing to the carts filled with star-forged steel. The elven warriors picked up arrows, spears, and blades with a coordinated speed and charged into the fray.

"Destroy them all," Erovos roared, and I almost blacked out from the sonic boom of his voice.

Suddenly, a grinding of stones sounded in my ears. My gaze darted up to see a giant hawk flying through the arch. Its wings folded in before sweeping out to soar over the battlefield. Three more hawks followed suit, filling the sky with avian warriors.

It took me a moment to realize they were the stone statues perched high above Hara'dune. The Sunshades!

Even though they must have weighed a ton, they drifted through the air as if they were weightless.

My eyes searched for the elve commanding them, and sure enough, I found Thaydril. His arms flourished through the air as he puppeteered the stone beasts.

The hawks flew over the weapon racks and filled their talons with Ever-burn spears. They tucked their wings and dove into the fray of demons.

The Wyn and Viltarran soldiers cheered as the birds barreled into the Voro-Kai and sliced them to death.

Erovos dropped me to the ground as his jaw unhinged and his deadly eyes focused on one of the majestic hawks.

The world eater's eyes widened in disbelief as the Sunshade continued to pump its wings, unaffected by his siphoning power.

I smiled. The stone had no life, so there was no essence to steal.

Another bird dove in a gust of wind, impaling demons with its spears, and as their hearts were punctured, or their limbs ripped apart, their remains rained down on their littermates.

Erovos turned his gaze to the charging desert elves, his jaw elongating. And with a gravitational inhale, he drained a whole line of gold-plated soldiers. Before their shriveled bodies could fall to the ground, Erovos hurled their energy at one of the great hawks. The stolen power hit the bird, and it screeched as its wing was blasted off its body. Unable to balance in the air, the great avian teetered and then fell to the ground. The Sunshade plummeted to the earth, crushing enemies as they fell.

The distraction was enough for Nepta to regain her balance. She raised her moon staff and slammed it to the ground, and with a rippled tremor, the earth cracked open. A horde of demons fell through the chasm, howling as they were lost to the earth.

The tides of war shifted. Instead of total obliteration, the playing field was evening out, but still, it was too close to call.

I couldn't stay on the battlefield much longer. Now was my chance to get to Indrasyl and heal her before any more lives were lost. But Nepta had cracked open the ground, and I couldn't ignore the call of rushing water deep within the earth.

· (·C· ● ·Ɔ·) ·

Erovos left the tree unguarded as he battled three armies and the great hawks. It was just the diversion I needed. Rowen had regrouped with Callum and a few other soldiers, their faces exhausted as they prepared for another wave of demons.

I called upon the water, just like Althea had done when she separated her soul flame from the giants. I dug deep into my inner well of power and called upon the water. Erovos may be a gravitational force, but so was I.

My body shined like the moon as I dragged the water out of the earth in a violent wave. It smashed into the Voro-Kai, drowning out their charging growls as they were swept away. Satisfaction rippled through me, even though it hardly made a dent in the never-ending swarm of demons.

Once I knew Rowen was safe and had a moment to catch his breath, I charged toward the Sylvan Mother Tree when suddenly, a claw wrapped around my ankle and wrenched me to the ground.

I whipped onto my back, ready to strike, but a flash of iridescent feathers shot past my vision.

A Voro-Kai, crawling with no legs, released its hold on me with a shriek and clutched its eye that oozed sludge. I didn't have time to process what had given me the opportunity to stab the demon in the throat, its cries turning gargled.

Rowen darted between me and the charging beasts. "Go!" he yelled, his face covered in blood, dirt, and sweat. "I won't let them touch you."

"I love you," I said as Rowen dug his feet into the ground and tightened his grip on his Ever-burn blades.

"You'll come back to me?" Rowen asked, his face turning from the charging Voro-Kai to lock eyes with me.

"Yes," I said, but it was a lie—a terrible lie. "Now, don't die."

Our chests heaved in unison as our gazes darted to each other's mouths, and in a desperate fury, Rowen and I collided like crashing waves. I wrapped my arms around his neck as he pulled me in tight. Our lips and tongues tangled in a wild and reckless moment. We didn't have the time, but we selfishly indulged in the obliterating kiss anyway.

I could taste Rowen's blood, fear, and passion in his kiss.

Could he taste my goodbye?

He would never believe I'd lie to him, but I had, and with the ugliest lie possible—that I would return to his arms.

I could only hope that one day we would meet on the horizon line like Althea and Donis, the first soul flames.

Rowen tore his mouth from mine in a savage growl and plunged his star blade into the nearest demon.

"Go," he urged again, facing the barrage of Voro-Kai.

I gazed upon my soul flame for the last time. His beauty was deadly as he kept the astral demons at bay, protecting and guarding me as he always had.

I tore my gaze away from my ferocious god and sprinted the final steps to Indrasyl—the tree that would be my tomb. It was a fact that haunted me in my waking, sleeping, and astral life.

I entered the tree's ancient and dying form. Her twisted branches unfurled like the wings of a dragon, inviting me inside her towering trunk. The chains that once ensnared me still hung from her hollow cavity, locked and latched from when my wrists were in them last.

My spine spasmed as I saw the black dress Erovos had dressed me in crumbled on the ground.

This was where my body had been forged as an elve.

My knees went weak. Not many die in the same place they were reborn. But I had to keep it together. I couldn't lose it now. Letting my emotions consume me would only waste precious time.

I walked deeper into Indrasyl's sheltering presence, losing sight of Rowen and the people I cared for. The only thing that kept my feet moving was the thought that if I succeeded—when

I succeeded—they would live long, happy lives in a flourishing land. I just wouldn't be around to see it.

The hollow of Indrasyl's trunk was far bigger than I remembered, with earthy chambers and twisting walkways between her roots. I walked deeper into her ancient form, gazing around the space that was the size of a large room.

I drew Mithrion with a shaky grip, readying to cut my palms open to feed the tree with my blood.

"Wait," said a voice that startled me as I poised the knife at the heel of my hand. I glanced up, and a choked sob caught in my throat.

"I thought you left," I barely gasped out.

"I would never leave you like that," Maddock said. His black hair was damp with sweat and stuck to his forehead. "After everything, that's still how you see me?" The hurt was evident on his face. His eyes flashed to the gown, then to me, wrath darkening his pained expression. It was as if he relived the day I returned to the village. When he'd knocked me out with my Light and caught my naked body from falling.

"You shouldn't have come here," I whispered, taking my place in the very heart of Indrasyl, my final resting place. "Tell Rowen I'm sorry."

"I won't," Maddock said, stepping toward me. All the color had left his face except for the deep purple smudges under his eyes. He stalked toward me.

"What are you doing?" I asked, fear creeping up my throat.

Maddock winced as if I'd stabbed him in the heart; then he drew his Ever-burn blade on me.

I raised Mithrion, a warning to stay back.

"It will be you who apologizes to Rowen for me," he said between hastened breaths.

My brows narrowed in confusion when he suddenly flicked

Mithrion out of my hand and caught it midair, just like Dyani had taught him.

"You said I might have to die for you," Maddock continued, his steps faltering as if he were drunk. "You said your forgiveness might come at the cost of my life."

He threw my words back at me, and the cruelty of how I'd spoken to him cut me like a knife.

"I'm here, ready to pay it," he said, his strong jaw jutting up. And for the first time, I'd allowed myself to truly see the sincerity in his soft brown gaze. But before I could speak, move, or comprehend what was happening, Madds sank to the ground with a cry.

I ran to him as his knees buckled, and I took the brunt of his weight as we sank to the ground.

"What's wrong?" I asked frantically, my hands hovering over his muscled body.

"My back," he rasped. "I tried sneaking around the back, but this place is crawling with demons."

I pushed him forward to see that he was covered in blood.

I ripped off his shirt and gasped.

He grimaced. "I know it's bad, but you should see the other guys."

The first thing I noticed was a huge and gushing wound. The second was a shimmering tattoo that covered his entire back.

"Maddock! Why didn't you show me this?" I asked furiously, trying to staunch the bleeding at his liver.

"You never seemed to be in a hurry to see me naked," he joked in a pained rasp.

My eyes traced along the silver markings covering his back. "The Marked," I barely whispered as his blood coated my hands. The silver embossment on his skin looked just like my scars.

His mark started between the dimples just above his pants, then extended up and out like a tree of lightning. The markings were thickest across his upper back, where the branches reached out across his shoulder blades.

I gasped in disbelief. "You're the one from the prophecy. It's always been you. The Synodic Son. The Marked. All of it."

He shrugged, his thumb tracing over one of the silver scars on my arm. "Maybe. Funny, how you're the one who gave it to me. The night in the crevice when you blasted me out of your mind. I woke up in the hospital with it. Since that day, it was always going to be one of us. I'm just choosing for it to be me."

"No." I shook my head. "Not like this. Never like this." I tried to speak, to refute what I was seeing.

"It's too late," Maddock replied weakly, and as soon as a drop of his blood landed within the core of Indrasyl, veins of Light spread throughout the ground. "Indrasyl has accepted me, Keira. She has accepted my sacrifice."

"No," I screamed to Indrasyl, pressing my hands harder to Maddock's wound. "You have the wrong person. It's supposed to be me!"

I'd told Maddock in confidence what I meant to do, never believing he would betray me to do it himself. He let everyone believe he'd deserted our army to keep me from guessing his plan. And I believed it so easily.

I was sobbing, pushing my Light into him to heal him. I regretted every horrible thought I ever had about him.

"I'm going to heal you and take your place," I said in a determined daze.

"Do not break this connection, Keira," he demanded weakly. "Indrasyl might not accept me again. And if you try, she might deny you. It is done."

"You did this for nothing. You don't have enough power. You only stole a small amount of my Light. It's nowhere near what is needed. Your death will have been for nothing," I cried, my hands slathered in red. "I'll still have to do this, and you could have . . . could have lived."

I hated him. Hated him more than when he'd violated my mind because now he had violated my trust.

His voice faded by the second. "You'll have to help me, Keira. Use me; use my body as a conduit. Do what needs to be done."

Inside the trunk of the tree, the battle was no more than white noise, but I knew the longer I prolonged Maddock's death, the more people would die, including Rowen.

"I'll hate you into the next life," I said, releasing my hands from his gaping wound and letting his blood fall.

"I know," he murmured. "Be with Rowen. Be happy."

I extended myself beyond, reaching the tendrils of my astral light toward Maddock. Our connection was already in place, formed through the soul flame bond he had stolen. Finding the threads of his existence was simple, and I latched onto each one, our bodies fully connected through the Alcreon Light that surged between us.

"Do it," he whispered against my cheek. We both knew he was right. He was dying.

With an anguished scream, I pushed all of Maddock's blood and my Light through him. It soaked into the tree whose roots were so long and ancient that they covered the entire earth. It would be a reset as the vines and roots healed the earth from the inside out.

Maddock arched back as I pushed the light of the heavens inside of him, using my astral projection powers as a gateway to heal Luneth. Indrasyl greedily accepted the blood I pushed into her through Maddock. I was bleeding him dry, and she was hungrily accepting his offer.

Maddock struggled to keep his eyes open as I fed his life force into the tree along with the power of the Alcreon Light.

"Come closer, Keira," he whispered, and I did as he said. How could I refuse him this last wish?

His lips softly touched my cheek. "I just wanted to taste you one time." His hands wrapped around me as he licked, kissed, and nuzzled his way down to my mouth. He hesitated as if waiting for me to push him away, but I didn't. Suddenly, he pressed his cold lips to mine, startling me. A little strength returned to him as he took my mouth, slowly exploring my lips as if it were the last thing he'd ever do. And it was.

When I first saw him in the hospital, unconscious and beautiful, he looked like a prince in need of a kiss to wake, only now, it was a kiss to sink into silence forever.

"It's better than I imagined," he murmured against my lips, then kissed me harder.

I felt a push through our bodies; something warm, golden, and painfully missed filled me as I kissed him back. Where I was giving him everything, he found the one channel to return something to me—my soul flame bond with Rowen.

I sobbed into his mouth as he returned what he had so violently stolen. The small missing piece clicked back into place, and a broken yet healed cry charged up my throat.

My bond returned to me fully, and I realized I was kissing Maddock. Not the man from the crevice, or the thief, or the bond stealer. Just Maddock.

He dove his tongue between my lips, exploring my mouth as he took and tasted what he wanted. My fingers threaded through his hair as I held him to my mouth.

"Ple-please, forgive me," he said against my lips then slumped in my arms.

Before I could say yes, yes that I forgive him a million stars over, his eyes closed forever. He would never get to hear that I forgave him. "Yes," I screamed, hoping some part of him was still close enough to hear me. I wanted to tell him there was nothing left to forgive.

Maddock slumped to the ground in my hold just as the tree around us illuminated in a blinding white light. The tree shook from deep within the earth, accepting the blood that carried the Alcreon Light, spreading and feeding it to the world.

Tears poured from my eyes. I couldn't stop them. The joy of Indrasyl coming back to life while Maddock lay lifeless in my arms was hard to reconcile—that one had to die for the other to live.

A comforting shadow appeared in my periphery, and I lifted my head to see Rowen joining us in the tree. He was covered in even more blood and sweat.

His emerald eyes were wild as he took in the sight. "What happened?" He panted as he ran toward us.

"It was supposed to be me," I sobbed, my tears crashing onto Maddock's cheeks.

Understanding settled over Rowen's face as he lowered himself and gently took Maddock from my arms, but I gripped him tighter, refusing to let go.

"I can't accept this," I cried, rocking him. "It was my life to give."

Rowen gripped my chin in his hand, forcing my gaze to his. "Don't say that. Do you hear me? This is what he wanted; the redemption he was seeking. Do not take that away from him, Keira."

My sobs were uncontrollable. "He didn't hear me say that I forgive him."

He gripped my chin harder. "He knows, my love. He knows. Say it back to me and believe it."

"He . . . he knows," I stuttered within his grasp.

"That's my girl," Rowen said as he released me, fighting the tears welling in his own eyes. I finally let him lower Maddock to the ground.

I picked up Mithrion and turned to Maddock to give him one last promise—that if I succeeded, I would come back for his body, but Indrasyl had other plans. She slowly blanketed him in branches and roots, pulling him into her cradle. No part of his body would go to waste. *Through blood and bone.*

I stood mesmerized as Maddock was engulfed in his tomb. And I couldn't help but envision my body being wrapped and cocooned within Indrasyl's embrace, living on forever in her roots.

It wasn't a bad way to go.

Rowen pulled me back as the tree closed in around us. The hollow trunk slowly merged together. Maddock's body, and the shifting bark, filled the hole of Indrasyl, making her complete. "Keira, listen to me. The battle still rages. We need to go."

As much as I wanted to stay and watch Maddock's funeral through to the end, I couldn't. This battle was far from over.

Though my bond was back in full force, there was a gaping hole deep within myself. It was as if I were an empty well ready to be filled.

"Let's end this," I gritted out. I didn't know how or with what energy, but there would be no sunrise in which this wasn't finished. One way or another, I would end this war.

Maddock may have sacrificed himself to heal Luneth, but Erovos hadn't been defeated. Nothing was to stop him from destroying the planet again or moving on to the next.

After what Maddock had offered in my place, I wanted to fight for him. For his memory. He'd given me the gift of time. And I'd be damned if I let Erovos ruin one more second of my life with Rowen.

I didn't wipe the tears for Maddock off my face. I'd let them stain my cheeks as I fought for his revenge. "I need to defeat Erovos. It might be on the astral plane."

"I will protect your body with my life," he swore as a wild, brutal forest swirled in his eyes.

"I know."

"Don't leave me again," he said as his eyes held mine. "You are my flame. If your light goes out, then so does mine. I don't have the strength to face this world without you."

"I'll never make you face this world, or any world, alone. I promise." This time, it wasn't a lie. It was the truth. Forever and always.

I didn't turn back to look at him as I raced towards Erovos. I knew Rowen was behind me. I didn't need to see him to know he was there because if I looked back, it might steal the strength I needed to defeat Erovos once and for all.

47

Rowen and I charged onto the battlefield. The stench of blood, death, and black ichor hit me like a brick wall, but there was no space for fear or hesitation.

I joined the battle where forest and desert elves alike fought for Luneth. The contrast of the Wyn's silver hair mixed with the gold armor of the Hara'dune warriors was luminous against the Voro-Kai. It looked like the sun and moon had come together to fight an insidious darkness. But with each passing second, the luminosity dimmed more and more as the Voro-Kai smothered out the light.

Only one hawk remained in the sky, pumping its broken wings to stay afloat. The other Sunshades were scattered upon the ground, never to take flight again. The cold bodies piling around me told me exactly how many souls the world eater used to take the great avians down. Too many. Far too many.

A Voro-Kai with Ever-burn arrows jutting from his face and chest charged by me. It grabbed a Viltarran soldier and slashed her throat open, diving its fangs into her neck.

My stomach twisted in dread as the battle raged on in chaos. There was no end in sight.

Suddenly, Indrasyl rumbled again, shaking every warrior and beast where they stood. A blast of Light shot skyward like a distress signal to the heavens, and a web of glowing roots illuminated the ground. The silver network spread across the soil like horizontal lightning.

Anywhere a Voro-Kai stood, hoof to root, they incinerated into smoke. Plumes of black dust erupted all around the field. It was as if the ground had become sanctified in holy Light, and Erovos' darkness could not walk upon it.

Luneth was fighting back.

But it still wasn't enough. The demons were catching on, avoiding the roots as they continued to scratch and claw and bite.

Suddenly, a light fell from the sky, piercing a Voro-Kai through the heart. The demon didn't even have a chance to blink before it exploded into a fine mist.

Another light fell, and another, and soon, it was raining stars.

Indrasyl had called for help, and the Elder Spirits answered. The stars pierced through demon and after demon in a murderous meteor shower.

I wove through the chaos, whirling Mithrion in elliptical arcs that carved through the remaining Voro-Kai.

A familiar cry caught my attention, and my head whipped to see Dyani sprinting across the battlefield. Her blades glowed like captured starlight as she ran like an Olympian, pumping her arms and legs with dire urgency. I followed her line of sight to what—or who—she ran to.

Rayal was covered in a swarm of premature demons. They were small but quick and ferocious. They latched onto her arms and legs and crawled up her back, biting into her armor. She couldn't shake them; for every one she pulled off, another took its place.

The fear on Dyani's blood-stained face was palpable. Claws and talons swiped at her, but she dodged every one, her eyes never wavering from her target. She charged onto a fallen Voro-Kai and used it as leverage to launch herself toward Rayal. In a series of impossible-to-see swipes, her blades danced over Rayal's flesh, slaughtering the demons that clung to her.

Rayal collapsed, but Dyani caught her in her arms, not letting the queen fall to her knees.

Rayal's golden eyes snapped to Dyani. Her face radiated with relief and something more than gratitude as she realized who'd caught her and kept her upright.

The fourth Sunshade plummeted to earth, shooting up bits of raw earth and rock.

I brought up my arm to shield my face, and when I lowered it, I saw a Voro-Kai encasing Callum's head in his giant palm. Its talons dug into the Viltarran warrior's face and scalp. Suddenly, a scrap of Ever-burn shot from deep within the trees and hit the Voro-Kai in the forearm. The beast hissed and released Callum, giving Rowen's friend the reprieve he needed to thrust his sword into the demon's chest.

My eyes darted to the tree line where I saw a tuft of white. I squinted, making out Ven with a slingshot, hurling bits of Ever-burn into the skirmish. Sabra was beside him, guarding him in a protective stance.

How the hell did they get here?

I shouldn't be surprised, but I would have to murder Ven later for sneaking into war-torn territory.

Suddenly, that iridescent ripple of light shot past my vision again, and I whirled around just in time to see a beast swiping at me. I ducked under its arm and used the momentum to kick up and around its back, hooking my legs around its beefy neck. I whirled around its head, bringing myself atop its shoulders. And with its head between my thighs, I did a forward roll down its chest, forcing it to flip over me and fall on its back. I landed in a crouch and plunged Mithrion into its heart.

I stood from my crouch, spinning in a slow circle to see the Wyn, Viltarran, and Hara'dune soldiers shouting in victory. Standing among them, to my relief, was Takoda, Nepta, and Alvar.

One by one, the Voro-Kai were defeated. Whether by earth, sky, or blade, they were ejected from this land forever.

Cheers erupted as the battle slowly ceased and the earth and heavens calmed.

Erovos was seemingly unbothered as his brood perished in front of him. The world eater smiled as our eyes locked across the field.

Rowen was suddenly beside me, and I squeezed his hand, telling him to stay.

I was exhausted, depleted, and worn, but I stepped forward, my gaze never wavering from the world eater's burning eyes.

"Erovos!" I yelled, flicking demon blood off my blade. "Let it all come down to me and you."

His razor-sharp smile widened as we met in the center of the field. "Very well, little light. Let us end this once and for all."

·(·C· ● ·)·)·

I charged at Erovos, winding Mithrion into a killing blow. The world eater vibrated and warped the air around him, causing my strike to miss. I swirled around and plunged again, but my weapon only cut through trails of mist.

"You think you can defeat me?" he asked in a humored laugh that chilled my bones. "Your armies, weapons, and Light are useless against me."

He was right. Even with our armies and Ever-burn blades, there was no defeating a black hole that could absorb the life and light out of everything. He dodged my attacks again and again. I couldn't get my hands on him. It was like trying to grab smoke and nail it down.

"I grow tired of this," Erovos said, billowing in shrouds of darkness. His chalky-white hands pulled back his hood, revealing his bony head. Then, his palms shot forward as he blasted me with harvested power, knocking Mithrion out of my grasp.

Rowen shouted my name across the battlefield, rushing toward me alongside a fleet of warriors. Erovos raised his arms and unleashed a sonic wave, halting everyone mid-run. They looked paused in place, but as I peered closer, I realized they were moving imperceptibly slow. It was as if the black hole before me had curved the fabric of time, causing them to exist on a different frequency.

The war cry etched on Rowen's face twisted my gut. He was frozen mid-lunge, looking like a charging statue. His broad shoulders and thighs rippled with raw power as the veins in his neck bulged. His sweat-plastered hair and short beard framed his ferocious eyes that were locked on me. His sword was raised in the air, ready to murder.

Takoda, Alvar, Dyani, everyone, was caught in Erovos' grip of time. They would never get to me. I was truly alone.

My gaze darted back to Erovos. "Retreat, or I will drain every last one of them dry," he said matter-of-factly, gesturing to my soul flame and the field of warriors. "Even if it takes all night."

"I will never surrender to you," I seethed as my fingertips pulsated with energy.

He hurled another blast of dark energy, but I pulled up a shield of Light at the last second. My arm juddered from the hit, but my defense held firm.

Erovos slammed into my shield again. This time, the impact

was so vicious that I bit down on my tongue, and blood welled in my mouth.

My heels dug into the earth as he hit me with a barrage of blows.

I gritted my teeth. Every muscle in my body burned and trembled as I held up my shield. The hits came faster and more frequently until it was a straight torrent of power. I cried out in exhaustion, begging for relief. Strength of will was the only thing keeping me going, but my energy was draining by the second.

Erovos was purposely wearing me down, waiting until I was too tired to lift even the smallest tendrils of myself against him. And despite my best efforts, my shield began to lower.

He finally stopped, offering me a brief reprieve, and we made eye contact through my silvery shield. "Let me have you, little light. Surrender, and I will spare your friends."

I was repulsed and sickened, but he was impossible to overcome. And I had tried everything else. I would have to let him in.

"Fine," I said with a deep breath of acceptance, and I dropped my shield.

I braced myself, but nothing could have prepared me for his obliterating slam. It was too fast and painful, and I lost sense of who I was.

Erovos grabbed me by the neck and lifted me into the air. I scratched at his hands as my legs jerked beneath me. Tendrils of darkness erupted from Erovos' back and raised around him like spider legs. The black threads curved over his shoulders, towards me, and I watched in horror as they pierced through my body.

I screamed in agony; the blinding pain nearly making me black out.

Was he suffocating or draining me? I couldn't tell, but I knew my time was well and truly up.

His hand lowered from my neck, but I remained suspended, held up in the air by his tenebrous arms. Erovos' power flowed into me like a poisonous IV, and I realized he wasn't killing me. He was turning me.

"Once my power has filled you, we will make them suffer together," a dissonant voice echoed in my ear. "As you can see, I've decided to spare you. Your new elven form is strong and impressive. Your pathetic human body would have been driven to madness, but now, I believe you will take my darkness well. Think of what I could accomplish with you by my side, the worlds we could consume together."

A tear slid down my cheek. Erovos was a celestial being, a miasmic shadow whose power eclipsed mine. I thought I could defeat him, but I was wrong. So very wrong.

How do you defeat someone with no weaknesses?

The realization hit me like a meteor shower—you don't. You join them.

I focused inward and latched onto Erovos' coils inside me. Instead of letting him feed me with his darkness, I would take it for myself.

"What are you doing?" he demanded as I glutinously stole from him. He tried ripping away from me, but I didn't let him budge. We were connected now.

His power couldn't be destroyed, but it could be contained. Within me.

His darkness bled through me, into my eyes, and the sky blinked out.

I choked on dread as horrifying images flashed in my mind: writhing bodies, melting faces, and vicious beasts played on a constant loop. Decaying flowers and bodies surrounded me; their shriveled vines and hands wrapped around me and dragged me down.

A burning clawed at my stomach and throat. I felt Erovos'

gravitational hunger, desire, and satiation after feeding. It made my mouth water. I turned my starving stare to the people around me, ready to feast.

Suddenly, something stronger than the hunger burned in my chest. My soul flame bond! It was whole, pure, and the most powerful thing in the universe.

I promised Rowen I would come back to him. And I would.

I didn't fight the hellish images in my head. It was impossible. All I could do was try to drown them out with thoughts of Rowen—his touch, his kiss, and his emerald aura encasing me. I thought of Maddock, of his warm eyes and charming smile. I focused on the memories of bringing water back to the village and liberating the desert elves. I thought of my new family and home, laughing with Ven, petting Sabra, and forming new and unexpected friendships.

The dark edges receded from my vision, so I kept going, kept thinking of every happy memory I could.

I imagined everything that was yet to come—the earth healing, marrying Rowen, and making love to him on our throne, in our bed, and any other secret nooks we could find. Of rebuilding Viltarran and creating a beautiful, meaningful, and fulfilling life together. Not just for us, but for everyone.

And last of all, I wanted to honor Maddock's sacrifice with a proper goodbye.

Suddenly, an idea struck.

If Madds could be the conduit for my powers, perhaps I could be one for Erovos.

I thought I'd done this when I trapped him in the crevice, but it hadn't been enough. I'd allowed him to stay in his body. This time, I would have to take it a step further. I would have to rip away his power, funnel it through my body, and put it somewhere it could never escape.

My senses stretched to the Wyn village and into the Sacred

Vale, where the Alcreon Stone hovered in midair. I latched onto the shattered pieces, and with a surge of my traveling abilities, I transported all the stones to the battlefield in a burst of lightning.

The shattered crystals now hovered and circled above us in our astral duel.

I channeled his cloying power through me and into the crystals. I yanked harder on Erovos' dark tendrils, ravenously pulling his energy into my body and transferring it into the stones.

Somehow, I could see it all. I was a creator, slowly and meticulously forging a new entity.

I shot my gaze to Erovos, and for the first time, a hint of fear flashed across his pallid face.

He looked down to see his astral form slowly peeling away from his body. "You have no idea what you're doing. You can't contain me!" he roared as he wrenched one of his dark tendrils free. He whipped it across my face, and my head snapped to the side.

My grasp slipped, and darkness encased me once again. The hunger returned stronger than ever. I was sinking, faster and faster. I didn't know if I could rise again.

Suddenly, six glowing entities appeared behind me. Their ethereal glow was blinding, powerful, and ancient.

Alcreon Light Bearer, do not give up, said a symphony of voices in my head.

I'd heard these overlapping voices before.

You must eclipse this darkness with your Light, the Elder Spirits hummed. *It is the only way to restore the balance throughout the cosmos. Feel your strength. You are reforged as an Ancient Elve.* The celestial beings bolstered around me, placing their heavenly arms on mine. *We are here with you,* they said as they helped me push the Dark Spirit into the Alcreon Stone. The Elder Spirits had once infused the stone with Light, but now they helped me infuse it with darkness.

Power buoyed through my veins, and the world eater bellowed in terror.

It was the final piece of the prophecy—when the first six stars align with the stones of shattered ruin.

Through blood, bone, and crystal, the prophecy finally clicked into place.

"You thought you were an all-powerful being," I said as the threads holding him together snapped and tore. "But when I'm done with you, you will be nothing more than a rock."

"I will find you again," he promised, his orange eyes raging. "You don't know pain, but when I find you again, I will teach you true suffering."

There were sinews connecting him to his splitting silhouette. "Good luck with that," I said, focusing on my happy memories, each of which was a speck of light that illuminated my vision. The stars spread and grew and multiplied until a blinding white light engulfed me. It was as if the Alcreon Light blasted out of me at the speed of light, causing me to be everywhere and nowhere all at once.

With a final push, I sealed Erovos within the stones, severing all our connections and cleansing his blight from my veins.

Erovos' shrieks finally ended as the celestial lights dimmed around me. I gently landed on my feet, my vision fully returned.

I stared at the world eater. His empty eyes blinked back at me.

"You do make quite the sacrificial vessel," I said, repeating the words he'd spoken to me before destroying my human body. And without a second thought, I blasted his corporeal form, watching as I obliterated him into smoke and ash.

A low-pitch hum vibrated above me, and my gaze shot skyward.

What was once whole, heavenly, and crystalline was now tainted, shattered, and gleaming an iridescent black.

The Elder Spirits glowed around me in nebulous forms that looked like galaxies. An unspoken communication passed between us as I thanked them for their help. *We chose correctly, Alcreon Light Bearer. It is we who must thank you for protecting our precious Light.* And in a flurry of shooting stars, they vanished, leaving me alone and surrounded by hovering dark crystals.

48

The war was over. We'd defeated Erovos' army and contained his corruption.

My legs buckled, and I sank to my knees in exhaustion, relief, and awe.

Time realigned as Rowen and the soldiers charged toward me. My soul flame dropped to his knees and gathered me in his embrace. "Are you hurt?" Rowen asked, frantically inspecting my body for injuries. I was in a daze; my tongue stuck to the roof of my mouth. "Keira, talk to me!"

Suddenly, the loss I'd pushed aside overcame me like a tidal wave. "He's gone. Maddock's gone," I burst out, crying, somehow expecting to see his face emerging from the crowd.

"I know," Rowen soothed, holding me tight against his armored chest. "I know."

"He didn't desert the army. That's just what he wanted me to believe." I laughed through the tears. "What a bastard."

Rowen let out a choked sound, threading his hands through my hair and guiding my gaze to his. "He was. But he loved you, and there was no better way for him to show you."

"He . . . he gave me my bond back."

My soul flame wiped my tears with his thumbs. "I know. I can feel it."

I gripped the edges of his silver-black breastplate. "He was always the one the prophecy spoke of. How did I not see it?"

Rowen's temples hollowed as he flexed his jaw. "You both fit the prophecy, Keira. It could have been either of you. I'm going to miss Maddock, and thank him every fucking day for his sacrifice, but you both went into Indrasyl to fulfill that prophecy."

Guilt punctured my lungs, and I winced. "Rowen, I'm so sorry I lied to you. It's unforgivable. I thought . . . I thought I was protecting you."

My soul flame's face was covered in mud, blood, and demon ichor, but his green eyes shone through with pained understanding. "I know why you did it, but if anything like that ever happens again, tell me. Please. We will figure it out together."

"I will," I promised as he helped me to my feet. I wiped the tears from my eyes, knowing now was not the time to mourn.

A hum vibrated in my veins, and my eyes lifted. Rowen's stare followed, his irises reflecting the dark crystals above. "What happened?" he asked as Dyani, Rayal, and Nepta joined us in the center of the field. "You asked me to stay back, but when Erovos knocked Mithrion from your hand, I couldn't stop myself. I ran to you, but everything happened so fast."

"You were flickering faster than a hummingbird's wings," Rayal said, holding one of Dyani's bloody hands.

The warrior agreed with a nod, her grime-covered face streaked with dried tears. "One moment, Erovos had you; the next, a blinding light filled the sky. Then he was gone, with these in his place," she said, her sharp chin jutting up.

I quickly recounted what happened with Erovos and the Elder Spirits, and how I trapped the world eater within the pieces of the Alcreon Stone.

"I can feel the Dark Spirit within the crystals," Nepta said, her voice steady yet cautious. The Elven-head appeared unharmed, though her face and ivory dress were covered in battle stains. "He is enraged and fighting for release, but he is not going anywhere anytime soon. We must tend to our dead and dying."

My head turned, taking in the blood, death, and raw earth around me. Only our dead filled the valley, and though so many had given their lives, more than half stood standing.

Takoda made his rounds with fresh noxlilies from his pack, prioritizing the severely injured first.

Our allies collected their dead in solemn reverence while others gathered weapons, pieces of armor, clothing, and body parts.

A single tear slid down my cheek as the fallen were carried away. Their lifeless eyes stared up at the heavens, the windows to their inner galaxies snuffed out forever. There had been a moment when I thought humanity wouldn't live to see the dawn, but as the sun pierced through the thick clouds, I knew their deaths weren't in vain.

The arch curved over the Lirien Valley, offering a peek at the other side of the world, now glittering with moonlight and rolling purple dunes. The desert elves carried their deceased in silence, returning home through the Eye of the Sun.

I still couldn't believe Rayal was here. Her arrival had been nothing short of a miracle, offering the reinforcements we so desperately needed. I shuddered to think what would have happened if she arrived even a second later. Yet, with her troops, the battle teetered on the brink of defeat.

Even the land, heavens, and Elder Spirits fought back against the world eater. Had we not all come together, aligning like the stars of a prophecy, Erovos' dark nature would know no bounds. And though the darkness was contained, the journey to our healing had just begun.

Even though I barely had the energy to stand, I checked on those bitten by a Voro-Kai. But as I inspected their injuries, I found no blight within their blood. It was as if my eclipsing blast had cleansed the darkness from their veins.

After I was sure no one would turn into an astral demon, I tended to Rowen's cuts and gashes. He had several that were a little too deep for my liking.

Light pulsed at my fingertip as I grazed my touch over Rowen's cheekbone, throat, and knuckles. "Thanks," he murmured and kissed me on the temple.

Ven and Sabra walked up to us as if they hadn't snuck into a war zone. My soul flame did a double take and ran his palm down his face. "I'm not even going to ask."

"Best that you don't," Ven said, petting Sabra behind the ear. The wolf's white fur was matted with black ichor, but she proudly smiled as blood dripped from her paws.

I knew what Sabra was capable of when it came to protecting Ven, yet I still quickly scanned them both for injuries, and thankfully, there were none to be found.

"After all I've taught you, a stick and string are your weapons of choice?" Rowen asked, gesturing to the boy's slingshot.

"Hey! This stick and string saved your ass like thirteen times," Ven remarked, pulling the sling back and pretending to take aim.

"Watch the language," Rowen said with a grin, clasping the young elve on the shoulder. "Sounds like I owe you one."

Ven beamed with pride. "You owe me a few."

"How did you get bits of Ever-burn?" I asked, knowing he'd actually inflicted damage on the demons he hit.

"I snuck into the forge and stole the scraps," he replied with delight. "Bailon thought it was Leer keeping the place tidy. And Leer never corrected him!" He laughed and shook his head as if we were all idiots.

"You never cease to amaze me," I said as Rowen and I laughed with him. The brief weightlessness in my chest let me know that despite all the loss and tragedy, we would find a way to smile again.

———— ·(·☽·●·☾·)· ————

The war cleanup continued, and I took a moment to rest and rehydrate. I sat cross-legged on the ground when suddenly, an iridescent light shimmered around me, and a small weight plopped in my lap.

Glowing feathers brushed against my skin in waves of silver, blue, and light purple, and a small but mighty chirp vibrated against my chest.

A starwing!

I'd seen the shimmering flash of its tail on the battlefield. It had saved my life twice. Once with the demon who'd grabbed me by the ankle and again with the demon who'd nearly sliced me in two.

I glanced around, searching for other starwings, but none were in sight.

Erovos said they were extinct. This must be the only one left, still bravely defending and protecting its home. I gently stroked the top of its head and noticed familiar scars around its body and wings. These ropey marks were from a net—a net I had freed this creature from over fifteen years ago.

"So we meet again, friend," I said, fighting back tears. My heart broke for the bird all alone in the world.

The starwing nestled deeper into my lap and closed its eyes. "I still have work to do," I said, but the bird ignored me and emitted sleepy trills of contentment.

"She knows you need rest," said a voice as warm as the sun.

"Rayal!" I replied as she joined me on the ground and we

hugged, careful not to smush the bird. "I can't thank you enough for helping us. But how did you escape Aedris?"

The warrior queen had removed most of her armor and wore fitted brown pants and a linen tank. Specks of blood and tiny scratches covered her face and hands. "It is I who owes you thanks. You planted the seeds of rebellion, and because of your defiance, I was able to overthrow Aedris with the help of my elves."

"You are now queen?"

"I am," she said, her eyes locking with mine in gratitude.

Thaydril appeared behind his cousin. Mud covered his embellished armor, and his black eyeliner smeared around his eyes like warpaint. "That was brilliant what you did with our step-uncle," he said, kneeling. "The second the collar wouldn't snap, the wards and restrictions placed upon us vanished. You wove your words masterfully."

Rayal nodded in agreement. "Not only did your words remind the elves of their rightful ruler, they also reminded Hara'dune—the land itself. The rebellion needed a spark to set it ablaze. We needed you."

"I'm just glad I could return the favor. You saved me in crypts," I said, watching Rowen sort the details of moving the war camp to the valley.

He didn't want to leave my side. I'd convinced him it was okay to let go of my hand. He'd reluctantly kissed my mouth, cheek, and palm before leaving to set up tents for the wounded, but his eyes kept flickering to mine as if he were afraid I would walk to Indrasyl and never return. My heart lurched as I remembered someone else had made that sacrifice.

My gaze shot back to Rayal and Thaydril. "You came just in time. Even a moment later and I fear you wouldn't have had an army to aid."

"I wish we could have gotten here sooner," she replied with a pinch between her brows. "The rebellion lasted almost three full days. It wasn't easy getting Aedris off the throne. He is now serving time in the sand pits."

"Well, isn't that poetic?"

Rayal acknowledged the bird on my lap. "She sleeps soundly," she said, joining me to pet my feathered friend.

"How do you know it's a she?" I asked, stroking its neck.

"See how sleek her crown and nape are, with no extra feathers or plumes? Definitely a female," she replied.

"She is the last of her kind," I said as a lump formed in my throat. "Wait. How do you know so much about starwings?"

"There is one in my aviary. Though I didn't know that's what they were called, or where they originated from."

"Is it . . . ?" I started to ask, too afraid of the answer.

Her eyes shone like marigold. "It's a male. I named him Ekee. It means *first star in the sky*."

A relieved sob escaped my lips. "How do you have him?"

"He was captured a few years ago, and someone sold him to my father. I never knew where Ekee belonged, but I knew it wasn't the desert. I couldn't release him into an inhospitable landscape, so I kept him safe in my sanctuary."

"Can you bring him back? We might be able to introduce them," I said, gesturing to the sleeping creature in my lap. "They are the last of their breed. They deserve to be reunited."

"Of course," the queen of Hara'dune replied. "I think it's time he returned home."

"Is there a word for *last star in the sky*?" I asked, resting my palm on my knee, but the female nudged my hand with her beak, and I immediately returned to stroking her downy feathers with a chuckle.

Rayal thought for a moment. "I believe the closest word would be 'Keeli'."

"Did you hear that, Keeli? You're not alone," I said as she fluttered her wings in my lap. A mate awaited her. And now that their habitat was healing, the starwings could hopefully thrive once again and fill the sky with their glittering tails.

I hugged Keeli closer. She'd asked me for help all those years ago when I was just a young girl in a torn nightgown. "I'm sorry it took me so long to help you. I was drugged by my parents and forced to forget you," I said as the bird craned her neck to stare directly at me. I could see the pain in her eyes as she conveyed how she'd watched her family and home perish. "I failed you then, but I won't fail you now."

Her small head cocked to the side as if she understood me. Then, she closed her eyes and rested her weary head on my arm.

We met fifteen years ago, our fates intertwined. I continued to hold the starwing that put me on the path I was destined to walk. She led me to my future, my soul flame, and the Alcreon Light thrumming through my veins. That same light spread through the ground. Indrasyl's silver roots shot out in every direction and healed the earth that was home to us all.

49

A few days had passed since the Battle at Lirien Valley, and the village felt as if it could finally breathe again. The war was over and all our healing could truly begin.

I walked along the lush pathways, brushing my hands against the leaves. Small vines followed and reached for me, curving around my fingertips as I walked by. Keeli floated behind me, squawking and marveling at all the greenery around her.

I wore a slate-grey dress laced with shimmering threads. Two thin straps wrapped around my neck, down my sternum, and then separated into wider panels that covered my breasts. The sleeves hung low off my shoulders and pooled at my elbows. The dark silver fabric draped down my body like a twilit pond.

"Are you ready to tell Nepta?" Rowen asked, striding alongside me, one of his calloused hands holding mine. We had requested an audience with the Elven-head at the Sacred Vale.

"I am. Are you sure *you're* ready?" I asked back, noting the slight tension in his fingers. "This is the third time you've asked me."

"Sorry," he said as he loosened his grip. "I guess I am nervous. I must tell the greatest leader I've ever known that I'm the lord of a citydom. I know next to nothing about ruling, and I'm worried she won't think me suitable. But more so, that you won't think me suitable."

I stopped on the path and pulled him toward me, wrapping my arms around his waist.

"You're the most suitable man I know," I said with a smirk. My hands lowered down his backside where I squeezed the defined slope of his ass. He chuckled, and my ploy to ease his nerves worked. "I'm serious, though. I don't know anyone more suitable. I don't know anything about ruling either, but I will be right there beside you, learning with you, ruling with you. You won't be doing it alone."

Rowen smiled, letting me trap him within my arms. "I must have done something right in another life to deserve you. I haven't even asked you if this is something you want to do."

I grabbed his face in my hands, feeling the scruff of his beard against my palms. "I thought I already answered that when I agreed to be your wife," I said as I wiggled my vine-entwined ring. "Of course I want to. That dream? The night before battle? That was our shared vision of the future, and I want more than anything to create that with you."

Rowen cradled my face in his hands, tilting my head back to fully take him in. He swiped his thumb over my lip. "Spirits, I can't wait to make you my wife," he said as he gently popped out my lower lip and took it into his mouth. My breath caught in my throat as he branded me with his smoldering kiss. His tongue stroked mine deliberately, slowly, and my mind went haywire as every bone in my body liquified.

Keeli squawked, but I was so lost in Rowen's kiss that I completely forgot what we were supposed to be doing.

"I can't wait to make you my husband," I murmured between

kisses, my hands trailing up the defined muscles of his back. "And I can't wait to fuck you as my husband." Our bodies melded closer together as my tongue curled into Rowen's mouth, and I tasted his moan on my lips.

"What's this, I hear?" Nepta said, coming up behind us on the path, and Rowen and I jumped apart.

So that was why Keeli was chirping.

Nepta may not be able to see what we were doing, but she definitely didn't need to *hear* it.

"I can understand now why everyone knows you two are soul flames. You certainly aren't hiding it," the Elven-head said with a huge grin on her face.

"I plan on making my soul flame my wife," Rowen proudly said, sliding his palm to the small of my back. "As well as the Lady of Viltarran."

If Nepta was shocked, she didn't show it. She just continued to smile.

Rowen cleared his throat and continued. "The queen of Hara'dune found a scroll bequeathing the citydom to me. We will leave once things have settled here, but I wanted to thank you for everything. For taking me in when I was broken with nothing but the clothes on my back. For protecting the love of my life within your village and fighting alongside her during the war."

"You are welcome, Rowen Damascus," she replied, taking his left hand in hers. "Go to Viltarran with my blessing. Your people need you. Both of you." She grabbed my left hand as well and placed our palms together.

She spoke in a language I couldn't understand but could feel deep within my bones. The flame in my chest thrummed and flicked in time with Rowen's. Energy moved around us as heat, flames, and Light coursed through our bodies like an infinity symbol.

"The Spirits bless this union," Nepta said, her voice thick with emotion. I looked down at our joined hands, where our vine-wrapped rings slowly hardened into silver. The earthy details and tiny leaves remained as the rings became everlasting symbols of our love. The final change was the moonlit diamond forming on the top of my band.

Happy tears pooled in my lash line as my gaze met Rowen's. "You're the best thing that's ever happened to me," he said as his eyes glistened with tears and choked emotion. "My sky was dark, void, and without meaning, but then you appeared to me, and I recognized you immediately, even in my utter darkness. You filled my night with stars, galaxies, and purpose. It was as if you'd found me in a thousand different realities and worlds and lit my sky in every one. I knew I never wanted to be parted from you."

"Before I met you, I felt you everywhere. You were in my pulse, my heart, and my soul long before I knew you. Time and space couldn't keep us apart, "

"Go on, Rowen," Nepta said with tears in her eyes. "Kiss your wife."

Rowen palmed the back of my skull and pulled me toward his soft but firm lips. We kissed and sealed our forever on a simple village pathway with a starwing as our witness. It was perfect, and Keeli cooed in approval.

Nepta's face beamed. "You both stood as pillars of light and strength when my village needed you most, but I have always known you were meant for more. Go forth in love and nourish your sacred soul flame bond. Use it as a guide to rule with kindness and wisdom."

"Thank you, Nepta," I said, throwing my arms around her small frame. "Thank you for always sensing something more within me and believing in me, even when I didn't believe in myself."

"Of course, child. I look forward to witnessing the prosperity you two will bring to Viltarran, Luneth, and beyond."

"What of the dark crystals?" I asked, making eye contact with Rowen. Keeli barreled into my arms as if the mere mention of the Dark Spirit terrified her. I clutched her close as her long tail cascaded down my arm.

"Driskell and I have returned them to the Sacred Vale," Nepta replied, offering the starwing a gentle pat to calm her. "They could not remain out in the open where anyone could find them. They must never fall into the wrong hands, for I believe Erovos' power can be accessed through the stones."

"Are you sure?" I asked. "We can take them or find a way to hide them in the Crypts where no one will ever find them."

Nepta shook her head. "The Wyn once guarded the Light that needed to be protected from the world. But it is you who guards that Light now, and we must protect the world from the dark crystals. It is our duty."

"You have Viltarran's aid in whatever you need," Rowen said, his voice steady yet sincere as he held me and Keeli.

"Always," I agreed, knowing the dark crystals were safest with Nepta.

"It is settled then," Nepta said, continuing to walk the path to the Sacred Vale alone. "I shall see you at tonight's ceremony. Make sure to bring a luminorb."

— ·(C · ● ·) ·) —

A memorial service was held at the beach for all the warriors, animals, and elves who had succumbed to Erovos' darkness. And for Maddock, the Synodic Son who'd sacrificed himself to save us all.

It was a beautiful evening. The stars and comets reflected on the calm ocean as the forest flourished behind us. Rowen stood by my side, his strong presence grounding as Keeli hovered nearby.

I wished we could've held the service near the Sylvan Mother Tree, but the valley was still recovering. The land had sustained extensive damage and needed time to heal. Though it gave me peace knowing Indrasyl was whole and complete, and that her healing roots already stretched to the Wyn village, I still missed being near Maddock.

I tried speaking with the Sylvan Mother Tree inside the Hymma, but it appeared she was in some sort of healing stasis. It took a lot to repair a world, so I understood. I hoped one day, I could speak with her again. Maybe even Maddock, too. Somehow.

He would probably say something like—*It took me becoming a tree for you to declare a ceasefire between us? Glad we could finally get to the root of our issues.*

He would say it with a smile, and I would roll my eyes at his inappropriate joke. What a smart ass! But even now, I couldn't help but smile.

"The fallen shall always be remembered and honored for their sacrifice," Nepta called out, her obsidian headdress and half-moon staff shimmering in the starlight. People and elves from all over Luneth had traveled to the Wyn beach, each one holding a glowing luminorb within their hands. "Release your memorial lanterns to the wind and let their light shine from this life to the next."

I opened my palms, letting the wind carry my luminorb to the sky. Tears streamed down my face as thousands of orbs soared and reflected over the water.

The sight was peaceful, infinite, and reflected eternity.

The luminorbs represented all those we had lost, but my eyes never left the one I dedicated to Maddock. I missed him so damn much, it hurt.

"Through blood, bone, and crystal, the marked son will breathe life anew unto the deadened lands of darkness," Driskell repeated the ending of the prophecy. Half of his long, white hair was pulled back into elaborate braids, and his eyes looked crazed with euphoria. "The prophecy has been fulfilled thanks to you all. Especially the Alcreon Light Bearer and the Marked Son. This is a celebration of life, and the healing of Luneth. We have much to be thankful for."

Gentle music played as people mingled and shared fond memories. I spotted Pia and Xala talking with Callum and a few other Viltarran soldiers. My eyes scanned over to Thaydril. He was dressed in an indigo robe and was talking to Leer. The clean-cut bladesmith looked equal parts intimidated and intrigued.

My gaze darted to Ven as I heard him recount war stories to Takoda and Alvar. The healer looked appalled, while the war captain beamed with pride. And through the sea of faces, I saw Rayal and Dyani walking toward me, followed by a shimmering bird.

Ekee's gaze was locked on Keeli as he flew right towards her, and my heart skipped a beat as she darted behind my legs.

Ekee fanned his tail in an elaborate display, and Keeli peeked her head around my leg. The male gracefully soared around her, then dove in impressive circles and swoops. His feathers glinted in the moonlight as he performed for her, but Keeli was wary.

The male changed tactics and disappeared into the trees. He returned a moment later with a morsel of food clutched in his bill. More interested now, Keeli reached her beak towards him and snatched his offering.

She gulped down her treat and chirped, finding Ekee's display and gift suitable. Their necks intertwined like swans on a lake.

Their bond had formed, and my heart soared.

"He was smoother than you were, Rowen," Dyani said with a playful nudge. "You almost messed up your chances with the Alcreon Light Bearer. How embarrassing."

"Don't I know it. I'll have to take notes," Rowen said with a chuckle as the birds took off into the air, flying around each other like helical comets.

"Looks like we play matchmaker well," Rayal said, her eyes reflecting the light of the starwings. The queen wore pants and a shirt with a gold diadem on her head.

"Thank you for bringing him home," I said as we hugged. "By the way, according to the deal I made with Aedris, my body is technically pledged to you."

Dyani and Rowen stiffened as the queen laughed. "I release you from your oath. Your body is yours and no one else's," she said with her full authority, and I felt something within me shift.

"Thank you," I said, noticing a pack slung over Dyani's shoulder. "Going somewhere?" I asked with a grin.

"I didn't get to fully take in the sights at Hara'dune," she replied, hoisting the pack with her lean arms that gleamed with Demil's silver armbands.

Rayal smiled as she took the warrior's hand in hers. "Is it all right if I steal your best warrior?"

"Second best warrior," Rowen said with a wry smile.

Dyani punched him in the arm. "Let's settle this once and for all. How many demons did you slay on the battlefield?"

Rowen huffed in disgust. "I don't count."

"Yes, you do," she rebutted.

"Fine," Rowen admitted. "Two hundred and fifty-two."

"Aha! That proves it. I killed over three hundred. And that was after I released my brother from Erovos' darkness. Believe it or not, I didn't count that one."

Rowen's smile faded. "I'm so sorry you had to do that, Dyani."

"Don't go soft on me now, Damascus. Just promise me you'll both come to visit," she said, her dark eyes darting between me and my soul flame.

"We will, I prom—" Before I could finish the sentence, Dyani pulled me into a fierce embrace. I hugged her back, not wanting to let go of the warrior who once hated me but was now my dearest friend. "I knew you wouldn't have to battle the world alone," I whispered in her ear, remembering the words she had spoken to me on our first mission with the Ever-burn blades. She squeezed me tighter before releasing me and quickly wiped her eyes.

"We both have so much to rebuild," I said to the queen. "But we don't have to do it alone. Let us help and be there for each other. Let's not repeat the mistakes of the rulers before us."

"Spoken like a true lady and the bearer of the Alcreon Light," Rayal replied as she squeezed my hand. Boisterous laughter caught her attention, and her eyes snapped to Thaydril and Leer. "I couldn't agree more, but now we must go before my cousin scars that young man."

We shared a final laugh and finished our goodbyes. And I watched as the queen and her warrior walked away hand in hand, their joined silhouettes disappearing into the crowd.

With a smile on my face, my gaze darted back to the birds dancing in the sky.

Erovos had nearly driven the starwings to extinction, along with countless other species, leaving wounds that might never heal. The devastation he caused would be felt for generations, but the first steps to healing the vibrant world of Luneth had only just begun.

50

I stared out at the ocean as Rowen rubbed my back in comforting circles. I couldn't bring myself to leave. I wanted to stay until every last luminorb disappeared.

My slate-grey dress and hair billowed in the wind, and Rowen tucked a flyaway curl behind my pointed ear. "Have I ever told you how much I love your silver freckles?"

"Not today," I replied, tucking under his arm as dawn hugged the horizon. We'd been here all night, and somehow, I still wasn't ready to say goodbye.

He leaned down and pressed a kiss to the sensitive skin below my ear. "I could spend an eternity counting them and recounting them."

"We have the time," I replied, relishing every moment in Rowen's arms.

Someone cleared their throat behind us, and we turned to see Callum. Takoda healed most of his wounds, but a bandage remained on his eye. "Beautiful ceremony," he said, joining us at the lapping waves.

"You're up late," Rowen remarked as I noted the faint bruises on his neck. Pia and Xala must have shown him a good time.

"And you're married," he replied, noting the ring on his finger. He clasped him on the shoulder with a wide, even-toothed grin. "When do you plan to take your bride back to Viltarran?"

"In a few days," Rowen replied. "Once everything here has settled."

Callum shifted on his feet, his contagious smile fading. "There is something I've been meaning to tell you. I hate to ruin your wedded bliss, but you need to know."

"What is it?" Rowen asked, his hand wrapping protectively around my middle.

"There have been sightings of a red-headed man and a woman with raven hair wandering the ruins of Viltarran."

My muscles tensed. "Caeryn and Aliphoura," I said, my eyes locking with Rowen's. I shuddered to think of how the red-headed man kidnapped me and broke my bones; nearly broke my spirit. Rowen had healed my body with noxlily petals, but the shimmering scars all over my body would always remind me of my time in the Crypts. "We never found Fou's body, and Caeryn hasn't been seen since."

Rowen scanned my face. "We watched Caeryn break her neck. He was devoted. Perhaps he carries her corpse?"

"Maybe," Callum said with an unconvinced look in his eye. "The reports have been of them rifling through the ruins. It's as if they are searching for something."

"Lord Leones' will," I gasped, my gut dropping. "If Fou's still alive, she would be searching for that. It's the only thing keeping her from reclaiming her title. If she ever found it, she could come for the throne."

Rowen's eyes darkened with the ghosts of his past. "Keep a close watch and let me know if there are any more sightings. We can't be too careful."

"Of course." Callum nodded. "Thaydril offered to portal me

and the warriors back today. We'll prepare what we can for your return."

"Thank you, but be sure to get some rest," Rowen said, patting his friend on the back. "We have a long road ahead of us. Nearly every building has been torn down. Only half the castle and a few neighborhoods stand."

Callum's blue gaze darted between me and Rowen. "We're ready. And I don't just speak for myself when I say I look forward to seeing what you two will do for Viltarran."

"We have some ideas," I said, wrapping my arms around Rowen. Unspoken words flashed between us as we recalled our shared dream.

"It will be good to see love and laughter return to the halls," Callum replied with one last look to the horizon. "Well, I best be off. My lord. My lady." He bowed at the waist and excused himself.

I tilted my gaze back to Rowen and rested my hand on his chest. "Being called *my lady* will take some getting used to."

"I believe you'll adjust quickly," Rowen replied with my favorite grin. He placed his hand over mine and toyed with the wedding band on my finger. I marveled at the man who was now and forever my husband. Though our nuptials had been quick and impromptu, I wished I had a wedding gift to give him.

My husband, the lord of Viltarran, stood before me in the early morning light. He was dressed simply, wearing his fitted pants and loose charcoal shirt with his ax at his side. He looked exactly as he had the first time I saw him—strong and handsome with muscled strength and quiet power. But there were two subtle differences.

The first was his face. The haunted shadows that clung to his features had disappeared. His gaze, once guarded and filled with the wounds of his past, was now clear, light, and brimming with purpose.

The second was his exposed chest. He only wore one necklace made of crystal beads. The other, with the silver medallion, was buried in the ground. Fou had placed a dark curse upon it to keep an eye on Rowen, and though we assumed her dead, it was still too great a risk to wear.

I felt the loss of his family heirloom deep in my bones. I had nothing from my life before, but I wanted Rowen to step into our future with a treasured piece of his past.

The sun was rising, and I was exhausted, but I couldn't go one more day without righting this wrong. It would be my wedding gift.

I turned to my husband and said, "Take me to your mother's necklace."

·(·C·●·)·)·

Rowen led me to where he'd buried his mother's necklace. It was just outside the Wyn village, up on one of the bluffs overlooking the sea.

He counted several paces from a tree, then knelt to where he'd buried the pendant.

"Can I see it?" I asked.

Rowen's eyes narrowed. "It's still cursed."

"I know. It's okay."

Without hesitation, Rowen drove his ax into the ground to break up the earth. After a minute of digging, he retrieved a small woven pouch.

I outstretched my palm to take it from him.

"Keira," he said with apprehension. "Someone could be watching."

"Trust me," I replied, keeping my hand steady.

He pulled the drawstrings apart and carefully lifted the

necklace out by the chain. He still didn't dare touch the medallion cursed by his ex-love to spy on him.

Rowen hesitated as if he feared the curse would rub off on me. There was no way Aliphoura could have survived, but still, there were sightings of a raven-haired woman wandering the wreckage of Viltarran. We couldn't be too careful.

He placed the necklace in my hand, and as soon as the medallion touched my palm, a pair of eyes flashed in my mind.

As fast as they appeared, they vanished.

Tendrils of Light spiraled up my arm as I cleansed the blight from the necklace with a silver blast.

"Someone was watching," I said, holding the medallion a moment longer, ensuring the curse and connection were severed.

"Did you recognize them?" Rowen asked, his brows narrowing.

"No," I said, handing him back his necklace. "But it's safe to wear again."

The light and love in his eyes were unmistakable as he traced the pendant with his finger. He put his head through the chain and situated the medallion on his sternum.

"I wish you could have met my mother," he said, seeming entirely whole. It was beautiful to see.

"Me too. She sounds like an amazing woman."

"She would have loved you."

"What was her name?" I asked, wishing she and Rowen had had more time together. She'd died unexpectedly, orphaning him when he was so young.

"Alenie Damascus," he said with pride.

"Alenie Damascus," I repeated, hoping in some way she could hear me. "Thank you for your son. You raised a good one. I'm honored to become a part of the family."

"Does that mean you'll take my name? It was my mother's. I

know she would want you to have it. Or I'll take yours, I don't care. As long as you're mine."

I looked at the ring on my finger. "I've never felt a connection to my name, and yours means so much to you. I would love to become a part of the Damascus family."

Rowen scooped me up and spun me in the air, my legs trailing behind me. We laughed as the world rotated around us, and after a long day of tears, the sound was music to my ears.

He lowered me to his lips and kissed me, passionately. I interlocked my fingers behind his neck, feeling a wave of pure and utter contentment.

The starwings had somehow found us up on the cliff and circled us with their shimmering tails.

Rowen and I had fought so hard for this peace, and looking at his once-cursed necklace that flashed with eyes I didn't recognize, something told me that we would have to keep fighting for it.

51

A few more days passed by as we healed and recovered.

Rowen and I had spent the afternoon packing, though, in truth, we didn't have much to bring with us. Our belongings were few and mostly consisted of books, sketches, a few clothes, and weapons.

"Are you ready to leave for Viltarran tomorrow?" he asked as I plopped onto our mattress. The canopy and bed were all that remained in our dome.

"I am." I smiled, perfectly encased in our haven. "I'm ready to start my life with you."

Rowen went to one of the packed woven baskets and pulled out something long, velvety, and green.

My eyebrows narrowed in confusion, then shot up in realization. Rowen stalked toward me with smooth, braided vines. "I've been thinking about tying you up all day," he said, standing at the foot of the bed. "Laid out and strung up just for me. At my mercy as I pleasure you all night."

Anticipation and panic swirled through my body. My mouth dried as wetness pooled somewhere else entirely. I was aroused just from watching him hold the rope, and I bit my lip as we held eye contact. "I don't know. I wiggled out of your last knot pretty easily."

His eyes simmered with heat, desire, and something like a challenge. He crawled onto the bed and caught my wrist, then the other. He put my hands together and held them in one of his large palms. I gulped as he wrapped the vines around my wrists, tying secure knots with adept precision.

He laid me back on the bed and lifted my bound hands above my head. My body surged with electricity as he hovered over me and tied the end of the rope to the headboard.

My chest heaved. The restraints weren't tight enough to hurt me but not loose enough that I could escape.

"You're mine," he said, his voice guttural and low.

"Does it look like I'm going anywhere?" I replied with a smirk, testing the bonds that didn't budge.

He sat back on his heels, his eyes obscenely tracing over every curve and indent of my body. "I wish you could see how you look right now. Completely and utterly at my mercy."

"You could do anything to me," I said as my nipples puckered beneath the thin fabric of my top.

His hands shoved up my lilac camisole, baring my breasts. He lightly grazed past my nipples with his scarred knuckles, and I shuddered as I erupted in goosebumps.

"I'm going to take my time with you, Lady Damascus," he said, and I squirmed.

His touch lowered to my satin bottoms where he slowly, torturously, pulled them off my body, revealing my bare and aching center.

I was laid out before him like his personal feast. "I'm going to make you feel so good."

I writhed against the binds, my hips pumping the air, searching for his hand, his mouth, anything. He chuckled darkly. The light bondage had me going crazy.

He started at my neck and kissed his way down my body. His lips brushed over my peaked nipple, and my body jolted, my hands staying in place.

I whimpered. Not being able to trace my hands along his muscled form was a different kind of torture.

I squirmed and wriggled under his ministrations, loving the rough scruff of his beard and the soft press of his lips.

He kissed down my ribcage, stomach, and hip bones.

I couldn't get away, and I didn't want to. I was completely at his mercy. Or he was at mine. I knew I could say the words to make him stop.

He spread my legs apart and grinned when he found me wet and glistening.

His fingertip traced my aching center as his other hand splayed across my abdomen. The points of contact ignited my body, but it wasn't enough. I needed more! "Please," I moaned. I couldn't take this torture anymore.

"My, how you beg and writhe for me," he said as he lowered his head between my legs. His breath skittered over my desire that dripped down my thigh, and my hips bucked the air. He chuckled again.

"Please," I begged again.

"Yes, my flame, I will touch you now. But only because you beg so prettily." His tongue darted out and stroked my aching bud.

Gratitude filled me as he finally touched me, and I jerked from the denied intensity. "Yes!"

I barely had a moment to adjust to his tongue before he drove his fingers inside me, and my back arched off the bed.

Everything coiled and bunched as I rode his fingers. I was so achy and plaint that my first orgasm was imminent. It wracked through me like a pulsating meteor shower. My body undulated with my arms trapped above my head.

When I finally touched back down to earth, my body was aglow and buzzing, but I noticed Rowen still wore his pants. And that upset me greatly.

I incinerated the ropes that bound my wrists and pounced onto my soul flame. Rowen's shadowed brow lifted in shock and excitement as I mounted him.

I pulled him from his pants. His cock was so hard and aching that I shuddered. He seized my moment of distraction and whirled me back under him.

He pulled off my top the rest of the way, then entered me with a slick thrust. I cried out as he filled me, commanding me to feel every inch of him as he pushed his way inside me.

Tension tightened in my core.

"Look at me when I make you come."

I opened my eyes to the green and welcoming forest of his irises, and he smiled as I came around his cock.

"Good girl."

I pumped my hips, taking him in and out of me, watching transfixed at how he could possibly fit inside me.

"I'm not done with you yet," he said and pounded into me mercilessly. My breasts shook, and my thighs trembled. I had no choice but to submit to the pleasure he demanded to give me. "You take me so good, Keira."

My third climax rocked through me in waves and waves of pleasure that seemed never-ending. When I came back to my senses, Rowen hovered over me, caging me within his muscled and veiny arms. I pumped my hips again, determined that he would be the next to come.

"Yes. Keira. Use that pretty pussy," he said, holding himself up as I fucked him from underneath.

Our eye contact was unflinching as I rode him from the bottom. His cock thickened and twitched inside of me. My pace picked up as I bucked and rode out his pleasure.

He growled out his release, using my body to extract every ounce of his pleasure. He crashed down on top of me and kissed me ferociously. His moan echoed down my throat as I kissed him back.

He curled me into his embrace and kissed my wrists. "I love you so much."

The ancient soul flame bond stirred within me. "I love you," I said, kissing his heaving chest. The fabric of his soul called to mine as if we'd been woven together long ago.

He pulled me in tighter as we basked in our sated bliss, and our arms held each other like a shield against the world.

Aliphoura and Caeryn might still be alive, plotting to come for Rowen's title. The future was uncertain, and our troubles might find us one day. But none of that mattered tonight. Or even tomorrow. We would head to Viltarran and build the dream Rowen and I had shared together.

With the promise of forever, and the eternal flames flickering in our eyes, Rowen traced and memorized every inch of my skin. And I his. Every blemish, beauty mark, and dent was mine to look at, now and forever.

I didn't know how long we laid there, lost in each others arms, or even in what world or plane we existed.

But as we lay naked, tangled in our forever, we kissed each other's scars and counted the freckles that turned into stars.

The End

ACKNOWLEDGMENTS

First and foremost, I would like to thank everyone who read and loved Synodic. Your support, messages, and posts on social media mean the world to me. I see you, and I'm so grateful for you. Thank you for being patient with me while I wrote Ecliptic.

I would like to thank my alpha reader, fellow author, and mom, Eileen Travis. The late-night read-throughs, discussions, and pep talks helped me more than you could ever know.

To my book fairy, Kat. I'm forever grateful you *discovered* me on TikTok and helped me get into bookstores and on author panels. You made my author wishes come true! Thank you to my editor, Judi, for jumping into my story. And to my new author friends, thank you for welcoming me into the space with open arms and encouraging me every step of the way.

Thank you so much to my incredible beta readers: Vanessa Altmayer, Gabrielle Connor, Amira F. Hassan, Nadia Noelle, and Trisha Shaw. Your feedback and insight were so invaluable. I can't fully express what it means to entrust my characters and story to you. I appreciate you so much!

I would like to thank my heroine, Keira. She found the strength to face her fears and, in doing so, gave me the courage to face mine.

Thank you to my beautiful fur babies for all the cuddles and kisses. Hearing your little heartbeats and snores while I write brings me so much comfort. You are my little galaxies!

To my real-life soul flame, Daniel, thank you for keeping me sane and fed and for walking our precious babies. Without you, none of this would be possible. Your unending love and support have helped me achieve my wildest dreams. I love you.

And, of course, you, dear reader, thank you for being here with me.

Kristin

ABOUT THE AUTHOR

Kristin Travis is a rising author known for Synodic and Ecliptic. The sci-fantasy duet is a slow burn to spicy romance with sexy men, forbidden touches, and lyrical writing.

Even from a young age, Kristin loved to read and write. She studied literature, poetry, and creative writing in college and is constantly honing her craft to take readers into ethereal and romantic worlds.

When Kristin isn't writing, she's creating spicy book content with her husband, Daniel, cuddling her two dogs on the couch, or chasing waterfalls and adventure.

If you enjoy Kristin's books, please leave a review. They are so helpful!

Follow Kristin on Social Media:

instagram.com/kristin.travis
tiktok.com/@kristin_travis

ALSO BY KRISTIN TRAVIS

The Synodic Duet

Synodic

Ecliptic

9 7 9 8 9 8 8 3 2 1 1 2 5